PRAISE FOR PURPLYND

"It is Sunday morning. I awaken with a familiar sense of struggle gnawing at my soul. Prayerfully, my inner voice whispers you need something. My eyes catch the inviting cover of *Purplynd* resting on my bedside table. Gently, I pick up the text. Slowly, I turn its pages. By merely touching the pages I remember the faith and faithfulness of Daisy. My hope is renewed by the spirit of justice that is embodied in Dancing Daisy's All-Day Day Care. Magically, my fingers land on the line in the book that reads, 'It was love that powered Daisy, not the love she was given but the love that she created.' I rose from bed, my energy shifted. Now I feel thankful and ready to create more love in a world that is struggling and hungry for love. *Purplynd* will capture your heart, your imagination, and transform your being. Read it. Savor it. Claim its magic over you."

—**Pastor Jacqueline Durhart**, Director of Spiritual Care, Starr King School for the Ministry

"An engaging, intriguing and thought-provoking read from start to finish, *Purplynd* draws you in, piques your curiosity and connects with something inside you that keeps you turning its pages . . . you find yourself learning more, relating more and wanting more."

— **Berena Hughes**, Freelance Editor

"Purplynd is an action filled mystery of love in a world of raw realism told by a creative story teller with imaginative expectancy and theological underpinnings. Readers will pause and think about awaking an under used freedom to ponder the contradictions of life. For starters there is the anger of love and the magic of the past. Do you need a pedagogy filter? Now you must buy the book and read more for yourself if you believe that the unexamined life is not worth living."

— **Dr. J. Aflred Smith, Sr.**, Pastor Emeritus, Allen Temple Baptist Church; Professor Emeritus, Berkeley School of Theology

"If you are looking for lyricism, hope and a fair bit of action, and you can use some complex thinking about the issues that matter in our world today, *Purplynd* won't let you down. I'm particularly grateful for a book that engages issues of justice that makes me feel cared for instead of lectured to. Thanks for the gift of utopian sci-fi in a world with too much dystopian sci-fi, BK."

— **Rev. Sandhya R. Jha**, Author of *Liberating Love*, Community Organizer, and Anti-Oppression/DEI Consultant

"*Purplynd* is so much more than a bunch of great words strung together by a master writer. It is a magic carpet ride to the edges of the imagination, the universe and one's moral fabric. It is a vehicle for an adventure of the mind and spirit; it's not just a great read, it's a and challenged what I had settled on as my integrity—all while on a beautiful, purple fast ride. It took me to places beyond my imagination, showed me red places in my soul voyage. It is a magical and wonderful, political and theological, inspiring journey."

— **Dr. Aleese Moore-Orbih**, Executive Director, California Partnership to End Domestic Violence

PURPLYND

BRIAN K. WOODSON, SR.

This is a work of fiction. The characters, places, and incidents portrayed, and the names used herein are fictitious or used in a fictitious manner. Any resemblance to the name, character, or history of any person, living or dead, is coincidental and unintentional. Product names used herein are not an endorsement of this work by the produce name owners.

Copyright © 2022 by Brian K. Woodson, Sr.
First Edition

Cover by Rafael Polendo (polendo.net) & Brian K. Woodson, Sr.
Cover image by: Matt Anderson Photography/Getty Images
Interior layout by Matthew J. Distefano

ISBN 978-1-957007-34-2
This volume is printed on acid free paper and meets ANSI Z39.48 standards. Printed in the United States of America

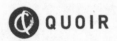 QUOIR

Published by Quoir
Chico, California
www.quoir.com

CONTENTS

CONTENTS

PURPLYND

IN ONE MURDEROUS MOVE, the supreme leader would quell a rebellion in its infancy and settle a score with the one purl on the planet he both hated and feared. His would be a decisive and powerful move that would quiet the noise about his ascension to the most powerful position in the empire. The dratsab controlled all the relevant places on the planet, and his unquestioned rule was unusually ruthless. He served the interests of the elite but answered to none. But a cancer began just outside the capital and had grown to infect significant cities in the realm. Clusters of unproductive purple, useless to the industrious and progressive parts of society, had become unmanageable. Enough of them had ceased showing up for work that the economy began to strain. Wages were beginning to rise and profits to fall. The ringleader of these circuses was one insignificant purl. If the dratsab wished to continue as the supreme ruler, he would have to eliminate this purl, thereby restoring order to the realm. The test of his power would be how quickly he cut off the head of the movement and pull out its heart. His predecessor, although handpicked and ruthless, had failed. He would not.

PURPLYND

PROLOGUE

PURPLE CAME IN THE same shapes and sizes as humans. They are not human at all, though it would be understandable if someone, perhaps a child, could not tell the difference, especially in the dark or in the earliest morning light. Purple have hands, feet, and features just as we do. They are as smart as we are. (Some would insist smarter.) Their eyes are more colorful and interesting than ours, along with other differences, of which you will soon learn, but the strangest thing about purple is something that would be glaring to us but went unnoticed among them. If you or I met a purl, it would be the first thing we would see, and until we got used to seeing purple, I am sure we would stare impolitely. But it would be a rare purl indeed who would notice and fewer still who would comment on the color of another purl's skin. This is curious because adult purple come in one of two unmistakable colors: red or blue. It wasn't always the case, but purple became unable, or perhaps just unwilling, to perceive what was obvious. Perhaps this inability is what caused the problem. Perhaps something else did. Still, this lack of perception on their part would be of no concern to us if our very existence was not entangled with theirs. You see, there is good reason to believe that Purplynd mirrors Earth, or perhaps it's the other way around. That is for you to decide.

PROLOGUE

PROTASIS

THE TROUBLES BEGAN, AS all such troubles do, in the middle of nowhere with no one watching. In this case, it was an insignificant suburb just outside the capital. There, unnoticed, was a wonderful daycare started by a kind lady who loved to dance. She would always go dancing with her friends and gained a reputation for being quite good. She loved dancing so much, her friends took to calling her "Dancing Daisy."

Well, Dancing Daisy used to work with a friend who kept children. She had taken the job just to help out until she found other work, but she was so good at making the children laugh, dance, and enjoy being at daycare, she never left. In fact, when the daycare closed, she started her own. It was called Dancing Daisy's All-Day Daycare because they kept the babies for as long as their parents wished. The business cards for Dancing Daisy's All-Day Daycare stated on the bottom in unmistakable red ink, "Don't worry if you're late...we never lock the gate!" Which meant, of course, Dancing Daisy's was no nine-to-five babysitter but a real-life, around-the-clock home away from home for little ones. Maybe that is why he was brought there.

Now, it had been a strange few weeks in that part of Purplynd. The days began to grow gray until every one of them had a dark and brooding sky. For the first few nights, the stars came out bright and shining, but after a while, even they were overtaken by the darkness. The dark air was particularly cold and strange in certain spaces that randomly moved from one place to another. Or maybe pockets of warmth were moving around? This was difficult to tell because anyone walking or riding outside would feel the pleasant warmth one moment and the desolate cold the next. No one understood what was happening or what the weather meant. The warmth was so wonderful, but the chill cooled to the bones and filled one with a sense of loneliness. And this was not that loneliness one feels from time to time. This was a loneliness which made you feel abandoned without hope, as if all life had left the planet, never to return, and you alone remained. In fact, as the weeks went by, purple began to experience more of the lonely cold than the wonderful warmth. Some even said the cold was taking over.

The purple in town began to loathe going outside for fear of being overtaken by bone-chilling loneliness. Purple, minding their own business, would be walking here or there, and the cold, without warning, would grab them. Most purple, male or female, in the iron grip of the chill, would weep. For weeks, this strange weather was centered over the town of Biscuit. Purple did not think coming home weeping was good for their health, so the purple of Biscuit stayed indoors as much as possible.

But at Dancing Daisy's All-Day Daycare, you wouldn't know there was a cold pocket anywhere. Of course, Daisy stopped taking the children outside the second day the strange weather began. On the first day the children begin to cry as the wave of a cooler breeze passed them, Daisy understood something she didn't need words to describe. And unlike some purple, she wasn't one to dilly-dally around with things that were wrong or off or even the slightest bit strange in a bad way. So, she brought her little charges inside and, for weeks, made the inside of Dancing Daisy's All-day Daycare so wonderful that the children were unaware of the danger outside. Parents would come to pick up their happy children and would begin to linger because Daisy's was so warm, peaceful, and inviting. Daisy would make sure the parents would completely wrap up their children before they left the house which kept, the children under her care, safe from the darkness.

As the weeks went on, parents would come in weeping because the short walk from the car to Daisy's door was so terribly lonely and cold that, in the few seconds it took Daisy to let them in, they were almost overwhelmed with sadness and grief. In fact, the weeks of growing cold and darkness got so bad that, all over Biscuit, purple began to experience a growing depression, despite remaining indoors and off the streets. The only purple forced to go out into the bleak and bitter loneliness that had captured the town were the ones with vital jobs. So, Daisy only had two toddlers the last week before he came. Their parents were school administrators and were the only ones who came to school the whole week. They picked up their children as soon as the last school bell rang and long before the now dim suns set and the darkness took complete control.

On the third evening at seven o'clock, three hours after the two children had been picked up, a knock on the door interrupted the quiet. The knock sounded musical, as if the wood of the door changed into something entirely different by being struck. Somehow, everything went still moments before the sound reached her ears. For many years after, whenever Daisy thought of that moment, she couldn't remember if the stillness came before or after the knock. But vivid in her memory was the second hand on the living room clock moving to seven o'clock with the loudest tick she had ever heard and, immediately after, the insistent loud knock on the door. As she remembered years later, she was convinced the clock didn't suddenly get loud; rather, for some reason, everything but the clock got really quiet.

And when she opened the door, instead of a breath of bitter, lonely cold, there was a pocket of almost overwhelming warmth. Its presence enveloped her so quickly, Daisy was not sure if the warmth came from behind her or from in front. She opened the door, and there she stood.

Daisy thought she was a female but later would wonder, for good reason, if the purl was male. She couldn't really tell because the figure was wrapped up like everyone else those days; her entire face was covered as if she (or he) was in a blizzard or sandstorm. Daisy's senses heightened; everything became vivid. She experienced a feeling of being suspended, somehow away from herself, all the while still being herself. The one at the door held something in its beautiful hands. Beautiful hands—those were the words Daisy would use whenever she told the story about that day. We all know what was in its hands, but Daisy could not have imagined how her life would change.

Standing in the door, surrounded by warmth and beauty, the figure, whose face and body was wrapped against the lonely cold, presented Daisy with a small, swaddled bundle. Daisy reached to accept it and moved as if to ask the figure to come into the house. She thought to speak, to invite her in and begin the "daycare" conversation. Why she was there? Who was she? What was in the bundle? All the questions you ask when you first take on a new customer and a hundred other questions, she had never asked anyone; but thought this might be her only chance to ever have them answered.

Without words and in an eternity hidden within a few seconds, Daisy understood mysteries. She found herself listening to the sweetest music she had ever heard. The music was unlike any she had ever experienced and danced inside her head like no music ever had. The sounds were so warm and familiar, as if she were singing and dancing them into existence.

Lost for a moment within eternity, she was startled as she realized the figure was speaking. But the music and what the figure was saying blended so well, she barely distinguished one from the other. A few words reverberated in her mind as she began to feel she had been chosen. The words "royal seed of Miis" sounded in her being. At those words, another part of her mind tried to wake up. She fought the memories attempting to speak in her mind in order to hear the music and the figure. "Child that Kha begot" were the next words she recognized, and the other part of her mind fired again. Something familiar, something important, from the past tried to break into her mind. Daisy was sure the messenger said more, but what took precedence was her realization of what she suspected was true: The bundle in her arms was, in fact, an infant. Just then, something within Daisy told her the figure was about to depart. Even before Daisy's eyes detected any movement, an alarm went off inside her soul. The female, or whatever this was, was leaving. But that couldn't be.

Daisy was being asked to take care of another child, and she was always happy to be a part of raising little ones, although this one—if it really *was* a baby inside this bundle—was entirely too young for her daycare. Plus, there were questions to be answered, contact information to be confirmed, and paperwork to be filled out. But none of these would happen because the figure that had appeared at her door was disappearing.

So, even though Daisy remained in the warm peace which began when the clock struck seven, a shutter of overwhelming shock hit her within a heartbeat. Suddenly, the baby in the bundle began to whimper. Daisy looked down to attend to her new charge. The baby was wrapped up in layers, and Daisy began to move the strips of cloth so she could see the baby's face. Daisy had a way of calming any crying baby. She would look at them while pulling all the love from her heart and pushing it through her eyes. When the baby saw it, he or she would quiet and become calm. Then Daisy would do whatever needed to be done—change their diaper, feed, or burp them, and, as they got older, fix whatever problem had brought them to tears in the first place. But that night, the strangest thing happened.

As Daisy moved her fingers, separating the cloth, the material changed the closer she came to the baby's face. The outer cloth looked like any nice baby blanket that had been in the lonely cold too long. Cloth, no matter how colorful and soft, became course and gray in the lonely cold. So, the cold, hard outer cloth was no surprise. Daisy just thought that the stranger and her baby must have been out in the lonely cold much too long, which made her want to undo the harm and care for the baby even more. The outer cloth was different from a normal baby blanket in which most purple would wrap a baby. What would normally be a big, folded square was instead thin strips about three fingers wide. This made it easier for Daisy to move the cloth away as she sought to uncover the baby's face. But what was peculiar was that the cloth became softer, brighter, and more colorful with each layer she peeled away. Daisy first thought the lights in the doorway had, for some reason, become dim; but as she moved the final layer away from the baby, she realized the light was coming from the colors of the cloth.

The fussing baby began to quiet, its eyes still closed shut, and Daisy began to rock the bundle up and down and pull the love up into her eyes so the baby could see all was well. What happened next was the strangest thing ever. When the baby opened its eyes and met the look of love Daisy had pulled from her core, something that had never happened before occurred. The baby accepted the calming gaze and reflected back something more powerful than Daisy had ever experienced. Instead of Daisy sending a message to the infant, something came from the baby to Daisy. It was a burst of warmth that was overwhelming. Something deep inside Daisy stirred. No words written or spoken could describe the warm embrace from his eyes. In that instant, every question she had ever asked had been answered. The embrace and kiss of every love of her life burst in a warm flash. Tears welled up in her eyes unlike any she had ever shed, tears of joy, peace, and assurance. They were tears of determination, grief, power, and love all mixed and mingled together. They filled her eyes, and then one slowly walked down her cheeks and jumped off her chin. The tear seemed to float to the baby and splash on the cloth by its cheek. Suddenly, that moment—with all its fullness and meaning—disappeared. In fact, only in her occasional dreams did Daisy remember the power and beauty of those first silent hours (well, they seemed like hours anyway) with the baby.

A pulse of panic pushed through her being as she realized how important it would be for her to give this child the absolute best daycare experience available in all Purplynd—or the universe for that matter. She was more determined than ever to get the information she needed from its mother, or whoever this was, in front of her.

But when Daisy looked up, the stranger was gone. Not walking back to her car, not walking down the street, not running away, she was just gone as if she had never been. Daisy could not keep back the panic rising in her heart. Then things got worse. As she was standing in the doorway, holding this baby, and wondering where its mother or whoever she or he was who had brought him had gone, someone or something in the distance was moving around in the darkness. Her first thought was that the figure was returning. She wanted to imagine everything was right and normal, but something was obviously wrong about that thought, something incongruent. The wonderful warmth embracing her in the doorway was fading, and, as she looked at the strange figure moving here and there, it abruptly stopped. Then turned. It began to move toward her.

Suddenly, the evening became a strange darkness that Daisy had never seen before. All had become charcoal black. Something was wrong. There was no reasonable thought attached to this emotion. Daisy was standing in her door as she had done a thousand times before, but a deep and different sensation overtook her. It was the feeling you get before the feeling that tells you, "You are about to throw up." It was a knowledge of something she had no way of knowing. Then, instead of becoming sharper and clearer as it got closer, the figure was losing shape and becoming even darker. The figure was like a shadow but not one made by light shining on something real. This was not the figure with the beautiful hands, and it was not just coming toward her but also for her. At that very moment, something changed; the darkness *saw* her, if that is the right word.

What Daisy discerned was the shadow that was once moving without definite direction found its mark and focused all its bitter cold and barrenness on her. The empty and hungry shadow was like a vacuum tube sucking life, goodness, and warmth into it, leaving in its path loneliness and tears. And, somehow, this darkness was coming straight toward her, rushing to consume her and the bundle in her arms. Daisy thought to scream. The wonderful warm presence had completely retreated into the house and called for her to follow. She sensed or thought or believed this shadow and the bitter cold that followed it, wanted her. And at that moment, a deep confusion washed over Daisy. She understood something was very wrong but very normal at the same time. At that same moment, she was both desired and undesirable. She was terrified. She thought she had taken the final exam on the value of her life and failed miserably. But she also felt she had never done her homework or studied, and so the failure was to be expected. The shadow was coming as her grade, and she was resolved to accept whatever the darkness brought.

As it swarmed closer, helplessness and hopelessness wrapped their fingers around her. The fingers froze her in the open doorway, holding her until the lonely cold could completely possess her. When the shadow reached her, it would be the end, and she gave herself to this fate. She was not ready for death, and she did not want to die, but in the grip of loneliness and despair, she felt she didn't deserve to live. Every bad thing she had ever thought or done came rushing to her mind and convinced her that death was her due. Every doubt she had ever considered came into her consciousness and suggested that there was nothing else to consider.

So, she accepted her death. She accepted her demise was necessary, if not welcome, and decided to open her arms and embrace the shadow racing toward her. This would be her end, and darkness would take her. No more reason to hope, no need to struggle to free herself from this final failure. She would die, and no one would know or care. The pain of living would be replaced by the eternal pains of death, but this she deserved. And so, without shedding a tear or whispering a regret, she consented to her total destruction and death. And as the command to open her arms moved from her brain to her limbs, a tiny impulse hit the tip of her smallest finger, and she remembered. The instant life and sensitivity came to her paralyzed fingertip; she felt the bundle and the baby. Suddenly, the life of the baby overwhelmed her desire to die. It was too late.

Panic pulsed through every corpuscle of her being and with it a powerful determination to protect the child. This was who she was and how she lived. Daisy protected children. She had long proved her arms were the safest place a baby could be. Angry fathers or mothers who sought to snatch a child from Daisy learned it was no easy task. No child had ever come to harm at dancing Daisy's, and this night was not going to be the first.

Love powered Daisy, not the love she was given but the love she created. It was love that gave her a reason to be on the planet. It was love that gave her purpose and strength. Love gave her ability to endure, to deliver, to secure. Love had done so all her life, and it would do so now. The demon of darkness could have her but not the baby in her arms. The anger of love is the most powerful anger there is, and Daisy had more love than most on Purplynd. But the shadow's hands had already gripped her tightly, and its face was now at the threshold.

And then it happened.

Without knowing how, Daisy moved or was moved. She pivoted to shield the bundle from the darkness with her body and, with the same movement, pressed her back against the wood to shut the door. But the door did not seem to want to close. A force was pushing it open.

The darkness would not be denied and was determined to have its way. Daisy's love moved from her heart to her bones and then to her back and with it, an extra kick. The door slammed and the lower lock clicked into its cradle. She turned and locked the dead bolt as if life depended on it. The snap of the dead bolt securing the door followed so soon after the catch of the bottom lock, they only made one sound. Daisy's eyes moved over the entrance to ensure it was sealed, and as she did, two beautiful hands appeared, and then they were gone.

Daisy came to herself and began to realize she was sitting on the sofa. She couldn't remember sitting down. She couldn't remember if she had walked or was carried or had floated to the sofa. If there was a word that combined all three, she would have consented that was, indeed, what had happened. All seemed surreal. Her heart hurt from beating so hard against her chest. She was terrified. She had almost lost the bundle in her arms to the vacuum of black that came for her. A shutter moved through her body with the thought. She remembered the fingers of the shadow reaching for the baby. She remembered darkness touching the outer blanket. She thought the touch woke her from the suicidal trance, but she was unsure if any of this was real.

Her mind was trying to distinguish reality from fantasy, but the line that separated one from the other was gone. She couldn't shake the thought that she had almost lost the beautiful baby to the shadow. She looked to the baby, to ensure the child was alright, despite her failure. She remembered looking into his eyes, and the memory of what had just happened began to descend into her like a receding wave sinks into beach sand. The images of what had happened at the door drifted into nonsense as if they were the remains of a dream, a full-color dream with all the bone-chilling terror and fairy-tale wonder mixed in, but it was the terror part that stuck. A frigid shiver moved across her skin. She was still a little frightened. She resolved to shake off the whole nightmare and get about the business of being Daisy. She decided to get up and get on with running the best all-day daycare in the town of Biscuit or the whole county, for that matter, and just as she resolved to wake up and put the dream behind her, she felt the bundle in her hands. Then came a shock.

The baby was moving. At first, Daisy thought the baby was fussing, as infants do from time to time. His uncoordinated arms and legs were moving every which way. It would have been natural for the infant to start crying. She expected the precious infant sound would be the next thing she experienced, but it wasn't. The baby wasn't fidgeting; it was fighting. Something was wrong, terribly wrong. The baby knew. She should have known. But how could she have known? Nothing like this had ever happened to her before. In fact, what was happening had not happened to *anyone* before or since. But in her arms, the crusty gray outer layers of the bundle begin to shrink, if that is the right word? What was happening was more like the bundle was getting bigger and smaller at the same time. It was as if the outer cloth had become a boa constrictor tightening to crush the child inside.

Daisy reacted. She moved like any mother would when her infant was faced with danger and death. She didn't think because she didn't have time to. She didn't pause long enough to realize how unnatural this was or perhaps how dangerous this might be. She dropped the bundle to her lap and started ripping the shards of lonely gray cloth from around the infant. Strength beyond measure filled her arms and fingers. The balance to keep the baby safe and still in her lap was that of a ballerina. All this while she went to war with whatever was happening in her lap. She tore away the outer from the inner wrap and, as she snatched it from around the child, each piece became a fistful of serpent which she threw to the floor. When the entire serpent had been removed from around the baby, Daisy quickly placed the infant beside her on the sofa and turned to finish whatever fighting remained. She turned, poised to strike anything that remained, determined to protect her child, but all she saw were pieces of gray serpent that seemed to have always been only cloth, except that it was returning to the flat shape that had once been the outer layer of the bundle. The lonely cold had a way of turning things, no matter how bright or beautiful, to gray, but the cloth on the floor turned from gray to charcoal black.

Daisy thought, whatever it was or had been, should not remain on her floor or in her house, for that matter, and decided to get rid of it. With the baby quiet on the sofa, she stood and bent to begin gathering the pieces. But when she went to pick up the first piece, it turned to dust, as did the next one and one after it. Daisy thought this was strange but given the absurd things that had been happening, accepted it as normal for the bizarre evening. She realized she would have to sweep up the now-charcoal dust and turned her mind to get the broom. She left the room and as she pulled the broom and the dustpan from the kitchen closet, panicked. With all the crazy, unheard-of things that had just happened, why would she leave the baby in the room by itself? She almost screamed. She ripped the broom from its holder and ran back into the room before the fear froze her. When she got to the room, all was well.

The baby was right where she left him, and the charcoal used-to-be cloth was still on the floor. She swept up the pieces that now were dust. She complimented herself mentally on how well she swept. The dust came up effortlessly. The charcoal substance wanted to leave her floor before the broom met it. The strange black dust filled the dustpan. Daisy decided, dust or not, it would be best if she put this in the outside trash instead of the kitchen garbage can. She walked to the back door and was shocked to see a large smash in the middle of the door as if someone, or something, from outside had rammed into it. The damage was so bad, she imagined the door would not open properly, but it did. Daisy wondered how, when, and what had damaged the door but just simply did not have the brainpower to even worry about it. The garbage can was just outside the door. Daisy unlocked the dead bolt and reached for the doorknob, and as she did, she noticed two handprints. When she saw the handprints, a peace washed over her. Whatever happened to the door, or whoever or whatever it was that damaged it or may have wanted to hurt her, was overridden by the presence of those hands. Instantly, the culminating fears of the shadow at the front door, the struggle on the sofa, and this damaged door faded to insignificance.

She would almost never talk about that night, but when she did, it was always with a confidence and security that came from the fact she saw those handprints. Without the image of those hands that soon faded and left no mark, the whole story would be different. The terror of the things that happened that night would have turned Daisy's beautiful, fire-engine red hair lime green. The experience of the shadow was so real and so powerful, it was enough the make anyone cower in fear and retreat into the safety of insanity for a lifetime or more. But, somehow, the presence of those beautiful hands erased the fear. Somehow, the sight of those hands evoked a deep knowing that left the terrors real but insignificant. The fact was, had Daisy not seen those beautiful hands, this story would have ended much differently, and there would probably be no one around to talk about it. We all avoided tragedy because of Daisy, and the courage and confidence she gained gave us all that baby boy. He grew up and changed everything, and, without Daisy, he never would have made it.

Daisy opened the door to her backyard, which was also the play area for the daycare children. When she did, the now familiar, lonely gray sky loomed in defiance of any stars that wished to appear. Somehow, the darkness didn't seem as foreboding as it had at the front door. Maybe this was because, compared with the shadow, it seemed illuminated. Or maybe something changed about Daisy, but she was no longer repulsed by the gray or afraid of it in any way. This was strange enough for Daisy to realize but not enough for her to think about. She reached into the house and grabbed the handle of the dustpan she had placed on the counter to open the door. It was there, waiting patiently for her. With her other hand, she lifted the lid off the garbage can. And just as she began to pour the charcoal ash remains of the outer wrapping into the trash, a strange thing happened. A cold breeze swept past her, blowing the black off the dustpan. Utter angst flashed in her heart at the thought of cleaning up the ashes she imagined scattered all over her backyard. There was no way Daisy was going to leave any of that black dust anywhere near her children. Just then, the breeze became like a brook or a fast-moving stream. The ashes jumped into the wind like a thousand swimmers anxious for the water. The ashes formed what looked like a rope against the lonely gray. Daisy watched it grow smaller in the distance until it disappeared in the gray sky. She turned to look at the dustpan, which was as clean as if it had just been washed. She put the lid down on the can and went back inside. She closed and locked the door and then washed her hands to return to the baby.

When she walked back into the living room, he was waiting for her, quiet and wrapped in the single beautiful blanket that was left. It was the cloth on which Daisy's tear had splashed. She picked him up and looked at him. In her entire life, Daisy had never felt such love for a child or anyone. She stared at him and held him as a mother would her firstborn child. His face was serene and beautiful. He had perfect tiny lips and nose; his royal blue eyelashes shone as if they were strands of light. She wanted to hold him forever, but the Daisy in her that was the Daisy of Dancing Daisy's All-day Daycare wanted more. She wanted to know if he was hungry or wet or warm enough. That Daisy wanted to go through her checklist and mark completed all the necessary items on the page. She unwrapped the baby from the blanket which no longer glowed but was still the most stunning she had ever seen. Its colors were like the burst of fireworks. The cloth had an intricate pattern that appeared simple at first glance, but the more one looked, the more it revealed. Everyone who saw the blanket marveled at its breathtaking beauty, so much so that Daisy took to covering the blanket with another one so as not to tempt weak purple from attempting to run off with it. More than one purl did, in fact, attempt to steal the blanket, but it would be years before Daisy would understand its beauty was not its most important feature. As Daisy moved the blanket away from the baby, his beauty captured her again. She stared and then touched his tiny hands. His fingernails, so perfect, looked as if they were made of pearl. His toes, crinkly and small, stayed motionless as the open air made his legs dance to the same music Daisy experienced, a lifetime ago, at the door.

He opened his eyes, and she fell into them. There it was again: a love beyond lifetimes, a gentleness born of incomprehensible strength. It called to her, and she answered. It took care of her in ways beyond words, and because of it, she would take care of him even if it cost her everything, and it would. In the bottom of the blanket, beneath the dancing legs that told Daisy it was time to feed the child, was a note. Daisy held the child to her chest, and he calmed a bit but began, as infants do, to search for its mother's milk. Daisy at once realized the dilemma and was surprised she wasn't as concerned as surely, she ought to be. The beauty of the note drew her. The paper was thick and rough and obviously handmade but had the surface and shine of fine silk. The intricate writing in gold leaf revealed no expense had been spared in its composition and added to its importance. She opened the note and began to read. Many answers to her questions about that night came in the words she read but so many more were created. As she read the note, the infant began to move as if he was uncomfortable. From the moment they are born, most purple infants make an awful fuss when they are hungry, but this one was different. Daisy was never sure if she felt the pain of his hunger before he did or if he telepathically told her what was going on with him. She just understood what the baby needed whenever he needed something. As he grew, she changed him as soon as he wet and was often ready for him to do the other thing babies do before he did it (which made potty training a cinch by the way). Anyone who paid attention could tell there was an uncanny connection between the two, and all this began when she opened the note that first night.

The note disabused Daisy of any notion that the strange parental figure who had dropped this precious package at her door would return anytime soon. Many thoughts filled her mind as she read. Some of the thoughts evoked stark terror and others, a love so intense it frightened her. The power of the love remained the most prominent and clear as all the other feelings swirled around her heart and mind. Motivated by this love, there was nothing Daisy couldn't do or wouldn't do. The emotions came with such power and intensity, Daisy was comforted by the knowledge that she was sitting down. It was as if the feelings were reality and everything else was a dream from which she would soon awaken.

Reading the note and realizing the strange figure with the beautiful hands would not be returning did give her some concern. She thought about the care this child would need and wondered about the danger the note spoke of and a thousand other related things. At the end of the note, there was a poem that told Daisy who the child was and much of what she would be required to do. She wanted to scream out loud in fear or weep because of the overwhelming burden that had just been placed in her arms, but love held both of these very logical responses to the note in check. The baby nestled in her left arm continued to let her know it was time for him to be fed, but the poem had a power that held her to the page. The words seemed to light up as her eyes moved over their letters. She wondered about the impossibility of the request the note as well as the infant at her breasts were making. The poem required an oath. It was an insane request. It was a sobering sentence that paused time as she considered its gravity. Her eyes continued to his name as her mind paused at the promise she was asked to make. She read his name, and the sound of it reverberated in her heart at the same moment her mind said yes to the oath's request. She turned her gaze at the beautiful infant in her arms. She looked and his eyes were open, calling her. She whispered the words of the oath and promised the infant in her arms to be faithful to it. Tears began to well up in her eyes as they fell again into his. An overwhelming warmth began in the core of her being and washed over her. She felt the wetness of her tears on her cheek and, at the same instant, felt a wetness at her breasts. She lifted her garments and began to feed the miracle in her arms from the miracle in her breasts. This union of mother and child formed a bond that would be tested by many trials but never broken. She let the note fall back to the blanket and, with loving, gentle tears that would not stop, said, "You are my pedagogy." Daisy never said his name without something powerful happening, and long before he began walking and talking, she stopped using it almost altogether. She just called him her Pedagogy, and for a long while, it was all anyone called him.

That is the story of how he came, and of course, there is more to tell about those first years. Daisy endured many perils as the baby grew. Strange things would invite themselves into their midst, and their lives were interrupted by sudden terrors which often came unannounced. The start of any day was no indicator of how it would end. But to know what Pedagogy did that upset so many powerful purple and ended Purplynd as it had been for as long as memory served, one must first know something about the world and history of Purplynd.

Daisy and Pedagogy lived in a time much like ours, but to properly comprehend the present, the past must be understood. There are important things to know about how things started to turn toward darkness long before the Purplynd that existed when Pedagogy was brought to Daisy. The inhabitants of Purplynd look like human beings and are not considered monsters in any human sense of the word. But as history makes plain, hideous faces and features identify true monsters less than the dark and devious deeds they do. Some monsters are born monsters, but perhaps the ones we should fear most are the monsters that are born as beautiful infants and become monsters by other means. There were certainly monsters in Purplynd, as there are currently monsters on Earth. But what was once true on Purplynd, and is still true on Earth, is that the monster's deeds are recognized more easily than the monsters themselves.

Purplynd is real. It is light-years away from us, but our mirrored moments suggest our destinies are shared. It is larger than Earth and has two suns. It, of course, has different names for its cycles that won't be mentioned here because it will not only sound weird but also be a little confusing. What we would call a day was divided into three distinct parts: day, bright-day, and night. What we would call a minute would take about ninety of our seconds, and their hour is made up of ninety of those long minutes. What you need to know to understand the catastrophe that came to the Purplynd of Daisy and her charge was that, for most of the history of Purplynd, purple gathered the things for their meals and did whatever chores needed to be done during the day, rested, ate, and socialized during bright-day, and slept at night. But that was long ago, before cities and brick buildings, before machines and metro transit. It was when purple lived in harmony with one another and the planet. Then one day, in one small village, something twisted everything.

THE BEASTS OF LAISH

THIS WAS HOW THE end of all things began. It was bright-day in the village of Laish. Laish was a circle of homes containing all the families that made up the community. It was like all the settlements in that day. To modern-day notions, such a place might be referred to as an encampment or a compound; but, in that time, that was how purple lived. A village was as large as the land around it could sustain, and Laish had about 120 purple from infants to ancients who worked, ate, and played together. After the bright-day meal, all the purple of Laish were relaxing in circles. Some were asleep in the bright light, surrounded by their loved ones. Some were singing, dancing, and playing their wooden flutes and drums. But most purple, especially the adults, were telling, or listening to, some tale.

Stories were always welcome in bright-day. A few stories were told as the final day's meal was prepared and presented, but the best, longest, and most interesting stories were told when every purl could give his or her undivided attention. A good story was not only connected to the deep truths and principles that were to guide Purplynd's existence, but they were also filled with unexpected twists and turns that held the attention of both the teller of the tale and all who listened. Once a story was told, it took two to three times longer than the length of the story to discuss its possible meanings. At that time in the history of Purplynd, there were no books or pens or writing, but purple had sharp memories and a keen eye for nuance. They would sit and listen to a story and delight in the art of lifting a phrase or part of the tale, add or subtract a word here or there, and, thereby, turn the entire tale in another direction. And if such was done with rhymes, it added even more delight. (Rhymers were rare and very respected in storytelling circles.)

The terrors approached quietly but long before they were seen, heard, or their odor detected in the still air, the birds announced their approach. Startled birds that would normally be about their own bright-day circles flew from their nests to someplace safer. The hunters saw the signs, too, as small critters called to their young and ran into their holes and homes. All these were the slight signals, unnoticed by most, that strangers were coming.

Now, in those times, it was rare to see purple from other villages. Occasionally, a hunter would see a purl who was not from his or her village; when this would occur, specific rituals and greetings were exchanged. These polite gestures ensured that kindness and not competition grew among all purple. At that time, purple considered all Purplynd one family. Some told stories of how all the villages of Purplynd were connected, and everyone was acquainted with the villages within a three-day journey in any direction. These villages were considered close family, and every three years, close families would meet for conversation and circles about their part of Purplynd.

But whatever crept toward Laish that day was from much farther away than a three-day journey. When the breeze blew toward the circles, the wise detected something was wrong. The circle with the most hunters was always the nearest to the village entrance, the loudest and most playful circle, the farthest away. The hunters caught the slight scent carried on the breeze and fell silent. Their minds began to search the index of their experiences to categorize the life in the woods heading toward them. The odor confused the musk of a decaying grass eater with the fowl stench of a carnivorous beast. Whatever it was, this new scent was from something they wanted to neither eat nor meet. As hunters, they recognized which beasts to pursue and which to avoid. Fortunately, in almost every case on Purplynd, the beasts one wished to avoid also wished to avoid purple. Villages were safe because predatory beasts on Purplynd loathed the smell of purple. But whatever foul-smelling beast or beasts were approaching carried a dark scent and no loathing of purl scent.

The curiosity mixed with wonder in the hunters spilled over to the others in the first circle. The storyteller stopped mid-sentence. In the middle of the compound, the slight scent awakened the few napping elders, who sat up slowly with furled brows and a concern only the most ancient are wise enough to have. Suddenly, just as the hunters decided to rise from their seated positions, *they* were on them. Preceded only by a rush of the birds nearby leaping into flight and the frightened silence of the children's circle, five male purple appeared at the outer edge of the village. It was nine steps to the first circle, and as they covered the distance, Quay—the best hunter in all the villages of the three-year circle—moved to retrieve his hunting lance.

If everyone on that day had a three-day cycle to ask themselves or others what Quay was doing or where he was going, none of them would have guessed. And if they had used a three-year cycle to think through and discuss what the five strange purple were about, they would not have come close. But Quay was always faster and quicker at some things. He was a master hunter with sharp instincts that were precise but inexplicable. And those instincts drove him toward his lance. His blood filled with rist, which thereby filled his entire self with strength, speed, confidence, and determination. He was resolute. *Rist*, the elders told him, was what filled his body when, as a young purl, he jumped the narrow place of the canyon, catching the tops of trees on the opposite slope, and climbed the face of the rock to save the one he loved. He survived what would have been a death leap for any purl. But the sight of Miis in danger filled Quay with death-defying power. And here again, Miis was in danger. He didn't know why she was in danger or how exactly, but there was no need to pause or think. Miis was in danger, their children and the entire village. Quay leaped over the other hunters, who themselves were beginning to rise at the sight of the entering strangers. He moved from being seated to six feet in the air quicker than the eye could follow. His hands hit the ground first, and he rolled to his feet at the foot of his lance. In one move and moment, he grasped his lance, stood, and began to turn toward the strangers, intent on protecting Miis and the rest. As he did, the air moving around him sounded as if a knife were separating it. This accelerated his sense of urgency and pumped even more rist into his veins.

His head completed the turn toward his targets; his strong, muscular shoulders followed and squared themselves to the strange danger. At that moment, a sight filled his vision—a large purl covered in a black animal skin with head and claws still attached. The mouth of the beast had been separated so that the bottom jaw was missing. The remaining beast head sat atop the head of the large purl with the two front fangs of the beast pressed into the purl's forehead and marked by dried blood around festering wounds. Four others, who were also covered with the skins of other untamed beasts, were close behind. What had never been seen before filled Quay's vision. The color of his skin. It was not one of the many shades of blue common among purple. His skin was an entirely different color. It was red, a red he had never seen before, deep and vermilion. It was a color that somehow carried the odor of darkness and death. The other thing he saw was a lance like his, only with what looked like a large, sharp stone arrow affixed to its tip. Quay understood this was what was moving the air around him. With all his might, he threw his lance toward the one covered in bearlike animal fur. As his hand opened to release the mighty throw of his lance, the arrowhead opened the blue flesh above his large heart and, entering, pinned him to the wall on which his lance had leaned.

As the blood filled his lungs and life left his body, Quay looked toward the farthest circle. As he sent his gaze in search of his children, he saw Miis in midair. She had moved when the arrow-tipped lance appeared. Miis was a master hunter, as well. She was second to none in all the villages of the three-year cycle except Quay. In every contest of a hunter's skill and agility, especially in the big three-year cycle games, which included all the hunters in that part of Purplynd and sometimes beyond, these two would always best the others. Often circle stories would weave in and out around whether Miis let Quay win so that she might win Quay. But, of course, just as that thought was digested, the question of whether Quay let Miis win to win her was broached. However, the stories were told and with whatever laughter and enjoyment was derived, there was neither doubt nor question in any of the villages of the three-year cycle that Quay and Miis were, by far, the most skilled and masterful hunters in all Purplynd. But on this day, Purplynd revealed there were mysteries hidden from the gentle purple of the three-year cycle.

Miis's running leap sent her through the air until her feet struck the beast-draped purl in the middle of his chest. The force knocked him down, and she rode his chest until his back thudded in the dust. Her knees bent low as the sweeping motion of a weapon-wielding hand raced over her head. She rolled to the left and between the legs of the purl who had just swung to kill her. She kicked him hard where his legs joined. He bent over in pain. She rolled over his back and ran to grab Quay's lance, which had barely missed the chest of the beast-draped purl just before her feet struck him. She pulled the deadly pole out of the wall of the first hut, where it had lodged, and turned to strike. Miis was fast and strong, but it was still *five against one* as the other hunters from Laish ran to enter the fray. She planted the blunt end of Quay's lance in the ground and pivoted back toward the five. She found her mark midair, and, as her feet hit the firm planet floor, she thrust the lance's business end into the side of one of the five. As she did, the beast-draped purl—recovering to his feet from her initial blow—plunged his weapon into her. The force was mighty enough to lift her in the air. Her mouth opened involuntarily, and she gasped and looked up. Her gaze was filled with the sight of her impaled Quay. This was the last image of her life, and she would have had it no other way.

Quay's eyes, however, were elsewhere. They found their mark in the farthest circle and met the look of his son. Quel, son of Quay, was a young hunter who had learned the ways of a hunter from his parents. Danger is swift and unforgiving in the wild. One has to be able to read the signs that will keep one alive while fires are burning, and prey is turning on you with ferocity. Quel had been taught large beasts were not felled by individuals, but by hunters working together. He perceived danger had entered the village when, in his periphery, he caught the first lightning-quick movement of his father's leap. The instant the strangers entered he mistook the beast-draped purl for a new strange beast. He began to clear his mind of the terror which sought to rise within him to clearly discern what manner of monster this might be. When his focus fixed on the reality that these were purple, however strange and malevolent they looked, the arrow-pointed lance appeared. He fixed his gaze on it and the motion of the purl with the beast fangs in his forehead. He followed its flight until it entered his father's chest. And as the arrow entered Quay, rist entered Quel and began to rise. He had been taught about rist, of course, but had never been in its power. He had trained well under the master hunters and was ready for his final tests, but now, with rist in his veins, he needed no approbation. Although the flight of the weapon was only a few seconds long, Quel's gaze was transfixed on it until the lance pierced through his father and lodged itself in the hut wall.

That was when Quel looked into the eyes of Quay. They told him volumes. Ready to enter the fight with the beasts of Laish, as they later came to be called, he paused for instructions. The eyes of a master hunter say much. Tactics and timing are in them. They can proscribe an arrow's flight or a hunter's attack. Words are often too loud and too slow to communicate the essential orders in the midst of a battle with beasts. Quel had long ago learned to read his father's eyes. He expected them to tell him how to attack these monsters that had entered the sacred space of their village. He expected them to tell him what weapon to use and what tactic to take. Instead, the eyes of the most fearless hunter in Purplynd told him to grab his sister and flee. The message was clear and commanding, but strange to Quel. He had never seen his father afraid, and it was not fear he saw at this moment. He had been long taught that hunters move forward toward danger when non-hunters are nearby. He was confident in his skills, and his father trusted him to fight well at his side, no matter what the threat. Quay and Quel were part of a master hunter's team. Quel had hopes and dreams of one day rivaling the mastery of Quay or Miis and was well on his way. He was, by far, the best apprentice of the young hunters. He expected those eyes to send him springing toward the invaders, and the rist filled him with confidence and desire to do just that. These thoughts took no time at all for Quel to think but still too much time, for his father's eyes rebuked his inaction. Quay's eyes shouted, *Flee now!*

And with speed and agility never seen in an apprentice, Quel lifted his sister into his arms and disappeared into the wood. With that done, the noise of the battle, that now would not include him, grew silent. Quay closed his eyes in death and Miis was there in all her power and beauty. He reached for her hand and held it. Their eyes met, and they entered the afterlife together. What followed next in the village of Laish is too dark to be mentioned here in any detail.

The five purple, one mortally wounded, ravaged through the village like fire through summer straw. In addition to the lances with arrow stone tips, they wielded something as sharp as glass and as hard as stone. With it, they pierced and shredded the flesh of every hunter and fighter who opposed them. Very few screams rose from the gentle purple of Laish because the violence was so absurd and unwarranted. The mayhem was so strange and unnatural. No purl in all Purplynd had ever experienced what we now call murder or war or rape, so there were no words for what happened at Laish. In fact, *Laish* became the word for war, murder, rape, or any type of gratuitous violence for some time on Purplynd. All the good purple of Laish were killed that bright-day—all except two.

Quel ran all bright-day through the wood with his sister in his arms. He used all the knowledge he had to not leave a traceable trail. At times, he climbed trees and traversed from branch to branch with his little sister on his back. Other times, he paused in panicked silence, listening for any following footsteps. The dark night descended, and his little sister finally fell asleep, but Quel would not rest. He tied his sister to him with vines and continued moving. The rist had fallen quiet in his veins, but a child of Quay and Miis had strength unknown to most, and that strength moved him through the black night without rest or food. Day dawned, and Quel continued toward the northern village, which was, as all villages, a three-day journey. The morning of the second day, another mighty purl would end the journey of Quel and his sister deep in the woods outside the village of his mother's purple.

Kha, the brother of Miis, had risen from circle two days before and stared south toward the village of Laish. He stood and moved to the edge of his village and strained to see or smell something. This unusual behavior caught the attention of several other hunters, who first checked their own senses to discern whether a danger nearby. Convinced otherwise, they counseled Kha to return to the bright-day communion. That night, Kha did not sleep well, which was almost unheard of for any ancient purl. Day and bright-day exact a toll on the mind and body; night is how both are renewed. Sleep was sacred. But Kha's mind was full of thoughts of his twin sister, Miis. He had not seen her since the last three-year cycle celebrations, but they remained inexplicably connected. They had always been fierce competitors, but where competition would make others enemies, theirs brought them closer together. Miis and Kha wrestled, ran, hunted, and competed more than any others. And when purple grew weary of the contests, Kha and Miis would turn and challenge each other, always becoming more connected and confident as they did. They grew older and more skilled and passed the master hunter tests younger than anyone in any village ever had.

Kha and Miis were inseparable. When Miis came of age, she was attractive for a purl, yet none of the eligible purple of the village courted her. Most were intimidated by her prowess and skills as a hunter, and the few other aspirants failed to meet the standards of Kha, who had an effective way of communicating the unworthiness of any potential suitor. That was until the third three-year cycle games during the master hunter contests. It was there that Kha met the only purl worthy of his twin. Kha and Miis were leading the master hunter team of their village in a dangerous hunt. They were in competition with the other master hunter teams of the three-year cycle, but only the team from Laish had any hunters capable of challenging those led by Kha and Miis. On the third day of the intense and long trek far away from the celebratory fires of the great communion, it happened. In a brief lull of the hunt, Kha's constant competitiveness with Miis almost cost his sister her life. In his defense, it must be said that it was nearly impossible to catch Miis off guard. She was constantly aware of her surroundings. The air, for her, was filled with information. She was able to follow the scent of anyone or anything and count the number of hunters in a party by their odors. She could tell from the sound of the claw's grasp what creature caught the branch of a tree or moved along the forest floor. Her eyes were sharp and keen. The bend of a leaf a hundred yards away or a trail a cycle old were as obvious to her as fruit hanging on a tree. From when they were young, Kha and Miis had always added to the tasks at hand. They would always add a challenge to the challenge that occupied them. But this time, unknown and unimagined by Kha, his twin was preoccupied in a way she had never been before.

All her senses were, at that moment, focused on a sight across the narrow canyon. Any other time, the unexpected quick sweep of Kha's lance would have been met with a back flip over the swinging pole to a perfect landing and punch to his chest. But this moment was unlike any that had come before for Miis. An unfamiliar new sense was moving through her, and her twin did not perceive it. And if he had somehow detected it, he would not have understood or approved, but that was a different matter. At that moment, what mattered was what usually happened, didn't. This time, the lance hit Miis in her back. The blow sent her forward, and her footsteps moved to catch up with her chest, but the ground disappeared before her feet found anything to grip. Her arms reached out to catch something, anything, that would stop her, but there was nothing to catch, and over the cliff, she flew into the deep canyon.

It was Quay who leaped to almost certain death across the canyon to save Miis's life, and that was the day Kha found the only purl worthy of his twin. Inexplicably, this was the memory that punched Kha in the heart and pushed him out of the circle the last bright-day. It was this memory of watching his beloved twin's body knocked into the canyon by his own hand that kept sleep from him most of the night. The complete and utter helplessness or the regret mingled with caustic guilt that washed over him woke him again and again. Thrice the nightmare woke him. He finally gave up on sleep, and, unrested, he moved before the dawn's invitation back to the edge of his village. That was when, far in the distance, faint sounds of something reached his ears. The forest that should have been silent, wasn't. It was all the invitation he needed to leave the village. He was a master hunter. He was unrested and in no pleasant mood. He did not get his lance, nor did he wake any other hunter as would normally be the case when danger approached. A hunger to see his sister's face drove him south, and since that was the direction from which the sounds were coming, he moved toward them. Confident his bare hands could meet and match any danger, he hurried to encounter whatever was ahead.

Kha moved swiftly but silently toward the sounds, careful to keep his scent moving away from what approached. Dawn followed him and began to paint the forest, first in shadows and then in pale colors that would soon be bright enough for any hunter to see. But Kha was seen before he found what he was searching for, and this had never before occurred. Later, in circles all over, Purplynd tales of this encounter would debate whether it was Kha's fatigue or the prowess of those who approached that bested the master hunter. What were faint steps suddenly became louder and quicker, heading directly toward him. Kha, steeled by the desire to see his twin, increased his pace toward whatever approached. He was ready for purl or predator when, suddenly, the image of Miis flashed before him, and he looked into the faces of his nephew and niece.

Kha opened his arms to embrace them both, and Quel fell into his uncle's chest. Quel told Kha the story of Laish and the five who had entered. The desire to continue to Laish gripped Kha even more with the story. He thought to send the two to the village and continue to Laish, but the fatigue of his nephew was too great to ask any more of him. The fatigue and sorrow that had been held back by the hunter inside finally captured Quel. He released the last reserve of his strength into the arms of his uncle. Kha, strong and mighty, threw the young hunter over his shoulder, picked up his niece, and headed back to the village. When they arrived, day had already finished half its course. Only the essential hunters and fishers had left the village because Kha's absence had raised an alarm, and the entire village had decided to wait on his return.

On that day, the circles began before bright-day. Quel told them all he remembered. Questions were asked about the purple of Laish that Quel could not answer. Quel told them many things about the dark night and how he escaped the nocturnal beasts that had no disdain of purl scent. He spoke of things only one who had journeyed through the dark night would know or understand. In retelling his own story, he began to realize the dangers he had conquered and wondered at the power of rist. But in all his telling and memory, there were three powerful images he would not shake for a lifetime. The first was the tip on the lance and the sharp-as-glass tool that pierced flesh as a lance would the air. The second was the look in his father's eyes that, in one command, drove him away and, at the same time, described an eternal and ever-present love for him. The third was the color of the skin of the five killers who ended life as it had always been—red.

All the elders and the male and female purple of note respected and affirmed Quel for reading and adhering to the instructions of his father. None questioned his ability to understand Quay's command or the logic of it. For hours, they spoke and wondered about the three main memories Quel shared. Kha assembled the hunters and a few others who would travel south at dawn to find the answers to the questions Quel did not have. They set the first great fire to mourn the deaths of the purple of Laish. And as they did, the exhaustion that did not take him for almost half a cycle, caught up to the son of Quay. He slept the rest of bright-day and all night. When he woke, Kha and the hunters were on their way to face, fight, or finish the work of Laish.

Kha and the most skilled hunters of his village moved fast. With their numbers and being alert to the malevolent intent of the five red purple, they did not care if they left a trail, for they were the hunters now. Kha passed the place where he met Quel and his sister and, soon after, lost any obvious trail that would reveal the course Quel had taken. Most master hunters could hide the path of their feet and hands. They were trained to move through the forest or wood lightly, leaving no more of a trail than a squirrel would in our world. But the path Quel and his sister left was much fainter. Even his scent had been camouflaged as only a child of Miis could do.

But Kha recognized what Quel had done, and he followed the scent of aloe until it disappeared into purl and then changed to blare, which was another plant whose fragrance covered the faint odor of purl. The best of the other hunters detected the fragrances—the scent of aloe or blare or amest and about a dozen others—but could not track them well. And each of the master hunters detected the occasional scent of purl, but none understood how Kha led them so well from one brief scent of purl to another. Kha knew because it was what he had done so many years before in a game of hunter and prey he had played with his twin. He was the first to smear the oils of different plants over him in an attempt to hide his path from his sister. Miis, of course, soon discovered what her beloved brother had been up to. Together, they perfected the art of disappearing to all but each other. None could follow Kha or Miis when they chose to disappear.

It took three days, a full cycle, to arrive at Laish. The hunters, although they were masters, would not journey through the night. They traveled all day and into bright-day but then rested. They were confident following Kha, who followed the invisible trail Quel had left. It was a trail that was not a straight line at all but one that switched back and forth more and more the closer they got to the village. Kha could have headed straight to Laish, but something drove him to follow the path of his nephew before it disappeared. He thought he had lost it several times and once was convinced it had vanished. The trail was several days old now, and no one would fault even him for losing the scent. But Kha was determined to know as much as he could about the journey of his nephew. It was, for him, linked unalterably to the fate of his beloved Miis. What awaited him at Laish, whether stories of victory or sights of defeat, would wait, but the story of Quel's journey would soon vanish into the forest. And there was information the forest could tell him that perhaps Quel could not or would not.

Kha climbed one of the tall trees in what had become thick forest to get his bearings, and the sight confirmed they were near the mountain foothills. He looked toward the rising second sun to chart a more direct course to Laish. Then, in the top of the trees where the air was thinner, he caught an unfamiliar scent. The eyes can detect dangers and move the body before the mind has fully understood. The ears can detect the speed and direction of threats, translate the bird songs carried on the breeze, and inform a hunter of what the eye has not yet perceived. But the nose of a purl can do both before the eye has seen the flutter of a leaf or the ear has detected the faintest of sounds. And the scent Kha first caught on top of that tree confirmed his decision to follow the curious path of his nephew. It was an unfamiliar scent, but there was no doubt about its darkness. It was a malevolent odor, and even though faint, the danger it spoke of promised death.

Kha descended the tree, determined to head in the direction of the scent and to meet whatever darkness it brought. The hunters followed him but were concerned about the look of resolve in his eyes. It was the look one has when the decision has been made to enter a struggle that can only end in violence. It was the look that accompanies the grip of one's weapon when one engages in battle to kill the beast intent on killing you. These were master hunters, unafraid of fear or death, and they fell in attack formation behind Kha. The faint scent grew stronger. The first of the other hunters to catch the scent immediately jumped toward the center of it. In one quick move, she flipped over Kha's shoulder and stood hunter-still. Kha stopped. The other hunters stopped, and, as each began to pick up the scent, they gripped their lances and turned up their perceptual senses.

The cold-blooded beasts of legend roamed the deep forest at night and that is why purple did not travel after the suns had set. There were three species of beasts on Purplynd in the ancient times. First were the beasts, both small and large, that purple hunted for food. The smallest ones were much like the hares and rodents of Earth, and the largest ones grew to the size and had the demeanor of elk. All these animals, whether large or small, were called wapiti. Wapiti were content to forage for food, eat and hide nuts, berries, and grasses, and live their lives avoiding being eaten. Then there were the beasts that preyed on and competed with purple in the hunt and consumption of wapiti.

The carnivorous beasts of this second species were called kaviri. Kaviri were like the carnivorous predators of Earth. Some hunted in packs or prides, and some hunted alone, but all of them hunted. Those who hunted alone were the fastest and most beautiful. Those who hunted in packs were typically smaller and lacked the majestic beauty of the larger beasts, but all kaviri hunted prey. They were faster and stronger and had senses that were sharper than purple, but for reasons none really understood, kaviri feared purple. Kaviri would flee the scent of a purl just as a bird would dart away if approached. The only exceptions were if it was nesting, sick, or cornered. Then kaviri, like any other wild beast, would fight to defend itself or its offspring.

But at the top of the animal chain was panthae. These beasts preyed on kaviri and had no fear of purl scent. None in the circles or villages had seen one, but many hunters had come across the unfinished carcass of a kaviri whose strewn flesh bore signs of a ravenous and cruel beast. Panthae were easily tracked, but there was no evidence they ever roamed in day or bright-day. To become a master hunter, one would have to find and follow a panthae trail and mark the cave from which it came. Few master hunters entered such caves, and then, only so far as the bright-day light would shine into them. Panthae lived deep within the caves, which opened in the foothills of the mountains. Boulders and brush often hid the entrances to their lairs, and occasionally, the blood trail of some poor beast would reveal them. And even though panthae never walked in day or bright-day, hunters would avoid the foothills and the mountain caves at all costs.

This was why the hunters surrounding Kha stopped. They all suspected what lay ahead of them involved panthae. But with the dark scent, the best of them could also detect a whiff of purl. It was confusing. Perhaps what lay ahead were the beast-covered purple that had entered Laish not long ago, perhaps something worse. Still, they were all master hunters, and fear merely informed them. Kha moved to the shoulder of the hunter who had leaped over him. Their eyes met, agreed on the battle plan, and communicated it throughout the band by glance and gesture. All were in motion. They moved with strength, stealth, and determination toward whatever awaited them in the wood ahead.

As the hunters moved in attack formation, the scent grew stronger and darker. The forest became thicker as they moved until only the faintest light of bright-day could be seen. Just as a rattlesnake would shake its tail or a wolf would begin to growl, any predator or prey on Purplynd that detected the presence of the approaching party would have begun to move away from the hunters or given them warning. But whatever was in the wood did neither, which meant whatever it was, it was not threatened by the presence of purple. There was no doubt what lay ahead was prepared and ready to pounce on the approaching hunters or to be pounced on. The master hunters followed Kha, knowing they were either springing or jumping into a trap of something deadly, but the rist that had risen in them made both prospects equally desirable. Kha was first. He extended his lance and, with a leap and whistle, jumped to the center of the scent followed by the fearless and faithful hunters with him.

What they found was deadly and dead, a large, half-devoured kaviri with the cruelest beast ever seen dead behind it. They could tell by its scent it was panthae, but the sight of even a dead panthae filled most of them with fear and dread. The panthae was dark, darker than could be imagined or described. It was turned away from the kaviri that had been severed in two by one clamp of its jaws. There was a large kaviri bone driven into one of its eyes, through its brain, and into the ground. There, motionless, and dead, it was still frightening. Its jaws, open for a final and fatal strike, displayed triangular flat teeth that were sharp as glass and hard as stone. The sight was unforgettable and would be described in many circles for many cycles into the future. The hunters began reading the scene by the evidence which remained.

Things many would miss if given a month of cycles to discover were plain to see for those ancient master hunters — a cradle high in a tree where a small child lay, the claw marks and circular movement of a surprised super-predator, the broken kaviri bone snatched from a freshly killed predator-become-prey. They read the battle and fell in awe of the purl who had waged and won it. The final strike that drove the thighbone through the beast could only have come from above. In fact, for much of the battle, the panthae seemed to attack the trees. The speed and precision needed to fight such a battle was rare. Besides Kha, only two others had ever been suspected to have such strength, courage, battle savviness, and speed. Still, neither he, his twin, nor Quay had never slain a panthae. Kha thought of his nephew, and pride filled him. He thought of his twin, and desire drove him. His heart called to him clarion. He left the scene and the slain beast and sped toward Laish with the master hunters in tow.

They entered Laish in attack formation. The master hunters encircled the encampment and moved quietly past the outer huts until they were in view of one another. They came in this way, not because of any possible danger but to honor their noble intent. The signs and silence in the outer wood had already told them what to expect in the village. They were told by the blood splatter on the petals of flowers and the sadness that seemed to hang on the leaves. They were told by the unnatural quiet of the wood. Creatures and the birds of prey encircled the village but, for reasons resembling reverence, would not enter. But long before these sights and sounds, the scent of the death and decay that had begun days before in the village of Laish told them that life had left Laish. When they entered, they, too, fell silent and still. To describe what entered their vision would be to communicate the utter and naked evil of what happened in Laish. To speak of those things would be to throw the seeds of otherwise unimaginable evil into innocent minds. There are things that once seen can never be unseen, things that reverberate in the psyche unmentioned yet unmovable. Some stories, once heard, encamp in the mind, poisoning every thought thereafter. This was what greeted the senses of Kha and the master hunters that day. Many of the hunters lifted their voices in a wail of mingled anguish, sorrow, and horror. Others collapsed and cried with loud moans of grief and anger, but from the mighty Kha, no sound arose. He who saw more, heard more, smelled more stood silent and still. The commanding eyes of Kha bid the hunters to stand fast, and this they were more than willing to do. The utter terror of what lay before them and around them grew a grief that threatened to freeze their hearts and corrupt their souls.

They had left their village with hope that their strength and skills could be of some help to the purple of Laish. They left willing to fight whatever or whomever was necessary to deliver their kin. But the scene before them condemned the confidence of those thoughts. The utter darkness of the deeds that had been done, as evidenced by the foul scene which lay before them, sucked the daylight from the sky. Now, the weariness of the long journey and its hopeless end began to descend on them. With the glance of Kha's command, they all sat down. Many were weeping; others sat silent, but all understood the need to be still and allow the sorrow to sink through them into the ground. They understood that what was entering their senses should not be held in their minds and bodies. The torrent of darkness seeking to possess their souls must move through them and into the rich, black ground on which they sat, so they sat still with their open palms pressed to the floor of their planet. They let what could not be held by their hearts move to where there was room. They sat still as their sorrow moved through them into the heart of Purplynd. And, in sacred silence, they all sat for the remaining hours of bright-day. All but Kha.

Kha was restless and would not sit. The rist, which, in him, had always been more powerful than in most, unsettled him. His longing for Miis was sharper now in her death than it had been in her life. What he sensed days ago, now lay before him. The connection between him and his twin had pulled him to his feet as the blade of the half-beast entered her chest, and she gasped. The alarm that began then foretold the scene before him now. The utter grief of the death surrounding him boiled his blood, and his sorrow began to sink—but not into the ground. He held on to it, and it hid in the shadows of his soul as something else rose to take its place. Within him, what the others were feeling raged. Within him, warriors of grief fought warriors of anger, and this war would continue for some time. For hours, the war waged within him, compelling his hearts and hopes to give way to anger and rage. Miis would have sensed what was happening in her twin. She would have understood what he needed, and she alone could have made him do it. She would have sat him down so the planet could absorb what no purl should attempt to carry. Kha knew he should sit, but he couldn't without her. He needed her. His twin held the calming part of him. Miis was his peace. He was her anger. Kha walked the village while the others sat still. He read what he could of what had happened there. He found the body of Quay and removed it from the wall. He found his twin and lay her body beside her spouse. At long last, when night had taken all light, he sat in the circle of his hunters. There, they would rest in deep grief. Sleep came, removed time, and gave them respite.

It was a silent night. The darkness hid the horror the dawn unveiled, but the sacred silence had prepared most for the tasks ahead. The hunters sat in respectful stillness until Kha exhaled a deep breath and stood. The hunter to his right stood after Kha was erect, and each of them rose as a wave moving around the circle. When the movement was complete and the hunter to Kha's left stood, Kha stabbed his lance into the ground. The sound seemed thunderous in the silence, and beginning with the purl who had stood last, each hunter in their turn stabbed his or her lance into the dust with a mighty thrust. When the last lance was planted into the black soil, Kha, the master of hunters, began the ritual of gathering the strewn and beloved dead around them. Many bodies had to be reassembled, but of these things, no more should be said. Each family was buried in the hut that had been their home, except the village leaders. Everything else—furnishings from the homes, toys, instruments, garments, and tools—were gathered together in the center of the village. It was the duty and honor of the kin and friends to find and bury the dead of Laish so that the last touches each purl body received was from someone who loved and cared about them. Many tears accompanied each burial, anointing the bodies with drops of love. Quay and Miis were buried last at the entrance to the village. Kha carried their bodies to the graves prepared for them. He caressed their swaddled forms as if they were infants. He lowered them into Purplynd, and, for the first time since entering the village, tears escaped the barriers of his soul and rolled down his cheeks. Each drop from his cheek summoned dusk and carried the fading light of bright-day into the dark grave.

Kha stood over his twin and the only purl worthy of her, and he spoke for the first time since entering the village. His words were great and noble. He spoke of his love for his twin and honored Quay, who had become a brother to him. With a quivering voice, he began to sing until, in full-throated lament, the song of life and love began.

The others joined in and eventually added verses of their kin. The holy hymn lasted for hours as the final tears of grief dropped to the ground. The chorus became a deep hum as, in the final act of ritual, all brought stones and placed them on the graves of Quay and Miis. The stones rose high above the head of the tallest purl and stood as a marker that the sounds of life would no longer enter Purplynd from Laish and that the silent sacredness of its resting dead should not be disturbed.

With the entrance to the village now closed, the hunters assembled again, encircling the mound of materials that had once been the possessions of the purple of Laish. A melodious moan moved among them, and one of the three tinkerers who had come with the company, brought flame to light this, the final fire of Laish. The flames rose toward the heavens and illuminated the darkness as it descended to end bright-day. The fire spread warmth toward the party as they sat like they had the night before, palms pressed to the planet. Purplynd sucked the sorrow from the souls of all who sat thus. Two did not. Kha chose to sit with his arms folded. He stared into the flames and beyond them. A force he had no name for kept the insides of his mind in motion. He thought these were the pangs of love and longing for his twin, but they were accompanied by an energy that wasn't love at all. Since before they had entered the village, Kha had been studying the signs of life and death that remained in Laish. He deciphered much of what had occurred. He could see where the fight began, and the thud left in the ground by the back of the beast that killed his twin. He saw where the hunters gathered and fell as they attacked. He saw the footprints of the children running to safety and where they had been slain. He saw, and could almost hear, the sounds of the slaughter. It was as if the dead cried out to him. The butchers taunted him as the shadows spoke. He searched and finally found the path the intruders had taken out of Laish. It was a path that called to him, *"Come follow me now."* These were the thoughts swirling in his mind as the flames of the fire licked the open air. The images ran frantically within him and, finding no exit, lodged themselves in the muscles and tissue of his being. Kha was being transformed from a master hunter into something else, and he did not know it. He only knew he could not rest, and this was not over.

There was another who did not keep still as the fire burned and quiet fell: Tyne, the tinkerer. Tyne was considered the wisest tinkerer in the three-year cycle. He had many of the sharp senses of a hunter but also possessed something else. Something in his mind allowed him to imagine things that never had been and to fashion things that, until they were made, purple believed could never be. From the moment Quel's story began, Tyne wanted to get to Laish. He wanted to see for himself what could be discovered there. He would see what most others would not. And while they were all overwhelmed by the tragedy and loss of life, Tyne was most curious about other things. At first, Kha was unconvinced tinkerers should accompany the hunters. So, instead of trying to convince Kha, Tyne used his influence to sway most of the council of elders to let him be included. It was the elders who had the final say, and Kha was only one of nine. Tyne was the fire starter and, under the pretense of maintaining the flame, excused himself from the rituals, which began and ended the party's presence at Laish. Had Kha's senses and attention not been so overwhelmed with the travesty in the village, the strange behavior of the tinkerer would have been obvious. But it would be a long time before the true importance of what Kha missed in this purl would be revealed and then much too late to reverse the tragic course that had already begun.

Morning met most of the hunters ready to make their way back to their own village. Some worried the travesty of Laish might visit their homes. Others were just ready to put the sorrow behind them, but all the hunters waited for Kha. He was the last to wake, which was unusual. Rest had avoided him until late into the night. In his mind, he blamed the residual rist in his veins for this, but long into the night, the flames held him entranced between consciousness and sleep. The last image he remembered was a dark shadow he thought was Tyne walking toward him in the firelight.

Kha woke resolved. The rest that comes when hard decisions are made, or difficult tasks are completed filled him with resolve. Realizing the whole party was waiting for him made him smile and suppress the chuckle that sought escape as he thought about how many times and ways circle stories would recount how the master hunter was the last to awake. With a deep sigh instead, he signaled that he was ready to begin the journey home. The party stood and, in the ways of ancient purple, bid farewell to the dead. Kha was the last to leave the village because he took his time saying his goodbyes. The entire party assembled just outside the village to the west. Kha came, and they began to journey home. The first stop for all would be the river where they would all wash what remained of the carnage off their bodies and out of the wounded part of their minds.

They arrived at a place beneath a waterfall where the water pooled, and the river was still. It was the place where the purple of Laish would have come to wash. There, they began the final ritual of death by slowly walking, one by one, into the waters. Again, forming a circle, they faced one another and began to submerge themselves over and over until they were clean. The blood that had remained on their bodies and clothes dissolved into the water, turning the pool a cloudy red. They watched and waited until all were clean and the waters had carried the bloodstains and much of the pain of death downriver. Usually, the ritual would then move to more celebratory activities. After a burial washing, the village would lend themselves to frolic and playing together in the water. Some would dive off the surrounding cliffs or tree branches; others would play any of the number of water games common to ancient purple. But after the washing and the watching of the water, no one began to play. Instead, a stunned silence froze them as they all stared at something uniquely strange.

There was one memory Quel shared they had not witnessed in all the horrors they had just buried, and here in the water, as bright-day showed all for what it was, they saw what they had before only imagined. Kha was the last to realize something had changed. He was staring at the river, holding on to the last sight of color in the distance, when he realized there was silence where there should have been a rising noise. He looked and everyone looked healthy and refreshed except they were all standing still and staring, their gaze fixed on him. He looked at them and then looked at what they were staring at and realized his skin was red.

The peace that had begun to rise in Kha as he washed and the waters cleared, began to dissipate faster than it had come. The color of his skin made him angry. The look in the eyes of the party made him angrier. He did not understand why the blood of Laish that he had walked through, sat in, and cleaned off the bodies of those he loved had not washed downriver as it had with the others. Some began to come close to him, perhaps to scrub the color from his skin. But the look of confusion and condemnation on their faces was too much for Kha to accept. He backed away from them and moved out of the water. The rest of the party came out of the waters behind him. Some wondered if the waters were cursed. The wiser among them suspected other things. This strange event called for a council to discuss what had happened and decide what should be done. The eldest and wisest among them sat in a circle. The others stood around them forming a ring. Some thought it best for Kha to return with them to the village. Others did not. Finally, it was decided: Kha should return to Laish and sit in silence until this red skin disappeared and his color returned to the blue hue of all purple of the planet. Two hunters asked to be allowed to stay with him, and it was thought wise, but Kha refused. The anger and all its power throbbed within him. It reminded him of rist, but he recognized what was moving through him was not rist at all. He used all his own power to suppress what was happening within him. He was sitting still but, at that moment, wanted to be wrestling a beast or strangling a kaviri. The questions asked of him provoked him more. He thought going back to his village was a waste of time because the trail of the killers was growing cold. If he had told them what was going through his mind or the pulses moving through his body, there were some in the party who could have helped him. Instead, he was polite and deferential to those for whom he had a rising contempt. Amid the din of the conversation occurring around him and the shouting happening inside his head, some part of him listened for the still small voice of his sister. She was the voice of calm, confidence, and quiet. He tried to focus on that voice, and as he did, the raging within him quieted, and he began to rest some in the midst of the council.

Finally, the circle came to a decision. Kha was to return to Laish. They would send him back to where the mystery began. They believed he was carrying something from Laish that he should have left. They were right, but they had no idea how right they were. Kha understood part of their reasoning, but he missed much of what was being said. So much was going on in his psyche. He did not want to be in this circle, and he did not want to be the subject of it. He did not want to go back to his village. What he wanted to do was hunt the murderers of his twin. He did not care his flesh was red, and he did not care what the collective wisdom of the circle was. In this state of mind, when too many thoughts came rushing and swirling into him, Kha had a habit of transferring the energy needed to think into muscle strength. He would run. He would hunt. He would wrestle purl after purl in a test of tease-and-tumble until exhaustion calmed him. This made him a great hunter and gave him great strength but diminished his capacity to sit in what the elders called 'sacred silence.' He needed Miis. She was his sacred voice. She was the one whose whisper could calm him. She was the only one that could, from time to time, beat him in a game of tease-and-tumble which, for them, became the game of tease, tumble, and toss because their match would end with one or the other being tossed into water or mud or anything soft and embarrassing. He thought of her, and it calmed him. He resolved, for whatever reason the circle was sending him back to Laish, he would go. He believed he should sit beside the grave of his twin and attempt to find the peace she had brought to him for so long while she lived. His eyes began to water with the thoughts of Miis. He stayed the tears with a brush of the back of his hand. He attempted to play this off as a brush to his brow. He looked at the quiet water and turned his mind in an attempt to give his full attention to the circle conversation which was reaching its conclusion.

Lost in the emotions and thoughts of his own, Kha did not hear the concerns expressed about his hearts. Nor did he hear the exact prescription for his time back at the village gate. He *did* hear that they intended to send two hunters with him, something he passionately did not want to happen.

He wanted to be alone or at least away from these with whom he had come. The anger that had quieted in him stirred, but he pushed it beneath his most polite and tender voice and asked if he would be allowed to go alone. The council was not moved. He argued the party had been away from their village and families long enough, and the trauma and terror of Laish would best be healed by their return. This was true, and the leaders sitting in the circle understood it better than he did. The younger hunters standing around the circle were all skilled hunters and had no fear of forest or foe, but the sights of slaughter, mayhem, and madness they had witnessed in Laish could only be permanently healed through the love and tenderness of the village. They wanted to return home, but they would heed the council's decision, and it had been made. More words were unnecessary. Either Kha would rebel, or the council would recant. It was unheard of that anyone would refuse to adhere to the counsel of a circle. Purple depended on one another and trusted that the thoughts of one mind must yield to the wisdom of many minds. It was and had always been that way. There were rare times when a decision required contemplation and time, but there was never this much tension and angst. Only Phee, one of the oldest master hunters, saw the red of Kha's skin deepen. She had taught Miis when Kha's twin was very young, and she was wiser than most in the ancient ways. Age had barely slowed her down, and her awareness of many things had increased as she grew older. All the hunters respected her guidance, and none would reject her conclusion on any matter. In the silence, all waited for her to speak and understood it would be the end of the matter, including Kha. Some time passed, and just as Phee inhaled the breath before her final decision was spoken, Tyne spoke out.

"I will accompany him!" he almost shouted. It was a stark interruption to the moment. Tyne began to argue that he was capable, and since he had neither wife nor child, he did not need to rush back to the village. He met the eyes of Kha with his own and told him to trust him. The glance connected Kha to the night before at the fire, just before he was lost to sleep. Kha remembered the fire and the connection to the fire starter he made without understanding or needing to understand how or why they were connected.

Kha remained quiet. Tyne finished his speech, and the circle fell quiet again. After some time, Phee spoke. "Kha, son of Khee, your heart is buried beneath the sorrow of Laish. You hold fire in your breast where water should flow. Darkness is descending on you. To see the bright-day, you must return to Laish. You are told there to stay until that which boils beneath your bones flows into the ground and remains. A full cycle you must rest, after which you must return to our village. There we will decide your course."

Phee instructed two very strong hunters to accompany Kha. She told them he must never be left alone and that one should hunt while the other cared for him. She told them which the foods he was to be fed. She called the names of specific roots and plants and instructed them that he was to eat no wapiti meat, no matter how well cooked. He was to rest and be massaged the three days of a cycle, whereupon they all should return to wash in the waters of the river and then home.

Another of the elder hunters spoke and declared it too late to journey farther. They would eat and head home at dawn. Tyne was told it was not a tinkerer's place to speak on these matters. He was reminded that to stand without a circle and speak into it is unkind, and he was not to repeat such a breach of decorum. All was settled. Young hunters were sent for food. The fire was started, and other preparations were made quickly because the deliberations had been long, and the bright-day almost spent. They ate, and they rested without any further conversations. On this day, one intense and long deliberation was enough. The darkness fell as a tall tree cut from its roots and was welcomed by all. Phee woke before the others. Her whistle made witness to the morning and called for the hunters to arise. She was already aware of what the others, after shaking the cobwebs from their minds, came to realize: Kha and Tyne were gone.

Phee wondered if Kha would make it through the night. His breathing was too measured and irregular, and the beating of his two hearts were out of sync. Only Kha could force out what was inside him, and Phee recognized what it was. The anger and energy swirling within him and being absorbed by his psyche and sinew would only exit by the embrace of peace. In the best of circumstances, this process would be aided by the expert love and care of the elders in a circle. The most powerful rituals of peace included and needed the village. The entire village would participate, singing softly at times, being silent at times, anointing the suffering one with oils and scents, while the one out of sorts sat with palms pressed against Purplynd.

Part of the conversation in the circle that last bright-day revolved around returning Kha to the village. Phee thought him too far gone to make the journey. She was right. She was not sure whether Kha was strong enough to resist the temptations within his soul. The cancer within him was a force that drives a purl away from other purple. It was a power that isolates and consumes a purl from his core. Mild forms of this sickness can occur when a tragic or sudden death happens. There are other, less explainable, reasons a purl might fall prey to this sickness, but it is easily detected in the village. Hunters are particularly susceptible to the malady because of the time they spend outside the community. The more comfortable a purl is with being alone, the more alone he or she becomes, and purple were not created to be alone. When this power is hot and strong within a purl, the only remedy is the ritual. It was rare for a purl to seek isolation, and the only elder in the three-year cycle who had ever seen a purl as sick as Kha now appeared to be was Phee.

Some suggested Kha and Tyne be tracked and taken to Laish. Others were now more convinced that Kha must be returned to the village. But with Kha gone, Phee was the elder who had the last word, and she was sensing the need for the party to return to the village. The seeds of the sickness that had taken Kha were in them all. It was plain to see. It was something Phee could smell, and it meant the most important movement was toward healing and home. Her eyes turned stern and gave the command that they were to start the journey and with speed. The hunters under her counsel now obeyed without further thought or question. One of the elders whooped a whistle, and like a startled herd of wapiti, off they flew toward their healing place. Phee took up the rear, waiting until all the others were some distance away. She was aware of a dark and cold presence. The darkness was too close to be safe and too far away to be recognized. The image and thought of Tyne came to her mind for some reason, but Tyne, or something darker, was waiting some distance away in the morning mist. It was what woke her. Whatever or whoever the shadow was did not follow the hunters but drifted into the distance in the direction of Kha's scent. Satisfied that the darkness would not follow them, Phee turned and, with her master skills, hurried to catch up to the party headed home.

Kha could not rest or sleep. Why Phee had set him near her to rest through the dark night, he did not know, but the gentle part of him welcomed it. Phee was kin and close. Since the death of his parents, she had been mother and father for both him and Miis. When he and his twin were just past their first steps, which, by the way, were much faster steps than most purple, she was there, helping her little sister with the marvelous twins. And through the tragic cycle of their parents' deaths, Phee had taken greater and greater responsibility for the twins' lives and growth. So, there in the circle beside her, Kha began to connect to good things again. The gentle part of him placed his palms against Purplynd and began to rest. But Kha did not rest well. The not-gentle part of him — he would want to say it was the hunter part of him, but it was more than that — did not want to be near Phee. Kha was much younger than Phee and several other elders in the party; in fact, he was the youngest elder of the village, but he was the head of this party. And, as such, he should determine the formation of the resting circle. Besides this, the two best hunters should always be set on opposite sides of the formation for safety. Was Phee suggesting he was any less of a master hunter because his skin was red? A voice inside his head that whispered that he was now aware of things she could not imagine, the voice declared, he was stronger and more focused than he had ever been.

The gentle and the not-gentle parts of his mind engaged a game of tease-and-tumble that kept sleep away from him long into the dark night. Until at last, his mind moved to memories of Miis. With this, his brow unfurled, and he was freed to rest. He lost consciousness, and the pull of Purplynd at his palms held him. But he did not rest long. A strange sound startled him. It was a faint sound but carried an urgent alarm. Something was out of place. He woke hunter-still, and, as he shook the cobwebs of sleep from his tired mind, he focused his senses on the sounds that woke him.

The hunters near him, as well as Phee beside him, remained in deep sleep. Had he been in his right and rested mind, he would have recognized that the sounds were coming from inside his mind instead of the outside world, but it had been many days since his mind had truly been rested. What rattled in his mind was the sound of a small kaviri running back and forth in a straight line some distance behind him. It was a dark, strange, and dangerous sound. Kaviri, especially small ones, did not run in straight lines. And kaviri would never remain or venture this close to purple. The only creature that would dare would be panthae, and he had never seen, nor heard, of a small panthae. Without taking time to think, he realized even panthae couldn't be born full-grown. With that thought, he picked up the scent of darkness. It was the same scent he picked up from the top of the trees after he had lost the scent of his nephew. The small creature that was running back and forth too near the circle was in danger or was a danger. Kha could not decipher which in the brief waking moment, but what was clear to him was that he must respond. As he stood, his palms pulled him back to the planet as if Purplynd was attempting to hold him against the danger, but he wrestled himself away from the healing it offered to face the threat.

Rising silently, Kha turned his back to the circle and walked into the darkness, following a sound and scent which seemed to remain the same distance away from him as he headed further into dark night. He was well into the wood and far from the circle before he truly woke. He found himself on a ridge when the first light of dawn broke. The moist forest beneath his feet made him wonder where he was and why. Awake now, he remembered the dream—if it *was* a dream. Determined to get his bearings, he looked behind him and his own trammeled path led in a straight line from the direction he had come. The path helped him realize that it must have been a dream, for it was a child's path, so obvious and heavy-footed. Kha smiled as he thought of what Miis would make of his sleepwalking tramp through the forest. He shook his head in wonder at himself and realized the elders were right: He was not at all himself.

The first star began to rise, and with its light, Kha began to desire his village. He was still exhausted and tired in his bones, but, somehow, the morning light lifted his spirits. The thought that he had no idea where he was or how he got there tickled him. Oh, how the stories would be told at circle. Kha resolved to find his way back to where his night travels had begun and then home. The child's path he had made through the night ensured the first part of this task would be simple. He took a deep breath, stretched his weary muscles, and turned around. And then he remembered.

He couldn't go back. He had been told to return to Laish. His first steps doubling back on his night trek trail were light. But as he headed back to the place they had camped, the forest began to get thick, erasing much of the morning light that had lightened his mood. And with each step, heaviness began to seep again into his soul. He wondered if the hunting party would be waiting for him. They were, after all, under his leadership. Or they had been, until the elders had circled last bright-day. The thoughts of that last circle were not welcome in his mind. He remembered he had been instructed to return to Laish. He remembered he didn't care at that time what they said or where he went. He thought his own behavior strange and wondered at it. He did not like the idea of going back to Laish. A gentle voice inside him called him to calm. The warmth of his sister's presence came to him in the quiet. The feeling made him long for home even more. Kha followed his own path for two hours, surprised he had wandered unconscious for so long. From time to time, the path he was retracing appeared to have been made by more than one purl. At the end of the third hour, he entered the circle where the party had slept the night before. They had gone long before he entered. The signs and sounds told him the party had departed hours ago, but he was drawn to the circle by a quiet within him that needed the company of his kin. He went to the place where he sat to be still and sleep the night before. He touched the place where Phee had been beside him. Purplynd called to him. It was as if the ground spoke. *Rest here.* There was something inviting, something warm about the place where Phee had been. Phee had become to Kha what his mother had been, but he was drawn to her more by the memories Miis shared of her than by the fact she raised him after the death of his parents.

The invitation was clarion. Whether it was Phee or Purplynd, the place where Phee had slept the night before was still warm and calling him. It was a gentle call. It was urgent but without any panic. It was deep and longing without force or compulsion. It resounded in the quiet core of his being. This calm call carried catastrophic consequences if not heeded. Kha was perplexed. He knelt, beginning to consent to the attraction of the place while a rising confusion within sought to push him to his feet. The solitude was comfortable for him, but, again, brought him the desire to return to his own village. The memory of its sights and sounds, the familiarity of its rituals, and how life moved through time were comforting and compelling. Being in the middle of a foreign forest drew his hearts to all the places that were familiar. In a saccadic moment, he remembered the alarm in his spirit cycles ago. He remembered the travesty of Laish. He remembered the danger, the darkness, and the despair of the journey to this point. And within a moment, he remembered the counsel of the circle was to send him back to Laish. For reasons he did not understand, he did not welcome the counsel of others in that moment. In fact, he wondered why any purl ever would. He did not need anyone to think for him. This he was capable of doing for himself and by himself. He did not know the independence that was growing in his mind and the color of his skin were related. Few would ever understand the connection. He just decided he would lie on the warm place that called to him, and there, he would decide whether to heed the council and return to Laish or return to his own village. Either way, it would be his decision and not that of any council. Kha decided to lay his cheek in the place where Phee's right palm had impressed the ground and rest. He would curl himself in the fetal position and reassemble his soul on the imprint of the purl who was mother to him. At long last, Kha began to lie down. He never made it.

The sound struck Kha before his eyes detected movement. No scent he could discern signaled caution, which is why the danger broke on him so quickly. He didn't have time to wonder why he didn't detect the danger or sense the darkness before it was too late because, in a rush of dust, fury, and noise, Tyne came running toward him. He came wildly into view, shrieking. Tyne was making an unfamiliar and strange sound. It was the scream of a frightened child mixed with a hunter's call to attack. It was a battle cry of victory and dominance disguised as plea for help. Both the sound and the tinkerer were coming straight toward Kha. Kha reacted. He jumped from the sacred spot Phee had left him, hit the ground, and rolled between the legs of the running Tyne. Tyne smiled in awe of the prowess and skill of the master hunter, but now Kha was between the tinkerer and the danger that pursued him. It appeared first as a dark shadow and quickly revealed itself as a large kaviri. It was enraged and attacking. Kha did not see that Tyne had stopped running and stood a few paces behind him, but the kaviri did and dipped its horns to culminate the attack. It lifted its head as its horns caught Kha and threw him high into the air, flipping him back first into the trunk of a tree. Tyne moved aside as would a master bullfighter, and the raging beast ran past him. Tyne then ran to help Kha, and just as he lifted him, the attacking beast was returning with all its fury. It headed straight toward the two figures. Tyne moved right and attempted to pull Kha with him. Kha was dazed and hurt but still capable of defending himself and aware enough to move out of the way of a crazed kaviri. He moved left, out of the way of the charging animal. The two purple were at cross-purposes with a beast between them. Kha ripped himself from the grip of Tyne but not before one of the sharp horns pierced Kha's chest, cutting a deep gash from which rich, thick blood began to ooze and then flow.

The wound removed any question that there would be a benign end to this contest. Rist rose like a great wave on a powerful sea and crashed hard into the body of Kha. If the wound was fatal, his body would have to wait to die because what rose within Kha was greater than death. The power had anger as its core component but was more than any anger Kha had ever allowed to surge in his flesh. It was pure rage with a blood lust. It was power focused for no purpose other than death. One of the beast's horns had stuck in the trunk of the tree, and in the moment, it took it to free itself, Kha, possessed by this new strength, grabbed its other horn, and pushed its head backward. With a fist as hard as stone and blows as powerful as thunder, Kha began punching the animal in its throat. The first few blows stunned the beast, and the successive strikes moved it from its desire to attack to a longing to flee. Kha, or some part of him, sensed the danger had passed and that the beast wished now only to flee. But something else inside him, something more powerful, bid him to strike harder. He released the horn in his left hand and continued striking blow after blow. There was a demented glee swirling in his veins. He continued the barrage of blows until the beast was dead, and even then, could not stop. The flesh of the beast tore, and Kha's fists began to splash in the bloody innards of the dead beast. The blood of the kaviri hit his chest and made his wound pulse with intense pain. Tyne moved behind him and pulled at his shoulders. Only then did he stop.

The dead kaviri carcass lay mutilated at Kha's feet. The muscles in his arms ached. Fatigue washed over his entire body. His breathing was heavy and labored. His chest rose and fell, and the intense pain of his wound began to take over his body. The loss of blood made him weak and light-headed. He stumbled backward a few steps and fell to the ground. He summoned his strength and sat up. With his left hand pressed on Purplynd and his right hand over the open wound in his chest, the wildness in his mind started to clear. The pain over his hearts began to throb, and he attempted to make sense of where he was and what had just occurred. Why would a kaviri attack him? His hands ached. The broken neck bones of his prey had lacerated his fists, but he did not know it. They were covered with mingled blood and fragments of beast. He attempted to lift his left hand off the ground to look at it. He wanted to piece together what he had just done but only lifted his hand a few measures off the ground before the weight of it pulled it back. His mind was foggy, and his vision began to blur. A hard blow to his forehead came from his blind side and his back hit the ground for the final time. As his eyes closed to Purplynd, the face of Tyne appeared. He was smiling. There was something in his hand.

Kha went in and out of consciousness. His open chest was pulled and torn. He felt himself being raised and made to drink warm, putrid grog, and then the light of bright-day went black.

What Kha did not know, could not have known, and never would have imagined was that the kaviri he had just killed had been provoked. Long before Kha rose to wander into the wood and while he was still sleeping, the fire starter had trapped an infant kaviri and tied its hindquarters with a vine. He would release it, and it would attempt to run, only to be dragged back and released again. Then Tyne took the terrorized pup back to where he had stolen it, broke its neck, and threw it into the nest. Doing so guaranteed the kaviri mother would recognize and remember his purl scent. Hours later, Tyne returned and stole another pup, but this one, he held up before its mother and taunted the beast by tossing the pup in the air as it squealed in terror and fear. Tyne then threw the pup against a tree and began to run. It was this enraged kaviri that came charging into the place where Kha contemplated rest.

There were other things Kha did not know. He did not know what it was Tyne poured down his throat. His compromised state of consciousness would later make it easy for him to doubt it ever occurred, but his memory was irrevocably marked by a process that had him waking to violent regurgitation over and over through the dark night of his transformation. Kha did not know the massive pain in his chest was not solely due to the kaviri wound but also because one of his hearts had been removed. Kha could also not have known what the whisperer was planning to do with his soul. These things would remain dark mysteries for a long time. Then they would be brought to light, only to be tragically forgotten again.

It was a long time before Kha awakened, and when he did, it was with a start. He was trapped. He woke sitting between two small trees with his arms outstretched and his wrists tied to the trunks of the saplings. He woke as if he were breaking into Purplynd from another world. He came to consciousness angry and ready to project that anger with all his might. Snapping the vines that bound his wrists to the small trunks, he rose to his feet but not adeptly. He was slow and unsteady. Shaking the cobwebs from his mind, he began to piece his memory back together. He looked for Tyne and found him not far away—crouching, watching, and waiting. Seeing no imminent danger, Kha began to calm himself.

The tightness across his chest hurt. He placed his hand over the now closed wound and barely recognized his own flesh. He looked at himself and accepted the red flesh as if he had been born red. It was the end of bright-day. Which bright-day, he did not know. It was not the same bright-day he fought the kaviri, but he was not sure how many days he had skipped. He would need help to understand just how many cycles had passed since his fight with the kaviri, and that help would not come for a long time. He had questions, but before he asked them, he would go and wash in the waters.

He returned to the edge of the pool where the entire party had washed away the blood and mud of Laish, which now seemed so long ago. At the water's edge, he began to remember things. He knelt to drink and a face he did not recognize stared back at him. That it was now irrevocably red he found strange but acceptable. But the hardness and violence of his own image, the darkness that lurked behind the eyelids plain to see, startled him. At that moment, he recognized the terror he had first seen in the kaviri he had killed to pass the master hunter trials. It was the look produced by horror and disbelief as inexplicable pain invites death. Looking into the water, he also saw his chest for the first time. The horn of the beast had cut him from the middle of his right breast all the way across the rest of his upper body. The wound had been stitched together with thorns and the small veins of a slain animal.

It was not unheard of to use the veins of a wapiti in an extreme attempt to save the life of a purl, but care must be taken. Only the gentlest of wapiti would ever be considered. Rituals with the community would follow soon after such acts. Finally, sitting with Purplynd would ensure no wildness would come into the soul of the purl or his or her children. Kha wondered what wapiti donated their life to save his, but no wapiti had. The strangeness of his own image quickly passed. Kha finished his drink and lowered himself into the pool beneath the waterfall to wash. When the water reached his wound, the scar across his chest erupted like a volcano and searing pain of lava moved beneath his skin. The pain was so intense, immediate, and unexpected, the master hunter reacted reflexively. Kha opened his mouth to cry, and the sound he made was more of a roar than the cry of any purl. The forest echoed with it, and the sound of his own soul frightened him.

With this new pain, Kha struggled to get out of the water. He made it to the shore and fell to his knees with his open palms pressed against Purplynd. Kha realized he had been changed. He understood this change was not merely the color of his skin and suspected it went deeper than the sound of his voice. He was angry, hurting, and suddenly exhausted. He was frightened, and this he had never been before. His thoughts ran to Phee. His heart called to her. Something small and weak inside him called to the woman who had become his mother. Like a lone, thin thread out of the full fabric of what he had become, it stretched back to his roots. Her voice, quiet and strong, spoke to him. It was a still, small, and clear voice despite the fires of pain, exhaustion, and anguish raging in his body. Her voice was like the sound of the silence between the lightning's flash and the thunder's crack. Phee, as if she was beside him, had heard his plea and called him to come home. Her call was a sweet and gentle request but one that granite could neither crush nor penetrate. Tears filled his eyes as the pain took full possession of his body. He resolved that if he would be able to rise and walk again, he would return to the village.

When a child shows promise in foraging for food and following instructions, he or she begins to be trained as a hunter. Most hunters became proficient in a particular part of the hunting task. Some were best at tracking. Others were skilled at throwing or fashioning lances. A few excelled at trapping prey, and at few mastered field dressing and preparing the parts of the capture that would be eaten. When a purl could do all the hunting tasks exceptionally well, they were sent to the three-year circle to be tested. If they survived the tests and the three-year circle of elders determined they were worthy, they became master hunters. Hunters were brave and essential for the life of the community. There were many hunters in a village, each with a role to play on a hunting party, but master hunters were rare. And then there were those who were not suited for hunting at all: Purple who would rather tinker about with things than hunt for food or do their part for the survival of the community. In fact, they weren't really good at contributing or connecting with others—until they were too good at it. While tracking an animal, they would easily get distracted by the design of a spider's web or lose focus because they were caught up weaving a new pattern with the grasses they had just collected. While fishing, instead of quietly waiting and watching the water for signs of life, they would be asking questions about this and that, or they more interested in how the boat was made. A father or mother with such a child, after a few distracted hunting or fishing trips, would bring the child back to the village, and everyone would discuss whether the young purl would be better suited as a tinkerer.

At first, these tinkerers (as they were called) fit in just perfectly. They were the ones who made things. First, they made flutes and whistles that mimicked the birds and creatures of Purplynd. Then they made drums and musical instruments of all kinds. They were the ones who crafted pots and utensils, tools and tables, and such. For the longest of time, the tinkerers would sit and sing with everyone else during the bright-day. They would tell stories about their tinkering right along with the stories of fish that got away or deer that got outsmarted or hunters who got lost. For most of the history of purple on Purplynd, this was how it was—hunters and fishermen, cooks and tinkerers, mothers and fathers—spent all day doing what needed to be done so that bright-day would find them singing, dancing, sharing stories, and enjoying the village life. Then the tinkerers began to involve themselves in questions that became mysteries. As time passed, their influence in circle grew until their mysteries drew them away from many circles and into their own. Among hunters, it was the master hunters who were revered by all. Among tinkerers, it was the whisperer who was feared the most and for good reason.

Tyne ran to Kha and lifted him to his knees, and as he did, rage rose within the hunter. For reasons he did not understand or think through, Kha wished to strike the tinkerer. Before his mind consented, his right fist swung hard toward the face of the only purl with him. In the past, it was only Miis who could counter the speed of a Kha fist. And, as his thoughts caught up to his actions, Kha wondered if hitting Tyne was the right thing to do. But before regret could register the strike, Tyne dipped down, and Kha's fist flew over the head of the tinkerer. With the movement, Kha's chest exploded again in pain. He roared, and black blood trickled from his wound. The pain paused the thinking part of his mind, and Kha only wished to attack. His anger was in charge of every muscle in his body, and those muscles wanted to strike. They *needed* to cause pain. He swung his hand wildly but powerfully back, lowering his aim, intent on a backhand blow while his left hand prepared to pummel. But Tyne's movements were so quick, or Kha's perception so compromised, the hunter did not understand how or why he missed his mark. As he reloaded his fist, his thoughts began to catch up with his actions, and he wondered if he should try again and what part of him wanted to destroy his friend. In those moments, Tyne unbent his back and, with cupped hands full of pulse, threw the dirt to the chest of Kha. As the ground of Purplynd hit the wound, the fire of pain began to subside. Kha felt the pulse hit him and, with it, relief from the pain as it stuck to his wet flesh. Tyne continued throwing the pulse until Kha was covered with the dirt of Purplynd. Kha's anger subsided, and his mind began to clear as he realized Tyne was actually helping him.

He still wanted to fall to the ground and rest, but Tyne insisted he stand while the thick pulse was applied. Kha stood with his arms outstretched until he could no longer hold them up. Tyne continued until his body was caked with the paste. He then told Kha to sit and rest his arms on his thighs, palms open and up, as he covered his face with the mixture. As the mud mask of pulse was applied, beginning at the crown of his head and moving past his cheeks and down his neck, the pulsing anger began to quiet.

Dark night came and brought peace or as close to peace as Kha had experienced since leaving the village.

"Now we must go," Tyne said softly to the master hunter.

Glad to be free of the pain and beginning to wonder about so many things, Kha's conscious mind did not register what Tyne said nor did his ears perceive the sound of his voice. He was attempting to sort out the thoughts and feelings swirling in his mind and heart. His body was both familiar and strange to him. He was who he had always been but was discovering a new purl emerging—one he did not recognize as himself. The paste covering his body was strange and foul. At first, he found it offensive, but as he calmed, he detected a hint of something sweet and familiar.

He began to be embarrassed about swinging at Tyne and amused that he missed his mark. He remembered the sound of his strange roar and wondered where it came from. He remembered the pain that had been more intense than any he had ever known and wondered where it originated. Kha welcomed the dark night. Somewhere within him, he connected the night with rest and renewal, and something deep inside him wanted rest more than anything else, but, at the same moment, a strange energy roiled within him. Most of him wanted to run. Most of him welcomed the dull pain in his limbs as invitations to move.

That was when the soft voice spoke again, "Master, we must go."

The sound of Tyne's voice and his gentle, pleasant countenance calmed Kha even more. Kha understood that Tyne was inviting him to more of this calm peace, but it took him a moment to decipher the words Tyne was speaking.

Kha began to speak, and a deep, guttural sound came from where his normal voice had been. "Where shall we go?"

Attempting to suppress the dissident sound, he strained to lift the tone of his voice as much as possible, but it still came out low and dark. His own voice was strange to him.

"And why shall we travel through dark night? The day will return soon enough, and we will travel then." Even as he said the words, Kha wondered why he had. The words were wise. They were true. It was the dark night. It was the time to rest and renew one's body and soul. But all the muscles in his body wanted to run, and his heart beat strong. Some part of him felt as if he had just wakened from a long rest. The wisdom he had just spoken was irrational. The truth was irrelevant. He wished to run, and what reason would there be not to? So, he resolved he would not rest but would instead run through the dark night.

He rose, and as he did, felt majestic. He looked down at Tyne, who acted surprised.

"I have decided we must go."

Tyne bowed in submission, "Yes, Master."

Kha turned south, intent on navigating around the pool and heading toward the village.

"Where are we going?" Tyne asked in a soft, submissive voice.

"I have decided to return to the village."

There was a hint of disappointment behind Tyne's eyes. "Yes, my master," was what he said but then began to mutter quietly as if to himself, "Then we shall defy the order of the circle. And who are they to tell the mighty Kha what he should do and where he is to go?"

The tinkerer muttered, but Kha did not catch his words with his conscious mind. He was confused by how Tyne addressed him. *My master?* He did not understand what Tyne meant. There was no such thing as a servant in those days, and the deferential deportment of the whisperer was at first puzzling to Kha. Tyne followed without question or comment. The illusion that Tyne was following him obediently gave birth to a feeling within Kha that he was powerful and that his purpose was just. He liked the feeling.

Kha began to move, and his first steps filled him with a sense of accomplishment and peace. He moved deliberately, intent on overtaking the rest of the party and getting home. His vision was sharp, but the darkness was sharper. Tyne followed the quick pace of the master hunter as if he was being dragged, but he was actually driving. The master hunter moved through the darkness filled with a powerful confidence that whispered from within him. He ran all the dark night. He ran unaware of any life around him until a figure he recognized appeared. From somewhere, his thoughts demanded he remember the purl in front of him, but within two steps, he concluded the darkness had tricked him. And he was compelled to run harder. Exhaustion began to take him, but he would not stop. Dawn began to break through the thick forest, and the light pushed him more. The work of the pulse-paste began to wane as it was almost totally scraped off by the brush and the driving pace. Tyne had been clipping his left heel every twenty paces or so but of this he remained unaware. When he came suddenly on what he thought was the sound of a strong stream, he stopped.

A master hunter does not easily lose his or her way in the forest whether it is day, bright-day, or the darkest night. But if he was anywhere near where he hoped to be, there should be neither stream nor water. The wood was familiar but not in a way that was welcoming. Kha was fully into the day, and the light of day mocked his navigational skills. He had exhausted all his strength and was weary, and now he was in an ill temper. He walked toward the sound until he came to the shores of a shallow river. In the distance, he heard the sound of a fall. He followed the shoreline toward the sound until he realized the dark night and all-day journey had brought him to where the journey had begun.

Kha was hungry and tired. The disappointment of being no closer to his village than when his night journey began took the little hope that had been in his thoughts since the night before. Stopping turned his mind toward the throbbing wound across his chest. Anger again began to rise within him. He had always been able to walk, run, or exert himself without much of a sweat, but now his heart hurt. His mood turned sour and sullen. He was hungry. It was the beginning of bright-day, and he found the light too bright. He moved from the water's edge and began to walk toward the woods. His thoughts began to spiral toward darkness. He wondered why the hunting party had left him. He wondered why they all hadn't turned to pursue whoever or whatever it was that attacked Laish. He wondered why Miis married Quay in the first place. The thoughts furrowed his brow, and like a dark fountain, continued to flow through his mind. He needed to act—to act in some way that would take his mind off the terrible things that were coming to his head. He needed to act because that was the way he always settled his mind. If he was well, he would have used the light of bright-day to pursue the killers of Laish or return to his own village. But the pains in his chest demanded other things. He had long spent the strength he had summoned the night before, and almost all at once, weariness and pain washed over him.

He headed toward the woods away from the lit riverbed, but his feet moved clumsily over the river rocks, and anyone seeing him would have taken him for an inebriated purl. Tyne rushed to him and helped him. With Tyne's touch, Kha let his remaining strength drain away. Tyne, who never looked strong, did not bend at all under the dead weight of the master hunter. He carried the master hunter to a boulder and sat him down. Then the tinkerer began making something like the paste that soothed the pain the night before. Tyne smeared it all over Kha again, and the body mask mollified his ill-tempered mood. This was a medicine Kha welcomed but did not need. It removed the pain from the kaviri wounds and the surgery he did not know had happened. Its pungent odor was terrible but less offensive than the mud the night before, and this mix made Kha even weaker and more lethargic. Tyne pleaded with Kha to stay still so the mask could do its magic and promised to find food for the two. The mud mask plastered over his body was thicker than the one the night before and seemed to tighten as Kha moved. The paste was either too strong or Kha was too weak to break through it or to move much within it. It did not feel like mud. It felt like something alive. It held him, and in his weariness, he welcomed it. Medicated and immobilized by the mud or whatever this was that had wrapped itself around him, Kha drifted into a silent, constricted, and dark sleep.

DANGER IN THE DARKNESS

SHADOWS DECEIVE. IT IS their greatest strength and, in a foreign forest, could cause death. The pool by the waterfall had washed away the mingled blood and mud of Laish, but much that was broken remained. Kha now sat entombed not far from where, cycles ago, those who had journeyed with him to Laish had left for home. The cold, dark presence possessing Kha was the same shadow Phee sensed three cycles ago as she directed the party to leave. In those moments, Phee recognized the darkness lingering in the woods, and the darkness recognized her. And now, there was more than shadows to fear. The entire journey home, Phee guarded the rear and directed all her keen senses to protect the party. The powers they had left near the river could not be trusted to leave them unmolested. She did not know where her sense of danger was rooted. Perhaps the killers of Laish had returned. Perhaps Kha had become one of them. Phee was convinced Kha was suppressing his rage in the last circle. But she didn't know how far down the road his soul had traveled.

It was vital that the party not rush home. The darkness they had witnessed was deep and raw. It had marred them and could have separated them from all who had not witnessed the carnage. It was a wound in their spirits. It was a hole in their souls. But the presence of a whisperer made things worse. The work of a whisperer can hide things deep in a purl's psyche beneath the soul. When Phee woke and Kha was gone, she knew dark powers had driven him away.

That first night after the river, she and the elders talked these things through. They decided the danger was real. Phee had no doubt. That was why their journey did not head straight to the village. The elders led the way, and each bright-day circle, they sat palms down. Ancient rituals were engaged in what many of the younger hunters had never experienced. The moans and songs seemed to sink deep into the soil of Purplynd, which was watered with many tears. The third day, Phee led the party to an ancient place. The oldest of the elders had heard about this sacred place but had never been and did not know the way. The forest there was thick, and even the light of bright-day barely pierced the canopy of the ancient branches that knit themselves together high above the purple who gently moved on its floor. Phee brought them to a small clearing where the light of bright-day illuminated the wood as if a giant candle was placed in the middle of an unlit forest. The clearing was made by a circle of poollé trees. There, the young hunters sat in circle, each with their back against the bark of a poollé. Some thought it coincidental that there was a tree for each of the party with two trees empty. But this was a circle Phee would not enter as a participant. It was one she would protect. She stood in its center, hunter-still. The clearing was close to the foothills. It was a dark and powerful place, and what roamed the surrounding woods had no fear of purl scent.

The ritual began with a slow and steady beat made by the males and females clapping parts of their bodies with their hands. The purple drums beat to a familiar rhythm, one that was often a part of circle celebrations. But here, the tempo was slow and deliberate. The beat was symphonic with parts particular to the different types of pain created by the journey and carnage. The slow and mournful slapping of thighs, chests, and hands matched the slowing heartbeats of the purple in the circle. The syncopated rhythm united the party in an intimate moment, and when the music and the breath became one, an elder began a mournful tone. Each purl joined in as they caught the melody, which they did, one by one, like a fire following a path around the circle. Time was suspended as the mournful moans and the music made by purple flesh moved through the party. The light of day faded and disappeared. The music slowed and, in a light none but those in the circle could see, the last beat of the rhythm was made by the leading elder placing his palms, one at a time, in perfect beat with the measured music on the protruding root of his tree. Each purl followed suit until, at last, each grasped the root of his or her tree and silence took possession of the circle. Only Phee could see what happened next, but it was felt by each purl in the party. A connection was made between purple and planet through the poollé. It was as if the roots of the poollé had entered their bodies or as if their fingers had somehow become the roots of their souls, reaching deep into Purplynd. Their eyes closed one by one, and just as everything that had happened in that circle, it began with the elder and moved purl by purl until all were resting in planetary peace. As each closed their eyes, the last image they saw was Phee standing guard, hunter-still, her skin glowing red.

This place was familiar to Phee. She had been here among these poollé before. This was an ancient place created by the ancestors for times when rist was of no use. It was created for times when anger and strength offered to answer things for which neither was created to address. It was a sacred place. Phee had been here long ago when she was a young master hunter, not long after her own sister was torn apart and died. Phee remembered this was not the first time senseless, uncontrolled violence had appeared. Red purple had released darkness into her world before. She knew of wounds and half wounds. Bent minds and broken spirits had taken possession of purple with whom she was connected. Horrors that striped the flesh with scars had harrowed the psyche of those she loved. And long after the physical scars had vanished, the wounded minds remained. Spirit wounds like poison infecting purple in subtle and unsubtle ways. Everything that hurts you does not harm you. And her teachers, now long dead, taught her well that everything that harms you must be made to help you. These are matters deeper than the physical muscles and the conscious mind; these are matters of the soul. They are matters of the part of one's mind that power one's being. The power of hate and the seductive supremacy it seeks to wield over one's conscious and unconscious being is a deadly force more powerful than rist. It could drive a thighbone through the eye of a panthae. And Phee knew that to move those experiences that harmed you into thoughts that helped you required getting beyond the pain and the fear of the pain returning.

Traumas have a way of hard wiring the brain. Tragedy can constrict the heart and trap it. Hunters must be free of fear's control at all times. This requires understanding and accepting the depth and power of darkness without bowing to it. Then, and only then, can tragedy become triumph. Then the harms become the solid rock on which a life can be built, impervious to the storms and hail that often rise in tempest. This is the rock Phee was standing on while the others were having their souls renewed. She summoned the trauma of Laish from every part of her memory. She brought the images of every purl torn and strewn. She brought the sights and sounds of their screams that echoed through the silence. She brought the odor of their death, the smell of the burning village, the feel of the blood-soaked planet, and the shadows created by the graves into her conscious being all at once. Then she pushed them out of her body into the soil of Purplynd, and the process caused her flesh to glow red as the evils were pushed out of her just as the bright-day ended.

The party drifted into the trance-like coma to heal their souls, and Phee stood guard so nothing could come to harm their bodies. This place was in the foothills near the mountains, and, like all places of great power, it was not far from greater danger. The poollé trees possessed abilities beyond any other plant on Purplynd. It was thought that those powers came from the deep, dark soil found only near the mountains. Not much more was known about the poollé because they were only found near the caves in the foothills of the black mountains. The same place where panthae lived and hunted. And, indeed, there was a cave not far from this sacred place. Long ago, three master hunters killed the panthae that had nested in the dark cave not far from where they were. They had used fire and smoke to draw the nocturnal beast to the light. Phee knew the delicate dance with death, the fearless courage and commitment it took to slay the beast. It was the poollé tree's embrace alone that kept the hunters who survived from losing their minds. The healing power of its leaves alone mended their torn bodies. The panthae that once lived in the nearby cave was dead. What she didn't know after all the years had passed was whether another panthae had grown to take its place.

The first night, Phee listened to the sounds of silence and searched the darkness. She was careful not to let the echoes of life that were in her mind create noise in the outside world. She listened for kaviri in the farthest distance. She sifted the scents to read of things living and dead that had passed near where the party lay. She strained to catch the scent of panthae and feared success. It was a long soundlessness. When dawn came, Phee left the circle to scout the area. Other elders had checked for signs of danger when the party arrived, but life has sound. Death, on the other hand, may be silent and slithers before it strikes, and the night had been too quiet. In the distance, her search found signs of small kaviri, and it was enough to calm her fears. The day was nearly half over, so she retraced her path to the sacred circle. If danger had advanced toward the party, she believed she would have heard it approach and been able to return to defend it. She should not have been so confident. Phee returned to the circle just as bright-day began. She covered her eyes with two poollé leaves and lay where the Purplynd suns would shine brightly and warm her skin. As the suns set, the cooler air would wake her, and she would again begin the night watch.

The light of the second sun faded, and with it, the cool breeze nibbled the blue flesh of the one who must wake. Phee moved out of the silence of sleep and began to kindle the fire of life in her limbs. She chased the cobwebs from her mind without so much as a twitch in her body. She inspected the air around her and cataloged the scents. She listened to the breeze and the breathing of each purl. Only when she was satisfied that all was safe did she stretch her limbs and rise. She ate a root she had brought back with her and drank water from a gourd she had filled. She began the watch and started to filter the silence. She moved her senses farther and farther away from the sacred space. All was silent. The stillness of the quiet troubled her. It was a hunter's sense, something that would take too many words to explain, but it was real. She moved from the center of the circle toward the southern edge, and as she stepped past the poollé, something grew sharp within her. It was akin to fear, but Phee wasn't afraid. It was her hunter's premonition. It was a sense that drew her toward a danger that she was confident she was prepared to confront.

The lives of the healing purple behind her depended on her abilities to fight long enough for others to awaken out of the trance. If necessary, she would whoop-whistle that particular sound that could be heard over great distances. It was what was known as "the death cry." The death cry was a sound that reached into the core of a purl. It was a sound impossible for a human voice to make and almost as impossible to imagine. If one mixed an eagle's cry with a lion's roar and added to it the bite of an eel or the sting of a jellyfish, one would be close to describing the death cry. It was a sound felt in the feet before heard in the ear. It was a piercing sound that mixed despair, desperation, and alarm. Purple were born knowing that sound. Phee would make it before she died if she had time, if the strike was not too swift. This is what it meant to keep watch. No beast in ancient Purplynd would kill more than one prey at a time. Even the kaviri, which hunted in packs, would only kill one prey at a time, and the same was true for the panthae. If this search beyond the sacred circle cost Phee her life, her death cry would allow the others time to awaken. And, while whatever beast feasted on her carcass, the cry would have saved their lives, even as it cost Phee hers. She was confident her skills were sharp enough to give her time to warn the others if it came time for her death. She was mistaken.

Phee moved away from the circle, pulled into the deep by the spirit within her. She stopped to check the world, to ensure her mind was quiet. Her hearts beat with a strong but strange rhythm, declaring themselves aware of something her mind was not. She stood hunter-still and forced her senses to search farther. The scent of darkness was gentle and slight, but she caught it. It turned her slightly east, and she began to follow it. The scent was distinct. She almost missed the first whiffs because they were a strange mix of familiar and unfamiliar things. She moved, following the trickle of scents until it became a clear stream. She paused again. She detected panthae, and its odor would have sent a cold chill over most. But not Phee. She began to recognize some parts of the scents now flowing into her nostrils. It was the same odor she caught when she jumped over Kha on the way to Laish. But there was something darker about this one. The river of scents was arching. It came from behind her, stretched toward the sacred circle and moved away from her toward the mountain foothills.

She wondered how close whatever this was had gotten to the circle or if it was already there. If not, would it come again? Then what was a scent became a sound, faint and in the distance. She steadied her pace, crouching more, with her hand gripping the lance, ready for battle. She could hear the four feet of the beast moving. She paused to decipher the direction. The pace was quick. It was not the quick burst of speed that meant the beast was charging something within its striking range. Still, it was not the stealthy pace of something looking at or stalking its unsuspecting prey. The beast was moving deliberately. The sounds suggested it was large. The fact that it was running in the night meant it was dangerous. Too much was unclear, but what *was* clear was the thickness of the dark scent which moved through those foothills. Phee carefully moved closer until she recognized two shocking things simultaneously. The beast had turned toward her. She froze, hoping the change in the beast's direction was unrelated to her presence. She shook her head to ensure the information coming through her senses was not the dark creations of her mind. Rist rose and washed warmly into her veins. The first shock was when she realized there was something wrong with the rhythm of the beast's footsteps, and the second was the scent of purl. But before she could see what was in the darkness, she knew it had seen her. Her periphery caught the dark shadow, and she reflexively moved to disappear. Her mind feared the approaching shadow was panthae, but the scent was confusing.

Phee moved out of the direct path of whatever it was that was approaching. The path of the dark beast didn't change, which helped Phee shake the thought that it had seen her. She was wrong. It had. But her confidence made her pause and focus on the coming danger. That was when she saw something move away.

She realized, to her horror, what she thought was one beast was actually two. It was why the footsteps were so irregular. One moved in her direction as the other maintained its course. She realized they were attempting to entrap her. Phee increased her speed and reversed her direction. She would have to cross the path of the lead beast to avoid the trap. She hoped she was still far enough away to avoid a battle with it but gripped her lance tighter anyway.

When she was in front of the approaching menace, she paused to get a glimpse of the foul-smelling beast. What she saw froze her and, therefore, put her life in grave peril. She thought her mind was misfiring. She thought a dark whisper was fogging her perception. She paused and focused as the shadow approached and recognized the frame of a purl. It was running toward her with a crazed look of danger and death. Its eyes looked straight at Phee but had to have been focused far beyond her, for it took no notice of her. Phee was frozen, trying to understand what she was seeing. Her pause was only a second or two, but those moments were long enough for the trap to spring. Then she saw it. An involuntary scream rose from her gut and, were it not for the power of rist, would have escaped her mouth, probably causing her death. The scream that wanted to be voiced was not the cry of a warrior but the howl of a wounded mother because the figure that rampaged before her, she recognized as her own: It was Kha. There was a scar across his chest, stitched together with black panthae veins. His skin shone red against the black night. There was a terror in his eyes that suggested a torment in his soul. He was running, attempting to escape the terror within him. Phee knew this better than Kha had known that his twin had died the moment he rose from circle not so long ago. But every moment of her stillness increased the danger. Staring, Phee forgot the second beast. She forgot she was moving to avoid a trap, and as Kha ran past her like a driven beast, Phee heard the wind separating behind her.

Phee back flipped over the sound. It was a branch swung so hard that, had it hit its mark, it would have broken her back; instead, with a loud crack, the branch broke against the tree trunk. Returning to her warrior senses saved her life, but the maternal moment and shock of seeing Kha meant the defensive move was made at the expense of her plan to escape. She landed on her feet, crouching, ready to move against her attacker. The wind again began to whisper as something speeding toward her separated the surrounding air. Instinctively, she moved her head and the whistle of something rushed past her ear. Whatever it was hit the trunk of the tree behind her with the sound of a lance piercing a kaviri. The urgency of her back flip had caused her to release her lance, and she prepared to fight hand to hand. Just then, the sound of something sharp slicing through the air caused her to dive in order to avoid whatever death had been thrown. Her leap through the darkness brought a surprise peril, for the ground descended sharply, and she fell downward and farther than she had intended. Over and over, she tumbled. Leaf and stone met her back, side, and stomach as she rolled until, with a heavy thud, her body hit the trunk of a large tree.

Her attacker was quick and quiet. The shock alone of seeing Kha that way would not have left Phee so close to being killed. She was an elder and well up in years, but age had made her more aware, not less. The years had increased her strengths but decreased the need to use them. The seconds she had spent tumbling were precious. Several times, she attempted to get her balance to no avail. Her body was moving too fast. The hard stop at the tree was painful but welcome. Phee had no time to assess her injuries. She jumped to her feet, with all her senses searching for what would happen next. She wondered if this was her time to die; if so, she was ready. A knowing deep inside reassured her that she was well-prepared for whatever would come next. When she gained her balance, there was nothing moving immediately toward her. Pausing to listen, she began to realize that her attacker had not followed her down the embankment. Nothing was coming toward her, but in the faint distance, she heard what she thought were the footsteps of Kha moving away from her and nothing else. Her sense of danger heightened as she wondered where he was.

Things were now beginning to fit together. Questions she had long pondered now found their answers, whispers on the wind from a thousand circles ago. The one who was so in love with her that she had rebuffed, the one who was always whittling at the edges of her life now revealed his true self. There was a time when she thought his affections were sincere. She thought his awkwardness was the kind common to any purl unaccustomed to courting a female as strong and beautiful as she had been. But something deep within her had cautioned her not to engage his affections. So, their lives had grown apart. She became a master hunter, and he became a tinkerer. She became the center of the community, and he owned the shadows.

She had wondered at his keen interest in coming with the party to Laish and had spoken against it. But after the journey had begun, Phee's focus was on the danger ahead and not any danger within. She had tried to ferret out the path Kha's heart was taking and thought the grief of Miis's death was the one thing that was tearing apart his soul. She had no idea there was a whisperer in their midst. She didn't know the darkness had traveled with them. And now the progenitor of the fears and anger that grew in Kha's heart had finally revealed himself—Tyne.

Phee remained motionless and expanded her senses. If Tyne had not followed her down, perhaps he was waiting for her to appear on the ridge from which she had fallen. Phee moved toward the suspected trap. Without fear, she moved as a master hunter, her senses searching to understand the wood through which she moved. At last, she came to the place she was attacked. She paused. Silent and still, she counted in her mind the living things around her. She heard no other purl in the quiet beyond the beating of her own two hearts and resolved that Tyne was nowhere nearby. She moved to find the objects thrown to slay her. It took some time to find the black objects embedded in the bark of two different trees. She thought first they were stones, but their edges were very sharp, and their triangular shape suggested otherwise. She took a small branch and tried to use it to pry the black bone-like object out of the tree, but it was splintered by the razor-sharp edges. She looked around and found the branch that had been swung to break her back. It was a hard and heavy wood for its size. With it, she removed one and then the other black object. Before they were completely in her hands, she realized what they were, and a terrible cold chill moved through her spine. An involuntary tear formed and fell from her eye as she realized that the razor-sharp and serrated objects in her hand were panthae teeth.

The whisperer had somehow fashioned throwing weapons from panthae teeth. Phee's mind raced to catch up to the truths swirling around her. Tyne must have somehow circled back to the panthae carcass Quel had slain. Or worse, he had slain the panthae himself. She tried to dismiss the thought that Tyne was hunter enough to slay a panthae, for that would make him far more dangerous than she now knew him to be. Her sister's death so long ago had taught her about the power and treachery of whisperers who had the will to kill.

The whisperer was fashioning Kha into a weapon. To complete his transformation and seal his destiny, Kha would have to hunt and kill his own. Phee realized the purple who remained healing among the poollé trees were in grave danger. Tyne's tracks led away from the poollé trees, and Phee wanted to believe he would not return that night. She found her lance nearby and, with it, headed off to the sacred circle. Phee now understood why Kha looked at her without seeing her: He was under a whisperer's whip. He was being driven by thoughts inside his mind that he was unaware were not his own. The look in Kha's eyes now made sense. He was becoming something that soon would need no whisperer to control. Kha had always been a strong hunter and natural fighter, but the potential for his power under the spell of a whisperer was nearly unimaginable. The panthae veins across his chest meant the Kha whom Phee had helped raise from birth no longer existed. Had Phee known one of his hearts was missing, she would have resolved to kill him just as she determined that Tyne would have to die.

It was true. Tyne was gone. The whisperer had moved to catch up with Kha. The spell that was holding him was not yet permanent. If left alone, he might find the strength to make it back to his village and find healing or a gentle death. But Tyne had other intentions, and turning the mighty Kha into a weapon under his control and command was chief among them. Fatigue was a key ingredient to the transformation of Kha, and the nocturnal run was intended to further remove the walls surrounding his conscious mind and allow the tinkerer to insert a few instructions. The confrontation with Phee had come at an unwelcome moment. He had not intended to be discovered so soon. In fact, he had no intentions of being discovered at all. Tyne had wished to tune Kha to the frequency of his whispers and release him to generate violence in the cycle of villages. Tyne had hoped to return to the village under the cover of lies he would weave. Now, that might not be possible. Phee's appearance was not only unexpected and had interrupted the process of turning Kha, it presented a grave peril to the tinkerer as well. Until then, Tyne had protected his identity and his plans. But being discovered before his weapon was ready would lead to his punishment and death. There was only one course of action open to him. He would have to immobilize Kha, find Phee, and destroy her before she alerted any others to who he was.

Tyne wondered why Phee was anywhere near the foothills. He had long wondered if she suspected he was not all he pretended to be. By now, she would have concluded there was more behind Kha's disappearance than grief. He thought the party was well on their way to the village and determined that Phee must be hunting him. He would have to kill Phee as soon as possible. He had underestimated her speed and agility and was angry with himself that he failed in his first attempt. Now, any element of surprise was gone, and Kha was not yet a weapon. He was not sure if the power he had developed over Kha was stronger than the bond between Kha and Phee. Tyne had, for so long, subtly created gentle tensions and distance between the two, but he had been careful not to overplay his hand in the village. He had kept careful distance, so he would not be suspected of any ulterior motives, but he always had them. When Miis married and left the village, Tyne intensified the whispers in order to expand the void within Kha—a void that Tyne ensured only his whispers could fill. All had gone as planned. Laish was destroyed, and his village would be next. The only force in his way was Phee. She would have to be destroyed.

Phee carefully made her way back to the party. She was looking for signs that Tyne or Kha had been anywhere near the circle. There was really no reason to believe they had. Phee had kept a careful watch, but a swirl of thoughts clouded her mind. The revelation of Tyne made her doubt so many things she had believed were true. It brought understanding and confusion at the same time. She now understood why Kha's childhood laughter and lightheartedness had changed to become such a dark adulthood. She was even more confused about the circumstances of her sister's death and about Laish. But all these thoughts would have to wait for answers. She would have to bring the matters to the elders' circle and find wisdom there. Once assembled, the elders would put the puzzling pieces of circumstance and character together. They would understand what had happened and know what must be done. But the elder circle was far from where Phee found herself. There was one more night before the party would return to the village healed of their wounds, whole, and ready. If it were not so, if they were already awake and ready, Phee and the hunters would be able to track Tyne and what was left of Kha and kill or capture them both. But there was no time to wait for the hunters to rise. Tyne would surely use the night to return, and that meant Phee would have to face him alone.

She welcomed the thoughts of the coming fight. It made her feel young again. It filled her with a hope that she would finally vindicate her sister's death, even if it caused her own. She was careful to bury the panthae teeth far from the poollé trees. The thought of using them as weapons did not enter her mind. The sound they made was unforgettable, and, should Tyne have any more, she was prepared to avoid them. Using an unfamiliar weapon was a sure way to be hurt by it. With confidence, she entered the sacred circle after ensuring that no danger was near. She placed two poollé leaves over her eyes, set her mind to wake up at dusk, and rested.

Tyne, on the other hand, found no rest nor sought any. Day and bright-day were spent entombing Kha, finding food, and feeding him. Kha's mind was a muddy mix of pain, anger, confusion, and hunger. The hunger replaced what would be hope in any normal purl. It was desire, raw and unfocused. It was part of the process that was transforming him, and not all of it was the work of the whisperer. After Tyne had wrapped him in the living cast, he went to find food for his subject. He brought back a subtle mix of greens and herbs laced with a particular powder that would ensure Kha did not think too much and not too well when he did. Then Tyne spent the last of bright-day sharpening sticks and gathering throwing stones. He had no intention of fighting fair and every intent on winning. He had lost the element of surprise, but tricks, traps, and deception had long been his favorite tools. He was confident they would be enough to kill Phee.

Tyne retraced the path he and Kha had used when they returned from the encounter with Phee. Phee would not know he and Kha had run in a circle. This would lead her to follow the path in the direction she last saw Kha heading and right into the traps he would set for her. The first traps he set were just beyond the sight of the entombed Kha. If, for some reason, Phee made it that close, it would mean his attempt to slay her had failed. Two saplings were bent back and tied with vines. Hair triggers were set to spring panthae teeth faster than any purl could move to avoid them should anything heavier than a bird walk near the trap. The traps were loaded with two of the three teeth he had left. If Phee escaped his traps and attacks or, worse, if he was lying unconscious in the woods, he was determined that Phee would die by these last traps and that Kha would not be turned to hunt him. In truth, Tyne's heart was as dark as a panthae cave. His thoughts were rooted in a festering hatred. He was given to evil. He did not care what others had to lose for him to win. How that happened or when the whisperer became what he was, is a mystery to be told later.

If Tyne did not return, he ensured that Kha would die a terrible death. Embedded in the paste in which Kha was wrapped was panthae larvae. Panthae larvae would not live long in the open air but buried in the plaster entombing Kha and kept warm by the heat of his red flesh, they would thrive. There, they would begin growing and maturing, and, within a cycle, they would begin searching for nutrition. The heat of Kha's heart would draw them, and they would begin burrowing toward it. Should the hair-thin, razor-sharp teeth of the growing worms reach a blood vessel, they would begin a frenzied, painful consumption of Kha. If Kha was strong enough to break through the plaster and kill the worms, he would live. But Tyne preferred his death and had, therefore, made the mixture extra thick and strong to ensure that Kha would not live without him.

Tyne had enough time to set two additional traps along the path before dusk. He had Kha's lance and had tied the last tooth of the panthae to its end. He did his best to conceal his path by walking in endless circles until he climbed high into the trees and hid. There, he waited to finally kill Phee.

Just as dusk settled and the last light of bright-day had been lost, Phee awoke, hunter-still. She gathered the information of the surrounding wood before she moved. Assured all was right and safe, she removed the poollé leaves from her eyes and ate them. Ingested poollé leaves can help the blood coagulate, reduce the sensation of pain, and stimulate stopped hearts, among other things which would come in handy in a battle. Their taste, however, is indescribably putrid to the point of being painful. Most who had tried poollé once would rather bleed to death or die of other causes than ingest another leaf. Phee was not among that group. It took an extreme act of courage, desperation, or, some would say wisdom, to swallow the leaf once its rancid flavor was registered by the senses. Of the few who ever had the opportunity to swallow a poollé leaf, all but two spat it out. Phee was one of them. Upon ingesting them, she doubled over in pain and agony for nearly an hour. She bit hard on a stick to bear the pain without screaming. When it was over, she ate a precious root and washed it all down with water from a hunter's gourd. She stood and took one last look at the party resting for their last night in the heart of the poollé stand.

She bounced the lance in her grip, welcoming its weight and balance. She moved out of the sacred space and headed to the place she had last encountered her foe. She moved cautiously but abandoned any attempt at stealth. She was looking for someone who was looking for her. She had no fear of meeting Tyne, and Kha, in the crazed stage of his transformation, would move loudly enough through the wood to be heard easily from a long way off. She wondered if she might still be able to turn him back. The spell was fresh, and perhaps he still had some loyalty to his village and his family. Phee was the symbol and embodiment of both. She wondered if he was beyond the reach of her love. She wondered if she could turn him into her ally. She reached the place where she had avoided the panthae teeth. She briefly examined the scene again and began to quietly approach the trail where Kha had passed her. The scent of his crazed soul was a day old but clear and would be easy to follow. He had run to her right; she turned left.

Turning to the left saved Phee's life, or at least delayed her death. The magic of the whisperer hid the fact that Tyne was not far from her. Phee did not sense the danger. Neither could she smell the scent of her enemy just a few yards away in the trees above. It was the power of the whisperer's magic and the fact that Phee was relying on other senses. She was following a quiet inside her. She was following love. It was a force more powerful than any other and a much better ally in battle than anger or hate. Very few knew this to be true, but Phee had learned of love's power long ago. Love turned her and led her to the left, but it did not alert her to Tyne's presence or explain the choice through her senses. Love simply invited her to the left, and she followed.

In the moment she turned, she did not think of Tyne, but he was there, pan-thae-tooth-pointed lance in hand, ready to strike. He needed Phee to take four steps in his direction for the perfect strike. Three steps would have sufficed. Three steps would not have ensured her death, but a strike from that distance would have severely maimed her. Now it was too late. She was moving away from his traps and toward his prey. Tyne knew if Phee continued following the path, she would ultimately come to Kha. And he was determined that this was to be the night Phee died. But now he had to abandon the hope of his plans and fight Phee one on one. He waited until he thought Phee was far enough away that he could move without her attacking him. Then he carefully found his way down from his perch without setting off the last trap he had set.

Phee couldn't explain why she had turned left. She had no reason to do it except something inside her told her. She was moving on instinct and confidence. The presence of danger was unmistakable. The blood that had not yet been spilled was in the air. She sensed danger was behind her but followed the trail away from it for about an hour, noticing that it arched. She also detected the strange repeating mark made by Tyne clipping the heel of Kha. Then she froze. The scent of Kha lingered from the night before. The odor of Tyne was there also, but there was something more, something moving toward her in the distance. Her search was over. She turned to her right, abandoning the trail, and moved toward that which was hunting her.

Tyne was angry. The lack of rest, the scuttling of his attack plan, and now the fact that Phee was moving toward Kha put him in a foul mood. And in this state, he abandoned the pleasant disposition that had hidden his heart from so many for so long. His mind was full. Thoughts of finishing the transformation of Kha, thoughts of the lies he would need to weave to return to the village, thoughts of not returning to the village at all, and thoughts of fighting and killing Phee drove him through the wood. These thoughts moving inside him made a muddy mixture of hate and anger. They inflamed the rist flowing through him. He didn't notice the noise he was making as he moved to intercept Phee or how fast or far he had traveled until, somehow, he entered a small clearing, and there she was.

She was standing there with her lance, looking at him, waiting for him. Even in the darkness, Tyne could see her beauty and majesty. She looked as if she loved him, but she was intent on killing him. She looked regal. He was a beggar in rags. She looked like the sweet water born to quench the thirst of every purl. *Every purl but him*, Tyne's thoughts swirled in his unfocused mind. Rage and rist washed over the tinkerer, and he ran toward Phee. He pointed his deadly lance at her breasts and rushed to slay her with one strike. Phee twirled her lance to deflect his and spun her body. With the other half of her lance and as a continuation of the defensive move, Phee struck Tyne in the back so that his momentum sent him tumbling past her. Tyne began an involuntary, low, guttural growl and found his fighting focus. The moments they fought brought years of training and practice to the aid of each fighter. The whack and thud of lance hitting lance reverberated through the darkness.

Phee found out that the lance Tyne was using was different and deadly as the panthae-tooth tip cut her again and again. What would have been a glancing blow now was one that cut, pierced, and tore flesh. Phee grew increasingly weaker. She remembered, as children, she alone thought Tyne was more hunter than tinkerer. When they had played together so long ago, she perceived what others denied existed. She saw ability and agility. She saw prowess that matched her own, but no one else did. Perhaps she was the only one to whom he showed it. She remembered that he wasn't always feeble and demure. She remembered now because she realized her death was near. She fought defensively at first, striking to knock him unconscious. She thought to tie him up and return him to the village where, perhaps, he could become again what he once was. But she was beginning to realize now that she never knew who or what he truly was. He was a master fighter. She found that she was not fighting a tinkerer but rather defending herself from a purl every bit her match. She struggled to incapacitate him. Blows that should have knocked him out simply stunned him. Her best moves were matched by counters that surprised her. She admired his ability to fight much more than the mealy-mouthed tinkerer she had thought he was. It was attractive to her. She was puzzled at why these thoughts should come into her mind as she was fighting for her life and losing.

It was close enough to dawn that the party at the poollé trees would soon begin waking. Their journey of cleansing was complete, and being thus renewed, they were ready to rejoin their families and return to the life of the village. They didn't know the danger they sought to protect their village from now resided in Tyne and Kha. And they didn't know that their protector and friend was fighting for her life not very far from where they rested. But Phee, knowing all of this, sought to warn them. Her battle was lost, so she decided to give the death cry. Just as she opened her mouth to cry, Tyne landed a hard blow to the back of her head. She countered with a hard strike to his side that broke a rib and punctured his lung. She tried to run away from him to give the cry. But as she opened her mouth to cry out, instead of sound, a warm, slightly salty liquid came out. She spit out the mouth full of blood to try again.

Another blow hit her head. She countered by thrusting her lance into Tyne's chest. She collapsed to the ground with no fight left in her. Tyne stumbled backward and fell to the ground with a thud.

Tyne arose in searing pain, his lung filling with blood, and slowing his pace. His eyes were swollen shut, and his jaw was broken from the blows of Phee's lance, elbows, and fists. He had fought many battles and killed more than anyone was aware but had never been in a contest like the one he was now leaving. The pain and brokenness of his body was very new to him. When he did not use traps and tricks, he used stealth, surprise, and his quickness to defeat others. But, most often, he enlisted the power of others to defeat his enemies. This battle he had to fight by himself and alone. Phee was a much greater fighter than he had imagined. His memory suggested that he was her match, but something he forgot made her formidable. Whatever that was, it was no longer relevant to him. He reached for his lance and used it to lift himself to his feet. His body's weight broke the panthae tooth off his deadly lance, as it became his temporary crutch. He hobbled over to the lifeless body of Phee and, with as much strength as he could muster, sought to drive the lance through her hearts. His final blow missed its mark, but he neither knew nor cared. Phee was dead, and he was dying. His only hope was to get to Kha before the panthae larvae matured and killed him. His only hope now was to teach his charge how to save his life.

Tyne had made a crucial mistake. He had miscalculated the age of the panthae larvae and the length of time it would take for them to reach Kha's flesh. He also had miscalculated the strength of the plaster he had used to immobilize the angry red purl. For, just as dawn broke the horizon with its first dim light, a sound shook the woods. It came from near the river. It reached the mountains and bounced back and woke everyone in the sacred circle. The young hunters leaped instantly to their feet. The older hunters remained still, awake, and aware. Their healing was complete. They were whole and ready to return to their village, but, for the second time in their journey, they heard a sound as bone chilling as a death cry but was not a death cry at all. It was something strange and foreboding. It was a sound that carried sorrow and danger. It was like a lion's roar but with a sharp, shrieking sound of pain. It was far enough way that the circle felt no immediate danger, but it was also clear to all that the sound did not come from any friend of purl.

Silence followed the loud, roaring sound, and with the quiet, the alarm left the healed hunters. They expected their protector to be where she was when they closed their eyes, but Phee was no longer in the circle. The ritual that took a full cycle seemed to only have begun moments ago. They felt strong and rested. They remembered Laish as if it were a cautionary tale from a circle story. Each bore evidence they had been changed; for most, it was a patch of green over their temple. The trauma they had endured was real, and they held dear the lessons it had taught but with enough emotional distance to keep it from controlling their actions or compelling their responses to life after Laish. The elders rose. The scent Phee had left most recently suggested danger. Nothing other than grave peril would have drawn Phee from the circle. And whatever threat she would have needed to protect them from would not likely have kept her away at the rising. They divided the group and sent the two best hunters to find Phee or her body and others to find food. This close to the foothills, wapiti would be hard to find, and the hunters and tinkers who remained were instructed to gather edible leaves and roots. A deep peace permeated the party, but all understood the urgent need to return to the village.

The hunters followed Phee's path. That she had returned to the place where the first encounter with Tyne had occurred was obvious to the hunters who read the faint evidence left by her footsteps. The evidence of the first attack made them wonder what weapon had pierced the trees. They followed the trail she made to the left and found the small clearing where the fight had begun. They took their time to read as much of the battle as they were able. They were confused as they attempted to imagine what kind of beast had purl feet. They wondered if the slayers of Laish had returned. A blood trail led them to Phee's body. They wept when they saw her. They stooped to inspect her body. Her flesh was still warm, but they could not tell whether she was dead or alive. Wounds that surely should have been fatal seemed stable. Places where her blood should have poured out of her body simply seeped. Vines were woven between their lances and Phee's motionless body was laid on the makeshift litter. Then, with as much speed and care as they had, the hunters headed to the sacred circle to bring Phee to the elders.

They ran with great agility and speed. They were careful not to further injure their leader but determined to get her to the elders. Seeing the light of the clearing brought hope to their hearts, and they carried Phee's body into the circle and laid it beneath one of the poollé trees that had remained empty throughout the ritual.

The elders needed to commune. A sense of urgency and danger filled their deliberations. The thought of waiting for Phee's body to grow cold so it could be buried was overruled by the fear of the return of whatever had left Phee for dead in the wood. Some argued that carrying the broken hunter's body back to the village would cost precious time. They wanted to leave two young hunters to stand guard until all hope of her returning to life was gone. Others thought she should be taken back to the village and placed in a healing circle. This thought was dismissed by the oldest among them, who cautioned that her body would not make it back to the village warm and her only hope was the poollé. All wondered if the attackers of Laish had returned.

As the elders sat to discuss these matters, the hunters and the rest of the party gathered around the limp body of the master hunter in what they imagined would be her final resting place. Then, as the hunters gazed at her torn body at the base of the tree, her right-hand fell from the litter and touched one of the poollé roots. Just then, a leaf from the tree fell on her chest and stuck to an open wound. The dark green leaf immediately glowed red as if the blood of her wound had set it on some strange fire. Then, as if the leaves of the tree were being commanded by an unheard voice, they began to fall one by one onto her body. One of the hunters brought this to the attention of the elders. When they turned to see, tears formed and fell from a few eyes. The decision had been made by the poollé; the party stood in awe as the tree sent its leaves to the fallen hunter until they had covered the front of her body. The makeshift litter was replaced by one made with branches from this same poollé tree as two straight ones, perfect for the purpose, fell from somewhere above. When the litter was complete, the tree sent leaves to it as it had done to Phee's body. The elders commanded that she be placed on the bed of leaves that had fallen on the poollé litter, and by doing so, Phee's body was encased in poollé. The leaves rose and fell as if a soft breeze moved them. They pulsed periodically with the strange red light.

The elders directed the party to prepare to move to the village. The meal the others had made was divided among them and would be eaten on the journey. The eldest took a single poollé leaf and placed it in Phee's mouth. When he closed her teeth on the leaf, her body shuttered and became frozen still. The two strongest hunters picked up the litter and turned toward their village. The elder turned his gaze toward the sky and, with tears streaming, gave the death cry; the woods reverberated with the sound, the souls of all living shook, and rist rose to run through the veins of every purl present. The party turned and then, led by the eldest, ran toward home as a pride of lions in pursuit of prey.

THE TROUBLES BEGIN

THE MOST RELIGIOUS OF religious books notes that Phee is the mother of all blues and Tyne is the father of all reds. But the complete story, whose beginning you have just read, exists on Purplynd in only one or two libraries. Fragments also exist in museums, but even if you knew to look for these histories, they would be found locked away with the rare and ancient manuscripts, forgotten by all but the most unusual curator. The ancient language through which they were first recorded many centuries after these things happened is lost. The stories of Quel, son of Kha, and the exploits of his sister were better remembered.

Since that time, it became very rare for any purl on Purplynd to perceive or talk about the color of another purl's skin, even though innumerable problems and the exploitation of countless purple occurred because they didn't. Still, what did separate purple was something different, something people on Earth would think was insignificant, if they noticed at all. But in the days when Daisy used to dance and Pedagogy made his mark and suffered his fate, purple were clearly divided. Purple were different, and the difference was thought to be bound in the very core their being, in what for humans would be DNA or genes. But even more than on our world, this difference was determinative. It was widely accepted and understood that all purple were not created equal. There were light-eyed purple and dark-eyed purple, and the two were considered different species.

Now the little town of Biscuit was of no consequence and would have disappeared without mention had it not been the heart and womb of the trouble. Biscuit held the seed from which the movement grew. The border of Biscuit began across the street from the end of Prometheus. It ended where the trash shacks blended into the city dump. The benefits of the large, incorporated capital with its utilities, pavement, and tax base ended right where Biscuit began. This made the homes closest to the border a convenient place for daycares, nail shops, and beauty salons. The light-eyed purple, who had the fortune to live in Prometheus, got their nails and hair done here on the edges of the town by the residents of Biscuit without too much inconvenience. Dark-eyed parents too poor to afford the licensed daycare facilities in Prometheus had their children raised and nurtured here and, thereby, did not have to venture too far into the dangerous and dirty town of Biscuit. This arrangement worked for the dark-eyed purple, and the light-eyed purple were content.

The light-eyed purple didn't know how or didn't seem to care about improving their lives until the roll-ins began. Funny how such a little thing changed minds about who they were and how the world should work. Some said the roll-ins caused the catastrophe that nearly ended the world and life on it. Still, whether they did or didn't, it was up to the dark-eyed purple to keep the world in peace, prosperity, and quiet. And the ruler of Prometheus, charged with the safety of the world and all purple on it, was the dratsab.

The trouble began one day on one block in Biscuit. Picardy Street was an unusual block. Entered at either end by a short block about three houses wide, the street split into north and south sides with a double row of houses that formed an island in the middle of the block. Picardy Street was a perfect place for a private fair because all access to the homes could be opened or closed at the east and west entrances. The oval shape of the block made it both larger and smaller than other neighborhoods in the city. There were almost twice as many purple than a normal block, and the neighbors were like a family. Children often raced around the island sidewalk when new sneakers or bicycles were acquired. Probably only one purl believed what started on that one block on that one day would take over the entire town of Biscuit and then spread to others. But once it did, the wrath of Prometheus would begin to focus on that town and every one like it.

It all started at what was called a roll-in, which started as an all-day block party that happened after Pookii and his crew drove their newest custom cars around the neighborhood and then to Picardy Street. When they got to Picardy, they just kept rolling around the island. Eventually, other custom-car shops joined the parade until the crowd that would amass for the show got too thick to drive through. Then, on the roll-in days, Pookii and his crew began to stop the cars, open the hoods, relax, and hang out. It became the summer thing. After a few years, it became a pretty big thing. The summer roll-in became a place where the hottest custom cars, motorcycles, and bicycles were on display. No hack jobs, no shade-tree wannabes—only the very finest work was allowed on the block. As the years went on, the neighbors started parking their own cars in other places to make more room for the show vehicles. Later still, the homes on Picardy Street began opening and cleaning out their garages, so they could be used as part of the roll-in. But the draw and power of the roll-in wasn't about the vehicles at all. It was the vibe. No guns, knives, attitudes, or anger were allowed at the roll-in. That was established early on and, through the years, took over. Even when rival gangs were active in Biscuit, there was a truce at the roll-in.

Equal to the exotic beauty of the vehicles was the food. The roll-in was *the* place to eat. At the first few roll-ins, the neighbors had hot dogs for the kids and some barbecue for the adults. But, as competition would have it, year after year, the grilling became more serious, desserts were added, and the drinks became more elaborate and colorful. No one charged money for food or anything else at the roll-in because Pookii said they couldn't. The roll-in was a place to share and care. It was a place for beauty and the best you could bring or be, and purple took great pride in bringing something to share at the roll-in. The food was free, but nothing was wasted. *If you can't eat it, don't get it* was the rule. Most purple savored little portions of everything and shared with their friends. purple ate what they wanted, when they wanted, and learned there would always be plenty to eat if nothing was wasted. Equal to the food was the beauty. Purple who attended the roll-in wore their best, brightest, most comfortable, and most beautiful things. Everyone was welcome, and, as the years went by, light-eyed purple from all around started attending the roll-ins.

The roll-in had become so popular, purple had to enter through one of the houses on either end of the block. There, they would be greeted and made sure that they understood and would follow the rules. If you needed it, before purple entered the block, they could shower, shave, and get groomed upstairs, where there were full barber and beauty shops. Beautiful, clean, and fresh clothing was available to wear and keep. No one entered the roll-in less than the best they could be. If someone needed a shave and a shower but didn't want to take one, they were sent elsewhere. If someone didn't want to keep the rules, they were escorted off the block. The roll-in was magic. It was a block party, summer camp, and theater all marvelously mixed together. But it wasn't like a fair or amusement park because it wasn't composed of servers and the served. The first part of the day was spent getting ready. Everyone had something to do. Hair was braided. Streets were swept. Meals were prepped. Cars were shined. (In the early days, this time was also used to tune and modify the vehicles.) Musicians practiced. Singers auditioned. The day's agenda and lineup were set and published. It was the part of the day everyone was doing something, so purple started calling that part of the day "doing it." "Doing it" was followed by the show. That was when the fun got big. That was when the vehicles got shown, the food was served, the music was played, and the dancing began.

The roll-in vehicles were works of art. The best food to be eaten in all Biscuit was found at the roll-in and the music concerts were awesome. Only the best came to play. They did not come to perform. They came to play and dance and to enjoy being enjoyed. As was mentioned, no money was exchanged at the roll-in, and there were no charges for anything; still, nothing was free. Every purl was expected to contribute. Even if all you had to contribute were kind words and gentle, sincere encouragement, every purl gave, and they gave well. From plumbing problems to music writing to dressmaking, purple brought their best to contribute to the rest, and almost all this was done during the "doing it" part of the day.

The second part of the day was devoted to demonstrating what you did, had done, or could do well. That was when the car shows, concerts, dancing, and eating took place. Gifts and talents were shared with whoever wished to be a part of the sharing. They called this part of the day "doing it well." "Doing it well" went until the day was done, and then everything stopped. Purple retired to the homes that had eventually moved from private property to community resources. Early on, as the roll-in was transitioning from a one-day event to a multi-day experience, one purl objected to his home being used to board overnight guests. He demanded he be compensated for the use of his home. But he wasn't. The next day, no one stopped by his front yard, ate his food, or paused to acknowledge he or his home existed. The loneliness was so devastating to him and his family that, the next year, he was the first to convert his home for the roll-in. In fact, his home became celebrated as the best place to stay on all Picardy Street.

Early in the evolution of the roll-in, it was decided that a curfew was necessary. The first few roll-ins went later and later into the night, and, of course, this caused problems. Some purple who had imbibed a little more than they should have, got loud and refused to turn off their music when they were asked. One, in particular, got heated. Pookii was called. By the time he arrived, a small crowd had gathered. The ringleader of the group had already intimidated all the purple around him, asserting he was going to do whatever he chose whenever he wanted. The small crowd started to part as a hooded figure moved toward the place where all the noise and attention had now focused. The ringleader clenched his fists and rocked back on his left foot, ready to fight to the death. These aggressive moves were intended to hide from others the fear rising within him. By the time Pookii was close enough for him to take his first swing, the terror of what he was about to attempt had erased all the inebriated courage he had. In the middle of his trying to decide to swing or not, Pookii said, "We're not doing it now, purl." Something about the way those words were spoken, or maybe it was how they were heard, calmed the purl and all the tension in the atmosphere. The purl felt both respected and corrected. Somehow, he understood that he didn't have to fight. In that same moment, he also understood that had he decided to fight, he would have suffered the worst beating of his life.

From then on, when the roll-ins were being planned, the time to shut it all down and turn the lights off was called "not doing it." The roll-in was a violence-free place until, of course, the last one. The roll-in was about the pha. Light-eyed purple were abused, belittled, berated, beaten, and treated as if they were beasts everywhere, especially in Prometheus, by the dark-eyed owners of the planet. But at the roll-in, everything was always peaceful, and everyone was invited to realize they were valued, loved, and respected. At the roll-in, time seemed to change from the rigid rush of clock time to an altogether different speed. "Doing it," "doing it well," and "not doing it" were as specific as time got. One reason was that pha was so needed, and every light-eyed purl had a deep hunger for it. But the other reason was that Pookii and his crew would not have it any other way. It was how the one-day event became two days and grew year after year until, at a full two months long, things changed drastically. Life itself slowed down during the roll-in. No one rushed, yet things were happening all the time. Pookii called it the "pace of peace."

"Some things take time," he would say. "And the things that take time should be given the time they take."

Purple all over, especially among the light-eyed population, hear about the roll-ins. Many thought the gathering's success was because of the unique and often exotic custom cars, but any purl who had been to even one roll-in understood it was about the pha. What one would not necessarily perceive, as the roll-in had grown to take over several streets beyond Picardy, was that anyone was in charge of what was happening. But those who needed to know knew Pookii and his crew were the power and the force behind the roll-in. And their power was uncontested until the trouble began. Pookii had a tight crew, most of whom had been in prison for too much of their lives. But, at that time on Purplynd, most light-eyed purple had spent an appreciable amount of time in prison, on parole, or one small step away from either.

The first of Pookii's crew was a purl named Bake. Bake spent the very early years of his adulthood as a stickup purl and bank robber. He never shot, killed, or harmed anyone, but he spent a lot of years behind bars. He learned to cook in prison and was the first barbecue master of the roll-in. Another of the crew was Bank. Bank had been one of the biggest drug dealers in Biscuit. Purple suspected but could never prove that he had business and connections in the city. Those who knew never said, and you could be sure that those who said didn't know. He was called Bank because most purple believed he fronted most of the money needed for the first roll-ins. The truth is only Pookii knew where the money came from, but Bank was the one who handled that part of the roll-in business.

Bud was the newest member of the team. He was expert in every bone-breaking art on the planet. The first bone Bud broke was the finger of a bully when Bud was in the first grade. He was five years old when a purl two years older than him was attempting to grab his sister, Daisy. It was clear Daisy needed help and the older purl meant her harm. Little Bud jumped in the fray, bit the purl's leg, caught hold of his forefinger, and bent it sideways until it broke with a loud crack. Life got rough from that point on. The little first grader was beaten for the incident. It wasn't the first beating he had gotten, but it was the first beating he remembered. His teacher spanked him and called his mother to the school. When his mother arrived, she beat him in front of everyone. She beat him as if she was crazed. Bud's cries became screams for mercy. Something changed within him that day. He didn't shed another tear for any reason for twenty-one years. From that point throughout his childhood, Bud survived many beatings but gave more than he took. He grew up going in and out of juvenile detention centers until, at the ripe age of sixteen, he was sentenced to an adult prison, where the beatings became professional. At twenty-seven years old, he had spent his last eleven years in a federal facility and had gained a reputation. Something about him was different, a rage released through his fists. Even before his workouts had produced his large muscular body, he was a dangerous purl to fight. He perfected the art of paralyzing bigger fighters with strategic blows. He was lighting fast and ruthless. The guards at the prison would pit the prisoners against each other and bet on the fights. The last five years Bud served, he never lost a fight, and every fight included his broken bone signature.

Prison was where Bud and Pookii met. The word had come through the yard: Someone needed to be taught a lesson in submission and the finer points of Promethean life. Bud's job was to teach that lesson with as much violence as necessary. He had done it many times before and always left his signature. This time was special. Word had come that this was someone the warden wanted broken, and Bud was told if he did this job well, he would be paroled within the week. At the time, Bud never needed motivation to fight. Something inside him left him always ready to hurt someone, but the offer of parole added incentive and gave him acute focus. The prisoner had not been convicted of anything. He had been picked up for no real reason, but Bud didn't care. Promethean police picked up light-eyed purple for whatever reason they wanted whenever they wanted. Whoever this was would get a thorough beating, a few bones broken, and then be thrown back on the streets educated. Charging, booking, convicting, and imprisoning purple took time and cost money. It was more efficient and so much less expensive to beat, cripple, and then return the purl to the streets. And Bud didn't mind one bit that it would be him doing the beating—and get paroled to boot. He wanted to smile, but the hatred that held him so tightly wouldn't let him. Still, he was more than happy to splatter some blood and maybe even make a grown purl cry.

They brought Bud to the intake shower cell and removed the shackles and chains confining him. This cell was where inmates were examined for contraband and showered. The room had a showerhead and soap dispensers, but often prisoners were hosed down with a fire hose. The sadistic guards justified the bestial act by arguing it was quicker. This area was also convenient for two other reasons. The blood that would undoubtedly be on the walls and floor could be washed down the drains in minutes. Even more important, there were no cameras in the shower cell, and, in prison, no evidence meant no crime had been committed.

Bud heard his victim before he saw him. The guards were cursing him, demeaning him, and threatening him as they did. But in between their voices, Bud caught the sound of a purl humming. It was strange, but Bud dismissed it from his mind as one would shoo away a fly that was buzzing around one's ear. A warm, familiar feeling flooded Bud's muscles, and he clenched his fists as the naked purl appeared in the shower. The purl was looking away over his shoulder when Bud told him to get ready for his first lesson. In the earlier days, Bud would have hit the purl before he was aware of what was coming. But Bud discovered that he enjoyed the look in his victim's eyes before the first blow came. That look told everything. Bud would know about how many blows it would take to finish off his victim by that first look. In that first fraction of a second, Bud would decide how many bones would be broken and how badly. The gentler and more afraid his victim was, the less brutal and numerous the breaks. But the tough, murderous, big types were in for a good beating.

It was as his right fist was hooking around to connect with the new purl's face that their eyes met. Bud had never looked into eyes like that before. It was confusing. The eyes of this purl held neither fear nor alarm of any kind. Bud was sure the purl understood that a hard right hook was headed for his jaw. Yet the purl showed no panic at the prospect of what was surely going to hurt, if not fracture, his jaw. And not only did his eyes show no panic, there no retaliatory energy in them. The purl was not switching into fight mode. Then a head-shatteringly strange thing happened, something that had never happened before: Bud's punch missed. It wasn't that he missed the jaw and hit the eye or struck the head. Bud missed completely. Bud was confused but took no time to think through what had happened or why. His victim was facing him now, and Bud loaded his muscles for a combination. They were his favorite punches: a left jab followed by a right as fast as lightning. Bud was so fast with this combination that, once, he gave a purl two black eyes before he hit the ground. They were his knockout blows. Usually, a number of body blows would serve to "tenderize the meat," as Bud would say, and then the combo to finish the job.

If he were in a bad mood or otherwise motivated, the knockdown punch would be followed by some kicks to the ribs or worse. His newest victim was in front of him. Bud sent the punches to their targets, but instead of hitting the mark, he smashed first his left and then his right fist into the shower cell wall.

Lucky for him, this was not one of the outer concrete walls, for then things would have been worse. As it was, the force of the blows broke the tiles that covered the drywall and made fist-sized indentations. The broken tiles lacerated Bud's fists, and as he drew his now-bloody hands back, shards of tile stuck to his knuckles. Bud began to fight confusion. Doubt flashed momentarily through his mind. He wondered if he could beat this purl. He wondered how the purl had avoided his blows. It was confusing, but he had no time to think, except to decide to move from boxing to wrestling. He opened his swelling hands and lunged to grab Pookii by his neck or pin him to the wall if he missed, but Pookii adeptly ducked under his hands, and Bud smashed into the wall he thought had trapped his victim. One of the serrated edges of tile cut into Bud's forehead, and blood began to stream down his face. Rage and confusion filled him. Pookii had not only avoided the lunge and moved away, but also turned on the shower. Cold water now began to drench the bloody prisoner. The wet floor and cheap plastic prison shoes Bud wore betrayed his last aggressive move and sent him face-first into the concrete.

When Bud regained consciousness, the guards were in the room. He was dazed, unsteady, and blood soaked. The guards were mocking him, but he could tell they were scared. He watched them hand Pookii a towel and his clothes. He had never seen a prisoner handed a towel or given his clothes. Usually, clothes were thrown into the wettest place in the shower, and the inmate and his clothes air-dried together. It was obvious the guards were afraid of whoever this was. Bud realized the beating he was supposed to give this new inmate was meant to give the guards confidence. They were afraid in ways no one would be able to understand had they not had an experience like the one he had just had. But the guards were not so much afraid of Pookii as they were terrified of what he showed them of themselves. It was in his gaze. It was in the way he looked at you. It made you feel like the core of who you were was being examined. It took a fraction of a second but lasted a lifetime. His gaze conversed with your soul. It walked through the entire history of your life and examined the choices you made at each important juncture. And if you were condemned, you were self-condemned, and this condemnation was utter and unalterable.

They stood Bud up and began to lock the heavy chains of his walking prison cell around him. They turned him and inadvertently faced him toward his opponent. That was when their eyes met again. Pookii looked at him, and Bud could tell the purl in front of him knew him. It was strange. Something flowed through Bud.

It was an emotion that he had not experienced in so long that he had forgotten it entirely. He thought he should feel ashamed or embarrassed, but he felt neither. He recognized he should not have attempted to beat this purl and, at the same moment, accepted that about a thousand other beatings he had participated in should never had occurred. He was utterly disgusted with his past behavior but had none of the disenchantment that usually came with realizing that he was absolutely wrong. As he looked at Pookii, his eyes welled up. This fight, if it could be called a fight, changed Bud. He was different. He didn't know how he was different or why he was different. He was just different and he was very glad he was. A guard pulled him toward the shower cell door, and the first tear in twenty-one years rolled down his cheek. Bud began to be shuffled to the door, but he had to know who this purl was. He had to know something more. He was at a junction on the road of his life. He needed help to take the path that now lay in front of him. And he sensed if he didn't get the answer to his question at that moment, he never would.

He looked toward Pookii, careful not to catch his gaze. "What's your name, purl?" he asked.

Pookii, fully dressed, drying his dreadlocks as if he was in a posh spa, looked at Bud and said, "Most purple call me Pookii."

"Yeah," Bud said, "but what did your mother call you?"

Pookii smiled as if the question meant something, as if Bud had unlocked a box and found a key inside. He stopped drying his hair and handed the towel to the prison guard who was standing by his side as if he were a valet. Pookii looked Bud in the eyes. The look answered Bud's real question. Bud wanted to be connected to the one who had just beaten him without the use of hatred, anger, or violence. Bud wanted to know if they would ever meet again. Bud wanted to know how to find him. Bud wanted to know if they could become friends. Pookii's eyes answered: *Yes, we are friends and will be for a long time.* It was all Bud needed to know. Now completely shackled, Bud could not wipe the tears that began to stream down his cheeks over, of course, his busted lip.

Pookii was taken to the solitary housing unit (SHU) and put in a cell. The guards were caught between two hard realities: their fear of Pookii and their fear of the warden. They had the solution: Noj Burg. Noj was a headbanger and sadistic corrections officer. He was the warden's chief enforcer. Noj had a little black box he called his windup toy. It was a heavy cube about ten inches square with a crank on the side and two protruding wires with alligator clips on the ends of them. Noj was the one to get things done. Confessions were his specialty, torture his pleasure. He enjoyed running electric current through the bodies of purple who would, because of the pain, say or do anything he demanded. But Noj had been called away to do some work for an employer the warden didn't know he had.

He left the day before Pookii arrived. The plan was to teach the light-eyed miscreant a few basic lessons on who was in charge and release him back into the streets. A few broken bones and a cracked jaw would keep him quiet. Add in a few after-visits from the Promethean Police Department (PPD), and light-eyed purple who didn't know their place went back to a quiet life of ignominy. Noj was the plan for Pookii all along. Using Bud was an improvisation. The whole process was to take a day, two at the most. Pookii would be back on the streets before purple realized he was gone. But the best-laid plans of policing the light-eyed purple often went astray. The order to take Pookii to the prison instead of the city jail had come directly from the warden. The problem was no one had told the warden Noj was long gone. That was when they came up with the plan to use Bud. The news that their backup plan had also failed left the warden in a funk. He hoped to have had the purl educated before anyone began inquiring about his whereabouts. Meanwhile, Pookii was in the SHU.

Pookii lay in the seven-by-ten-foot cell, staring up at the ceiling, and filled his mind with a memory. It was a memory from when he was young, long before anyone called him Pookii, a memory from the time when everyone called him the name his mother gave him. He had taken a job at the university where his mother had been taking a few classes. He was twenty-eight, all male and muscles. He was digging a hole in the middle of campus when he met her. It was summer, and the Purplynd suns were at their brightest. His shirt was buttoned at the bottom to catch whatever breeze chose to pass by. Sweat soaked the short sleeves that outlined his biceps and triceps as he forced the spade into the ground. As a slight breeze filled his shirt like a sail on the sea, it caught the eyes of a student walking by. Like most males, he had no idea this was the day his hearts were to be given away and never reclaimed.

Daisy had just finished the final of her negotiations class. Negotiations was one of the more difficult classes in the prestigious university's law school. The verve one gets when an arduous task has been overcome filled her. Daisy was walking on air. She had finished the last examination of her law school life. It had been a long and grueling journey. As one of the rare light-eyed purple allowed to pursue law, she had endured every test and trial thrown at her. She had been tested in and out of the classrooms. Most of the purple she met were determined to disqualify or dissuade her from completing school and becoming a lawyer, but she had.

She walked across the quad with a bounce in her step and in other places a male purl would appreciate. She was feeling confident, and she had every reason to be the most confident purl on the planet. She was beautiful inside and out. She was brilliant and tough-minded. She was very well-educated, all the while never forgetting the ghettos from which she was reared. She couldn't help but smile, having the weight of the world, if only momentarily, lifted off her shoulders. That was when she saw him.

On any other day, her head would have been filled with obligations, equations, and case law. The image of a purl planting a tree right in front of her would have been pushed to the periphery of her vision and out of her mind. And if she did see him, she would be much too shy to say anything at all. But that day, with its beautiful bright suns' light, the sense of success pushed her beyond her normal behavior. She felt flirtatious and frisky, and there he was. She headed straight toward him.

Her intent was to say hello as she walked by. She thought she would enjoy the admiration of a stranger, all the while giving him the kindness of being seen. She slowed her pace as the hem of her skirt danced from side to side. The sashaying frills of her skirt entering Pookii's periphery made him look up.

"Hi there," Daisy planned to say, but just as the *h* formed in her breath, their eyes met. Something deep within her moved, and the feeling was so strong it frightened her. Her instinct was to hurry away from him and sort out what had just happened, but his gaze wouldn't release her. His eyes held her in a careful caress as if she was fragile and precious, yet at the same time strong and secure. His eyes held her as a loving parent would hold a newborn. He smiled, and Daisy realized she was staring. She was falling into a wonderful pool of sky blue. His eyes were warm and safe. She wanted to lay in the garden of his gaze forever, but as soon as she realized she was staring, she forced herself to break away from his eyes and found her eyes stuck, taking in the beauty of the muscles his shirt opened up to reveal.

"I'm Daisy," was what came out of her mouth as the other part of her mind thought about how dumb it was for her to say it.

"That's my mother's name," the purl replied.

"I assure you it is my own," she said, recovering the quick wit that had always served her well in life. He laughed, and it pleased her. That was how the conversation that changed both of their lives began. Daisy stood, holding her books to her chest, talking. She was determined for some reason to have a conversation, and finally, Pookii thrust the spade into the soil and stepped out of the hole he was digging. With that act, they began to tie a knot that has yet to unravel but one that cost more than Daisy could have imagined. They were connected. It was something they both understood the moment their eyes met. The conversation wove in and out of their lives as two needles would knit a sweater or perhaps baby booties. The gentle laughter and deepening joy grew until a figure heading in their direction entered Pookii's periphery.

Pookii had been enraptured by the cadence of Daisy's voice. It made him smile. It sounded like the song of a bird he had once heard long ago, deep in the woods. The sound of the woo song had reached his ears long before the image of the bird was found by his eyes. Something about that birdsong had called to him. Pookii moved without making a sound and made his way through the forest without disturbing any of the life that was around him. When he finally got within sight of the bird, the beauty of it was overwhelming. He sat and studied the bird and memorized its song. In times of stress or danger, he brought the song of the bird to his mind. And the beautiful purl standing before him talking took him to that same place of safety and peace. He never took his eyes from her face. He studied her lips, her eyes, her nose, and the lobes that could be seen hidden in the beautiful curly dark hair. He didn't avert his eyes, but he kept in his sight the approaching figure as a hunter would watch a predator advance toward him.

Daisy was unaware of anything or anyone except the moment she was sharing with the one who had been digging into Purplynd and who was now sinking into her hearts. It seemed important to Daisy to let Pookii know she was not from the upper classes. She never hid the facts of her upbringing in Noth, a seedy small section of shacks outside Prometheus where some light-eyed purple were allowed to congregate and eke out a living. She didn't know why she thought it was so important to tell this tree-planting stranger her life story. But somehow, it was vital. So, she kept talking. She was lingering in a moment of tranquility and joy she didn't want to end. Then something strange brushed her shoulders. Like the chilling breeze that accosts the warm, sunny autumn day, letting you know winter is on its way, she became aware of something. It made her pause, and when she did, she realized Pookii also recognized that something had changed. Then the sound of a familiar voice erased whatever magic she was enjoying at that moment. She sensed something unpleasant was coming toward them. She was right.

The unpleasant something that sent the cool breeze across the conversation was trouble in the form of a purl named Nos. Nos was a purl from an important family. He had been raised to rule and carried the disposition of one who expected others to understand this was both his and their reality. Nos's family had sponsored Daisy's entrance into the law school as a benevolent act. His grandfather had befriended her mother and had always treated Daisy with gentleness. Nos was attracted to Daisy and had long ago let her know it. At first, she was flattered but soon realized Nos wanted her more as a prized possession than as a life partner. She had not dated much throughout her life. She had goals, and they drove her. Pursuing and excelling in education and caring for her siblings ate up each day quickly.

It was in law school that she began to understand the power of her attractiveness, and it was Nos who provoked the revelation. He was used to getting anything he wanted. He could buy, deal, or steal with impunity, and for some reason, he set his sights on Daisy. But one date in the first year of law school was all it took for her to understand volumes about herself, her limits, and the life of the privileged. That date began her true education in the law and steeled her determination to become an advocate for the ignorant and powerless purple. But none of her rebuffs dissuaded Nos. She had communicated as clear as she could that she was not interested in a relationship with him, but the more distance she attempted to put between them, the more determined he was to have her.

When Nos reached the two of them, he interrupted the conversation abruptly but smoothly. He was polite but dismissive. Pookii had experienced this type all his life. He was used to being ignored or thought insignificant. But his identity was clear to him. And he understood most purple were blind to the things he saw clearly. He had no interest in a macho contest with the red purl who interrupted his warm, gentle break. The thought that Nos might wish to match wits or weapons with him tickled Pookii, and an involuntary smirk brushed across his face as he began to move toward returning to his work. Nos possessively grasped Daisy's arm, and Pookii witnessed her eyes register the distaste she had for the act. He perceived Nos was the kind of purl who had a need to control others. But the conversation he had just enjoyed suggested that Daisy wasn't the purl to try to control. It was in her eyes. It was in her story. She was strong in ways a self-absorbed purl would miss. In fact, Pookii thought Daisy was strong in ways she hadn't realized yet. He also sensed her strength would be put to the test in the next few moments. These thoughts increased the power her beauty had over him, and, as she turned her attention to Nos, he returned to the hole and shovel.

Nos demanded Daisy pay attention to him. He didn't do this with angry words, but everything about how he spoke, and his presence suggested that nothing was more important in the world than him. They began to quarrel. He had been looking for her. He had found out where the Negotiations final exam was and had just left that classroom after waiting for and not finding her. Daisy, for her part, was perturbed he would use his influence to get the information on her possible where-abouts. She wondered who had told him where she was likely to be. Nos revealed he had given up on finding her and had just happened to see her on the quad. Daisy was not at all pleased. She realized that had she not stopped to talk to this stranger, she could have avoided Nos. She didn't want to hate him but didn't at all like the emotional confusion that came whenever he was near her. He had a way of making her feel indebted to him while appearing to be genuinely attracted to her. He had a soft, quiet way of speaking, but she always suspected that nefarious motives were at the base of all the kindness he showed her. She was sorry she had stopped because, had she not paused, she would have avoided him. But somehow, and from somewhere deep inside her, meeting this tree planter was worth whatever cost came with it. As this thought passed through her mind, the grip of Nos's hand tightened on her arm.

Nos had graduated two years before and had a reputation of dominating others and whatever else suited him. He was the grandson of the chancellor and the son of the Promethean dratsab. He did not have any right to access information about Daisy's possible whereabouts, but he had the power, and he believed in power. He believed in gaining as much power as possible, and he believed in using it.

Part of the happiness of that day for Daisy was the distance she could put between herself and Nos. It was also the chance to escape the influence of his powerful family. It was true that they were her sponsors, and Daisy believed that had they not found her and believed in her potential, she would probably be digging through the trash of Promethean society, attempting to build a life in Noth. Still, a deep joy was opening in her soul at the thought of finally being free of their influence and away from their constant surveillance. The grip of Nos was annoying for reasons she didn't understand, nor did she take the time to think it through. His grip was a mix of aggression, possession, and control that made something strange rise within her. She pulled her arm away sharply. Then it happened.

Rage appeared on Nos's face like the flash of flame from a lighted match. It disappeared quickly, and before Daisy could think about what it might mean or reveal about the one who had so gently and persistently pursued her, a hand was moving toward her face.

Nos had lost control. What was happening inside him appeared to the outside world. Why it happened was confusing to him. He was a master of controlling what he presented to the world. Since he was a small child, his grandfather had taught him how to control and command his thoughts and emotions. It was the first step on the path of developing the leader he was born to become. This was a new and uncomfortable feeling of vulnerability. The anger that gripped him was severe, and he wasn't sure why it had so suddenly erupted. Nonetheless, his answer to Daisy's disrespect was on its way. He was comfortable with the slap across the face his hand was delivering. Daisy had never experienced this part of his power, but he was confident that he would be able to continue his courting of her after it had done its work. There were many whom he had so instructed, and they all had eventually realized their error and adjusted their behaviors. But he had altered his entire approach to Daisy. The chancellor had given his blessing of his pursuit on the condition Nos be gentle with her. But at this moment, the chancellor's lessons were buried somewhere inaccessibly deep, and Nos enjoyed the surging power that sped his open hand toward Daisy's face.

Daisy's mind moved back and forth from the words coming out of Nos and the conversation he interrupted, which contributed to her being less aware that Nos intended to strike her. As the hand came toward her face, Daisy attempted to move from its path, but Nos's swing was too fast. Her move took much of the strength of the blow away, but it was still hard enough to push her lower lip into her teeth and make it bleed. The fact that a purl would attack her was no shock to Daisy; she had been raised in Noth. The thought that a highbrow sophisticate would slap her was no surprise either, but the fact that it was Nos who did it caught her off guard. She dropped the books she was holding against her breasts, and the warm thoughts of embrace she felt as she talked with the tree planter disappeared. It was replaced by what purple called a "Noth attitude." Daisy never took a beating and had no intention of starting now. Nos looked in her eyes. Daisy did not cower or cry. There were no tears welling up in her, no sense of helplessness. Instead, there was a look of power and presence. It infuriated him. It was the gaze of a purl who thought herself his match. He lunged at her, and the fight began.

It was a real fight. There were a lot of fists that flew toward Daisy's face but none that squarely hit their mark. It was a bruising battle for one of the participants. It was an enraged Nos who was lunging and swinging as Daisy adeptly avoided his best blows and attempts. She would flip and twist as if she had been trained to fight all her life. When she couldn't avoid him, she swept out his legs or rolled into his swing and tossed him aside. After the last good flip, Nos lay on the ground confused, beaten, and angry. He had vacillated between controlled and uncontrolled rage, but nothing he did convinced him he could defeat her. In fact, she was toying with him. He was convinced that Daisy could have hurt him badly if she chose to. The thought increased his fury. Daisy, out of breath, stood a short distance away, looking at him. She was bleeding from her lip and had her hands on her hips. There was a smile on her face. She looked satisfied. She looked as if she had just played a game and won. She was disheveled but regal. Nos's anger grew as she turned her gaze to the tree planter. Their eyes met and they connected in an intimate joy. There was a link between them that made Nos feel insignificant. In that instant, she became just another light-eyed purl to Nos. He stood, reached into his pocket holster, and pulled out a revolver.

The confusion swirling in his mind could not overwhelm the anger of being tossed around as if he was a child. The added irrelevance he felt blinded him with rage. He aimed the gun at Daisy's head. The lessons of his grandfather about the care that was to be given to this particular purl whispered for him to stop. He couldn't stop. He pulled the trigger. The gunshot rang throughout the campus, bouncing off the buildings, freezing the conversations of those who recognized the sound. They turned their heads toward the blast. Some of those who had already paused to watch the prolonged fight between Daisy and Nos began running away as the gun was pulled.

Daisy never saw the gun. All she saw was Pookii. She was caught by his eyes and, strangely, not at all startled by his movement. Both his hands grabbed the shovel handle to use as a fulcrum to send his body to flight. His feet extended toward Daisy. She saw them moving through the air as time slowed, and she welcomed their approach. Those feet hit her shoulder and chest and moved her backward just before she heard an explosion and felt her forehead burst. Bright-day disappeared, and a starless night embraced her as she fell to the ground in a dreamless sleep.

Nos watched Pookii's body flying toward Daisy. He pulled the trigger again. He had intended to shoot twice, to place two bullets into the cranium of his victim. It was how he had been trained. It was instinctive. He was an expert marksman, and this was not his first time shooting a purl. His second shot missed because Pookii had moved Daisy out of its path. He was undecided on his target for the third shot. He couldn't choose between ensuring the Daisy's death or that of the purl headed toward him, so the third shot flew into the building that housed the chancellor's office. The fourth shot was aimed at the face of the one flying into view. It missed at almost point-blank range.

Pookii grabbed the hot barrel of the gun and twisted it outward, breaking Nos's trigger finger and disarming the murderer. He tossed the weapon to the side. Then, uniting every muscle in his body and the power of his soul, he sent a force through his backhand to the face of Nos. There was something about that slap, something hidden in the sound of it. Pookii understood what it was. It was the sound of utter contempt. It was the sound of legitimacy and dignity being removed. It was a judgment from which no appeal would be heard. Nos realized it. The others around heard it but were confused. Some thought another gun had been fired. But those who actually witnessed the slap understood what had just happened, and it confirmed a possibility they had never imagined. The backhand removed all the status and authority Nos had enjoyed. It was as if he, and his family name, had been reduced from royalty to peasantry. It was not just the backhand. For those who saw the flash of Pookii's presence as the sound occurred, the tree planter was somehow, in that instant, much more than a tree planter. It disoriented them. They felt like bowing, but the sight and the scene demanded otherwise. The blow was strategic, painful, and effective. Nos fell to the ground unconscious.

Pookii ran to Daisy. Blood was streaming from her forehead. He reached into his shirt pocket where he had several leaves and placed them on the open wound. They flashed with a red glow and, as they became blood soaked, turned dark and began to pulse. This stopped the blood from flowing. He cradled her in his arms and called to her.

Daisy was crossing over into the next world. Majestic mountains came into view. She heard the water of a brook, and the sound it made was like a sweet song of peace. The wonder and colors of the place drew her. Warmth and beauty surrounded her. There was a welcome in that place she had never experienced but had always desired. She agreed with her soul to release her life and live forever wherever she was. There, she hoped to follow the brook and find the source of its melody. The mountains in the distance whispered to her that they held a home built just for her. A powerful wash of hope rolled over her. She would be glad to spend all eternity in the joy of that place.

Just as she was opening her hand to release her life on Purplynd, she heard a voice. It was a commanding and strong voice filled with authority and power. But strength was not all that was contained in the melodious bass tone; in it was a love deeper than the ocean and even more powerful than the beauty of that place. It was a confusing sound. It was calling her back to Purplynd. She was sure she had never known such a love in her life. The love she heard in that voice held her completely and accepted her totally. It was a love that needed her as much as she needed it. It told her to come back. It said he needed her. And she knew she needed him. Turning from the blissful vision, Daisy opened her eyes and saw his. Pookii cradled Daisy in his arms, and warmth began chasing away the creeping cold where their bodies touched.

Sirens screaming in the distance were getting louder. The opening of Nos's pocket holster had set off an alarm. The dratsab's family enjoyed privileges and protections others could not imagine, and the simple opening of his pocket holster was enough to send teams of assistance toward him just in case he needed any. Of course, uniformed police officers were on the way, as well.

Daisy had one hand and her hearts in that beautiful place. She had decided to leave Purplynd and find her home in the mountains, but for the moment, she was lost in the voice. She could feel something warm moving into and through her from the cradle of his embrace. She wanted to talk to him. She wanted to continue the conversation Nos had interrupted. She wanted to invite him to her home in the mountains, even if she felt she already lived there. She wanted to ask him to never leave her. She opened her mouth to speak, which she thought took entirely too much strength to do. When she did, he placed a leaf in it. This action confused her. When the leaf touched her tongue, her jaw snapped closed. The lights went out. The beautiful place disappeared. The sound of the brook and his voice went silent. She fell into a black void and was gone.

The first gunshot had been detected by sensors and set off all sorts of alarms. The emergency medical technicians and seven highly trained security officers were on their way. Normally, Nos's private security would not have allowed him to be out of their sight, but Nos had insisted. He had plans for his encounter with Daisy. If all went well, he would be able to consummate his three-year pursuit of her in some hidden place on campus. There were many such places, and Nos had used them all. If she resisted or things got a little physical as they did from time to time, he had a plan for that as well. In either case, he preferred there be no witnesses. His secret service detail had just lost two of its longtime special agents, and the new guys had not yet proved they would look past anything he decided to do. So, Nos demanded they remain in their vehicle outside the campus gates. He reminded them, he was on the very secure law school campus, and if the chancellor was in his office, there would be plenty of surveillance.

The agents arrived at the scene first. The gathered crowd increased the anxiety and general confusion. As they ran to the body, the lead agent barked his commands through their earpieces—two agents to control the crowd and two to neutralize the threat, while he and the others went straight to Nos. They ran, guns drawn, shouting at the crowd to move back. Video feeds to the authorities confirmed there were two purple on the ground, one was bleeding and the other was the son of the dratsab. Very few purple were aware that the chancellor was not on campus. This left the EMT on duty just a few hundred feet away in the basement of the chancellor's building. Alerted by the holster alarm, they, too, were running to the center of the quad toward the still body of Nos. The secret service agents arrived first and checked for a pulse. He was alive. The EMTs had a shorter distance to run, arrived right behind the agents, and began triage on the unconscious son of the dratsab.

Daisy's head hit the ground. The blow didn't hurt much because it was just a few inches in the air, but she was displeased. She furrowed her brow. Something had interrupted a wonderful dream—a dream she desperately wanted to continue—but she had to wake up. So, with no small amount of angst, she opened her eyes, and there it all was. She returned to that wonderful place she had been and always wanted to be. She sighed in joyful acceptance. But something was different. It took her a moment to think through what was missing. She began to catalog paradise. The singing brook was there, although she didn't immediately notice the change in its song. The mountains were in the distance, and they still called to her. The beauty was still powerful and welcoming. The air still wrapped itself around her with every breath as if it were a warm embrace. She thought to close her eyes and take a deep breath of the warmth and release herself to its embrace when she realized what was wrong. It frightened her. The incongruence of what she felt and what she remembered was tragic. She widened her gaze and attempted to open her eyes wider than they had ever been. She tried to examine the picture before her, pixel by pixel. She searched from the distant horizon to the grass beneath her feet, and there was no mistaking it: The colors were gone. The beautiful, vibrant colors that were so powerful that she could feel them had become gray. The world in which she first felt true, deep love had changed, and only a shadow remained.

She knew what was wrong, and it made her angry. She didn't know how she knew, but that wasn't important. The color was gone because he was gone. The one in the house in the mountains, the one who loved her, the one she loved with all her being was gone. He had been taken. Most female purple, when faced with such an utter and essential loss, would cower in helpless grief and tears. They would look for some purl to help them. They would cry out loud in hopes that someone would hear their anguish and deliver them. But Daisy needed no rescuer. She needed no deliverer.

Like a kaviri provoked by a robber in its nest, like a panthae awakened by an intruder's noise, Daisy needed no help outside her own purlness. And, at that moment, she was filled with a sense of determination and strength. The warm power of warrior's blood filled her being, and she rose to accept the battles she was sure would come. The troubles began in the mountain foothills and that was where they must end. She took one final breath of the warmth as if it were her last embrace and began walking toward the tree line. The woods increased her sense of danger, and she determined that a weapon would be welcome. She looked, and she found what she thought was a branch. Looking closer along its perfectly straight length, she realized it was a spear. She bounced it in her hand. As she did, she recognized it. It was hers. It was hers but not because she claimed it at that moment. It was hers. It had always been hers, and she accepted that it belonged to her just as she accepted that her home was at the foot of the mountains. When one knows, one does not have to wonder, and Daisy knew.

She was a warrior. What needed to be done, she had to do. She began to run toward the mountains. She ran for days without noticing when she rested. She ran without making noise or leaving a trail. She ran at a warrior's pace, swift and quick, all the while being aware of everything around her. The life in the wild surrounding her spoke volumes as she moved through it. She could smell the trails of kaviri and prey. Then, getting closer to something, she slowed her pace.

It was evil, and she could taste the malevolence in the air. There was a scent, and she followed it. It was a faint scent. It was the scent of an injured purl mixed with so many other things it confused her. If it was a purl, it was like no purl she had ever encountered. Daisy bounced the spear in her hand, and a warm power washed through her being. She slowed her pace even more and picked up a trail so faint most would have missed it, but she was a master. She followed it until she came to a small clearing. She paused, aware of imminent danger. There was something painful in the circle.

The portion of a second she needed to interpret the peril was too long, for before she could complete the turn to face her foe, she felt the force of a branch pushing the air into her lower back. She flipped over the deadly blow. The branch hit the tree with a loud thud. Daisy's feet searched for solid ground from which she could fight her enemy, but the ground sloped steeply away from her. Over and over, she tumbled. Leaf and stone met her back, side, and stomach as she rolled until, with a heavy thud, her body hit the trunk of a large tree. There, gathering her wits, she saw him. Standing over her was a large purl. There was a spear in his hand. His frame blocked the light, and his face was covered in shadows. He raised the spear high into the air and, aiming for her hearts, began to strike the mortal blow. Daisy accepted the death that would come when the wood hit its mark and closed her eyes. The figure bent his body to add more force to the blow. The searing pain set her chest on fire.

Daisy opened her eyes, and a purl was standing over her. The colors of the world had returned. She was in an ambulance. The EMT had just pulled a large needle out of her chest. He seemed pleased. Her head hurt. Daisy closed her eyes and fell into a dreamless sleep.

As soon as they confirmed Nos would not be injured by being moved, the agents swept him to his feet. Each of the two strong men placed a firm grip under Nos's armpits and began heading to safety. They would take him to the chancellor's office, which was the safest spot-on campus and, in fact, one of the safest places in all Prometheus. As they moved him, his feet barely touched the ground. The cobwebs began to clear in his mind, and Nos could see over his shoulder that they had taken the tree planter into custody. He could see Daisy surrounded by the EMTs and wondered if he had killed her. His security team ushered him into the office, secured the outer room, and called in their report. Nos, safe in the chancellor's office, stood behind the bulletproof glass and began gathering his wits. Daisy was placed on the gurney, put into the ambulance, and rushed to the hospital. Her books were still strewn on the ground. He stared at the bloodstained dark grass where her head had lain and at the hole the stranger had dug. The tree, with its roots protected by a circular cloth, was sitting not far away, still waiting to be planted.

His grandfather was obsessed with several things, and this type of tree was one of them. He had attempted to plant several such trees in prominent places on his properties. He would usually plant them by a window so that he might gaze on them for most of the day. Invariably, they would die. Nos cursed the tree under his breath. Had the tree not been in his way, he would, at this moment, be deep into the seduction of his prize. He wondered if he would have enjoyed her screaming objections more than her quiet submission to his power. The thought came with a shrill rush of warmth that cascaded from his brain stem through his shoulders. With the chancellor gone, he could do anything he wanted, and standing in the office of one of the most powerful forces in Prometheus was affecting him. The sense of power and privilege the office of the chancellor evoked flowed through him and almost made him forget the humiliating strike from the tree planter. He was standing in the office with his special guards outside. A horde of attendants were at his beck and call. And yet, he could not shake the memory. It came from the shadows in the quiet. It was the pain of the backhand. It was the horror he felt when he remembered the light in the eyes of the purl who was his superior.

Now, Nos needed to take something from someone. He needed to exercise his power to reassure himself and remind others of who he was and the power he possessed. He was so shaken by the fight he was not his best self. He did not understand why he lost. He did not understand how Daisy fought so well. He thought she could have killed him or harmed him in any way she wished at any time in the battle, and that angered and confused him. He had never in his life been so totally beaten in a fight. He hoped he had killed her and, in his same confused mind, hoped he had not. In the swirl and turmoil of his emotions, he welcomed his grandfather's office. It had always been a place of refuge and comfort. It was not long before one of his grandfather's assistants brought him a fresh set of clothes. The attendant informed him that the dratsab was reviewing the events and managing the news report of the incident. He was told to remain where he was until he was sent his next instructions. He was told to expect a phone call. The animosity between Nos and his father was thick and flowed both ways. There were only two purple on the planet Nos feared, and one of them was the dratsab. He went into the private bath, showered, and dressed.

The evening had come when the phone rang. The dratsab was a very efficient ruler and had taught Nos many important things about life and power. He wasn't the kind of father who kissed his child when they needed it or the kind of dad who taught them gentleness or hope. There were no hugs from him. Life was too dangerous for tenderness. He was the kind of dad who taught his child lessons about the value of life by not caring if they died. He was the one who taught the difficult lessons, and some of them came quick and hard. They were the kind of lessons that sank deep into the soul and psyche of a purl. He was the father who made sure they understood some purple were prey, and the rest were to be taught to obey. These lessons didn't leave Nos and his father lovingly close. So, Nos reached for the receiver, dreading the conversation he was likely to have. He hoped it wasn't the dratsab, but who else could it be? He was not sure if Daisy was dead, but he had left the tree planter alive. He was in line to be the next dratsab, but others this close to the office had been killed because of weakness. He picked up the receiver, choked down all his fear and anxiety, and, with as much coldness as he could project, identified himself. The voice on the other end asked if he would hold for the chancellor. Nos sighed in relief. He respected his father and feared his power, but he loved his grandfather.

He and his grandfather spoke for nearly an hour. The conversation began with the chancellor asking Nos if he was okay. He asked in a way that swept past Nos's defenses. With the love and care woven into the chancellor's voice, Nos's eyes watered until one of them overflowed, sending a tear streaming down his red cheek. The chancellor had reviewed the surveillance footage from several angles. He had spoken to the dratsab. Everything was being managed. Nos relaxed and let the tension flow out of his body. His grandfather told him many things and Nos listened to him. He helped him over the fear of the dratsab's reaction and gave his grandson step-by-step instructions. He assured Nos that he was still heir to the dratsab and suggested that his ascension would come quicker than anyone thought.

Nos was unaware that many of the things the chancellor told him were lies. Some of the lies would reveal themselves in time, but others would sink his soul into darker and darker deeds, particularly those lies in which Nos participated and were perpetuated by his own will and way in the world. They talked about Daisy. In the end, all was well. They did not talk much about the tree planter. Nos was too ashamed, and the chancellor had other reasons. The memory brought anguish deep within Nos's soul and brought pain back to his face. The chancellor dismissed concern about the tree planter and helped Nos see much of what he remembered about his attacker was not true. The chancellor reminded Nos that he had seen the tapes and had, in fact, studied them. He assured Nos that there was nothing to worry about and that the tree planter would be dealt with.

The next morning, the news reported the story of the deranged gardener whose attempt to kill a light-eyed law student was thwarted by the selfless, quick courage of the son of the dratsab. There was speculation about whether light-eyed purple targeted other light-eyed purple when they aspired to accomplish things that required the intelligence of dark-eyed purple. There was a ceremony planned to honor and award the courage of the dratsab's son. Prayers were solicited for the nameless light-eyed purl who lay in critical condition at the University Medical Center Hospital.

Daisy stirred. An unfamiliar beeping disturbed her rest. She opened her eyes to see what was making the noise. She didn't know where she was, and she began firing up her mind to orient herself. The blue sky of bright-day peeking through the window began to bring clarity and comfort. Hurried footsteps came close. She thought to turn to see who it was, but, before she could, a wave of sleepiness washed over her, and she decided to rest just a little while longer.

It felt like only a few moments had passed when she opened her eyes again. And there he was. It felt as if her bed had been raised some, at least more than she remembered, but she was unsure about everything at that moment. She realized she was in a hospital and attempted to remember what had brought her there. Memories came flooding into her mind, but she was unsure of which were real and which were dreams. She looked at him and, at the same, saw a bouquet of daisies. She looked at the space beneath the window shade where the bright-day sky had appeared, but all the light of day was gone. She remembered his face, and suddenly, the noise of the gunshot flashed across her mind. She raised her hand to her forehead and placed her fingers under the neatly combed bangs of rich blue hair.

More confusion. She didn't think she liked bangs. The confusion in her eyes drew him. He came to her bedside and held her hand. There was tenderness and kindness in his touch. She welcomed it. He welcomed her back and said he had been waiting, praying the gods would return her to him. She was confused. He understood. He spoke so softly and with such familiarity it made Daisy question how well her memory was working. He kissed her tenderly on the forehead and on both cheeks. He called her his darling and said he had cried by her bedside until the doctors promised him that she would recover. He spent hours talking to her and promised he would return in the morning. He said he was so happy to have her back with him.

The days passed, and the tender visits continued. He talked about the day when it all happened and wondered how something so terrible could lead to such a wonderful clarity. Daisy was getting better but remained a little confused. She asked one of her nurses to find a newspaper from the day after her injury and was told that one had been kept just in case. The newspaper stories confirmed what she had been hearing, even though reading them made her feel there was something very wrong. She gradually accepted the stories Nos had been telling her were true. She didn't remember loving him or him loving her, but all the signs pointed in that direction.

A team of specialists from the chancellor's office were the only physicians allowed to attend to Daisy. They were each an expert in their field. They had been assembled by the chancellor to work on projects that even the dratsab's intelligence agencies had no access. The chancellor had them rushed in from all over Prometheus after he had reviewed the surveillance tapes. The doctors gave Daisy a clean bill of health without mentioning how many weeks she laid unconscious. The leaves that were attached to her injury stumped them. They observed them gradually disappear. They wondered as her skin changed and the leaves erased any sign of the wound. They had no explanation. Daisy was oblivious to all of this. She only knew she felt wonderful and was ready to leave the hospital. She was kept for days while they poked and prodded her and took samples of everything.

When Nos came to drive her home from the hospital, he brought with him a letter from the dratsab inviting Daisy to work in his legal department. The letter offered her a job in which she would spend the first several months preparing for the bar exam and, after passing it, would begin working in the department of Light-Eyed Affairs (DLA). It was a dream job for Daisy. She had always wanted to find a way to use her intelligence and energy to help those like her. On the drive from the hospital, Daisy realized the last place she had lived was in campus housing. When she mentioned it, Nos told her he had secured an apartment for her in his building several floors below his own. The apartment came as part of the job offer. She wondered at the wisdom of living so close to Nos and so far away from Noth. But she let the thought fade into the benign confusion that had permeated everything since she woke up in the hospital.

Life for Daisy began to speed up, and she fell into a rhythm that soon helped her accept the course her life had taken. She began her work and was very soon an attorney in the Department of Light-Eyed Affairs. She rose through its ranks as if a secret hand was propelling her success. Her ability to practice law was unmatched, and although she was often challenged, she was rarely beaten. She took to wearing sunglasses to hide her light eyes as she went in and out of her office building. It kept the stares down from security and others as she walked straight in the building while all the other light-eyed purple waited in long lines to enter the heavily protected DLA facilities. As time moved on, she found it easier to just wear contact lenses. Nos showed his approval when she did. He called her his dark-eyed goddess. He meant it as a compliment, but it was also a statement against who she really was. Nos asked if she wanted him to get his grandfather's medical team to change her light green eyes to a dark brown. That such a procedure was possible was kept secret from most and was absolutely illegal, but as the son of the dratsab, Nos could do many things with impunity. He offered this to Daisy, in part, to demonstrate his power. His arrogance hid the fact that the suggestion had the opposite effect. With improvements in lens technology, Daisy could keep her contacts in for longer periods and only took them out when Nos was not around. Secretly, she loved her light green eyes because in her dreams, he loved them.

Daisy continued to move through the Promethean aristocracy and bureaucracy as she fought for the light-eyed purple. She accepted the courtship of Nos, even though her coworkers understood they were a couple long before she accepted this as her reality. His continued kindness was hard to deny. The Nos she remembered in law school was so different from the one who politely, but continually, moved to contain her world in an ever-diminishing circle. Her work in the DLA kept her focused and without much time for a social life.

Two years passed, and her life was full and wonderful except for the occasional vivid dream that called to something deep inside her. Those dreams connected to something true about who she was and where she was supposed to be. When she was dreaming, she felt wonderful. But when she woke, she was disturbed. The dreams seemed essential to her life and her purpose on Purplynd, but she had no one to talk to about them. When she mentioned them to Nos, his disapproval was so obvious and belittling she stopped talking about them. If Nos had been wise, he would have listened carefully to the dreams and told them to his grandfather, but arrogance and power have a way of making one blind. Sometimes the answers to life appear and are ignored. Arrogance hides wisdom's thread in haystacks.

So, Nos continued to ply the plan his grandfather had given him long ago and was delighted in his own success. Daisy, against her will, had begun to care about pleasing Nos. Perhaps it was his kindness toward her. In her mind, he had softened in his interactions with others, and she began to want to please him. Still, there were the dreams. They were so powerful, and they were true to her in ways she did not understand. In the end, the attorney in her told her to weigh the facts against the fantasy. Nos was real. The dreams, or whatever they were, were not real.

The little time she had that was not consumed by DLA work was occupied by Nos, who always seemed to know when she had an unencumbered moment. This did not give her much time to spend in Noth or any of the other light-eyed townships. There was no time to enjoy casual moments with the light-eyed community and no time to have a relationship with anyone other than Nos, even though, somewhere deep inside her, there was someone else, someone with whom she longed to be, someone who was the best part of her. But Daisy realized this only in the split seconds before she awakened on sunny days after a full night's rest. Besides, she told herself, life was busy, and Nos was real. So, she was not completely surprised the night he proposed to her.

He had dressed in a gray dinner jacket with silk trim on the lapels. A custom-made, vibrant violet, double-collared shirt made him look especially handsome. He got down on one knee. She noticed his skin glowed red when he asked for her hand. She did not know why she noticed that. Strangely, the night before, she had one of the most vivid and troubling dreams since her trip to the hospital. Without that dream, she would have accepted his proposal without much reservation. She was not in love with Nos. At least, she was not in love with him in the way she thought she should be. When they talked about their relationship and in those rare times when Daisy shared her heart with him, Nos would dismiss her uncertainty. The woman in her dreams would easily tell him no. If she was the woman she was in her dreams, she would have left him and the palace prison he had built to lock her in long ago. As she thought this, her mind whispered, *Dreams are empty fantasies. Nos is here and real. As the wife of the dratsab, there is much you could do to help your purple.* This whisper came out of the darkness and presented itself in her mind as wisdom. An argument against spending her life with Nos rose to be recognized but the thought was logical and practical. She was a lawyer. She dealt in facts. The sparkle of the large diamond on the engagement ring invited her to search for the colors in her dreams. Just then, a violet ray shone in the ring. She could not remember something. She thought that whatever it was, it was essential to know at this moment. She searched for a memory or meaning. There was something in the way, like thick brush obscuring the light she needed to see.

She began to clear the confusion, but before she could see the light of bright-day, she heard herself say, "Yes." She noticed that the color of her new fiancé faded to its normal rouge even as his eyes seemed darker than normal.

When Daisy woke the next morning, her stomach was upset. Nos had insisted on cooking their meal. She thought the gourmet dinner was part of his proposal plan but wondered what ingredients in the spicy food had her system so upset. The thoughts to stay home were dismissed when she remembered an important meeting she didn't want to miss. Any other purl would have wrapped herself in her blankets and hid from the day, but Daisy had strength beyond most. She had needed that strength to live for most of her life. Her strength was what helped her climb out of Noth. Her strength, perseverance and tenacity were what helped her finish law school. And these three also allowed her to exist in the dark-eyed world without being crushed by the benign, ubiquitous hatred they had for light-eyed purple. So, feeling as sick as a junkyard dog, she was determined to make her meeting.

There were very few purple with the strength Daisy had. Two of them were from when she was very small. She only remembered their voices and how they marveled at how soon she learned to walk and how strong she was. She didn't know why she thought they were strong, but, in her mind, they were. Who they were had been long-lost. Daisy had forgotten all about them until the dreams started.

Then there was the tree planter, whom she never mentioned to Nos or anyone. She thought he was strong. He often appeared in her dreams. In fact, she had seen him the night before Nos proposed. When she looked through the classified files of the DLA, she could find nothing more than reports similar to the stories in the newspapers. She remembered his name. How could she forget? But he had disappeared. When she was quiet and alone, she missed him. When Nos was gone on a trip or away for a while, everything was different. In those times, she would dream and rest and question things about her life, like the story she had been told in the hospital. Somewhere in her soul, something was wrong with the story she was told and her own memory of that day. But, in most of her conscious thoughts about the incident, she wanted to know what had happened to him. Had he been disappeared like so many light-eyed purple and buried in a shallow, unmarked grave? Was he in the wild beyond Prometheus? And what should she do about finding the answers she wanted? These thoughts brought her to the only other purl she knew who had this same kind of reluctance to believe everything she was told—her best and oldest friend, Daisi.

The two had met in kindergarten. The first time the teacher called the name Daisy from the attendance sheet, they both answered. Then they each accused the other of taking their name and began to fight. Fighting among the light-eyed purple of Noth was usual. There was not enough of anything, so purple fought. The purple of Noth didn't always fight fair, but they always fought. And a few became very good at it. When they were in the fifth grade, a purl about two years older than Daisy started picking on both of them. He was asking for something inappropriate, and for some reason, they were both afraid. He had just cornered Daisi when her little brother, Bud, bit him and then grabbed his finger until it broke. From that point all the way through high school, the girls were the closest of friends. They began to be called Daisy 1 and 2. Their friends would write their names "Daisi" and "Daisii." Every purl acquainted with them both called Daisii "Tu." But no one in the dark-eyed world called her Tu, and, as she entered the higher education institutions of the dark-eyed purple, the only way her name was written was "D-A-I-S-Y". She had long ago lost contact and connection with the purple of her past, but Daisi had recently appeared out of nowhere and on her calendar.

Daisii didn't know her friend had attended to her safety while she was in the hospital after she had been shot. She didn't know Daisi had written to her many times. She didn't know how protected she was from information and influences outside of the bubble the dratsab had created for her. But Daisi had called and needed her. It sounded urgent, as many calls to the DLA sounded, but this was Daisi, and she had made her way through the labyrinth of offices and purple to get to Daisii's administrative assistant and then to Daisii herself. So, no matter how sick Daisy was, she wouldn't miss this meeting.

It was very difficult for light-eyed purple to enter the city and almost impossible for one to be permitted into the upper offices of the DLA. The plans to allow Daisi into the executive suite of the DLA and to Daisii's inner office were elaborate and difficult. Daisi would have already been standing in many long lines. Daisii could have asked Nos to use his influence to have Daisi picked up and brought to her without any problem, but that would have come at a price that Daisii was sure she did not want to pay. So, she threw up one last time, brushed her teeth, gargled, and dressed for work.

Daisii threw some medicine in her purse just in case and headed out. The elevator doors opened to reveal two attractive female purple already on their way to the street level. They looked a bit disheveled for that early in the morning and were giggling over some secrets as the elevator doors opened. They got quiet as Daisii entered the elevator and remained silent the long ride down. Daisii thought their presence and behavior was strange, but the day was full, and Daisi was probably already waiting, and there was this ring on her finger.

Pookii had been in the SHU for ten days. From the warden's vantage, things were getting irksome. This was supposed to be an in-and-out procedure, twenty-four hours at most. The whole prison reverberated with the news of the inmate who busted up Bud. The guards were edgy and more aware than usual that they were not in control. On the outside, light-eyed purple began asking questions about Pookii's disappearance, and their complaints and conjectures were getting louder. What the warden had meant to be a quick lesson to a purl who didn't know his place was becoming a problem. A firsthand account of the circumstances of Pookii's arrest began spreading throughout the light-eyed hovels. The parole he had offered went around all the usual procedures and paperwork, which signaled to Bud that the warden was desperate. Bud used that desperation to his advantage. He made sure all the paperwork was signed and in his possession before he was taken to the shower room. In the confusion afterward, he used his network to push the paperwork through and got released eight days after meeting Pookii. The warden had pulled enough strings getting the initial parole deal through and didn't want any additional light to be shone on his prison. He could rearrest a light-eyed purl at any time, and the arrest of a purl with Bud's reputation wouldn't be questioned. The problem was that the DLA had just begun a prison investigation throughout Prometheus. His prison had been announced by his friend Nos as the one selected to be inspected.

Nos and the warden were co-conspirators and had collaborated on many nefarious things in the past. They had a similar view and approach to the opposite sex, and both loved the accumulation and projection of power. The warden didn't know why his prison was selected or what Nos was up to but trusted that he would use the investigation as a means to increase their power and influence with the dratsab. Nos had just left the mainland, and the warden didn't know when he would return. The new DLA director was on a mission. She had gotten on a crusade to clean up the prison system. She was the girlfriend of the dratsab's son, but the warden didn't know whether he was setting her up for failure or something else. He believed Nos would fill him in on his plan when they found a private place to talk. He understood this would have to wait until Nos returned and they met face-to-face but had no idea when that would be. Meanwhile, Noj Burg had finally been found and would soon be back at the prison to train the light-eyed purl who was causing so much trouble.

Daisii entered her suite of offices from the private corridors where only the dark-eyed staff had access. She greeted her private administrative assistant, who asked whether she was ill. Daisii had no idea Nos had planted that assistant — the purl with whom she was closest to in all the DLA offices—or that he had called on his way to the airport to tell her Daisii was ill and would probably not come to work for the next few days. Nos would often call for reports of Daisii's activities and interests. On this call, his tone was so suggestive that the young administrative assistant was thrown a bit by his directness. The son of the dratsab had a reputation, but she could not tell whether he was seriously propositioning her or testing her. She found him both creepy and intriguing at the same time. He was extremely powerful, and she liked the idea of power. Sometimes, he spoke in a way she could feel in her bones. She found this power both dangerous and seductive. The conversation was brief, but the sexually charged aggressiveness of Nos made her forget to report to him that Daisii was scheduled to meet with a light-eyed purl who was a friend from her past. She realized her omission soon after she hung up the phone but reasoned that if Daisii wouldn't be in for a few days, she would have time to tell Nos later. In fact, it would give her an excuse to call him. She was so surprised to see Daisii when she walked in that she almost dropped a handful of papers she was carrying to the shredder. From there, she was on her way to tell the light-eyed purl in the waiting area that Daisii would not be able to see her.

Daisii walked past her administrator's desk and into her private office. She went straight to her private bathroom to check her hair and makeup in the mirror. The question her assistant asked made her wonder if she didn't look well, and she wanted to make sure she looked better than she felt. She took off her sunglasses and stared into her own light green eyes. She had taken out her contacts to put drops in her eyes as part of restoring herself from the restless night. Looking into the mirror, she was caught by her own eyes. They spoke of something true. They opened her past. Her own eyes invited her beyond the events of her life into something deeper. There was something beyond her, yet *in* her, and this thing gave her a sense of peace and a connection to something she needed. She looked at the shining and expensive ring that was now on her finger. The large stone was real, but her eyes told her there was something not real about the ring and a lot more of what was now her life.

Daisi was her first appointment for the day, and the purl in the mirror had told her to spend the entire morning catching up with her old friend. Just then, a knock on the office door shook her out of her contemplations. Daisii walked into her office and closed the bathroom door behind her. Her assistant showed Daisi into the office, and, as soon as her old friend came into view, tears welled up in her eyes. Her assistant lingered. Daisii politely told her to leave, being very careful to hold back the emotions that were welling up. When her assistant closed the door, Daisii almost ran from behind her desk to embrace Daisi. Now the tears rolled freely down her cheeks. Daisii looked into the light eyes of her long-lost friend and embraced her again. She felt like she was breathing fresh air after being underwater for years.

Daisi called her friend "Tu" and began to talk as if she only had a minute for her whole story. In fact, that was what she had been told. She had been told the DLA director had granted her five minutes and after those minutes expired, she would be escorted out. When Daisi told her that she had been given that time limit, Daisii got an idea. She went to her desk, picked up the phone, and told her assistant she would be leaving and to cancel her appointments for the morning. She took Daisi's cell phone and her own, placed them in a special case, and locked them in her desk drawer. She handed Daisi an extra pair of dark glasses and put on her own. She took some cash from another drawer and told Daisi to put it in her purse. Then they walked out of the back door and through the private corridors of the DLA building and disappeared into the morning.

The new DLA director came back to the office on a mission. The sickness from the morning was long gone, and Daisii was at her full strength. She met with all her afternoon appointments, and they gave her even more excitement about the direction the DLA was taking under her leadership. She finished the day and left the building. Seeing Daisi connected her to her past in ways that were refreshing. Daisii had worked hard for years to improve the lives and fate of light-eyed purple. It had been her mission. But all her work was from the ivory tower of the DLA. She had become respected in the dark-eyed world, and her close connection to Nos gave her deference, which she used to further reforms on behalf of the light-eyed. Still, all this work was done from Prometheus. She didn't know whether it was looking into the mirror or meeting Daisi that made her feel so different, but something brought life back into her in a new, old way.

Daisii promised Daisi that she would come to Noth and spend the weekend. Nos was out of town, and no one other than the dratsab would question her whereabouts. She left her phone in her office and took Daisi's phone home with her. She would be able to use this mix-up as a cover if Nos questioned why he couldn't reach her over the weekend. Initially, Daisii left her and her friend's phones in the office, so they could talk without every word being recorded. Nos had the power to access almost anything he wished, and Daisii thought it wise not to share the conversation with her childhood friend with the dark-eyed intelligence services or Nos. As they talked, something inside Daisii began to awaken, even though Daisi didn't tell her much. Daisi was wary of the conversation and did not trust politicians or the bureaucratic part of the government. Few light-eyed purple were aware that the director of the DLA was light-eyed, and it would not have made much difference to most if they were. The dark-eyed were never trusted to act purely or honestly in the interest of light-eyed purple. So, Daisi studied the body language and listened to every inflection of Daisii's voice to see if her old friend could be trusted with the information she so desperately wanted to share with her. The promise to come to Noth would give Daisi more time to assess whether her friend was still someone she could trust with her life.

Daisii left her plush apartment at dusk. She had come back to grab a few things for the two nights she would be away. As she packed the oversize purse, she realized all the things she had that were hard, if not impossible, to find in Noth. She wanted take some of the things as gifts to her old friends but realized that such would be too bulky to carry inconspicuously and might not be received in the right spirit. She took off the audacious ring Nos had placed on her finger because it would make her stand out among the light-eyed impoverished of Noth. At best, it would cause envy; at worse, some poor thug would be tempted to take it from her. The thought made her smile. She remembered the rough-and-tumble life of Noth and smiled at how domesticated and docile she had become. A picture of her last fight flashed in her mind. The image of her throwing Nos over her shoulder came to her in slow motion. When his body bounced on the ground, something inside her began asking questions. But the memory began to fade as soon as it had come. Daisii paused. There was something she needed to remember, something urgent about this memory she no longer had. Her brow furled in frustration. Daisii searched her mind. She tried to get past the hospital. She tried to get to that last day on campus, but nothing came to her except shadows. Daisii shook her head to chase the fog away. There was nothing in the past to remember, Nos always told her; there was only the future to plan. She and Daisi had made some plans for the weekend, and the thought of getting off the reservation and out of Prometheus was exciting. Alone, the weekend would have been filled with fretting about the mysteries she could feel were important but remained hidden from her conscious mind, but now, she had a weekend with old friends. She looked forward to reuniting with the purple of Noth.

She went over the list of things they had planned. She left her engagement ring in the jewelry soak on her vanity. She had no idea of the ways that Nos could track and manipulate the object he had so recently placed on his fiancée's finger. And she didn't know how this simple act would save the life of purple she cared about. Daisii left the eye-darkening contact lenses in their case. It was a small but significant thing that gave her peace as she readied herself to escape Prometheus. All was ready. She checked the apartment one last time. She locked her door with her voice command and initiated the program that turned lights on and off and made noises to simulate someone living in the apartment. It was a program Nos had designed for himself and installed in all his private residences. It helped him disappear and could provide alibis when needed. Nos never imagined it would be used by anyone other than himself. He was wrong. As Daisii left the building, the security at the reception desk noted a female wearing dark sunglasses, even though the suns had disappeared for the day. He had seen females coming off the elevators to the upper floors in many states. He had worked at the high-end apartment building long enough to suspect that she was covering up a black eye like other guests of the son of the dratsab. His training taught him to note that the woman was the same height and frame as the new director of the DLA, but if it was her, he reasoned, she would have spoken and been dressed much better.

Daisii made her way through the city to the place they had planned to meet. Daisi had sent her to a working-class restaurant on the outskirts of Prometheus. Daisii's peace and joy increased with each mile she rode away from the city. Daisi had a friend who worked at the restaurant as a waitress, and it was not unusual to see an occasional light-eyed purl or two. Daisi waited outside, unseen in the shadows. She had told her friend to watch for a green-eyed blue purl wearing a red top. Daisii arrived. She had removed her dark glasses after she got off the long train ride that took her from the heart of Prometheus to the edge of the city. There were enough light-eyed purple in that section of town that no one would think she didn't belong. She had dressed as Daisi told her, and when she told the hostess her name, she was taken to a table in the back. It was just a few minutes later when Daisi walked into the restaurant and right to Daisii's table. Seeing Daisi again was wonderful. Daisi took her overstuffed purse and transferred Daisii's underwear and clothes into a bag she had. Daisii watched as her long-lost friend checked her garments for tracking devices and thought she might be being too careful but accepted that she had forgotten the danger and threats light-eyed purple suffer every day. Daisi gave the purse to her waitress friend. The waitress would take it back to downtown Prometheus after her shift and leave it in a shopping cart at the all-night supermarket.

The weekend in Noth was incredible. Besides the incredibly bad-tasting shots she drank on a dare from her old friend, the weekend was the best one of her life. Daisii thought the shots were called poollé because they tasted like poo, but she never backed down from a "Daisi dare," so she did it twice. It wasn't long after the shots that she got very sick. She ran to bathroom and puked as her best friend rubbed her back to console her. After that, Daisii washed her face and drank something else Daisi gave her and went to bed. She slept like a newborn baby and had the most vivid and colorful dreams that night. She had no idea the terrible-tasting shots she shared with her friend had anything to do with her dreams or how wonderful she was beginning to feel. She was surrounded by a love that reminded her of who she was and why she went to law school in the first place.

She and Daisi talked for hours, and Daisi explained why and how hard it was to get to her. Daisii thought the difficulty was just a matter common to all big bureaucracies, but the stories began to make her wonder. Daisi told her about Bud. Daisii loved Bud. He was like her little brother. She remembered him breaking the finger of the older boy who had tried to molest both her and Daisi. She remembered how he screamed and cried when his mother came and abused him in front of everyone. More than the physical pain, it was the betrayal that broke his hearts and hers. What no one but she and Daisi knew was that Daisii cried every night for a week after the beating. That was when the two of them decided their life paths. Daisi decided to go into the military, and Daisii was going to law school. From that day, each of them dedicated their lives to those goals. It would be a long time before anyone else recognized where they were headed, and no one would have guessed because Daisii was the best fighter in the neighborhood, and Daisi was the brains.

Each used their innate gifts to help the other, and those years together knit them closer than any passage of time could erode. Daisi told the new director of the DLA about Bud's change. She told her something unbelievable had happened and how it happened. Daisii did not believe it, and Daisi didn't blame her. She promised on Sunday, she would see for herself. Daisi also mentioned she had tried to visit her friend when she was in the hospital but didn't say anything more. That part of the conversation was like someone pushing a poker into a fireplace and looking through the white ashes for an ember still hot enough to start a flame. Daisii wanted to know more, but something in her mind felt cold and went dark when she thought about the hospital. In that moment, when she was wondering about the shadow covering her memory, Daisi was staring into her eyes, reading thoughts hidden in the shadows of her mind.

Daisii slept well and enjoyed her wonderful dreams on both Friday and Saturday nights. By the time she woke up and dressed on Sunday, the family had already gathered. Daisi was cooking in the backyard when she walked out. Everyone began to greet her. Bud was surrounded by his old friends but when Daisii appeared, he ran and embraced her. He held her and then pushed back with his hands on her shoulders to look in her eyes. Tears were streaming down his cheeks, and when Daisii saw Bud's tears, she couldn't stop hers from flowing. She couldn't wrap her head around Bud weeping. Bud was the strongest, meanest, most frightening purl she had ever known. And she had known Bud all his life. She witnessed the darkness descend on him and engulf all that was gentle and loving within him. If ever a purl was lost to redemption, it was Bud. She was building prisons for the likes of him. But here he was holding her, and in his arms, protection and love flowed out of him and into her. He was changed just as Daisi had said. They held each other for a long time, and everyone in the backyard understood because each of them had had the same experience with Bud since he was paroled.

The bright-day celebration was wonderful; everyone there called Daisii "Tu." They ate and laughed and told tall tales of adventures, some of which were hard to believe. And during the whole time, Daisii couldn't keep her eyes off Bud. Every time their eyes met, hers would begin to water. When everyone had eaten and the bright-day was over, Daisi, Bud, and a few others took Tu to the corner of the backyard under a large tree. They sat down and told her about Pookii. They told her how he was taken without having committed any crime or offense; they told her that he had not been charged and had disappeared. They told her the only way they found out where he was and what had happened was when Bud had gotten miraculously paroled. Daisii had no idea who this Pookii was. She had never heard of such a purl, even if something about him was familiar. But the change in Bud was real, and anyone who could affect this type of change did not belong in prison. When the weekend was over, she left her renewed friendship, determined to get this purl released. She had the power, and it was the first time she was unquestionably determined to use it.

The warden was unhappy. He was unhappy, first, because he didn't like to be told what to do and, second, because he didn't like to be reminded that there were purple more powerful than he was. But the letter was clear, and it came from the director of the DLA. He didn't know how she got the information but wasn't surprised about it. Nos had spies everywhere, and she was Nos's girlfriend. He wondered why Nos hadn't been the one to tell him or why he cared about this particular purl. He wondered if Nos was aware of the letter at all. He wondered if the director was beginning the process to replace him. He suspected that he was not one of her favorites. Her prison-reform talk in the papers had always worried him, but Nos had always reassured him. The direct, clear, and authoritative letter suggested that the director was aware of some very uncomfortable things about what was happening in his prison. The communication made him wonder what other knowledge she had, but most of all, he wondered if Noj had already begun his interrogation. He was determined to get Pookii back out on the streets as soon as possible. He would then write a letter thanking her for her concern and assuring her he would find those responsible for the unlawful abduction and reprimand or charge them, if necessary. His mind had already begun crafting his defense, and he convinced himself that all would be fine if Noj had not mangled the purl beyond recognition. His first step was an angry visit to the deputy warden's office, where he publicly and demonstrably questioned and accused the deputy of illegally holding Pookii. Plenty of purple witnessed his feigned outrage, and the deputy warden promised to immediately take care of the release. The warden stormed back to his office, hiding the glee of having put his plan into action.

It was only seconds after he left that the phone in Noj's office started ringing off the hook. But it was too late. Noj and his submission crew had already left for the cell where Pookii had been buried alive for nearly two weeks. In fact, they were already on their way through the labyrinth of gates and bars on the way to Pookii's cell when the warden did his little acting scene in the deputy warden's office. Noj had his black box with him and was longing to make someone scream after his vacation was cut short, and his purl service folder dinged because no one could find him. He was supposed to have been fishing but was actually involved in some other wholly illegal activities for which he used his dark proclivities.

When they arrived at the cell, Noj used his torture machine to strike the outside of the door and started yelling orders through the steel. He told Pookii to get on his knees with his back to the door and cross his legs. He stared at his wrist monitor watching Pookii's non-compliance. Something cool washed over him as he realized this purl was going to require a brutal lesson. He yelled his commands again, adding invectives and curses. Still, Pookii simply stood erect, his hand folded behind him, looking directly into the photo optic fiber lens whose location he was not supposed to know. Noj told one of the jailers to open the cell door. Just as the key was inserted, two large guards came running toward him and his men. He thought they were re-inforcements and mumbled to no one in particular how much he was going to enjoy mutilating the purl behind the door. The door opened out just as the reinforcements reached Noj. Pookii stood still, staring straight into the empty soul of Noj as the guard who had just arrived whispered in his ear.

Rage, with nowhere to be released, was ignited and then flowed through Noj. It was not just what was said in his ear that infuriated him. It was the look in the eyes of the purl in that cell; there was no fear or cowardice in them. Noj had seen strong purple before, but what incensed him was that there also was no anger in them. Noj had never seen such, and he deeply needed to destroy this purl. Noj needed to put fear in him. He needed to make him cry and beg for mercy. But the threat that came from the deputy warden was strong and clear. Noj was an evil man who took delight in the screams of his victims, but the deputy warden was a stone-cold killer who never asked twice and never gave forgiveness. There were few purple Noj feared in all Purplynd; the deputy warden was near the top of that list. Noj backed away from the open cell door.

It was just a few hours later when Pookii, dressed in his own clothes, walked out of the prison unshackled and unbowed. As he passed the last set of locked doors, Noj was waiting. Their eyes met. Noj, at that moment, vowed to destroy the purl who walked by him. He embraced both hatred and resolve. Something nearly physical entered his being, and he welcomed it.

Pookii was given some pocket change to catch the bus and was dropped off on the freedom side of the chain-link, razor-wire-topped fence. After he was released, the warden was called and informed that the mission had been completed. The warden then sent a letter to the DLA director informing her that, due to an extremely rare case of mistaken identity, a light-eyed purl was very briefly detained in the prison. He thanked the director for bringing the matter to his attention and assured her that, in all the years of his distinguished career, this was the first such instance he had encountered. This last lie was a bit over the top, but it was his attempt to assess where he stood with the director. If all was well, she would certify the same in the public reports by somehow referencing how rare it was for the wrong purl to be detained. If she didn't, well then, he would know she was no friend.

Nos returned to the city, confident and resolved. He always loved spending time with his grandfather, and the last two weeks in the wilderness had ended wonderfully. The chancellor had exotic interests, many of which Nos didn't understand. The chancellor and Nos flew to an island and then were driven to the distant mountain foothills where they met with the rest of the chancellor's team at a bar. Together, they hiked several days in the wild. One night, they met some natives who were so primitive they didn't know who his grandfather was, and they left one member of the team with them to restore some artifact his grandfather had brought. But the team spent most of their time investigating the different plants and trees they came across. Some of the purple on his grandfather's team seemed to be on an archeological mission. They were constantly searching for bone fragments or mounds that may have once been near settlements of ancient purple. The chancellor and his team met and conversed about things Nos did not understand. Most of these conversations were convened at the close of day in a special tent where their samples were gathered, cataloged, and packed. But Nos didn't care at all about the science. He was there to be with his grandfather.

Nos was never sure why his grandfather included him in his affairs. He was not sure why he was invited on this trip at the last minute but was excited about giving the chancellor his report on how things were progressing. After his grandfather's evening meetings, he would come into the tent they shared and spend the rest of the time with Nos. Nos loved these moments. There, far away from civilization, they discussed and adjusted the plan for Nos's ascension to become the next dratsab. The chancellor was happy with the progress Nos was making with the new director of the DLA. He told him about the engagement, but the chancellor was not as pleased about it as Nos thought he would be. It was, after all, his plan. The chancellor asked several questions about how the food was prepared and the precise portions of the potions Nos had used. Everything appeared to be in order, but the chancellor worried that the potion might have been a little strong. He was aware of something Nos was not, namely, the precise potion proportions Nos used had killed a purl whom the chancellor had in the same predicament years before. The chancellor appreciated that the large engagement ring contained a locator and had been coated with toxins to help ensure the magic would take. Still, the chancellor thought Nos relied too heavily on technology. He realized the timing was unfortunate. He would have preferred if Nos were close enough to monitor Daisy through the first several days at least. Nos assured the chancellor that he had covered every base. He was confident in his spies and his technology. Nos thought the trip was wonderful. He was excited that his ascension would occur quicker than he had thought possible, and he was anxious to get back and move the plan forward.

Nos frequently met with his co-conspirators at his favorite restaurant in all Prometheus. It was owned by the dratsab, and it was a place Nos could truly have private conversations. He could do anything he wanted without the slightest fear of being reprimanded, counseled, or questioned. He had, in fact, already done many nefarious things in the dark corners and hidden rooms of the Promethean Panthae. The part-nightclub, part-restaurant was named and built by the now chancellor and father of the dratsab. He named it after an ancient creature he claimed had mythological powers. Nos had been drawn to its secret dark corridors long before he was old enough to imagine right from wrong or sit at the bar and partake of its potent liquors.

The dratsab had taken ownership of the Promethean Panthae from his father. He did not ask for it as a gift or offer to purchase it, but rather used his power as a highly placed Promethean government official to steal it. The change of ownership was public and brutal. There was no love lost between the father and son, and the hostile takeover meant that some of the secrets of the Promethean Panthae were never revealed to the dratsab. Instead, the chancellor revealed them to his grandson. Knowledge of these hidden things was the first indication to Nos that one day he might ascend and become the dratsab. It also made the restaurant feel like a safe and powerful place for Nos to discuss the kind of things he had called his friend to talk about.

Nos met the warden at the Promethean Panthae the evening he returned. It had been almost two weeks since he had left with his grandfather, and he was anxious to move his plan forward. He also wanted to enjoy some female companionship before letting Daisy know he was back in town. The chancellor had made Nos swear he would never strike Daisy or consummate their connection until he gave him permission. It was part of a long conversation at the law school many years before. Nos didn't understand why, but the chancellor was powerful and ruthless. Obedience would get him the dratsab he feared that disobedience would remove the favor he enjoyed from his grandfather. He didn't know whether the chancellor wanted Daisy for himself or was protecting her for some other reason but gaining the power he lusted after meant following the instructions of his grandfather completely. When he arrived at the Promethean Panthae, the two female purple who were in the elevator the morning he left were there with another companion. The four of them disappeared into the nether parts of the Panthae.

When the warden arrived, he was taken to the basement and then to a private, hidden elevator that went farther down into the darkness. It opened to a corridor that looked more like a cavern than a hallway. It was dimly lit and oppressive. Its curved walls were rough and cold. As he walked to the only lit doorway, he realized that he was unsure how deep beneath the ground he had descended. A lone mammoth of a purl stood guard at the door. The guard opened the door, and the warden entered Nos's underground office. The warden and Nos had grown closer over the years. They had engaged in and enjoyed the same types of entertainment while they were both in law school. They had also shared in committing and covering up crimes for each other. The two became close when the warden took the blame for the rape of the daughter of a cabinet-level government official. It was one of Nos's dark deeds, but he managed to move all the blame away from the dratsab's son to himself. Then, during the trial, they succeeded in destroying both the young purl's reputation and the case. She and her family were driven out of power in humiliation and shame.

The warden had been to this deep office only a few other times. One of them was when Nos had informed him of the plan to make him the warden. The prison was an important tool in subjugating the population and consolidating power. The way he had come into the underground office was the only way in he was aware of, but he suspected other entrances and exits existed. He sat still and waited. The plush, dark room had a fully stocked bar and an overstuffed lounge sofa, but the warden sat in the stiff chair, facing the desk as if he were a child called to the principal's office. He thought he and the son of the dratsab were on good terms, but there was no need to take chances. As warden of the largest prison in the country, he was well aware that there were ways of monitoring every move purple make and assumed that the fiber-optic cameras were watching everything he did.

A few moments later, Nos came into the room from behind the warden with a sudden outbreak of noise and light. Sounds of females giggling and kisses goodbye filled what was silent space. The warden was careful not to turn around. Instead, he sat still and stared at the empty desk in front of him, waiting for permission to relax. The letter worried him. He wasn't sure what Nos was up to but hoped this was the meeting in which he would find out. Nos could shoot him in the middle of the street without consequence, and the warden was sure he could die in that office before the hour was up or the visit over. The door closed, and the sounds of purple disappeared. The warden felt the hand on his shoulder before he heard Nos's voice. The icy touch helped him realize that he was sweating from the fear of what might happen next. But Nos seemed happy to see him and excited about something. He offered his friend a drink, and with the first bite of the dark whiskey, the tension began to drift out of the warden's mind and body. They sat in the comfortable, overstuffed chairs, and Nos began to describe the plan for his ascension to the dratsab. The warden was aware that the chancellor was the power behind his friend and also that Nos was not a novice at elaborate and dangerous plans to appropriate power. Details were discussed that could only be whispered in the subterranean lair. The conversation itself could have brought the wrath of the dratsab down on every name mentioned and their families, but Nos was committed. Something significant had happened, and Nos was empowered by it. The warden was enraptured by the prospect of becoming even more powerful and was committed to every dark deed Nos described. After a good, long conversation and several drinks, Nos invited the warden upstairs to eat. They left the office through the same door the warden had entered. The guard who had been at the door when he arrived was nowhere to be seen.

On the elevator ride up to the basement, the warden wondered at how relaxed he was. By the time they had walked through the kitchen, sat, and ordered their meals, he was at ease. He decided to ask about the DLA director and the letter reprimanding him. He wondered if it had come at Nos's directive and how that fit into the plan they had just discussed. Nos knew nothing about the letter and dismissed it as part of Daisy's frivolous crusade to save the light-eyed race. They laughed together and exchanged some derogatory remarks about light-eyed purple. Another round of drinks came, and they toasted to their control of light-eyed purple. The warden then told Nos the letter had not only questioned how he ran the prison but had also ordered the release of an uncharged purl. He alluded to how badly Noj would have mangled Pookii had the director not insisted on his immediate discharge. Nos began to wonder who Pookii was and why Daisy would want him released. The warden told him it was just some uppity, light-eyed, double-hearted purl who needed to be taught a lesson. He did not mention he had ordered his capture and conditioning in the first place.

The alcohol consumption had put the warden in a relaxed and confident mood. He finished the drink and was immediately brought another. This was Nos's table, after all. Nos asked to see the purl whom his brand-new fiancée had sprung from prison while he was away. The warden turned to his wrist, called the prison, and ordered Pookii's file and picture be sent to his wrist device. In just a few moments, his wrist buzzed with the information. He crossed his left wrist over his plate to show Nos the picture of Pookii. As the image on the device appeared, a look came across Nos's face that sobered the warden instantly. Nos grabbed the warden's wrist and pulled it closer to unmistakably identify the purl. The sudden violent move shook the table. As the image became clear, the effect of the alcohol drained from Nos as water from a broken vase. There was no mistaking whose face it was. Nos rose in a sudden move that upended the table, still holding the warden's wrist. His left-hand rose to strike. Before the fine china could hit the floor, Nos had slapped the face of the warden with such force that he and the dishes shattered on the floor at the same moment. The warden didn't dare move. He lay in the shards of glass as the broken bottle of wine emptied its last drops onto the floor. He looked at Nos, wondering if he was to die even before his offense was revealed. Nos sat back down on the curved leather bench of his booth. The crimson flare that had erupted through his flesh began to fade to its normal rouge. Attendants scurried to clean up the mess and restore the pristine table setting of the dratsab's son. The warden was helped to his feet while all checked to see if it was all right with Nos to do so. The warden stood still.

Nos remembered the last time he had seen that face. It all came back in full color. He remembered looking over his shoulder. He remembered the agents snatching Pookii away from Daisy. He remembered he was whispering in her ear. He remembered Pookii had disappeared. He was told that law students who had witnessed everything surrounded the officers who were arresting Pookii and refused to let him be taken. He wondered why the dratsab or his grandfather hadn't caught and killed Pookii soon after. He wondered why his grandfather had insisted on him coming on the long trip into the wild. He wondered why Daisy freed Pookii and what she remembered. He wondered who he could trust, even as he resolved he could trust no one. He understood he would have to kill his way out of his predicament, but he wasn't at all sure who should be killed first or why. He needed more information. He needed the warden alive for now. He calmed himself. He breathed the darkness deeper into himself. A dark quiet came. His eyes became the color of coal. He told his friend to sit down.

The myriad of thoughts, suspicions, and fears took time; all the while, the warden sat beside him, silent. A fresh meal was set before Nos, and he began to eat, not because he had an appetite, but because he wanted to put the warden at ease. A meal was placed in front of the warden also, but he was much too afraid to move. Nos smiled at him and told him to eat. The warden obeyed. Nos pushed all his anger and rage far from view and gave every indication that he had regained his composure. He even smiled and began talking about the food and making light conversation to put his friend at ease. More information was needed from the warden, and he opted for asking for it delicately rather than torturing the truth out of him. The time with his grandfather had reminded him of the power of seduction and subtlety. The warden began to be convinced that the fit of rage was not directed at him but rather something related to the purl on his wrist device. Somehow, he mustered the courage to ask Nos who Pookii was, hoping to understand better what amount of danger awaited him.

"His name is Pedagogy," Nos said.

The warden recognized the name. He thought for a while and then asked if this was the purl who shot and tried to kill Daisy so many years ago. Nos's skin pulsed red when the warden asked the question. But no one detected his change. Nos didn't know whether the warden was baiting him. He didn't know if the warden knew the truth. He studied his facial movements and listened for signs of the warden's allegiance. Nos asked his friend to elaborate on his question. The warden related that he only vaguely remembered what he had read in newspaper accounts of an incident at the law school a year or so after he had graduated. At that time, he had not yet worked his way into the dratsab's circle of control and would have had no way of knowing the day after the incident, an all-points bulletin had gone out to find Pedagogy. Nos read the warden's body language. He examined every phrase he spoke and watched the dilation of his pupils. Nos was convinced most of what the warden was saying was the truth. There was little he knew about Pedagogy, but, still, Nos perceived the warden was withholding some information. He was sharing, but not everything. His fear was so dominant that it made him difficult to read. Clearly the warden was afraid of him, but Nos began to suspect the warden feared something or someone else much more. Nos smiled. He asked his friend if he would like one of the ladies to drive him home.

THE BABY GROWS UP

THE NOTE DANCING DAISY read the day Pedagogy was delivered into her arms was folded into three sections and ended with a poem. Together, they told of marvelous and mysterious things that would happen to Daisy and the baby she held in her arms. The note told her many things she knew must be true because she felt the power of the words as she read them. There was much in it but no urgency to read all of it. Instead, Daisy read until it confirmed there was no one who would return to take him from her. But as she heard the words in her heart, something warm stirred within her. She looked from the note to stare with wonder at the bundle in her arms. She nursed him, and tears filled her eyes each time their eyes met.

Pedagogy finished nursing and drifted off to sleep. Daisy didn't want to move. She didn't want to put the baby down even for a moment. So, she watched him sleep. There was still a part of her, most of her actually, that didn't think any of this was real. She expected to wake up and resume her life, but she didn't want to wake up. She wanted this to be real. She wanted this child to be hers. Somehow, the child in her arms was a bridge over all the scars of her life, including the destruction of her womb. Thoughts of unattended chores moved through her mind. There were always things to do, preparations to be made, but she didn't want to move. She didn't want to wake from the dream. She drifted off to sleep.

Daisy woke suddenly. Her mind moved through the dream she had been having of a child brought to her in the strangest way. She wondered why she was on the couch and not in her own bed. She looked up at the clock. It was three o'clock in the morning. She began to pull her mind into the present and felt the bundle in her arms. It was real. The child was in her arms and awake. Daisy knew the infant needed to be changed. He wasn't crying or fussing, but she knew because he was telling her. Daisy carried him to her bedroom, cleaned him, and changed him. As she opened the blanket, she marveled again at its beauty. The inside of the blanket was even more intricate than the outside, but both were rich with colors that seemed to almost vibrate, if that makes sense. It didn't make much sense to Daisy, but if you had asked her that night, she would have said she heard the colors as much as she saw them. She nursed Pedagogy back to sleep. She laid him beside her, and they slept.

Morning came and, with it, several phone calls notifying Daisy that neither of the two children she had been expecting was coming. In fact, she and her newest charge would be alone for the next three days, which gave Daisy time to think through her new life. She could hardly believe the dreams of her childhood and the hopes of her youth had become a reality. She remembered the tears that stained her cheeks when the doctor told her she would never be able to have children. The thought of those tears of sorrow brought new tears of joy. The time alone with Pedagogy was precious. In those three days, Daisy rearranged her bedroom to include the things she would need for her charge, including a bassinet right beside her bed.

The two of them grew closer and found a rhythm of rest, relaxation, and work that convinced Daisy that the daycare would be fine. The short break flew by, and the evening before the children would return, she decided to wash the beautiful blanket that held Pedagogy since he had come. Its fabric was so soft and warm it was hard to imagine exchanging it for anything Daisy had or any other cloth existing on Purplynd. She nursed and changed Pedagogy. She held him until he was sleeping soundly and laid him in the bassinet. She took the blanket to the kitchen to hand-wash it in the stainless-steel vegetable sink. As she washed it, she marveled at the intricate patterns. The inside of the blanket was different in important ways. Its singing colors suggested something more urgent than the outer side. She wondered from where it came. She wondered if Pedagogy came from the same place.

She used the gentlest soap she had, and when she had finished washing, she wondered briefly if it needed it or if her washing had made a difference. She walked toward the backdoor, mesmerized by the beauty of the blanket without paying too much attention to where she was going. She opened the door and stepped out into the backyard. The colors glowed in the light of the lonely gray that had surrounded Biscuit. Then, just as she draped the blanket over the clothesline and was reaching for a clothespin, she felt a cold breeze whip past her shoulder. Before the hairs stood up on her bare arms or the shiver pushed up the bumps on her skin, Daisy felt her stomach sink. She wanted to scream but didn't want to waste the time or energy it would take. How could she forget something so important so quickly? The colors on the blanket grew dark in her periphery as she looked toward the backdoor. The door began to pick up speed as it moved to close. It was about to slam shut. Without thinking, Daisy released the blanket and ran toward the fast-moving door. She was fast but arrived too late to avoid her hand getting slammed into the doorjamb. She began to push the door open, but something was on the other side, pushing it closed. Her child was in danger. She was desperate. She cried out the name of her child that was written on the note and pushed with all her strength; as she did, she felt a warm wind rush from behind her and slam against the backdoor, knocking it off its hinges.

She ran over the door and straight to the bedroom. Coming into the room, she saw the white legs of the bassinet turn brown and then black as darkness rose from the floor. She looked for her Pedagogy, who was fighting the sheet attempting to cover him as a shroud. Daisy threw the sheet off Pedagogy and out of the bassinet. As it hit the air around the cradle, it turned brown and then black before it hit the floorboards. With Pedagogy in her arms, she ran toward the front door. As she did, she felt herself pass through a warm pool of air swirling into the room, the last part of which was almost hot. She passed the couch and was at the front door when she wondered whether she was safer in the house or outside it. She looked back toward the room and saw the swirling, warm wind had in its grasp the sheet and bassinet, both of which had turned black and began disintegrating into dust. In the middle of the bassinet was a circle so dark it looked like a hole. The warm swirl of wind carried all the blackness toward the kitchen and out the opening where the backdoor had been. Then, just as Daisy thought she had made the right decision to stay in the house, there was a loud boom. She froze. She felt the baby pushing her arms in pulses as she held him. But the pulses came from her heart beating so hard she could feel it. In the quiet after the boom, she searched the silence for the sound of the wind. Standing still, her eyes stared at the opening to the kitchen.

The quiet helped her heart calm. Daisy began to blame herself for everything that had just happened. She began to wonder if the bassinet or the sheets contained some dark force. She wanted to cry as the sense of complete inadequacy began to rise to take over her emotions. She checked Pedagogy to ensure that the sheet, bassinet, or frigid breeze had not harmed him. She held him up to look him over, beginning at his feet. When their eyes met, Pedagogy was smiling. He looked as if they had just played a wonderful game and won. It was a look of confidence. His eyes connected with her heart and said, *I am glad we chose you.* Daisy received the unexpected affirmation, and the funk and depression which sought to capture Daisy vanished. Her eyes began to water again. The thought that she was chosen and had not made a mistake washed over her with joy. With her newfound confidence, she walked to the kitchen. The back door had been slammed back into its frame. Daisy tried to twist the knob just to check if the door was operable. It wasn't. The door was sealed shut. She was safe. She looked down at Pedagogy, who had fallen sound asleep. She thought to lay him down but was afraid to go into the bedroom. Something inside her suggested she try.

Cautious to enter, she paused in the doorway. As she did, an overwhelming sense of peace and safety emanated from the room. The warm, swirling wind had washed everything. The room was brighter. The walls appeared as if they had received a fresh coat of paint, and all the furniture had been polished. The air was as fresh as a mountain meadow. It pulled her from the doorway into an embrace of peace and safety. Daisy felt safer in that room than she ever had felt anywhere. She breathed a sigh of relief at the thought that everything was as it should be, and it settled her. She understood there were very real terrors in her world and, somehow, those terrors had come closer than ever before, but at that moment, she was unafraid of them. It was the baby. It was her love for this baby that gave her the courage to face anything. She laid her Pedagogy in the middle of her bed and rested with him for a while.

There were things to be done before the children returned in the morning. Daisy got up and left Pedagogy in the safety and comfort of the room which was now more his than hers. As she moved through the doorway, a sudden shock hit her. Her stomach began to turn inside out, and her heart pounded when she remembered — the blanket. The last she remembered; she had let go of it near the clothesline. Daisy panicked. She was convinced the swirling winds battling in the house would have taken the blanket far away from the clothesline where it had been draped. She hoped it was still in the backyard, perhaps blown into a corner. She feared it had been swept to some other part of Biscuit and could not imagine how she could convince anyone to return it to her.

Arriving in the kitchen, she remembered the backdoor had been sealed shut. She rattled the handle anyway; it did not budge. She moved the curtain and peered through the window into the backyard in desperate hope of spotting the blanket. The beautiful cloth was nowhere to be seen. Her heart sank further. She couldn't see the whole backyard from the window and began to worry about the plan forming in her mind. Her thought was to go out the front door and around the house to search the backyard. But she didn't want to be that far away from Pedagogy for the amount of time it would take to run around the house. She was afraid that if she took the chance, the front door might become what the backdoor now was, sealed shut with her on the wrong side of it. But the blanket was too important. She didn't know why it was important or how it was important, but if she had to risk everything, she would.

That the blanket was as important as Pedagogy was an insane thought. At that moment, Daisy didn't know how illogical it was. Darkness appears in the mind long before it is perceived by one's sight. Once perceived, darkness moves in to capture the heart, kill the spirit, and suffocate hope. She didn't think about how quickly danger could overwhelm her or how powerful darkness can be. The darkness was dangerous and powerful, but the blanket belonged to Pedagogy. And she would do anything for him. She had already faced death more times recently than she had her whole life, and she was no longer afraid. She resolved to search for the blanket before another wind came to possess it. She had a sense that it was close. She had confidence. She would feel it inside her if it was really lost. She convinced herself the blanket was still in the backyard just beneath her view. She believed it was pressed against the house at the foot of the door. She decided to prop open the front door, extend the dead bolt to ensure it would not close or lock her out, and run around the house to the backyard. She told herself that the gate on the side of the house to the backyard was not locked. But it was.

The gate was six feet high and locked. She began locking it after the lonely, gray skies had appeared. Why she thought otherwise at that moment was a testament to the fact she wasn't thinking clearly. She took a deep breath and turned toward the front door. As she did, her brow furrowed in determination and her hand involuntarily formed fists at her first resolved movement to enact her plan. Then it happened. As she turned her head from the backdoor window to the front of the house, something flashed in her periphery. She was almost out of the kitchen when it caught her eye and turned her head. It was right there — the blanket, folded neatly on the edge of the table, dry and ready for use. She sighed out loud, and her heart pulled her to Pedagogy. She took him his blanket. When she opened the blanket in the room full of fresh air, the glow it had when she first saw it returned. She wrapped Pedagogy in his blanket. He welcomed it. He nursed and went back to sleep. Daisy went and finished getting everything ready for the children who would return to Dancing Daisy's All-Day Daycare in the morning. She wondered how things would change with Pedagogy present. For no logical reason, she wondered how long she would be able to maintain the daycare. The note told of several adventures she and Pedagogy would experience, and she knew most of them would not be in Biscuit.

The children began returning the next day. Just two children came the first week, but after that business started to pick up. By the end of the month, the regular children had returned, plus a few others. The lonely gray began to lift, and, by the end of the third month since Pedagogy came, Biscuit had returned to its natural cycles of daylight. Time moved on, and things returned to better than normal. Business was so good that Daisy hired a young purl named Tepa to help. Her very first intuition about Tepa was that she didn't fit. Something about her wasn't right, but before Daisy could pause to discern what her heart was attempting to communicate, Tepa began talking. Her voice was very soft and inviting. She presented herself in such a warm way Daisy just had to hire her.

Daisy was even more of her loving, gentle self with Pedagogy in her life. There were no more blankets turning into snakes or flying bassinets. And, except for their nightly ritual and an occasional dream, Daisy didn't think about any such things. Her life was full. Her love for Pedagogy astounded her. It didn't diminish her love or care for any of the other children, but Pedagogy always came first for her. Some parents noticed Pedagogy was a quiet baby; he never cried or fussed. Some questioned why Daisy would attend to him before he cried. They wondered how she knew when to change a soiled diaper or when he was hungry because no one ever heard him make any sort of fuss. But Daisy was learning to trust her inner feelings and to listen for Pedagogy's messages in her heart. The hard lesson came after the daycare became busy and Daisy had hired Tepa.

It was late in the day after a long and busy afternoon. Daisy was on her way to check on Pedagogy when she observed Tepa putting toys away without thoroughly cleaning and disinfecting them. Daisy paused to show Tepa where all the supplies were and how and where the toys were cleaned and stored. Just as she finished, the last parent came to pick up her little one. They chatted for a little while. Life had returned to a brighter reality in Biscuit and Dancing Daisy's was the center of it. The parent wanted Daisy to know what a difference she could see in her little girl. The parent was quite chatty for some reason, and Daisy didn't want to interrupt her. She enjoyed hearing how good her daycare was and how highly purple thought of her. After a while, Daisy excused herself and showed the parent and her child out the front door. The self-congratulating smile adorning her face as she entered the bedroom evaporated at the sight of her charge. Pedagogy was in the bed with his head turned toward the wall. When Daisy went to him, her heart sank. Pedagogy had been crying but now was quiet. She removed his soiled diaper, and the rash covering his bottom was plain to see. Caring for the rash over the next few days was painful for both of them. Each time Daisy changed and medicated Pedagogy, they both cried. And each time, through the tears, Daisy promised her baby she would always come when he called her.

Months ago, she would have fallen into a slight depression. She would have cycled over and over in her mind what she had done wrong and how terrible she was for causing Pedagogy such pain. But she was healed of that darkness. Her failures and mistakes made her more determined to succeed. Somehow, Pedagogy inspired the best in her, and each day brought her more strength, dedication, and determination to do all the note said would be required. Daisy would have to be very strong to do some things the note required. She was not at all ready at the moment, but she believed she would be when the time came.

As Pedagogy grew, he interacted more and more with the children brought to Dancing Daisy's. The children loved him and were happiest when he was at the center of their activities. The bedroom, which had become his room, was the favorite place for the children to play and gather. Tepa called his room the magic room because the children would leave before soiling their diapers, and there was never any crying while the children played there. Daisy's bed had been moved to the spare bedroom. In its place, there was a beautiful convertible crib she and Pedagogy had found one day when they were out for a long stroll. It was a day when Daisy had wanted to get away with just Pedagogy. The few children who were at the daycare were asleep, and Tepa was more than able to take care of them, so she put Pedagogy in the stroller, and off they went.

The beauty of the day called for exploration. The suns were warm and inviting. And, perhaps for that reason, Daisy decided to walk into Prometheus instead of staying in Biscuit. They walked through the well-kept streets and past the stately brownstone houses. Meandering through the neighborhoods was wonderful and adventurous. Their hearts brightened by being together and away from the daycare. Daisy sensed Pedagogy appreciated her undivided attention, and she enjoyed the time alone with the gift of love that had come into her life. As they walked, they marveled at the little shops stuck right in the middle of some apartments and houses. They would occasionally pause to look in a window or wave at a shopkeeper. Then they paused at a peculiar place. It was a strange shop which seemed all a-jumble. It was what some would call a bric-a-brac. The place was packed and had no straight aisles or any obvious sections, just several discernible paths around and through things. The jumble of this and that, of here, there, and over one's head made the shop look dark as if one had entered a thick forest. Still, a warm and welcoming sense came over Daisy as she entered. The small front door hid the secret that the inside of the store was quite large. Daisy pushed the stroller down the crooked aisles, passing some inviting ones because they were too tight for the stroller. She didn't know why she was there or how she had gotten there or exactly where she was, but a warm sense within her suggested that she and Pedagogy were right where they were supposed to be.

Just as she was thinking it was time to find their way out, she was greeted by the strangest purl she had ever seen. The voice startled her, and she would have been shocked if Pedagogy hadn't giggled at that moment. The sound of her "hello" came from somewhere in the shadows of the shop. When the purl appeared, her sky-blue eyes glowed in the dim light of the shop. She wore what looked like a cloak with the hood draped on her shoulders. There was something magnetic about her. Daisy wanted to stare at her face, but the purl stooped down and began talking to Pedagogy, who was enraptured by her attention. His feet started to dance, and the sound of his laughter drew Daisy close to whoever this was who brought so much joy to her Pedagogy. The purl asked about Pedagogy. She asked how things were going. She asked questions as if she were aware of more than anyone should have been about the child and Daisy. She never even hinted that Pedagogy was not Daisy's birth child.

If she had, Daisy would have bolted away. Instead, somehow through her questions and the sound of her voice, she affirmed the perfect match of mother and child. Daisy began to think this was one purl she could trust with the whole truth. She felt she could share anything and everything with her. The purl asked what brought them to the shop, but, before Daisy could answer, she asked if Pedagogy had a bed. Daisy said he didn't and, at that moment, realized how the crib she was using was not really fit for her Pedagogy, and she would have to purchase a proper bed for her growing child soon. The figure turned her attention from Pedagogy and stood up. She looked at Daisy, and their eyes met. Daisy looked away. It was as if the purl was looking through her eyes into her soul. Daisy averted her eyes because she wasn't sure if her soul was pure enough to withstand the gaze of the stranger. She wasn't sure what was happening. The beautiful eyes were gentle yet piercing. The sharp points within Daisy made her afraid to be seen.

"Follow me," she said. "I have something I think you will need."

Daisy picked Pedagogy up out of the stroller. Somehow, the figure before her told her the stroller was too wide for where they were going. Besides, for reasons only a mother could know, she wanted Pedagogy in her arms and close.

They wound their way through the shop to somewhat of an uncluttered work-space. Dusty half-finished pieces of furniture hung on the wall in the shadows just above their heads. Pedagogy began wiggling and reaching for one. The figure smiled at the baby's reaction. She reached up to retrieve the ornately carved head-board and foot of the bed Pedagogy chose. When she did, the sleeves of the robe revealed muscular arms which made Daisy wonder whether the robed figure in front of her was truly a female purl. The purl asked Pedagogy if it was the one he wanted. She spoke to him as if he were capable of carrying on an adult conversation. When she brought the pieces down into the light, Daisy drew an involuntary breath.

The pieces looked as if they had been created for a child of royalty. The wood was seamless and subtle with a rich, multicolored, undulating grain which swam from one side of the headboard to the other. The headboard was a flat panel of sea and sky held together by what looked like two tree trunks. The trunks bent in toward the bed, and their branches reached to intermingle in the middle of the headboard. The branches were rich and thick and rolled out from the smooth panel to create an overhang. The foot of the bed stood on two additional trunks, but the branches wove themselves together without a solid panel to hold the trunks in place. The majesty of the bed was indescribable. Daisy was a bit frightened because two truths appeared in her heart the moment the beautiful headboard came into full view: She thought Pedagogy should have the bed, and there was no way she would be able to afford it.

Pedagogy wiggled and wanted to be free of Daisy's embrace. She put him down, and he went right to the bed as if he intended to assemble it and take a nap right then and there. Daisy asked about the wood and the bed. She really wanted to know how much it would cost but was afraid of the number. The purl with the sky-blue eyes told her the bed was very old. She said the wood and the carving were both of poollé trees. When those words registered in her mind, Daisy's heart stopped. She remembered the note she read the first night Pedagogy appeared. The note that was tucked in his blanket that evening told Daisy to read it to the child each night for his first three years. Only half the time had passed, and Daisy had been faithful to the promise she made to herself to follow everything it said. There were several instructions in the note and a long poem at the end of it. The last line of the poem she read to her Pedagogy every night said,

"From death and danger; he shall rest beneath the poollé trees."

Daisy was a bit frightened. Until the note, she had never heard of a poollé tree. She spent months trying to find information about poollé trees. Most of her research suggested that poollé trees were part of mythological stories of ancient times. And until this moment, no one had ever mentioned their existence. It would not be the last time the note and the words she read to her Pedagogy every night collided with the circumstances in their lives.

She was afraid to ask what the purl knew about poollé trees. Her focus was on getting that piece of furniture. She wanted to know how much the bed would cost. She was sure it was worth whatever was asked because, to her, it was already priceless. With Pedagogy on the floor, attempting to climb up the headboard, she asked the figure how much it cost. The figure replied it was not for sale. Daisy's heart dropped. Questions began to fill her mind: *If it was not for sale, why did she show it to us? If it was not for sale, why take it off the wall?* Anger, as an appropriate response to this answer, began to rise within her. But before she could furrow her brow, or fashion a response, Pedagogy spoke. It was a loud, unintelligible baby sentence, but the figure who had been looking at Daisy turned all her attention to the child. She went down on one of her knees and bowed her head. Daisy thought she was just going to play with Pedagogy, but something was different. She wasn't playing with the child; she was being reverent. Daisy asked again for the price. The figure, without lifting her bowed head, told her again the bed was not for sale but this time with something worshipful in her voice. Daisy bent to pick up Pedagogy. The figure remained frozen. The long, thick locks of her green hair hid her face. Daisy was indignant. The questions and more were buzzing in her head. The figure looked up at Daisy. As she did, her face shone a beautiful, iridescent royal blue. Daisy sought to focus, and in doing so, the purl's skin color disappeared. She wanted answers, and she wanted the bed that could be configured as a crib. It belonged to Pedagogy as much as she did. She wanted to know what would override the answer she had been given. The figure, returning her gaze to the floor, spoke something frightening.

A part of Daisy wanted to run out of the shop and continue with the wonderful walk she and her Pedagogy were enjoying. Entering the shop had brought her back to the realization that her life was not normal. As much as she wanted to pretend that he was, her Pedagogy was not a normal child. Her life had changed eighteen months earlier, and, as normal as things had become, she now believed there was much more to reality and existence than most purple understood. Strange, unexplainable things happened and when they did, there were reasons and meanings from which one ought to take note and learn. She believed somehow that she would always be protected and that the dangerous and dark things could be defeated. She didn't sense she was in danger, but a part of her still wanted to take her baby and run out of the shop.

The note Daisy read to Pedagogy every night was private. It had to be. Daisy was always careful to be sure no one was close to hearing the words she whispered to her baby. And the more she read them, the more she understood and the more mystery she embraced. But here in this shop, a purl she had never seen or met before spoke words no other purl should have known from a note no one should have known existed. Daisy could not yet recite the whole note from memory, but there were parts she couldn't forget. The words spoken by the figure kneeling at her feet were some of them. Daisy was shaken as the voice said:

"Then find the one to him that's true

To finally set him free."

Daisy recognized they were the words just before the last line of the poem. Daisy's lips moved quoting the last line, as the purl before her said it out loud:

"From death and danger; he shall rest

Beneath the poollé trees."

The figure looked up. Daisy wanted to know how she knew those lines, and then again, she didn't. It was time to leave. Something outside the store had changed, and the purl's knowledge was frightening. She had an urgency to put Pedagogy in the stroller and head home. She began walking toward where she had left the stroller. She wanted the bed but had come to know when danger was approaching. The figure rose to follow her. The sense of urgency increased. Daisy, strapping Pedagogy in the stroller, made what she thought would be her last case for the bed. She was moving to get to the safety of her home and, standing behind the stroller, asked one last time how she could persuade the figure to sell her the bed. It didn't matter what the reply was. Daisy was convinced and determined at that moment of two things: She was going to get her child to safety before the danger came, and he would have that bed. The figure spoke, and her voice froze Daisy.

Their eyes met, and Daisy stood still. The figure asked, "Will you keep your promise?"

Daisy's eyes began to tear. How did this purl know so much? How could she ask questions that revealed she knew too much already? As Daisy looked into the glowing, sky-blue eyes, she knew they had already searched her and found the answer to the question. But Daisy, with the tears now streaming down her face, told the figure she would.

The figure told Daisy there was no need to purchase the bed because it already belonged to the Poollé Kii, son of the blessed. Daisy wanted to know how this figure knew the name of her child and so many other things she thought was information she alone held. But more than anything, she wanted to get to safety. She turned toward the front door, but the figure touched her shoulder and asked her to follow her instead. Daisy understood the purl was aware of the same danger she was. They went out of the back door, and the purl helped Daisy and Pedagogy into a waiting vehicle. Another figure carefully placed the convertible crib and the stroller into the back of the truck. As soon as the furniture was secure, the two large, hooded purple sped off with Daisy and her Pedagogy in the back seat. Pedagogy laughed as the vehicle sped off. Daisy looked at him. She looked into his beautiful light blue eyes, and her heart joined his happiness. She thought Pedagogy understood much more than an eighteen-month-old child should. She believed he understood more about what had just happened than she did. His eyes said not only that the danger had been averted but also that it had been fun.

Daisy didn't know exactly where she was in Prometheus or how to get back to Dancing Daisy's, but no one asked. The purple drove her right to the daycare's front door. The two were kind and very gentle. They helped Daisy to the house and moved her remaining furniture out of the bedroom and into the spare one. Then they assembled the ornate crib. Pedagogy participated in the whole affair. He walked around his room as if he was supervising the ongoing work. He had what seemed to be conversations with the purple who would pause whatever they were doing and pay attention to Pedagogy when he spoke. It was as if they were old friends or more like he was their much elder sibling and in charge of everything happening in the room.

When the crib was assembled, the room looked majestic. The purple had also brought and placed in the room an ornate dresser which matched the crib. Pedagogy showed his approval by putting his blanket on the bed as its final adornment. The purple told Daisy they would return when the child was three years old to convert the crib into the bed it could become. Daisy thought it strange that the figures mentioned Pedagogy's third birthday. Perhaps it was a coincidence. Even though the thought of it being a coincidence entered her mind, Daisy was beginning to believe there were no such things. The purple left, and all was well. The newspapers the next day told of a terrible fire that burned down an antique shop in Prometheus.

BREAK FROM BISCUIT

Dancing Daisy's All-Day Daycare was operating at capacity and gained a reputation for being the most wonderful place to give your baby a start. Children who began life with colic came to Daisy's and found joy and peace. Often a crying child would be carried into Pedagogy's room or simply brought to where Pedagogy was, and the child would become calm and content. As word spread, more parents wanted their children to be cared for by Daisy, so much so, some mothers asked to have their child placed on the waiting list soon after they found out they were pregnant. More and more dark-eyed purple began asking Daisy to care for their children. Daisy realized her limit when one unfortunate incident occurred. A parent had asked, insisted really, that her three-year-old's birthday party be held at the daycare. The parent promised to pay all the expenses and even offered to have some family members help with the children. The party had all the bells and whistles, including an inflatable castle which almost took up the whole backyard. There were also custom-made cakes, piñatas full of candy, and more purple than Daisy had imagined. A few dark-eyed purple were at the party, and Daisy didn't know if they were relatives, guests, or Promethean spies. Daisy did her best to keep things under control. A few purple paused by Pedagogy's room, but Daisy thought nothing of it until everyone had gone home. She was uneasy during parts of the day but dismissed her feelings as natural concern over the large number of purple in her home.

Daisy kept Pedagogy in her sight for most of the party. It had been almost three years since that first night and the beautiful hands. She did not to talk too much about her child. Most purple did not ask. Most did not know Pedagogy was at the heart of what was different at Dancing Daisy's, but Daisy did, and she cherished the change that had come over her since that night. She was stronger and more courageous. She had a greater capacity to love. And she understood her life was an essential part of something much larger and more vital than the gentle, repeated breaths which made it up. Her job was to protect and nurture this young child until he did what he had come to Purplynd to do. Daisy didn't know what Pedagogy's mission was, but her assignment was to safeguard this child until he no longer needed her. The note told her that and many other things, some of which she understood and some of which were too mysterious to decipher. And over the months, she had learned to trust her senses. She had learned to understand Pedagogy. She had learned to read his eyes, and she listened intently as he learned to talk. This had served them well so far, but, somehow, in the noise of the party, she missed something important. The three-year anniversary of Pedagogy's arrival was just a few weeks away. Daisy had complied with the note's instructions and safeguarded it, the blanket, and the child. Several times, a parent or one of the children had looked longingly at the blanket, and there was even one time a parent attempted to take it. But since Tepa had come and taken some of the burden off Daisy's plate, things began to take on a calmer rhythm, and no one asked any more probing questions or attempted to take anything from the house.

One of the things that made Daisy's baby seem normal was his attachment to the blanket. As an infant, Daisy kept him wrapped in its softness. As Pedagogy learned to crawl and then walk, he always kept it close, but as he got older and after his crib was put up, the blanket stayed on his bed or in his room. One of the top things on Daisy's list as she prepared for all the adults and others who would be at the party was to put the blanket out of sight. The blanket remained beautiful, even though the brilliant colors that glowed bright that first night had faded some. Still, something inside her whispered for her to hide it from prying eyes. The thought came several evenings before when Tepa placed it over Pedagogy after she had insisted on putting him in his crib. Daisy had rocked Pedagogy to sleep on the couch, and he was sleeping in her arms. She was tired from the day and had said so several times, but she got lost in the memory of her first night with Pedagogy. Tears welled up in her eyes as they often did when her tender heart was touched. It was right then that Tepa intervened and offered to put Pedagogy in his bed. Daisy agreed, but something about the look in Tepa's eyes suggested that Daisy add putting away the blanket to the list of party preparations. Unfortunately, she got busy, and that particular task fell off her to-do list. The blanket full of colors and patterns was beautiful, but what Daisy did not know, and could not imagine, was how important it was to the life and destiny of her child. She had kept Pedagogy, the note, and the blanket from harm and from being scrutinized by the authorities or any others for nearly three years. Then it all fell apart.

The cakes had been cut. The piñatas had been broken open. Plenty of laughter and fun had been enjoyed by all, and it was time to clean up. Work-purple came to deflate and remove the castle. Parents were coming to retrieve their children for the evening, and Daisy was glad it was all ending. Pedagogy acted first. In the midst of Daisy saying goodbye to the parent who had sponsored the event, Daisy caught Pedagogy running into the house in her periphery. For reasons even Daisy didn't think through, she abruptly ended the conversation and ran after him. Pedagogy ran through the kitchen, past the living room, and to his room. Daisy and her child arrived at the doorway to the room at the same moment. Two dark-eyed purple were in the room. Daisy asked them what they were doing and insisted they leave. They told her they were admiring the crib. They asked many questions about it, all of which Daisy avoided answering. She told them it was a gift from a friend and asked if they would please leave. They continued to ask questions politely as if they were legitimate guests who just happened to see the bed and wanted to know more about it. But Daisy didn't believe they were just guests; something in her stomach told her otherwise. She escorted them to the front door.

They left without inquiring about any family members still at the party or insisting on saying goodbye to the birthday purl, which made Daisy even more sure they were not who they pretended to be. As they were leaving, Daisy wondered at a camera in one of their hands. Then, just as the door closed, it hit her. Her heart stopped. She ran back to Pedagogy's room and to the crib. It was gone. The blanket was not on the bed. She ran back to the front door, angry with herself that she had forgotten to secure the blanket before the party started. She looked to the street and up and down the block for the purple who had just left, but they were nowhere to be found.

She hurried through the house as the fear that she had lost the blanket grew in her heart. Tepa saw the anxiety in her boss's face and took care of seeing the final guests and the Work-purple out of the house. She had even taken Pedagogy with her, who loved watching the castle come down and the process of getting it back into the truck and ready for the next party. When Tepa and Pedagogy found Daisy sitting in the living room, she was despondent. She sat with tears welling up in her eyes and her head bowed. She didn't want to admit to Pedagogy that she had lost the blanket. She didn't want to admit it to herself. Tepa asked what was wrong. Daisy told her she couldn't find the blanket. Tepa lit up as if she was the heroine and told Daisy she had taken the blanket off the bed and put it in the dresser because she thought it best for it to be out of sight. They all went into the room. Tepa went to the dresser and opened the top left dresser drawer. She didn't notice that it was not quite closed. She opened it and rifled through the clothes—nothing. She began to panic and rifled through the entire dresser, unaware that Daisy had already done the same. The blanket was nowhere to be found. She turned and looked at Daisy. Pedagogy looked at Tepa. He was aware of something about her that Daisy wasn't. A tear escaped Daisy's eye and rolled down her cheek. Pedagogy ran to his toy closet, opened the door, and almost disappeared into it. He backed out of the doorway, pulling his blanket with two hands. When it was free from being buried beneath toy trucks and stuffed bears,

Pedagogy gathered his blanket into both of his arms, turned, and ran into Daisy's arms.

The party reminded Daisy that the time had come for her to perform the first mysterious task the note had instructed. For several days after the party, the fact that she had almost lost the blanket reminded her that she had made a promise, and Purplynd was not particularly interested in her keeping it. The coming anniversary added to the intensity with which she read the note each night. She was reminded that on the third anniversary of the day she received the child, she was to travel to a specific place deep into the wilderness near the foot of the mountains. Daisy didn't know which mountains she was to go to or how to get to them. And, if she did happen to get to the right mountains, she had no idea how to find a place in the wilderness she had never been to before. She had said this out loud one evening after she had read the poem to Pedagogy. He had fallen asleep as he always did on the last line of the poem, and right after, Daisy would always lean over and kiss her Pedagogy. That night, she kissed her sleeping child and wept as she wondered out loud how she would be able to fulfill her promise when there was so much she didn't know. She was alone in the house, or so she thought. Business had gotten so good that Dancing Daisy's All-Day Daycare rarely had overnight children. Even though the days were full, her clients were now parents who had careers and vocations that allowed them to spend the evenings with their children. Tepa had gone home after the last child was picked up. In the quiet and solitude of being alone with Pedagogy, Daisy let her guard down. She had been careful all these years to ensure no one was close enough to overhear the evening ritual with her son. But since the big birthday party, she had become progressively uneasy. The anxiousness increased when a letter arrived from the Department of Light-Eyed Affairs asking if all the children in her care had had their inoculations. Two days later, another letter came reminding her about licensing renewal. And finally, a week after that, a letter came informing Daisy there would be an inspection of her daycare coming soon and informing her of what documentation would be required for each of her children. Daisy wondered why the DLA was interested in her daycare all of a sudden. Then she remembered the two purple she had chased out of Pedagogy's room.

She wondered what she would do or say if the inspectors asked about Pedagogy. She thought about Tepa and wondered if she would help secure the secrecy of Pedagogy when the inspectors showed up. Tepa seemed to love Pedagogy and had always been interested and invested in him. Daisy couldn't see that Pedagogy didn't seem to share the admiration. She had no idea that her first intuitions had been right. Tepa had been sent to work for Daisy by a purl who had been informed about Daisy's curiosity about poollé trees. Daisy had gone to libraries and even old bookshops to research the stories and myths about the poollé. She thought she had been clever enough to hide her curiosity and didn't really know how dangerous it was to ask questions. She used public computers to protect her anonymity but didn't know how deeply into her life a purl with access could dip. She was unaware that the two purple in Pedagogy's room had been looking for something. And she didn't know they would soon return but this time as inspectors from the DLA.

As the thoughts of what to do were moving in her mind, her gaze rested on the angelic picture of her sleeping baby. A sudden noise shattered the peace. She dropped the note in the crib under the carved poollé trees and went to investigate. She didn't see what happened to the parchment when she did. Daisy was ready for whatever and whomever. When she stepped outside the door, the figure of a full-grown purl appeared in the shadows. It happened so fast that she was startled. But Daisy was ready. Her fingers curled into a fist, and she readied herself for whatever would come. She remembered the look in the eyes of the purl in the antique shop when the darkness was descending. Daisy felt prepared to fight the enemy of her child, and with the feeling came courage and confidence. She turned sharply toward the figure with her fist loaded for the first punch and then recognized her. It was Tepa. Daisy relaxed her fists and asked what she was doing in the house. Tepa told how she had forgotten something and was returning to get it when she heard Daisy in the bedroom. She said she came to the bedroom to see if she was all right. Tepa was looking past her into the bedroom. She was looking at something that glowed brightly and then dimmed in the crib. Daisy had no idea that anything had happened behind her, but her sleeping Pedagogy did not need Tepa peering over him. She closed the door and offered to help Tepa find what she had left, which they found right away. Daisy wondered why Tepa would come back for something so small. She wondered how long she had been in the house and how much she had overheard. She didn't know it, but Tepa had been at the door for some time, straining to decipher the words she spoke to the child. With Tepa gone, Daisy lay down and, after a while, went to sleep. Fear would wake her up.

The morning came, leaving only three days before the inspectors were scheduled to arrive, and Daisy had still not told Tepa she was going to put Pedagogy in her care. The letter had come more than a week ago informing her of the DLA inspection. Together, Daisy and Tepa had assembled all the information needed for the inspection. Daisy thought Tepa was especially suited for the care of the children over the last few weeks, and she marveled at how, when Tepa first came to work, she had wondered if

Tepa really liked children at all. But now Daisy believed that Tepa loved Pedagogy as much as she did. And, even though it took some time, Pedagogy was enjoying Tepa more each day. Pedagogy even took Tepa into his room and put his blanket on her. Daisy thought this was a wonderful act of acceptance. She was curious but decided to just take in what was unfolding in front of her. Pedagogy opened his dresser and pulled the note out from its secret hiding place. Daisy didn't know Pedagogy knew where she kept the note, but apparently, he did. He took it and sat in front of Tepa to read it. Daisy wondered why Pedagogy would do this. She felt that perhaps Pedagogy was choosing Tepa instead of her for the rest of his journey. Daisy's heart began to pound in her chest. The light coming through the windows dimmed as if dark clouds had taken over the sky. A chilling breeze swept past her and rushed to the child sitting in front of Tepa. As soon as the icy wind touched the paper of the note, it began to turn black. Daisy tried to run toward Pedagogy but was frozen. She wanted to move, but her body would not respond. Then the horror increased. The now totally black note became dust. Tepa stood up and took Pedagogy's hand. They turned and looked at Daisy to say goodbye forever and began to walk out of the room through the window. Daisy wanted to scream and stop them, but the words would not come out. She fought whatever force was holding her with all her power but was unable to break its grasp. She was not going to let the shadows take her child. If she called to him, he would not leave her, but she could not speak. Determined to stop Tepa from taking Pedagogy, Daisy finally screamed which broke the grasp of the black shadow that held her. As she called his name out loud, Daisy sat straight up in her bed.

Daisy dismissed her nightmare as just anxiety about the trip, and, by the time the day had worn on, she had forgotten all about it. She got dressed and started her morning. Nearly everything was ready for the inspection, but there was a lot yet to do for her trip to the mountains. She had prepared Tepa to run the daycare for the week and a half she would be away. She had told the parents she would be away, and some had decided to take their children out of daycare for that period, which made the load on Tepa very manageable. Daisy was still unsure exactly where she was going and planned to finish her research in the next two days. The surprise inspection had thrown everything off. Pedagogy was awake, and she went into his room to find he had gotten up and dressed himself. They were going on a trip, and he was excited about it. He had put his pants on backward, and the sight made Daisy chuckle. She fixed the error as they began their day with their ritual hugs, kisses, and breakfast. Tepa arrived earlier than usual and was entirely helpful as the day progressed. Tepa took care of everything, attempting to show herself invaluable. This gave Daisy time to work on her list for the trip.

The number one task was to rent a vehicle, which Daisy thought would be easier than actually finding exactly where she was going. She was wrong. Inexplicably, none of the vehicle rental places would rent to her. Each of them had their reason: There were no vehicles that could go off-road, they could not rent the vehicle out for a whole week, or they had booked all their vehicles. What Daisy thought would be the easiest of her final preparations turned out to be nearly impossible. Tepa, seeing Daisy's angst over the whole ordeal, suggested she try hiring a driver. A driver would, of course, come with his or her own vehicle and save Daisy the trouble of driving for hours. Daisy thought about it and then welcomed the suggestion. She began calling limo services. After contacting several companies, one in particular was very helpful. Most were too expensive, but this one had an off-road vehicle and was reasonably priced. After the long ordeal, Daisy believed she had hit the jackpot. The purl asked all the right questions yet didn't pry. If Daisy hadn't been exhausted by the search that had taken almost the whole day, she would have suspected the purl was too perfect. When asked what mountains, Daisy only told him the ones to the west. She said she would give him the exact location when they left, to which he agreed, unlike any of the other services.

With the vehicle secured, Daisy relaxed and congratulated herself on getting it done. The inspection would be in two days, and Daisy decided it was time to bring Tepa in on her plans to hide Pedagogy from the inspectors. Daisy thought Tepa had proved herself trustworthy. She had a growing confidence that Tepa was her ally. The note had cautioned Daisy not to share it or its information with anyone. It told her that help would come when she needed it, if she was true to her promise. The note said she would know the helpers because the helpers would know her. And over the past weeks, Daisy began to believe that Tepa was one of the ones who had been sent to help her. So, after the children had been quieted and were napping, Daisy called Tepa to the kitchen table. She began to tell Tepa how much she appreciated her and had come to depend on her help. Daisy told her that she needed a special kind of help that might put her in danger with the DLA. She said that if Tepa was not comfortable with the prospect of getting into trouble with the dark-eyed authorities, she would stop and not say any more. For most light-eyed purple, the fewer dealings one had with the dark-eyed purple, the better. The dark-eyed purple had all the power and used it against the light-eyed ones whenever it suited them. There was a special bond between the light-eyed purple that Daisy could count on. Light-eyed purple had to protect one another from the unjust, and often random, violence of the dark-eyed world. But she didn't want to endanger the only friend she believed she had.

When Pedagogy came, Daisy had stopped going out dancing. First, because Pedagogy was so small and demanded all her attention, but life with her child had replaced the joy of dancing with the joy of life itself. She fell away from her network of friends, and the ones she had been closest to stopped calling and checking on her soon after Tepa had arrived. It was another reason Daisy felt so close to Tepa; she thought that perhaps Tepa had been sent to replace the friends she had lost. She said much of these things at the table with Tepa listening. Tepa was polite but quite uninterested in any secrets Daisy thought were important. She had a way of relaxing Daisy and inviting her into a place of peace and safety, which made Daisy want to share more with her than she would with anyone else.

Daisy told Tepa how Pedagogy had come to her. She told her that she wanted to keep the knowledge of Pedagogy from the DLA and that she wanted Tepa to keep Pedagogy away from the house while the inspectors were there. Tepa was reassuring in a way that made Daisy comfortable, glad even, that she was sharing the story of Pedagogy with her. She finally had a friend with whom she could share her love and responsibilities. Pedagogy was such a complete joy, but as she was sharing the story with Tepa, Daisy began to realize the immense burden and how much of a lonely obligation it was. They discussed how Tepa would take Pedagogy away from the daycare for the entire day of the inspection. Tepa suggested that the inspection might take the whole day, if not more, and perhaps they should plan for her to take Pedagogy away overnight. Besides, Tepa reasoned, Daisy still had things to finish before their trip. Daisy felt that these were reasonable suggestions. For some reason, she thought to tell Tepa about her trip to the mountains. She was enjoying the strange new tea that Tepa had made for her and decided to take another sip before she told Tepa her whole plan.

Daisy didn't remember if Tepa had asked or if she just wanted to share more of her story, but, just as she lifted the teacup to her mouth to take another sip, Pedagogy screamed. It was a sharp, unfamiliar sound that scared her. Without understanding what, how, or why, she knew something was terribly wrong. The shock of the unfamiliar sound made her release the teacup which floated to the floor and broke into pieces. Turning to run to her child, her periphery registered a shadow escaping the hot tea as it splashed out of the shattering cup. Tepa began to rise as well. Daisy noticed her look of dismay as the cup drifted to the floor. She tried to remember what she had just told Tepa. She wondered whether she had violated her oath to keep Pedagogy safe. The scream certainly suggested that he was not safe. She would not be able to live if anything had harmed her child. She ran to the door of his room, and just as she reached it, the doorbell rang.

The worst fear Daisy ever had was harm coming to her Pedagogy. The scream and her heart were now suggesting that his life was in danger, and there was nothing she could do to save him. Whatever had alarmed Pedagogy was real, and even though she stopped everything she was doing at the sound and ran to attend him, she was afraid she was too late. The other children woke, crying at the sound of Pedagogy's alarm. There was a possibility the DLA inspectors had come earlier than scheduled because they would often do so to catch purple unaware and unprepared. Daisy had never before been afraid of a visit from the DLA, but since Pedagogy came, she feared they would come and take him away from her. The DLA had no respect for the life of a light-eyed purl. Terrible stories about what they allowed to happen to orphans filled Daisy's childhood. She wondered whether she should give Pedagogy to Tepa and tell her to run, to take him to safety. Tepa had mentioned that she was willing to take him to her mother's home across town. Some quiet part of Daisy wondered if she should give Pedagogy to her at all. But there was no time to think this through. When she reached the crib, she scanned for the cause of his alarm. Nothing was obvious. Pedagogy wasn't fighting or moving violently. Her scan of the room did not detect anything out of order. She picked up her child, who had grown almost too big for the crib. She looked in his eyes in an attempt to better understand the dangers they were both in, but nothing registered.

The bell rang again. This time, the very ring itself carried a sense of urgency. With the baby in her arms, she hurried toward the kitchen and gave her charge to Tepa. She told Tepa to run. Daisy turned toward the front door as a strange chill moved through her mind. In her periphery, she caught a look of disapproval in Pedagogy's eyes. Whoever was at the door wanted in immediately. Tepa took Pedagogy and hurried out the back. Her plan was to run through the backyard and along the side of the house and escape with the child. She smiled to herself, knowing that she had accomplished her assignment. She had spent almost two years working her way into the trust and confidence of her employer. She didn't have the note or the blanket, but she had something much more important to the one who had sent her on this mission; she had the child. She thought this would satisfy him, and she could find a new life far away from Syng.

Syng was a very powerful purl who owned an elite establishment that catered to the rich and powerful purple of Prometheus. He had found Tepa after a rich, dark-eyed young purl left her crying in a back booth. He befriended her and had a powerful way of calming her fears and quieting her inhibitions. After a short while of nurturing her, he offered her a job. She worked at the Promethean Panthae for some time and proved her worth many times in many ways. The job to win the Daisy's trust was well within her skill set and was her ticket out of the limited possibilities of light-eyed life. Syng had promised her an expensive surgical operation that would change the color of her eyes. She hoped with dark eyes and her ambition, she would go far. She had planned to use her connection to Syng and the tricks he taught her to ascend in power. He had promised to help her do just that and taught her many dark arts, including how to make some very potent teas with which the mind could be bent and the judgment of a purl corrupted. Syng taught her life could be manipulated to afford her many of the pleasures she had sought in other ways, if only she would follow his guidance. And this, she had done. Now she had the child, and nothing could stop her.

Things happened so fast that she didn't have time to give Pedagogy the laced candy that would have put him to sleep. She didn't know who was at the door. She just thought that the tea she had given to Daisy and the power of her suggestions had worked more effectively than she thought possible. She was careful to mix the potion according to Syng's instructions. She had seen them work on others and longed to learn how to make them herself. She thought that once she delivered the child, Syng would begin to train her in that, too. In fact, she didn't hear the front doorbell ring either time. She thought they were part of Daisy's delusions, so she played along. She was so happy that she had finally finished this long assignment. She was happy to get away from the children, whom she really hated, and return to the dark lairs of Syng's Panthae. The purple she had let into the birthday party long ago were some of Syng's. They were supposed to return as DLA inspectors in two days. They were coming to get the blanket and the note. Her job was to tell them where the note was hidden and where the blanket was kept. Her main task was to win the trust of the child, but she never did. For reasons she could not understand, despite the warm charm she showed him and in denial of all of Syng's tutelage, Pedagogy never took to her. But now she had him. He was struggling in her arms and was heavier and stronger than seemed reasonable, but she had him.

Daisy reached the door, and an overwhelming fear and alarm burst in her body. As her hand was moving to the doorknob, it twisted, and the door opened from the outside. The power of the large purl standing in front of her startled her, and her heart skipped. There were two cloaked purple at the door, and one of them began to run to the side of the house. Her mind went to Pedagogy and Tepa. He was going to intercept them. She moved to intercept him. The large purl at the door stood still, staring into the house. He stood frozen and took in every sign, from the footprints of Daisy coming to the door to the potion-laden tea on the floor. He smelled its putrid ingredients. Footprints and odors revealed that Daisy had taken the child from his room and transferred him to another, and whoever that purl was had a dark scent. The child and the dark-scented one had gone through the back door. These observations occurred in what would be a flash to any regular purl. But in the second or two he took to read the signs, Daisy slipped past him to follow the purl who ran to the side of the house. As Daisy passed the cloaked purl at the door, she was struck by his eyes. He did not have the dangerous dark pupils of a DLA inspector. In fact, with his head covered by an oversize hood, his sky-blue eyes seemed to radiate light. His skin also pulsed a beautiful blue.

Pedagogy did not approve of Daisy's choice to give him to Tepa and started fighting her as soon as they were through the back door. He kicked and twisted and punched. He grabbed a fistful of Tepa's hair and began to pull. Tepa responded and managed to pin one of the child's arms under hers. She held him tighter and head-butted him, which made him let go of her hair and stunned him still. Most children would have screamed in pain and displeasure, but Pedagogy made a different choice. As they turned the corner, Pedagogy began to resist again. As she was running and struggling with the child, a large figure came running toward her. She didn't have time to discern whether the figure was friend or foe, and her preference was to treat everyone as an enemy until it was proved otherwise. It was two days too early for Syng's inspectors to show up, but there was always a chance he had men around. She took another step and decided the light-eyed figure was no friend. She abandoned her hope of reaching her vehicle and decided to turn around and run out the back of the backyard. She pressed the distress button on her belt buckle that signaled to Syng that she had the child and was ready to be picked up. The joy of completing her mission had quickly turned to fear. She heard Daisy's voice. It made Tepa hate her more.

Tepa was confident that Syng's purple would find her, but it would take time. Dark-eyed purple hanging around Biscuit would have drawn attention, and light-eyed spies were unreliable, so Syng had sent his protégé in alone. She would have to elude Daisy and the purple for about an hour or so, and then all would be well. Tepa was fast, and the suns were setting. If she made it to the darkness, all would be well. As she turned to head out the back of the yard, Pedagogy revealed that he had a plan of his own when he bit into her shoulder. Tepa screamed at the pain. An uncontrollable rage ran through her body. To be fair to her, it was a reaction to the sharp teeth and powerful bite, but she pulled the child from her and with both hands threw him as far away from her as possible. Daisy saw her baby in midair and horror exploded within her being. She had seen Pedagogy fight his captor and sensed that the figure running in front of her was not from the DLA or a danger, but she was determined to get to her child. He was thrown with such force that it was sure to hurt him. Daisy wanted to scream but didn't have time as Pedagogy's body turned in the air and began its descent headfirst toward the concrete. If his head hit that concrete, Daisy feared the worse. He was thrown with such force that she was sure he would be severely hurt or killed. The horror froze time, and everything happened in slow motion. What Daisy missed because all her attention was on her child, was that the large purl in front of her had launched himself toward the child as soon as Tepa began to throw him. His flowing cloak told the tale of his journey as he leaped into the air over Pedagogy, caught him in his arm, and tucked him to his chest. The purl finished his aerial flip and landed bowed on one knee with Pedagogy pressed to his chest.

Tepa continued running toward the back of the yard. The rage running through her veins made her faster. She realized she lost control when she threw the child. She told herself it was a reaction. She told herself she had no other choice. The sharp, unexpected bite set off her primal instincts. Whoever the large purl coming toward her was, he was much too big for her to fight. She had blown her cover. The only thing she could think of was to run for her life. She saw the purl leap toward her to catch the child and didn't care whether he saved him or not. She realized his choice to save the child would cost him time, and she would use that time to get away. She heard Daisy scream as the child left her arms, but a quick look over her shoulder proved that neither Daisy nor the purl was following her. Then, just a few steps from the fence, she saw another large purl running through the back door toward her. Tepa hit the eight-foot fence with a leap. She flipped over it in a move worthy of a warrior. When her feet touched the ground on the other side, she went into a controlled roll. Finishing the roll on her feet, she continued running. The footsteps of the purl following her motivated her to keep going. She headed for the trees not far away and hoped for the darkness.

The large figure Daisy left at the front door had run through the house to intercept the one who had taken the child out of the house. As he exited the back door, Tepa was headed to the fence. He could easily have caught up to her and was almost at the fence when she cleared it. It was obvious to him that she had been trained, but it was also clear she was no master. A master would have fought for her life and not fled to save it. And if her task was to procure the child, a well-trained warrior would not have left him under any circumstances. Nevertheless, he had decided to pursue, subdue, and capture this purl. In full stride, he jumped, thrust his palms against the planet, and launched himself into a twisting front flip that landed him on top of the fence. He surveyed the landscape and detected Tepa's scent as it followed her toward the woods. But before he could continue his pursuit, the other purl whistled. It was a brief, almost silent sound, but he knew what it meant. He back flipped with a twist off the fence and ran back into the house. He stopped in the kitchen and knelt by the broken teacup. He blew on it, and the puddle of tea spilled around it. The cup and the tea turned to a black dust and, in a stream, rushed out of the door and over the fence. The purl then quickly closed and sealed the door.

The purl who had caught Pedagogy held him to his chest and stood to his feet. He could hear Tepa running away, and nothing was moving toward him, but he was unwilling to take any chance with the Poollé Kii. Pedagogy rested in his arms and preferred them to Daisy. He buried his head in the neck of the large purl. Daisy noticed. What Daisy did not know was that Pedagogy was healing the wound from the headbutt. There was a faint glow coming from beneath the hood where Pedagogy held his forehead, but she didn't understand what was happening. She felt strange. She felt like her child was rejecting her, as if he had deemed her unworthy. Anger began to rise from her stomach. She turned to demand the purl hand over her child, but just as she did, the purl blew a stream of his breath into her face. The thought to be enraged at the act occurred to Daisy, but before the thought was fully formed, the sweet odor of his breath hit her. It was the kind of scent one would find wonderful, but instead, it combined in a putrid way with whatever was rising from her stomach. Daisy was going to be sick. She turned her head and threw up. The tea and sweet biscuits Tepa had insisted she eat came pouring out of her. Daisy turned her head to the grass and retched again. The contents of her stomach rushed toward the grass. She was frightened to see a black mist rise from the regurgitated food and fly toward the back fence and the woods. She looked to the purl holding her child. She was embarrassed and confused. She wiped her mouth with her sleeve and realized she was feeling better than she had for the last several days. She didn't remember feeling ill and was confused on how she didn't realize she was not herself. She looked into the light eyes of the purl. They were looking deeply into hers. His bright yellow eyes glowed as the Purplynd suns were setting. They were searching her soul.

The large, hooded figure with the glowing yellow eyes told Daisy that they must go inside and hurry. He had not yet given Pedagogy to her, and Daisy was uneasy about it, but there was a palpable urgency to get inside. The suns had not yet set, but a peculiar darkness had already begun to descend. Important things had changed. Daisy closed and locked the door. She looked at her Pedagogy, who was nearly too big for her to carry but fit perfectly in the arms of the large purl holding him. Her heart was pounding through her chest. The thought that Tepa was not who she thought she was scared Daisy, and she began to descend into a bottomless pit of sorrow and guilt. Confusion filled her, and anger began to rise again within her. She wanted her child. This purl, whoever he was, had no right to keep him from her. She thought to take her child from whoever this purl was. Just then, Pedagogy jumped out of his arms. Daisy caught a glimpse of his eyes. There was so much love and power in them that Daisy calmed herself and abandoned her descent into anger and despair. There was something else in his eyes, but Daisy didn't yet understand what Pedagogy was communicating. He ran toward his room, and the large purl who had been in the kitchen followed him.

The purl who remained looked at Daisy in a way that made her question whether she was in her own home. He invited her into the kitchen and began making a special broth with ingredients from a pouch tied onto his belt. Moments later, Pedagogy and the other purl came back into the kitchen and sat at the table. Pedagogy sat close to Daisy, which calmed some of the emotions still running through her. The purl finished the brew and placed it on the table in front of Daisy. She had to drink it, and everyone waited until she did. The look in Pedagogy's eyes told her it was necessary for her to consume the broth. She touched the bowl to her lips and began to drink. It was warm but not too hot. It had a strange inviting flavor. Pedagogy tipped the bowl, letting her know that she should finish the whole thing at whatever cost. Pedagogy had never asked her to do anything that was not for the benefit of good and wonderful things. His hand of encouragement pushed Daisy past any doubt she had about consuming the strange brew. She began to swallow and decided she would gulp the whole thing down at one time. She drank the entire contents of the small bowl and decided on the last swallow that it was not at all a pleasant experience. Her stomach began to churn, and seconds later, her brain felt like a fire was burning parts of it.

Daisy realized she had been poisoned. She wondered why she drank the liquid at all. She wondered why Pedagogy had encouraged her to drink it. She remembered that she had begun to wonder if Pedagogy wanted her alive. She wondered if he wanted to get a new guardian. Since Tepa had come, she had seen them grow close, and now her child — the gift that had come to her three years ago—was ready to leave her. She looked at the large purl who had met her at the door. He seemed poised to strike. The other purl and Pedagogy were staring at her. They knew she had been poisoned. A tear formed in her eyes, and she wanted to close them and die. Just then, she realized she would be sick again. She didn't think she had any food left in her. She turned as quickly as she could and rose to head toward the bathroom. As she did, she realized she was not going to make it. Her movement placed her in front of the other purl. He was holding a sack in his hand. It was just what she needed. Her mouth opened, and an awful dust came out of her. She threw up a black bile that had the flavor of death. It filled the pouch the purl held open for it like a serpent leaving her body against its will. As soon as it was out, the purl pulled tight the drawstring on the pouch and tied it. There was something living inside it, attempting to escape. The purl went to the backdoor the other purl had opened. He threw the bag high into the air. The bag exploded in a bright purple flame and disintegrated.

The whole experience left Daisy on the floor, exhausted. The purl who had run to the side of the house and who had saved Pedagogy from harm, if not death, removed his hood and bent to help Daisy get up. Daisy recognized that he was one of the purple who had driven her from the antique shop long ago. He told Daisy they had come to take her to the mountains. Daisy wondered how they knew about her upcoming trip. She had only mentioned the mountains to the driver who had finally agreed to take her. As with all the others, she had been careful to give them as little information as possible. And the driver she had hired was due to pick her up in three days right after the DLA inspections were complete. Daisy began to tell him these things and ask more questions. She was confused about Tepa. She wanted to know what had come out of her and how it had gotten in her in the first place. She needed clarity and answers. She believed this purl could help her. He told Daisy there would be time for her questions on the journey but now they had to leave quickly. He convinced her that Tepa would soon return with others who intended harm to her and the child. Had Daisy not seen Tepa throw her child to his harm and not just thrown up a black serpent, she would not have believed him. She trusted these purple because Pedagogy trusted them. Without another thought to delay her, Daisy called the parents to come pick up the remaining children and hurried to her room to pack.

Tepa reached the woods, panting. She heard footsteps behind her and the sound drove her beyond her normal running limits. Exhausted, she stopped and listened. Her heart was pounding. She was in the woods north of Biscuit but had no idea where. The darkness she had longed for had come and covered her path into the woods, but she wasn't sure where she was. With no strength left, she fell panting to the ground. She didn't know that the footsteps she had been hearing were coming from her imagination. The darkness she had placed in the tea for Daisy had found her and driven her into confusion. She had run for almost an hour, but the toxins that drove her were now gone, and she began to calm. She lay until her heart and breath quieted to a gentle rhythm. She pressed her ears against Purplynd to rest. The energy she had used to conjure and confuse Daisy, as well as the exhaustion from running for her life, convinced her that sleep was wise. She closed her eyes and drifted out of consciousness. She woke panicked by the sound of heavy footsteps rushing toward her. She tried to shake herself out of her sleep and escape. It was too late. They were already on her.

ESCAPE TO THE MOUNTAINS

IT WAS DEEP INTO the darkness when they left. There was a car seat next to the driver that was obviously for Pedagogy. He had already fallen asleep, and one of the large purple gently strapped him into his seat. Daisy sat in the rear seat behind the driver, and the other purl sat behind Pedagogy. They drove the first hour without headlights or sound. Daisy sensed the importance of the silence. She guessed the vehicle they were in could not be easily tracked. It had slick tires like a drag racer's and was not like any she had seen before. It made almost no sound as they sped through the darkest backstreets of Biscuit. Daisy's head began to clear. The doubts, fears, and confusion that had been growing in her heart dissipated. They drove for hours. Daisy drifted in and out of sleep, but the purl beside her and the driver remained alert and poised for anything that might arise. She woke to the light of the rising suns streaming in through the windshield. As she gathered her thoughts, she realized that meant they were headed east. The thought made her worry. She had convinced herself they were to travel west. She was sure Pedagogy had helped her and confirmed they were to head to the west. She wanted to ask but did not know whether it was appropriate to break the silence.

Daisy stretched forward to check on her Pedagogy. The purl at the wheel told her Pedagogy would wake soon. She didn't know how he knew, but the rising suns were Pedagogy's alarm clock. As she wondered about where she was and what was happening, the driver spoke to Pedagogy, who had just awakened. He told him they were almost at the transfer point. The purl next to Daisy told him everything had gone well and there was no indication they had been detected. Daisy wondered why they were speaking to Pedagogy as if he understood and was in charge.

The vehicle turned off the paved road and into the woods. The grass trail was just wide enough for them to fit, and the driver slowed the vehicle to navigate his way through the woods. The trail turned constantly and moved up and down steep and not-so-steep valleys and glens. Daisy would not be able to find her way back to the road if she needed. The driver followed a hidden trail that moved them through the woods. If there were signs to mark the trail, Daisy could not make out where those signs were or when they were seen. After hours of winding through the foothill woodlands, they entered into a clearing with a large log cabin and an enclosed corral. Majestic mountains rose high behind the house. The vehicle stopped in front of the house, where another cloaked purl stood waiting. When the vehicle stopped, the purl knelt on one knee and bowed its head. The purl sitting beside Daisy leaped out of the vehicle, seemingly before it had fully stopped, and opened the door for Pedagogy. The other purl had already unbuckled Pedagogy by the time the door was open, and, as soon as it was, Pedagogy jumped out. He walked to the kneeling purl and pushed her hood off her bowed head. When he did, the curls of the purl's beautiful, long green hair bounced and danced in the morning suns' light. Pedagogy kissed both of her cheeks, after which she almost jumped up. She took Pedagogy in her extended arms and held him high. She began to slowly twirl and pull the child into her embrace. Pedagogy loved it as much as she did.

Just then, in the woods north of Biscuit, two agitated, large, red, dark-eyed purple lifted Tepa to her feet. Tepa pulled out their grasp and had already tightened her fists to begin the fight she planned to wage against whoever they were. *They* were large, and the fight would be a hard one to win, but that was never a real discouragement for her. Only after she had sent her first roundhouse toward the chin of the purl closest to her did she recognize him. Unfortunately for him, her hand was quicker than her memory and faster than his reflexes. The hard smack to his jaw began the conversation.

They were Syng's men. Syng had sent them when Tepa had activated the switch on her belt. It had only taken them a little more than an hour to get from Prometheus to Biscuit and to locate the transponder that had fallen out of Tepa's belt. What made it dislodge was a mystery. But the two had to find and follow her path through the woods, which they had no real skill in doing. They spent the entire night wandering in search of Tepa. They would not return without her, and by the time they had doubled back to check for her at Dancing Daisy's, Daisy and the child had long since disappeared. It was their last venture into the woods that they happened to find the female purl. They only found her because of the sounds she made as she struggled in her sleep.

Tepa told them to take her back to the daycare, but they refused. Syng had sent them and was anxious for her return. The night of waiting had worn his patience razor thin. The trap he had set to capture the child, his guardian, and any other clues to Daisy's interest in poollé trees had snapped shut with no prey. His purple's reports of not finding Tepa, the child, or Daisy infuriated him. Syng was not one to take bad news well, and they didn't want to bear the brunt of his displeasure. The ride back to the Promethean Panthae was quiet. Tepa spent her time attempting to piece together what had happened and what she would tell Syng. The men were tired from an all-night search, the result of which they feared would not please their employer. They stopped the car in the rear, near the private entrance to the club. The large purl opened the door for Tepa, who got out indignantly. It didn't help that the purl pulled a long stray vine from her hair as she passed him. Tepa had missed it during her backseat grooming effort. She slapped his hand away from her. They walked past the construction of an elevator shaft that went deep down into the darkness. They walked down four flights of stairs to a level Tepa didn't know existed. They knocked and then entered a plush office. The office was well lit but held a darkness that struck Tepa as soon as she entered it.

Syng was waiting. He rose from his chair and went to greet Tepa as soon as she walked into the room. He hugged her softly and asked if she was OK. He told her he had been worrying about her and how, when she signaled, he sent his purple to ensure she was safe and secure. He offered Tepa a drink. She refused. He insisted. The sweet drink made her body relax. Syng was a master at conjuring brews for various uses, but the love that he was showing her convinced her that he wouldn't drug her. She had nothing to hide, she argued within herself, as she thought through her most recent actions. Syng talked with the purple who had brought her. He didn't like their answers.

Over the next three days, Syng searched for answers. The more information he received, the more questions it created. He sent his "inspectors" who returned without adding useful information. Tepa begged to be allowed to return to the daycare early in her interrogation. She promised she could get more information than anyone else. Syng was unconvinced. The inspectors closed the daycare and, after they had turned away the last parent, tore the home inside out. They were looking for whatever they could find, including the note Tepa swore existed. Nothing in the home suggested anything special about it or the purple who had lived there. Syng talked to his driver who had promised to take Daisy to the mountains. All he confirmed was that he had promised to take Daisy to the mountains in the west. He wondered if the driver and Tepa had conspired to deceive him. Unsatisfied with his answers, he had the driver taken to the outskirts of Biscuit and killed. He would accuse Daisy of his murder if necessary. Syng asked Tepa who the purple were who had come. He asked her how they knew to come at that time. He wondered why she had given the child to them.

He was convinced she was lying. Things didn't add up. The potions she had ingested and the drugs he had injected did nothing to make things clearer. Syng had begun with a warm welcome and embrace of Tepa, but his patience had worn thin.

What began as his interest in someone who shared an interest in poollé trees had become a mystery, and that mystery had become a challenge. It was an exceptionally rare scholar who studied the role of the poollé tree in the ancient myths. Their existence and power were hidden in the oldest texts and those in no language currently spoken. Knowledge of poollé was linked to power, and Daisy had an interest in poollé which meant she had an interest in power. Perhaps she was practiced in the ancient arts, for how else could she have bested his protégé? Syng hated not knowing. He hated loose ends. There were those who would do anything to possess the power he had. There were certainly those who would do what he had done to obtain it. He feared that Daisy might be one of them. He had questions he was sure Tepa could not answer, and he had come to a dead end. Until he found the woman and the mystery child, there would be no more answers. So, he tortured Tepa for three more days. He did this for the pleasure of it. Her screams quieted the torment within his soul. The splatter of her blood across his face brought him dark delight. If anyone heard the screams of terror coming from the bowels of the Panthae, the utter fear those sounds provoked sealed their silence forever.

The home in the woods at the foot of the mountains had a clear, cool stream running behind it. Parts of the home looked ancient but walking through it made Daisy wonder if it had just been built. There were no cobwebs or dust. The interior sides of the outer walls were smooth and polished. In most places, it was impossible to see where the logs were joined. The other walls inside the house were light and inviting; they looked as if they had just been painted. The windows and skylights made it seem as if there were no ceilings at all. One strange thing was that there were no finished floors in the entire home. The floors were the ground except the places where a rare rug had been placed. Stranger still, the ground within the house was warm. The entire house generated fresh air, and breathing it healed the heart and brought freshness to one's soul. Being inside the house filled Daisy with a sense of safety like never before. The green-haired, sky-blue-eyed purl who had reverently greeted Pedagogy showed Daisy around the house and then excused herself to prepare their meal. As she was speaking, Daisy recognized that she was the same purl from the antique store. Daisy's eyes watered as she thought about the times she felt alone. She realized that somehow, since Pedagogy came into her life, she had never been alone.

The purple had taken Pedagogy's crib from Biscuit and, as soon as they arrived, began reassembling it in the house. Daisy thought she understood how the crib would convert into a bed, but when they had reassembled it in Pedagogy's room, the bed had been transformed into something majestic. It seemed the wood itself had grown, which Daisy told herself was impossible. Daisy had learned to take her cues from Pedagogy, and he was more relaxed than he had been in quite some time. It wasn't until the next day, as Daisy played with Pedagogy on the banks of the stream, that she realized she hadn't seen Pedagogy this energetic and playful since Tepa came to work at the daycare. Daisy accepted, even before it was talked about over dinner, that she would probably not see her home in Biscuit for a long time. She wondered if they were near the place the note spoke of but was told that place was much farther away. The conversation at the table was one part mystery and two parts reassuring. Daisy learned that Tepa had been poisoning her in small amounts since she had arrived. She also realized her own thoughts and actions could not be trusted until all the darkness Tepa had sewn into her had been removed. That explained the darkness that came out of her after she had consumed the broth. It nearly broke her heart to realize that the darkness created by the poison caused the attack on the antique shop. The dinner was unlike any Daisy had ever made or eaten. The food looked like any other but tasted thousands of times better. Even the water had a more refreshing flavor than any Daisy had experienced before. Everyone ate and drank and talked as if all in the world was right. They chatted and laughed as if it was their daily routine. Daisy's heart welcomed the grace and peace filling the moment.

Pedagogy's room was the largest bedroom of several. The female purl had arranged the bedroom next to Pedagogy for Daisy and laid out clothes for her to sleep. Daisy changed, and the sleeping gown embraced her in warmth and love. She couldn't help but smile and nestle her cheek into its collar. Just having the nightgown on made her anxious to go to sleep. Daisy had kept the note that she received in the blanket in a pouch pressed against her body and under her clothes. When she changed, she was delighted to find a pocket in the gown just over her heart. She placed the folded note in it and buttoned it closed. She was sure these purple were trustworthy but feared her time with the note was nearing an end, which made it even more dear to her. Besides, keeping the note and reading the poem at the end of it to Pedagogy was her task to do. Coming to this cabin in the woods renewed her dedication to Pedagogy and the promise she had made the first time she read the note. She went to his room to, once again, engage in the ritual that had been theirs since that first night. She locked the door behind her and thought herself foolish for doing it. She sat in a chair that was positioned by the bed as if it was placed there specifically for the purpose of reading the note. It was a high seat Daisy had to climb into, and it had a place for her feet to rest exactly where she would have wanted. Once there, she looked at Pedagogy, and his eyes met hers. His eyes looked at Daisy as if she had been gone for a long while and had just returned. He was so glad she had returned to him, and the look of love and welcome in his eyes brought tears to hers. She read the letter and the power she experienced the first time she read it to Pedagogy returned.

At the last line: "From death and danger; he shall rest Beneath the poollé trees," Pedagogy drifted off to sleep. Daisy stayed there still and wept for a while. It was as if the enormity of the task she began all those years ago hit her all at once. With the comprehension of how immense that task was came the immediate realization that she had already completed it. Being in this house gave her a sense of closure and finality, even though no one suggested that her role had changed. And it was certain that their lives were forever intertwined and there were many challenges ahead, but she sat watching her baby sleep with tears rolling down her cheeks. Finally, when she decided to rest, she chose the soft, spacious couch that was in Pedagogy's room. She curled up under the comforter and slept, enveloped in the warm embrace of love.

When she awakened, Pedagogy was already up and gone. The door to his room stood wide open, and the sight of it made Daisy sit up. As her mind gathered itself, she realized where she was. Daisy laid her head back down and closed her eyes in search of the sweetest sleep of her life. It was gone. Still, she lay there waking up, not wanting to leave the most comfortable couch on Purplynd as a growing sense pushed her toward the day. She looked through the window and could see Pedagogy playing in the sunshine. He was safer than he had ever been. She went into her bedroom, expecting to find the things she had hastily packed. They were not there. Other clothes were laid out for her, and after she had showered, she found they fit her as if they had been tailor made. She was not surprised, which made her smile. She was beginning to accept there were powers beyond her own that would help her through life. The thought increased her peace. There was even an inner pocket in the garment into which the note, again, fit perfectly.

Daisy walked past the dining table and realized she had missed a wonderful breakfast. Coming into the kitchen, the green-haired, light-eyed female purl was putting away the last of the morning's dishes. She asked if Daisy would like some breakfast and, before Daisy could tell her she wasn't hungry, presented her with a cup and saucer full of delicious hot tea. Sweet biscuits soon followed, and the purl sat with Daisy as she ate. There was a window at the table where they sat through which they could see Pedagogy and the other purl talking and playing. The peace of the moment was almost overwhelming, and when Daisy mentioned it, the purl chuckled her consent and agreement. She told Daisy the feelings she was experiencing was pha. Pha, she was told, was the power that created Purplynd, and it was the power that held it together. Daisy had a thousand questions and thought she was in a place where all of them could be answered. She wanted to ask all of them at once. The few sips of the tea filled her with a sense of peace and a gentle excitement. Before she spoke, the eyes of the purl suggested she take a bite of her biscuit. As she did, the thoughts of doing anything other than eating the biscuit disappeared. The texture and flavor of the magnificent pastry danced in her mouth. Daisy had no words to describe what was happening. It was as if her mouth had never been used to its full potential. Each bite twirled in her mouth and tickled her taste buds until it disappeared. Daisy was enraptured by the meal and didn't even realize the purl had risen to start other tasks. When she finished enjoying the experience, the day called to her.

Daisy rose to join her Pedagogy outside and thought once more to ask at least one question. As she began thinking about which one of the many questions she would ask the beautiful green-haired purl, their eyes met. Daisy understood that the time for questions and answers would come, but that moment was not it. So, she continued out into the yard behind the house. When Pedagogy saw her, he ran and jumped in her arms. The purl he had been with disappeared, and Daisy sat with her Pedagogy for hours on the banks of a stream, enjoying the pha. When, at last, the bright-day crested, Daisy began to feel hungry. Just then, Pedagogy took her hand and told her it was time to eat. The thought of sitting together increased her pha, as she believed it was time to get some answers to her questions. They went into the house, where the meal was just ready to be eaten. After that dinner, the two purple, Daisy, and the Poollé Kii talked until the night came. This they did each day they were at the ancient house at the foot of the mountains. The answers added deep understanding to questions Daisy had since that first night. They also added mystery and the wisdom that there was much more adventure ahead. This is what she was told.

Everything they had packed at the house was being driven back to Biscuit by the purl who drove them to the mountain. They were not sure if Tepa or any other purl had placed locating devices on any of them, and even if they didn't, the clothes could be used to trace and find her. For the safety of her and the Poollé Kii, it was best not to have any traceable items as they moved forward. Daisy was told the danger to the child was very real and had always been. She was chosen because of her pure heart and steel will. She had been watched her whole life, but the guardians were not sure of her worthiness until she named the Poollé Kii and swore her promise. It was her promise that gave her the ability to lactate. Her heart held the right combination of love, wisdom, and strength. The knowledge that she had been monitored and that Pedagogy would have been taken from her had she not been fit to care for him in the way he deserved increased her sense of joy and peace. She loved her child more than her own life and wanted what was best for him, whatever it cost. That was why the realization that she would never return to Biscuit or to Dancing Daisy's All-day Daycare was as welcome to her as a rainbow after a storm.

She was told that a powerful purl was searching for her and the child and that they would have to stay in this mountain home for a while. Daisy didn't know how long a while would be but could think of no other place she would want to be. Being in this place filled her with a sense of hope and power. She was safe and loved. She was in a place where she could share her deepest confusion or her silliest whim and receive only love and understanding in return. She was told that when it was time to leave, they would go to the place near the mountains the note spoke of. Her Pedagogy's blanket contained in its design the map to get them to the exact place they needed to go. Not even the wisest of the guardians could find the place without it. The purl didn't know who had trained Tepa or how many purple she had been working with. They spoke of those who preferred war, death, and confusion to peace or the peaceful. Daisy remembered from her past those in Prometheus who found pleasure in the death of innocents. In fact, Daisy was an important part of the battle for the whole of Purplynd. She was told the child she had raised was a descendant of Quel-Kha, son of Quay, child of Miis, the greatest master in the history of Purplynd. She was told that the wisdom of Quel-Kha was hidden in the Poollé Kii and that the hope of all who loved peace and all who sought pha was in him. These were the lessons she learned as she and her Pedagogy awaited the arrival of the purple who would take them to the place of which the note spoke. There, her journey with the note would end, and this made the last nights of reading it all the more sacred to her.

Daisy was told things about Purplynd no school had ever taught. She had known Purplynd was a living planet, but she learned, around the fire in the home by the mountains, that it was much more alive than she thought. She also learned a lot about the poollé trees and about their connection to that life. She learned there is wisdom that can never enter the world of words but is more real and more important than all the books ever written. She learned darkness and light are at war and every purl must choose on what side he or she would fight. The two purple spoke as if this war between light and darkness would be waged soon in ways it had never been. Most of these things Daisy learned while sitting around the table or around the fireplace as the bright-day ended. Her Pedagogy was always present and attentive. He contributed to the conversation in ways that astounded Daisy. Whenever he would speak, the others would listen with a respect and deference which made Daisy suspect that she might have been too casual with her own child. Some of the words Pedagogy spoke were in some other language, and there were times he spoke that would result in the two purple bowing low enough to place their foreheads on the ground. She learned that the poollé tree was very rare and ancient. One poollé tree could live for many thousands of years, and the seeds of a poollé tree could lie dormant for many thousands more. The most ancient of the trees were the seedlings of the poollé that existed before purple walked on Purplynd.

What Daisy wasn't told was the poollé were not just botanical trees but that they also had the power of bridging the distance between plant and purple. She wasn't told but began to suspect that the life and essence of purple were connected to the planet itself and the poollé trees somehow linked the two. The talks around the fire taught her much about herself and her life. She learned the things she was taught in school and the intellect of purple was not the only wisdom on Purplynd. In the mountains, she came to respect the role other living things on the planet played. Daisy found out that the dark-eyed purple who controlled Prometheus and most of the planet were not the legitimate rulers nor the only power. Somehow, the poollé trees and these strange purple in the mountains were part of something dangerously important. She and her child were caught in the middle of this. There were moments in the stories that filled her with fear. They were not at all trying to scare her, but the purple and her Pedagogy would get caught up talking about all that had happened, and the stories would become so vivid and real the hair on Daisy's arms would stand up, and at times, a shiver would run down her spine. Pedagogy and the others would sense when fear captured her, and they would stop the story. This was, in part, why Daisy didn't know some important things that could have saved her life.

There were other things that Daisy was deliberately not told. She understood poollé trees were alive in mysterious ways. She pieced together from the many conversations that they could communicate with certain purple, but she didn't understand how. She wondered if the trees talked or had some kind of sign language. She asked questions, which were answered sometimes with other questions, sometimes with mysteries, and other times not at all. Daisy suspected there were things she either couldn't understand or was not ready to hear. She was right. She wasn't told that there were particular poollé trees that carried the mind and memory of powerful ancient masters. She also did not know that when a purl who shared the bloodline of one of these masters ingested the leaves of one of these particular poollé trees, some of the memories, mind, and mastery of that ancient master would become a part of that purl. The merging of mind and memory was a process that took time and careful guidance. Only with the help of the guardians could one remain whole and sane once a match was made between purl and poollé. This was one of the things that Daisy was not told.

The green-haired purl and the other purl did tell Daisy there was once a poollé tree that had embraced the dying body of a great ancient master. The mind and memory of this master had been absorbed by that tree and then divided into several trees as the generations of poollé moved through the eons. Daisy was told that her Pedagogy was a descendant of one of the greatest masters of the ancient world, but what she wasn't told was that the particular poollé strain of his ancestor had been found and assembled. She wasn't told that she had been the keeper of those powerful poollé seeds since Pedagogy had arrived. She wasn't told any of these things for her own safety and for that of Pedagogy. The last thing she wasn't told was that the guardians who knew the correct ritual to merge the mind of this particular poollé tree and purl had been assembled. An attempt by any other purl or team would end in death, insanity, or something much worse.

The days in that house by the mountain foothills disappeared into a time-altered reality. Daisy fell into a comfort with the rhythms. She began to take walks with the green-haired purl in the mornings to gather fruits, berries, and an occasional sliver or two of bark. She learned many things as she interacted with the woods that came alive around her. Animals that she had only read about or seen in books sang and played in their natural habitats. The green-haired purl moved lightly and quietly through the woods. She moved through the woods as a bird glides through the air. The leaves and trees wrapped themselves around her as if they were her garment. The leaves on the ground and the grass beneath her feet seemed to lift her as she walked. Daisy marveled that she left no footprints or trail that could be discerned. Daisy tried to learn how not to make so much noise as she walked.

Before Pedagogy came into her life, when she would dance, everyone always marveled at how light she was on her feet. When she used to go out dancing, Daisy had a reputation for gliding across the dance floor as if she floated on a cushion of air. But here in the woods, she walked with large, noisy, lead boots compared with her green-haired teacher. She began to understand the planet in ways one would become familiar with a friend on a long journey. She witnessed Pedagogy grow in that environment in ways that were unique and vital. The warm dark nights, like a womb, welcomed her to deep and renewing rest. Each day found her more alive than the previous. Then, one night, it all changed.

There were a few purple who Syng trusted to do whatever he asked. He had groomed, taught, and tested their loyalty, and they understood that obedience and silence were required to be this close to the kind of power he wielded. It wasn't the first time he had used them to clean up this type of mess, and the rewards for being one of Syng's chosen few were attractive; money, sex partners, and small fortunes were offered for the nefarious work. Every purl who worked for Syng had been enticed in some way, and most were hooked on something only he could provide. But not every purl in Syng's employ knew as much about him as the closest few. All understood him to be a wealthy, powerful employer. He was politically well-connected and peculiar like most of the very wealthy. What they didn't know was that each of them had been chosen. Syng left as little to chance as possible and would select the purple he allowed around him only after careful investigations. He had gained a reputation for being one of the few wealthy purple who would employ formerly incarcerated purple and supported prison reform. He led the drive that finally allowed prisoners to work and earn money while they were paying for their crimes against society. Only a few knew that this was simply a way to suppress wages in the work world outside the prison fences and to maintain an almost slave labor force within them. They also did not know that the profiles Syng maintained gave him access to the precise purple he wanted for the monstrous parts of his business. Syng would select certain purple in his employ and allow them to get attached to a lifestyle of privilege and access. Then they would be tasked to participate in an act that left a naked fear in their soul. It was that fear that kept them loyal. And it was that fear, above all else, that made them deadly.

Syng was sure he had gotten all the information out of Tepa that she had. The torture that proceeded after was for other purposes. His last evil acts were performed on her lifeless frame. Exhausted by his own demented acts, he sat in the darkness until his red skin glowed. There were questions. He still wondered how Daisy found out about the poollé and why she wanted to know more. He wondered who the father of her child was and why she didn't talk about him. He wondered if it was the father of the child who showed up that last night. He wondered if anyone other than those he desired to know knew about this subterranean lair. He wondered if the paperwork for the expansion of the restaurant had ever been approved. The plans he had submitted were incomplete because they didn't show the subterranean maze of rooms or the true depth of the elevator that led to them. Syng had paid off some officials and threatened others. He was confident he had projected his power sufficiently enough to get an official approval, so he didn't wait for permission to begin the work. The dratsab was in his pocket. It was only a matter of purple following the orders that came from the dratsab, and all would be well. But the approvals were overdue, and none of his contacts could tell Syng why. This, too, troubled him. There was no one he could trust and so much at stake. The swirl of thoughts haunted him. It contributed to his bestial torment of Tepa. He dwelt there in the darkness for days, drunk with the insanity of his own debauchery and nurturing doubts until the odor of death demanded remedy. He washed his body and burned his clothes.

He called for three of his purple to dispose of the body. Syng sent other purple to Biscuit to find answers to his questions about Daisy, the daycare, and the child. The days had turned into weeks since the disappearance. Syng feared the more time passed, the harder it would be to cure the pain of his unanswered questions. He was careful not to overplay his hand or expose the depth of his curiosity because he didn't want to alert any official channels. He was connected to power in significant ways but didn't want to shed light on any of his private projects. He was not a man of patience, and he began to blame his caution for the lack of progress discovering the whereabouts of Daisy. Many years passed, and the events faded into a hidden dark place of his memory. Then, after a long time, there was a break in his favor.

Daisy had become so comfortable at the home at the foot of the mountains she lost track of how much time had passed. Pedagogy had grown, and she welcomed more each day what she began to call his family. But, in an instant, Daisy cursed the calm that had renewed her life and hope. She believed Pedagogy's care and safety was her responsibility alone, and she blamed herself for the terror that had arrived. Her first thought was to grab Pedagogy and run. They would be lost in the woods, but at least she wouldn't be trapped in the house. She cursed the fact that she had let the lure of her comfortable bed persuade her not to sleep every night at his bedside. Now she would have to get him from his room before they could make their escape, and although it would only add a few moments to their flight from danger, she needed every second.

They had been joined after some weeks by the purl who had driven the vehicle back to Biscuit, and he had arrived by foot. The five of them had dwelt in the house by the mountains, resting as if it had been built for them and their leisure. Everything was pha until this moment, and in it, Daisy wondered if it had all been a trap. She didn't know how they had found her, but she could feel their strength and see them in the shadows: two large purple cloaked and hooded, standing in the darkness. They were at the front door, and they had come for the Poollé Kii; she could feel it. There was no time for thinking; she needed to get her child and run. She tried to move but was frozen. Someone or something was holding her. She wondered if the green-haired purl or something else had her strapped to her bed against her will. It didn't matter. Daisy was determined and had learned some things about her own power and strength. She summoned her will and, with determination, broke through whatever was holding her and sat straight up in the bed. With her eyes open in the darkness, she tried to convince herself that it was just a nightmare. She had had nothing but sweet dreams since she arrived, dreams of dances and celebrations. The pha had been so powerful that Daisy began to translate it into a sense of her own power. She felt betrayed by all of it now.

Daisy couldn't shake the feeling that it was more than a dream. Her heart was racing, and sleep was long gone. She decided to rise from her bed and get to her Pedagogy. If there was nothing to fear, she would be content to sleep beside her child. She climbed out of the bed, wishing she had a weapon, and remembered the large swords above the fireplace. Daisy had no idea what time it was, but it felt like it was the darkest part of the night. She rushed to the door of her chamber and was shocked as she opened it to find the green-haired purl standing in front of her. It was as if she expected Daisy to open the door at that very moment. This was no dream. The look in her light eyes told Daisy she, too, knew dangerous purple had come for the child. Now Daisy was even more desperate to get to her Pedagogy. But she could read in the eyes of the green-haired purl that her idea to run was not the plan they would engage. She could also feel a peculiar strength in her green-haired friend that she hadn't before. It was as if her gentle green-haired host was not a host at all. It felt as if she had been playing the part of a hostess when she was actually an...assassin. Now it was urgent for Daisy to get to Pedagogy. Daisy summoned strength from somewhere deep inside and stared into the eyes of her host. She began to clench her fist just as the green-haired purl moved out of her path. As Daisy turned down the hall toward Pedagogy's room, she caught a glimpse of the green-haired purl's eyes. They told her she would not be allowed to enter the room of the Poollé Kii.

Things were happening fast. Danger was close, but Daisy was catching up. As she reached the door to Pedagogy's chamber, she realized the prohibition against entering made sense. She didn't know what time it was. She had no idea whether she had slept one hour or most of the night. Pedagogy would sense she was out of sorts, and her anxiety and fear would wake her child. If he asked her what was wrong, she would have nothing to tell him. She knew something had changed; danger was very close, and running was not an option. But there was too much she didn't know to wake Pedagogy. As she reached the door, she looked back at the green-haired purl. Their eyes met. The light-eyed purl was headed toward Daisy. Her eyes revealed she was aware of the figures that stood in the darkness, but there was no fear in them. Instead, there was that peculiar strength and something else that made Daisy wonder if she shouldn't fear for her safety. Just as Daisy decided not to wake her child, the green-haired purl was at the bedroom door. She gripped Daisy with both her arms and turned her until they were face-to-face. The purl's sky-blue eyes glowed in the darkness. They stared into Daisy's. Daisy understood she was to go to the center room and wait. The instructions were clear and unequivocal. They were orders from her superior and her own choice. She was sure that whatever was about to happen was beyond her skill set. The purl released her, and Daisy headed for the center room as the green-haired purl stood guard outside the Poollé Kii's chamber door.

The first thing Daisy saw as she entered the large center room was that two of the swords which hung above the fireplace had been removed. Turning her head from the fireplace to the front door as if she was following the invisible path they had taken, she saw them. Each had its tip resting in the soil and its hilt steadied beneath the palm of a purl. The polished metal reflected the fireplace flames, and the razor-sharp edges anticipated battle. The gentle purple who had driven Daisy and her Pedagogy to this mountain hideout and showed her and the Poollé Kii every kindness stood as sentries facing the door. As Daisy sat down, she realized her child's playmates and tutors were warriors. The absence of danger allowed them to appear docile and harmless, but now, standing in their full height, weapons at the ready, they revealed themselves to Daisy as the fiercest and deadliest purple she could ever have imagined.

Daisy sat in the silence. The two purple standing guard neither moved nor spoke. The green-haired purl at her child's door also made no sound. Daisy was sure they were aware of her. They could hear her breath and the fast beating of her heart. They were aware of everything she imagined and more. Then, in the darkness, the two sentries began to glow red. At first, Daisy thought it was her imagination. When she realized it was real, the hairs stood up on her arms. She wondered whether these purple had always been red. She couldn't remember. She never thought it was important, but at this moment, she believed the color of their skin was the key to life and death. The glowing red color moved down from the crown of their heads past their bare, muscular arms and legs and into the ground. As it did, it was replaced by a flash of iridescent blue before returning to the shadow, outlining their frames in the darkness. Then all was still again. Daisy's heart returned to its regular beat, and she kept her eyes on the sentries standing guard between all she loved and the danger just beyond the front door. Daisy thought they were waiting for whatever was outside to attack. She was wrong.

The sky began to lighten as dawn began to arrive, and with it, Daisy knew her child would soon be waking. Her heart began to beat as if it wanted to explode. She wanted to go to him, but a deeper wisdom prohibited her. If a battle began, she would only be in the way. Perhaps the house held a secret escape. She couldn't make sense of the female purl's message to her. Daisy was learning to understand more of what these purple would say through their eyes and gestures. She was not to make any noise, that eye signal was clear. She knew she was to stay out of the way. She knew the swords were not ceremonial. She wanted to be useful. She wanted to give her life if necessary. She wanted to be with her Pedagogy. All these thoughts raced through her mind as she sat waiting. Then a light appeared as the door to Pedagogy's chamber opened. The voice of her child broke the silence. The female purl was speaking softly to the Poollé Kii. Then the door closed, and the light disappeared. Daisy wanted to run to her Pedagogy, but her duty was to stay where she was. It was hard. The minutes it took for Pedagogy to appear seemed like hours. Just as the rising suns began to brighten the sky, the coming daylight revealed that the shadow figures that woke Daisy in fear were more than real. The first sight of the dark silhouettes emerging from the night's blackness sent a violent shudder of terror through her. They stood tall and motionless, two figures with cloaks and hoods that covered their frames and the features of their faces. Their hands were clasped at their waist, covered by sleeves that draped to envelop them. Daisy's eyes studied the figures that did not move. They were large and imposing. Her gaze searched for movement or anything that would suggest that there was less to worry about than she imagined.

Suddenly, Pedagogy's opening door cast a glowing light across the room. It was the light and the sound of approaching footsteps that allowed her to finally break her fixation on the dark shadows she saw through the windows. Pedagogy walked into the room wearing a white cloak Daisy had never seen. Beneath it, he wore clothes embroidered with threads that glowed in the dim light. Across his small chest, the pattern of the glowing threads matched the relief that was on the headboard of his bed. They were the symbols of the Poollé Kii, but it would be some time before Daisy would recognize this or many of the other signs that had surrounded him and her. With the entrance of Pedagogy, the two sentries in the room spun their swords in circular motions, which stopped as the sword tips met above their heads. The angle they made matched the pitch of the high ceiling above them. Pedagogy walked into the room as if he understood more than Daisy imagined any child his age could. The female walked behind him and took her position behind the guards with her back to them, facing Pedagogy. All was ready. Pedagogy walked over to Daisy, who remained frozen. He climbed up on her lap, hugged her neck, and kissed her. Tears ran down her cheeks. She stared into the glow of his light blue eyes, and all the terror that had gripped her turned into peace.

The brief moment Pedagogy spent in Daisy's lap was enough to fill her with the confidence she would need to face whatever came next. By the time Pedagogy climbed out of her lap, the green-haired purl was kneeling. She was waiting for the command of the Poollé Kii. She could take the bejeweled sword that remained above the fireplace and join to fight the figures that had arrived or go meet them without it. The figures were either danger or help, but only the Poollé Kii would know. Daisy could not see it beneath the robe she wore, but this purl also glowed from red to blue at the feet of the Poollé Kii. After her color had returned, she lifted her head to gaze into the eyes of her Kii.

Daisy witnessed this, and the pounding cadence of her heart was the only sound breaking the silence. She searched with all her senses but heard nothing except the stillness. The green-haired purl stood, turned, and moved toward the large front doors. She moved slowly and silently. Her first three steps brought her directly beneath the two swords still being held by the warriors defending the Poollé Kii. As her foot moved through the plane formed by the razor-sharp edge of the swords, the two figures outside that had been frozen in the darkness moved with lightning speed, and reaching within their cloaks, drew swords of their own. They moved with poetic synchronicity and swiftness. As they pulled their swords from the scabbards hidden beneath their cloaks, the morning suns reflected in the mirror finish of the blades as lightning flashes. The swords moved in the same beautiful and deadly motion and ended with their tips in the ground. Four hands rested on the hilts in the exact same position as inside purple had moments before. The move was so smooth and quick Daisy did not know whether she had seen it, heard it, or sensed it in some other way. But there was no time to decipher how she knew what she knew. It was the knowing that held life and death. The movements of the figures caused their cloak hoods to rest on their broad shoulders exposing faces as capable of death as the razor edges of the swords in their grasp. The green-haired purl moved past the two guards and stood at the double doors.

Daisy was captured and frozen by the light eyes of the purple on the other side of the doors. She sensed their power and her powerlessness. There was nothing she could do. If she was to die, the most noble thing to do would be sit where she was. She sat as a queen at court. Her role in the next moments was to witness. She straightened her posture in the chair that had become her throne. The Poollé Kii stood motionless in front of her. After some moments, Daisy sensed his chest rise and heard him release a long sigh. It was the cue for the green-haired protector who, at the near silent command, pulled open both doors. The morning light rushed into the room and cast shadows of the figures in the room. The sword still held high in the outstretched arm of the guarding purl on the left moved backward slightly and tapped the other sword. Both swords turned in the air as they were released. When their tips pointed to the hearts of the figures beyond the entrance, they froze and began to fall straight down. The two guards each swung their arms backward as their left foot moved forward, and their bodies bent at the knees. Without moving their eyes which, like the swords, were fixed on the danger before them, they caught the swords by their grips and rose to their full standing height. The moment the sword handles were in the grips of the guards, the figures outside flexed their muscular frames, sending their cloaks off their backs and onto ground behind them.

Without a word said or a glance exchanged, the Poollé Kii and his guards began to move toward the open door. Daisy was sure everyone heard the noise of her heart pounding. She wasn't ready for her Pedagogy to die, no matter what the poem said. She was sure the guards were prepared to fight to the death. She sensed that they were ready for the fight. There was no fear in them. They were well-trained, and this was not their first battle. But Daisy could also feel that the figures they approached were warriors of a different sort. The warriors outside seemed not to have conquered their fears; they seemed never to have had any. They projected a power to contend with beasts and a sense that death was the component that gave their lives meaning. The green-haired purl was facing the Poollé Kii as he and his guards walked toward the open doors. She measured the distance between her and the sword that still hung above the fireplace and calculated the time it would take her to retrieve it and join the battle. The Poollé Kii had forbidden her to take it down. Her weapon of choice was the long pole, and she believed she could beat any swordsman with it, but her Kii had commanded she leave it by the door to his room where she had stood guard all night. The two guarding the Kii passed through the doorway into the morning with him three paces behind. As they did, the figures back flipped into fighting positions. The guards wanted to attack while they were mid flip, but the child Kii forbade it. He commanded them to hold, and they froze in obedience with their swords positioned to strike.

The Poollé Kii walked through the portal into the morning toward the warriors. He stopped one-half pace in front of his guards and stood between them and the large figures. He threw off the white cloak that had covered his clothes, and the embroidery on his tunic shone in the morning light. He spoke words Daisy did not understand. She thought they were in another language. But the words he spoke made seeing clearer. The imposing deadly figures that had haunted the house all night now appeared as the epitome of Purpleness. They were no less warriors, and they remained poised to strike with the large swords, but the words of her Pedagogy changed something significantly. Daisy did not know what. The Poollé Kii spoke again, and this time, the green-haired purl turned and ran into the house. He spoke again, and his guards brought their swords to the resting position with the tips in the soil and their hands resting on the pommel. Daisy thought this was strange. She thought this gave the attack advantage to the intruders, for the large purple remained in their attack position. She didn't understand the Kii's command to his guards demonstrated that he did not fear the threat the figures posed. Her eyes were so intensely focused on her child that she missed the green-haired purl's movement until she knelt before the Poollé Kii. Her back was to the fearsome purple, whose swords still glistened in the morning light, poised to strike. She took what she had brought, draped it over the right shoulder of the Kii, and fastened it around his neck with a clasp. It was the inner blanket in which he had been wrapped that first night. It was glowing now as it had then. The colors were alive with light. When the green-haired purl finished, she bowed with her forehead touching the ground and remained motionless.

As the blanket came in full view of the imposing purple, they began to move. There was a sound they made as all the air in their lungs was forced suddenly through their nostrils and open mouths. It was a sound that had the power of a train horn. Yet where one would expect an ear-piercing stream of noise, there was symphonic precision. The sound was so clear it registered in the eyes and had a flavor. Daisy experienced the sound with senses she didn't know she had. It rang in her chest as much as her ears. Daisy could never quite describe it. She could also never quite forget it. The sound they made was accompanied by the two purple moving as if they were one mind and body. Their bodies went into the air and moved in and out of the fetal position until, finally, they threw their bodies toward the ground. When their flawlessly harmonized move was completed, they had assumed the same posture as the green-haired purl. At first, Daisy thought the acts were wonderful displays of reverence. She marveled again at the love and awe these purple had for her Pedagogy. She wondered at how privileged she was to have been a part of his care, and then it hit her — the swords. Why did she think these figures had suddenly become benign?

Something warm moved completely through her body. She didn't have any time to wonder what it was, where it came from, or why she was feeling it. There was no time to think. She leaped from her seat and ran toward her Pedagogy. As she reached the door, her fears were confirmed. The swords were falling as if they were arrows. They were heading straight for her child. Daisy leaped toward the blades. She had never moved that fast before. It was as if time had slowed to help her cover the necessary ground. Her gaze was fixed on the deadly razor edges falling slowly. She was confident she would be able to throw her body between her Pedagogy and the blades. Then, just as she was intercepting the razor edges of the falling swords, the two free hands of the Kii's guards caught her. The swords hit their marks, and everything went black.

Daisy tried to open her eyes, but her eyelids were too heavy. She tried to remember where she was and what was happening, but the darkness pulled her back into the deep. This happened several times until she forced her eyes open. Her open eyes took some moments before they focused. The fog hiding her memory began to lift. She recognized her room and realized she was in the bed that she had slept in since the night after she arrived. She didn't know how she got to her room. She tried to piece together what had happened. She remembered the swords and checked her body for wounds. She tried to decipher what was real and what was not. She listened to the sounds of the silence that surrounded her. The suns were shining, and the light of the late morning washed into her room in as if welcoming her into the day. The light suggested that everything was well, but Daisy was not so sure. She wondered if she was dead. She wondered if she was dreaming and attempted to stand up. She was successful. She walked out of her room and into the house. The quiet became unsettling. She was confused to see most of the furniture covered with large sheets. There were neither signs nor sounds of life. Fear began to rise within her. She was drawn to the front doors. She walked across the warm Purplynd ground and opened them both. She stood still and tried to remember. She began to see. The footprints of the guards and where they stopped to protect her Pedagogy appeared. She stared and began to see the shadows of what once was. The footprints of her Pedagogy were there. The shadows of the frightening warrior figures flipping and throwing their swords high in the air revealed themselves. She remembered. She saw herself leap through the air and the hands of the guards arresting her forward motion and pushing her back. The falling swords struck the ground and sunk deep into Purplynd less than an inch from the shoulders of the figures bowing at the feet of the Poollé Kii. She saw the green-haired purl spinning in the air toward her, and where she had fallen to the ground unconscious.

Hope and confusion filled her. She shook from her mind the thoughts and shadows that just showed her the past. She wanted to believe she was alive and what she had just seen was true. She turned to enter the house. Something fluttered in her periphery. She turned toward the movement. She studied the tree line and began to breathe in the many scents in the surrounding air. She stood very still, staring. She was calm but more alert and aware of the world around her than she had ever been. She was ready to fight, even if she had no idea why she would need to. Time had slowed and was waiting for her. She was content to let it wait. Then something moved in the distance: a tiny shadow at the tree line. The small dark image in the distance grew larger. It was coming toward her. Daisy was still. She was ready. The figure grew until Daisy recognized it was a purl. A cautious few moments later, she recognized the green-haired purl walking toward her. The sight made her feel pha. She was carrying something large. It was a basket full of roots and food harvested from the woods. A warmth flowed over Daisy. She was not dead, and the sight and sounds of the green-haired purl proved she was also not alone. She waited at the doors for the purl and realized her heart had found a peaceful rhythm. When the green-haired purl reached her, Daisy touched her arm. Their eyes met, and Daisy was sure all was well. They walked into the kitchen and began to sort and wash the roots, flowers, and vegetables from the large basket. As they did, Daisy suddenly felt as if she hadn't eaten in days, which was true.

She didn't know it, but Daisy had been unconscious for a full cycle. The purl gave Daisy a biscuit that filled her with energy and quieted the hunger that had suddenly gripped her. As they worked in the kitchen, the green-haired purl answered Daisy's questions. She told her the large figures that had appeared were guardians. They were the wisest in the ancient ways of the poollé and they had the charge of guarding the line of Quel-Kha. The guardians were masters in all the ancient arts, including combat. They had come to assess the blood and spirit of her Pedagogy, to assess if he was really the Poollé Kii, and to see if he had the strength to endure the process of becoming. If they thought he was whole and capable, they would take him to the sacred grove. If they detected corruption, they would have killed him and his companions. The green-haired purl and the guards believed Pedagogy was the Poollé Kii, but they were not guardians. They were warriors and keen in many arts but not yet masters of them all. The guardians had come at that precise time. They had observed the child's movements over the past weeks. Their presence was felt but not seen. They had appeared and listened all night to the child's breathing and studied the steady beating of his hearts. The final tests of his character came the morning when he appeared before them unafraid. These things proved he had warrior blood and was capable of much more than most, but when the threads of his garments glowed and the blanket of his birth radiated the light of the ancients, the guardians were satisfied that Pedagogy was the Poollé Kii.

Daisy asked why the green-haired purl and her companions did not seem to welcome the guardians when they arrived. She was told they had sensed their presence weeks ago, and this was only because the guardians wished them to know that they were present. The green-haired purl and her two companions were a maté. A maté is a set of three warriors who trained, thought, and fought as one. A good maté could match a guardian in battle if those within it were well tuned and well trained. Daisy was told the three purple she had lived with these many months at the house were part of the best maté alive. The purls within a maté are connected so completely and inseparably in mind, body, and purpose that, once formed, they are given one name. And because they were the best, they were called Ilii. A battle between Ilii and a guardian could end with four dead purple, which was why two guardians had come. Ilii would not have defeated two guardians, but they would have died trying. The green-haired purl added that if Pedagogy was who they believed, he might have made the difference. Daisy wondered what the green-haired purl meant. She was puzzled how a child, not yet four years old, could participate in a battle of adults with swords and poles. Seeing her confusion, the green-haired purl paused and let silence teach her what it could. When the lesson was done, Daisy looked at the purl preparing what she understood would be her last meal in the house. It had been almost a year since this house had become a home and school for both her and her child. The time had flown by, and she had changed in ways she was only now realizing. She looked at her kitchen companion, understanding things she didn't know how or why. She remembered things she had learned through experience without remembering the experiences themselves. Daisy was confident for reasons she didn't even understand. She was not dead, left alone in the house, or otherwise separated from everyone she loved. Something was different within her. She, and the world, had changed in every way that mattered.

After Daisy's long, silent pause, the green-haired purl confirmed many of her thoughts. They were leaving, and something had been revealed about her that Ilii didn't know but the guardians did. It explained why the guardians waited so long in the woods and why they had not revealed themselves sooner. They had detected it immediately. Something that put all their lives at greater risk. Ilii realized it only when Daisy flew to intercept the falling swords. She was moving under the power of rist. This meant warrior blood ran through her veins. Once the warrior awoke in a purl, it would move to align itself with the family from which it came. With its pure water and food, Daisy's time in the home at the foot of the mountains had removed all of Prometheus' poisons and pollutions from her, and she became more of who she was created to be. She became more a part of the family from which she came, and this could be an asset or a threat to the Poollé Kii. The specific move of the guardians as Pedagogy stood before them provoked the rist in Daisy's veins. But only after she had moved did Ilii understand the danger of her presence. When Ilii intercepted her, they struck her unconscious and laid her in her bed. The guardians lit a sacred fire beside her and searched her dreams for clues of her ancestral history. They listened closely to the sound of her heart to ensure that it was strong, and, when they were sure she was not a child of any untoward thing, they released her to rest. The first experience with rist for any purl would require an extended time of rest. Rist pulls all the energy and power of a purl into acute focus, and all but the very strong are left weakened afterward. Daisy had been depleted by her first encounter with rist, knocked unconscious by the guards, and then had her thoughts tapped by the mind-probing gaze of the guardians. Although she lay asleep and oblivious to most of this, some part of her was aware of the tests she was taking as she lay unconscious for a cycle. She would have to call on that part of her past in the future.

The meal had been prepared and the table set, and, just as the last plate was placed on the table, hoof beats sounded in the distance. Daisy and her companion went to the door to watch the party approach. Four large horse-like creatures thundered toward them, with one small beast following close. Long before they reached the house, Daisy could see the guardians riding the first two creatures. The lead guardian rode his beast with the young Poollé Kii sitting in the saddle in front of him. The Poollé Kii was holding the reins, which were huge in his small hands. He had taken the reins just as they broke the tree line. He pushed his mount into a run because he was delighted to see that Daisy had survived, and he couldn't wait to hug her and feel her cheeks pressed against his own. It was a rare purl that could survive what Daisy had. When he left days ago with Ilii and the guardians for some special training and to acquire his mount, there was no guarantee that Daisy would be alive or well upon his return. She was both, and he was delighted. The distance was covered in no time, and the dust of the pounding hooves marked their trail straight to the front doors. When he arrived, Pedagogy stopped the mount abruptly, making it rear up on its hind legs. While its front legs were high in the air, he ran to the high point of its head and jumped. Flipping twice in the air he landed with his arms extended and his feet in a primary fighting stance. Ilii bowed their heads, acknowledging the prowess and perfection of the move. The guardians were equally impressed but, being not easily given to open expressions of emotion, showed none. One would have had to read their eyes to know how their hearts filled to see the Poollé Kii at that moment. They were aware of how much he loved his Daisy. With the knowledge that her life was at precarious risk, he left her side to go do what the Poollé Kii must, and this impressed the guardians. He gave himself entirely to his training without allowing the pollution of fear or fret for the only mother he had ever known interfere with the tasks at hand deep in the mountain caves. And now to create a move that had art, innovation, and deadly skill as an expression of love and joy filled them and sealed their dedication to the Poollé Kii.

The Poollé Kii, the guardians, and Ilii arrived about an hour into bright-day. After his perfect and original battle move, Pedagogy ran and jumped into the arms of Daisy. He hugged her neck as she twirled with him in her arms. He received her love and kisses with joy. Ilii wondered at the love and closeness of the two. It was a marvel that drew them close to Daisy in ways she would not know or understand for a long time. When the twirling was done, Daisy carried her Pedagogy, who was almost as long as she was, into the house to eat the meal that had been prepared. The horse-like beasts were also treated to their favorite grasses and berries which had been grown in and around the corral especially for them. Daisy noted that Ilii were almost as deferential to the guardians as they were to Pedagogy. Daisy found the meal delicious and satisfied her in ways she could feel throughout her body. After the meal, Ilii cleared the table, washed, and put away the dishes. They all knew it would be some time before they would be used again.

The seven of them sat in a circle near the fire and talked. Daisy was fascinated by the stories. She didn't know they were part of renewing the mind of Pedagogy. The Poollé Kii sat in the middle of the circle and fell asleep very soon after the guardians began to speak. He lay placid and peaceful. Daisy imagined that she hadn't seen him look so satisfied since the first night he lay nestled beneath her breasts, nursing. The thought brought a tear to her eyes. Ilii mentioned they thought he would have long ago fallen asleep from exhaustion. They marveled at the strength and stamina of the Poollé Kii at such a young age. Ilii then picked up him without disturbing him in any way and placed him in his own bed and returned to the circle. After some stories Daisy hoped never to forget, the guardians began a long slow, deep chant. Ilii joined in, and the circle began to sway in rhythm to the sound of an ancient song. The guardians and Ilii rhythmically placed their palms on the warm Purplynd. Daisy thought herself too tired to understand the images in front of her and wondered if she was asleep as she the purple before her glowed royal blue.

Daisy prided herself in being a light sleeper. She woke just as dawn was lightening the sky. Since these would be the last moments in her wonderful bed, she decided to linger. She listened for sounds of life in the house, and the silence suggested no one was awake. Daisy had great hearing and the time in the mountains had only made it better, so she spread her arms and legs beneath the soft, heavy comforter on the bed. She imagined the blanket in which Pedagogy arrived felt as wonderful to him as her bed did to her at that moment. She lay there enjoying the softness and remembering the stories of the night before. She thought of how Ilii had taught her to tell distances by the songs the birds sang as they called to one another. She thought of the sound of critters drinking at the creek and learned to listen for them to scurry as she approached. She thought of the foods she had learned to find in the forest and how she had learned to walk quietly through the woods, and then BAM! Daisy jumped at the explosion of noise. She sat still in the bed and listened for another noise. Her heart pounded in her chest. Surely, the others would have heard the noise. She wondered why she didn't hear any footsteps or voices. The silence worried her. Daisy got out her bed and began to walk toward the door. When no other noise followed, she decided to grab her robe and see why the others had not been awakened by the sound. She walked by Pedagogy's room, and he was not there. In fact, his entire room had been prepared for his absence. Daisy ran through the empty house and to the front doors. She pulled them open, and there they all were.

The guardians and Ilii were standing beside their mounts, waiting. Other beasts had come in the night; three were packed with large bundles. Daisy's saddled mount stood waiting. Pedagogy was face-to-face with the small beast that had come riderless the day before. They were having a conversation that both were enjoying. Ilii held their long pole, and Daisy realized by the look in their eyes that it was the green-haired purl who had struck the house to rouse her out of the bed. No words were said. An entirely too self-conscious Daisy ran into the house to change her clothes and get ready for the trip. She was embarrassed. They had spoken the night before about the journey ahead. They planned to move before first light. Ilii had begun packing and preparing days before. Daisy had left her things neatly stacked on the dresser before she went to bed. For reasons she didn't understand, she was still not quite herself. She had gone to bed while the others made their final preparations and promised herself that she would put her things in the large saddle sacks just as Ilii had shown her upon waking. Apparently, she was more tired than she realized. She rushed into her room to get dressed and packed, but all of her things had already been removed. She realized Ilii had been in her room. They had packed and removed her things without her hearing them. Daisy reminded herself she was among purple who were unlike any other. They had marvelous abilities that inspired her to become what she had not before imagined was possible, and she was sure they had powers beyond these. The stories they told suggested all their abilities would be needed in the journey ahead. Their dedication to the Poollé Kii matched her love for her Pedagogy, but she had nothing more than a mother's love to contribute to the group. She wondered if it mattered. She remembered a line from the poem. Tears came to her eyes just as the shudder passed through her body. Love was all she had. She was determined that it would be enough.

The group traveled toward the mountains and then turned east. The guardians determined the direction and the pace. They traveled for three months into the wild, past mountains and streams, through thick forest and open plain. Each night they would camp, and the guardians or Ilii would remain awake, watching. In some places, a fire would be lit, and a hot meal served, but many nights, they were careful to make neither fire nor sound. During the day, Pedagogy always sat in the saddle with a guardian or was carried on a guardian's shoulder while the party walked beside the beasts to rest them. Daisy relaxed her mothering as he became closer to these purple masters. The first few weeks, he slept on and off in the saddle, resting in their arms. But, as the weeks went by, he became more and more alert and aware. The small beast Daisy had seen Pedagogy talking to was growing as well. At first, it just danced and played around the other beasts while always staying close to Pedagogy. Near the end of the journey, the beast wanted Pedagogy to ride it. Pedagogy was taught how to take care of it, and the bond between them grew. Daisy learned the beasts were of a rare and special breed: a breed of beasts bred for warriors in ancient times. The animals traveled in bands of no more than seven or eight, and each band was commanded by a leader. The guardians, Ilii, and Pedagogy had found its mother deep in the mountains, and she was the mare ridden by Pedagogy and the guardian. Both this beast and its fold had a circle of iridescent color in its blue mane. Pedagogy had been there at its birth. There was a connection Daisy didn't understand between the beasts and their riders, and the beasts themselves seemed to know more of where they were going than Daisy. There were many adventures through those months, some very frightening. Daisy wouldn't realize how much she had been changed by those three months until her life depended on it.

Daisy had gotten used to life in the wild: sleeping beneath the starry sky, the cold, crisp morning air, and the quiet had become a new type of music to her. It ended abruptly. She sensed it before anyone told her it was true. They had ridden further into bright-day than they had ever before, and the beasts were restless. For three months at each camp, the beasts would encircle the purple, eat, and rest as if they were sentries. In fact, for most of the journey, Daisy was convinced the beasts were as responsible for the route they took as the guardians. But the last two nights, they were anxious and unnerved. The beasts acted as if the guardians made them go where they preferred not.

Their uneasiness reminded Daisy of a night about a month and a half into their journey. It was near a waterfall that flowed into a river. That night, the beasts did not sleep at all but rather stood encircling the camp, facing outward. It was one of the most frightening nights of the journey. The guardians stood watch as they had the night they arrived at the mountain home, only this time they stood back-to-back. Daisy and Pedagogy lay between them. Ilii lie around them. If Ilii slept, it was very lightly. They lay flat on their backs, holding their weapons. Daisy imagined they slept. But they did not sleep at all. Rather, all night, they watched the night sky and the treetops lest death seek to arrive from above. Still, Daisy sensed danger of a sort she had never before. She tried to stay awake but fell asleep, only to have dreams filled with nightmares. Daisy had no doubt she was in one of the sacred and scary places the guardians spoke about in the stories they told. The beasts on that night seemed ferocious and dangerous. Daisy remembered waking as one of them momentarily growled in the darkness. A chill ran through her spine that she never forgot.

On this night, the beasts were fidgety and uncomfortable. As soon as their burdens were unloaded and their saddles removed, they started moving their hooves restlessly. They wanted to run but were waiting for the mare whose fold was with Pedagogy. Pedagogy gave the beast some berries, whispered in her ear, and then patted her neck as he said his goodbye. The mare raised her head high and reared on her hind legs as if to say farewell. She then let out a sound Daisy was able to interpret but not translate, turned, and ran off with her fold with the other anxious beasts close behind. Daisy wondered why she didn't panic as the only means of transportation for the last three months ran into the woods without them. She was confident the family she had grown a part of were capable of thriving in any circumstance, and no one else was alarmed that the beasts were gone. Then another strange thing happened.

After dinner, as they were sitting together in circle, one of the guardians asked Daisy to recite the poem. This was strange because there had been no indication the guardians knew the poem existed. She was unaware, each day, that the guardian and the Poollé Kii recited the poem at dawn. She had kept the note hidden and as secret as she could. Still, she was not surprised they knew. Had she not been under their guidance and protection for three months, and had they not won her complete trust, she would have attempted to keep the words from them. But she remembered the night at the waterfall. It had taught her to trust that the guardians knew things that were essential for her life and that of her child—their Poollé Kii. She remembered, before that night, Ilii had been quiet and extremely aware of their surroundings all bright-day. When they finally made camp, there was no fire made or meal cooked. She and Pedagogy were given biscuits and some dried fruit, but none of the others ate or spoke. As the night turned dark, Ilii held their weapons at the ready, and one of the guardians drew its sword. The other guardian held Pedagogy's hand and threw a satchel over his shoulder. The two of them walked into the water under the three full moons. They walked until the water reached the chest of the child and stopped. Daisy almost jumped into the river as she saw her child dip beneath the swift current, but before she could stand up, his head reappeared, glistening as the water reflected the light of the moons. She watched as the guardian pulled Pedagogy's blanket out of the satchel and placed it in the hands of her child. Pedagogy lifted the folded blanket in his hands, tilted his head to the night sky, and shouted something as loud as his little voice could. The leaves on the shoreline trees shuttered in response. Then he held the corners of the blanket and threw it open and down to the surface of the water. As the blanket touched the waters flowing around the Poollé Kii, his skin began to glow purple and then a bright royal blue. As the blue light emanating from the Poollé Kii reached the blanket, it also began to glow in the night with the light Daisy had first seen on the night she received her Pedagogy.

The Poollé Kii standing in the water appeared as more than her Pedagogy. His skin continued to glow royal blue in the darkness. The blanket grew brighter and then sparked. Light began to leach into the water and flow down the river. The bright spark of the blanket was what the guardian was waiting for, and immediately after it occurred, he rushed the child out of the water. One of Ilii took the Poollé Kii, dried him off, and wrapped him in layers of warm cloth. The guardian wrung out the blanket, and the excess water spilled as light into the water and flowed down river. The two guardians held the blanket up to the light of the moons. The blanket glowed and seemed translucent. The guardians stared at it. Daisy was told later that the guardians were reading a map that the blanket could only reveal when the Poollé Kii held it in these waters under the full moons. It was the map that had led them precisely to where they were. It was also a map of the life journey of the Poollé Kii. It showed the path to his success and the dangers that could lead to his death. So, when Daisy was asked to recite the poem, she complied. So, much had happened in the year and three months since she had left Biscuit. She knew she was caught up in something greater than anything she had imagined.

She recited the poem, and as she did, tears welled up in her eyes. Then the guardian asked the question that Ilii had asked before. It surprised Daisy that Ilii knew to ask. But the guardian's question came with something else. His voice and tone took Daisy back to the first night the guardians appeared. There was danger and power in the question. It felt as if the razor edge of his sword were asking. Daisy wasn't afraid but realized in that saccadic moment how grave a task she was being presented. Would she keep her promise? With tears streaming down her cheeks, she said she would. Her answer satisfied her inquisitor. She wept at his approval because she knew what he saw in her eyes was truer than any words she could say, no matter how strongly she felt them. The guardian knew. She had passed the test.

That night, the guardians stood as they had when they first entered Daisy's dream months ago. They faced the direction in which the horse-like beasts seemed terrified. Two of Ilii stood guard, facing the direction the beasts had run. Daisy and her Pedagogy lay in the center of them all. As the child in her arms slept, Daisy wished she knew how to fight, so she, too, could protect her child. As the thought passed through her mind, Ilii turned to look at her. Their eyes met, and Daisy heard in her heart that the love she had for her Pedagogy was all she would need. That thought sent her into a dreamless sleep. The long night had its tests of which Daisy would remain unaware.

Pedagogy began to stretch and stir. Dawn was on the horizon. He wished he could lie and sleep for hours. The thought came into his mind that there would be times to rest, but this was not one of them. The thought was familiar. It was as if he were having a conversation between his four-year-old and forty-year-old self. Pedagogy sat up, yawned, and opened his eyes. As he did, Ilii were there to wash his face and hands. The day was filled with activity and preparation. Daisy filled in where she could, and the skills she had learned in the house by the mountains came into full use. Pedagogy went off with Ilii and returned dragging a bird almost as large as himself. He was very proud to show Daisy that he, too, had played a role in the day's preparation. Daisy wondered if Pedagogy had caught and wrestled the bird himself. She dismissed the thought when she realized that the bird would have had to have been killed. She didn't want to think that her child had faced that danger or done such a deed at his young and tender age. But he had.

Ilii, Pedagogy, and Daisy spent the day preparing for the bright-day meal. Daisy knew this was a special day. All the signs pointed to a grand celebration, and she would have been caught up in the joy of preparing for it except for the guardians. They stood as still as statues. There was no indication they had moved since the night before. They stood there in the trees, facing an open meadow Daisy only noticed when she had wandered to gather some wild herbs for the meal. They wore the same cloaks that covered them from their shoulders to just above the soles of their feet. The hoods covered their heads, and their hands rested on the pommel of their broadswords. Daisy believed there was good reason they stood there. She couldn't imagine what the reason was, but she knew it was real.

Then, just as bright-day began, the thunderous sound of hoof beats filled the air as the ground itself shook. Ilii took the Poollé Kii into a tepee they had set up only hours before. Without sound or signal, the guardians began to move toward the clearing. They moved as if they were one very dangerous purl with two broadswords straight toward the sounds. The green-haired purl had also disappeared at the thunder, and by the time Daisy looked to find her, she was coming toward her. She brought a beautiful cloak that shone with a yellow light and gave it to Daisy. Daisy adorned the regal cloak and accepted her elevated role. Ilii appeared with the Poollé Kii who had been dressed and robed. The five of them followed the path the guardians had created and walked to the edge of the trees. The guardians had walked to the specific place the blanket map had told them to find. It was not exactly in the center of the field but clearly off to the left. They had to study the night sky and the daylight signs to find the exact location the blanket had shown. It had taken until this moment for them to be sure. And the moment the spot was revealed, they moved toward it. They began walking slowly as if they were stalking prey and then began moving faster and faster until they were running to a specific spot that was attempting to evade them. Suddenly, they both leaped into the air, spinning their swords. The edges of their swords met at the height of their jump, and a spark was seen even in the bright-daylight. They landed face-to-face on one knee with their swords planted in the ground near the outside shoulder of each of them. Just as the swords struck the ground, four of the horse-like beasts came thundering from across the meadow.

Daisy watched the pageantry, believing it was all ceremonial, but something inside her wondered if she was missing something very real but invisible to her own perceptions. The four beasts carried guardians robed and armed like the two who had cared for Daisy and her Pedagogy. They rode hard and fast toward the kneeling guardians. Daisy's heart began to race. The four beasts covered the open field faster than she could gather their intent. Just before they reached the two kneeling figures, their swords flashed a bright reflection of the suns as they drew them. The beasts began to encircle the two guardians and continued running around and around. Dust began to rise until Daisy had no idea what was happening in the distance. The thunder of hooves pounding the ground continued, and she thought for a moment that they were headed toward her. She tried to peer through the dust using all the hunting skills she had learned over the past year. Just as she believed she could perceive what was afoot, they emerged from the dust heading straight toward her. The four beasts were riderless. Daisy wondered what had happened or what was still happening in the dust where the guardians were, but the approaching creatures obscured any view of them. Before the fierce beasts were too close, they slowed to a trot and then walked until they stopped in a semicircle about twelve feet in front of the Poollé Kii. One of the beasts covered the rest of the distance and came to the Poollé Kii. The green-haired purl placed Pedagogy on the beast and mounted it behind him. Daisy and the others climbed atop the others, and the beasts walked to where the dust was settling.

When they arrived at where the guardians were, Daisy found the ground had been cleared and laid bare in a complete circle. Six guardians stood equally separated around the perimeter of the very large circle. Their swords pierced the ground and seemed ablaze. Daisy didn't know whether the swords were reflecting the suns' light of bright-day or emitting their own. Ilii and Daisy dismounted. The Poollé Kii alone rode his beast to the center of the circle. The beast bent down, and the Poollé Kii jumped off it and stood. The horse-like beast left the circle and walked its circumference with the others behind her. Then the beast led them away in the direction they had arrived. The guardians each stepped forward in front of their swords, which remained stuck into the heart of Purplynd. All but one bowed before the Poollé Kii. The guardian whom Pedagogy had ridden with for most of the journey did not kneel but approached the Poollé Kii and called for Daisy to enter the circle. Then Ilii brought Pedagogy's blanket and folded it at his feet. The guardian then asked Daisy for the letter. She took it from the pocket beneath her heart inside her garment. As she removed it, she felt the warmth it had brought her and feared she would lose the comfort it had conveyed. She fought back the tears filling her eyes. As she was handing the note to the guardian, one tear broke through, ran down her cheeks, and leaped off her face and onto the letter. The tear sparked the folded page, and a light appeared where it hit the parchment and began to dissipate. The guardian took the letter and, with speed and agility that was hard to follow with the eye, cut the letter into six equal pieces. Daisy's heart sank. Pedagogy was excited. The guardian threw the pieces into the air. At that very moment, the other guardians leaped from their kneeling positions and, flipping in the air, each caught one of the pieces. The sixth piece fell slowly and landed on the blanket folded at the Poollé Kii's feet.

Songs were sung and words spoken in languages that Daisy did not understand. Before the last song was sung and as the last sun set, each of the guardians removed their sword and placed their piece of the parchment into the opening the sword had left. They each took a flask from their belt and poured glowing water into the hole and onto the planted parchment. As each one did this, light rose from Purplynd. The Poollé Kii was last to take the piece from atop his blanket and plant it in the hole left by the sword of his guardian. Then, he sat in the center of the circle to begin the final tests of his lineage. The tests would take three cycles to complete. If he were an impostor, they would surely kill him. If he bore only some of the Quel-Kha seed, he would survive the tests, depending on how strong the blood of Quel-Kha was in his veins. His guardian and Ilii believed he was of the seed of Quel-Kha, but the four guardians who had come had tests that would remove all doubt. If he were truly descended from Quel-Kha, he could live as a warrior or maybe, with time, become a guardian. But, if the six strands of poollé united in him, it would confirm that his lineage was pure. If his mind were strong enough to restore the memories of his ancestors and he found his true mate, he would be the Gha-Poollé Kii, whose destiny was to defeat the reign of evil, restore the balance of life, and rule the planet. But this bright-day was just the beginning of the ritual. There were days of tests ahead. There were terrors that Daisy would have to witness and fears she would have to overcome before any of them would know whether the one they called the Poollé Kii was, in fact, the one who had been promised to come.

LOVE, DEATH, AND DANGER

AFTER THOSE MOMENTS IN the wild, Daisy and Pedagogy settled on the outskirts of the light-eyed city of Noth, not far from the place where the last ceremony took place. Ilii opened a laundromat where the poor purple of Noth came to wash their clothes. Daisy and her growing child lived in the cottage in the back. Ilii kept them both safe and out of the eye of any dark-eyed authorities. Pedagogy helped in the laundry and, as he grew older, became quite handy with the machines. He didn't attend the underfunded light-eyed public schools that served more to catalog and discourage the light-eyed population than to inform them in any useful manner. Instead, he and Ilii took many camping trips that included lessons on life, danger, and history. Their trips also included some contests Daisy could not have imagined and would have been horrified if she had known.

As her child grew into his teens and beyond, the camping trips became journeys to faraway places, and the time in Noth was occupied by Ilii and Pedagogy's passion for restoring vehicles. In the summers after his teenage years, Pedagogy and Ilii would drive their nicest and most elaborate vehicle creations in parades through town or even as far away as Biscuit. Meanwhile, Daisy contented herself to run the laundry, and all was well until something caught her eye. That day, one glimpse at a newspaper changed everything for everyone. Some purl had left a Promethean newspaper in the laundry, and while Daisy was cleaning up the laundromat, she saw an advertisement in it for a lecture on the ancient legends of Purplynd. The ad held her gaze.

"Hear the stories of the ancient purple, potions, and plants!" the ad announced. "Learn the magic of the past and find its power," it promised. The advertisement called her. That evening, Daisy walked to the cottage still thinking about the lecture.

By the time she woke in the morning, she had decided to go. If Ilii or Pedagogy had been home or aware of her thoughts, they would have warned her of the danger. But Daisy was left to her own mind, and she was confident it was strong enough to protect the information it held. No memories from the past came to caution her. She forgot about the darkness that had once captured her. She forgot Tepa. She forgot the poison she had unwittingly consumed. She forgot the terror she felt from time to time as she cared for the child who came to her as a gift. She forgot that she had once put him in the arms of danger. She did not imagine that she was about to do it again, only this time neither of them would escape. As the days passed, her desire to hear the lecture grew stronger. There were forces at work which she was unaware. And then, the night of the lecture arrived.

That evening, she left the laundry early. She wrapped herself in a scarf to hide as much of her facial features as she could without it being conspicuous. She walked to the other side of Noth, careful to check if she was being followed. She thought it would be ridiculous for anyone to follow her, but she wanted to practice for the journey home, and she wanted to be able to tell Pedagogy she had used the utmost caution coming and going. She waited at the bus stop where the light-eyed purple would catch the bus to the border of Prometheus. A small crowd grew. The bus came, and Daisy boarded. As the bus wound its way through the outskirts of Noth, it became crowded before it reached the train station into the heart of the city. The light-eyed workers flowed out of the bus, most of them toward the train, some to other buses. Daisy moved with the flow. She had studied the route over and over so as not to stand out as someone who didn't know how to get where she was going. She wore sunglasses to hide behind, but as the suns were setting, if she didn't take them off, they would make her stand out. She reached the ticket booth for the lecture with enough light for it to be somewhat reasonable for her to have them on. She knew that the audience would be mostly dark-eyed purple, which made her feel confident that she wouldn't run into anyone from the laundromat. Still, being surrounded by such dark-eyed company made her uncomfortable.

Daisy took her assigned seat and breathed a deep sigh. It had been ages since she sat around the fire in the mountains, listening to the ancient tales. Sitting in the darkened theater, she felt safe and wonderful. There were so many pieces of the puzzle she longed to put together, and the ad convinced her this lecture would answer her questions and address her curiosity. Her mind moved back to the fireplace and the dirt floor of the home at the foot of the mountains. She remembered Ilii and the ancient tales that were so real. She began to pull the stories from her past to the present. The things she had seen and done began to drift back into her mind. Caught up in her memories, she barely heard the introduction of the speaker and woke out of her near trance as the introduction ended. The speaker was invited to the podium. The audience rose in loud applause. Then he appeared. It was strange because the first thing Daisy noticed was the color of his skin. She thought perhaps the sunglasses she had just removed were playing a trick. It was only a glimpse as his figure appeared and then disappeared through the standing crowd. Daisy shifted to see around the purple standing in front of her to confirm what she saw. Everyone was standing and applauding, and she couldn't get another look at him until everyone was seated. He began to speak, and the audience embraced a hushed silence. His voice was melodious. He spoke in a rhythm that was soothing but powerfully invited the hearers into his story. He told intriguing tales about the mysteries of the ancient past. He mentioned some names Daisy recognized and some she did not. It was wonderful, and time passed as if it were a dream. The lecture concluded, and Daisy made her way back to the far side of Noth. Her mind was so full of the things she had heard that she forgot to check if she was being followed. She was in awe of the things she remembered and the new things that had just been presented. She was drawn to the one who knew so much of things she thought were secrets entrusted only to her. The delight of listening to the stories she had come to love made her forget the momentary shock and horror she felt when she saw his skin glowing red the moment he appeared on stage.

When the red glow of the speaker's flesh appeared, Daisy wanted to flee. The thought to leave came as an instantaneous pulse that ran through her being. There were no clear thoughts accompanying the jolt. She did not "think" about running away. There was no intellectually discernible information she understood provoking her to flee the theater. It was just a feeling. It was just an instruction that momentarily pulsed through her being. Her search to confirm that his flesh was red was an attempt to give her some reason to leave. But by the time he was again in view, he was already speaking. The sound of his voice calmed her every fear and erased all else. That was why the next day, as she held the program in her hand, she had no memory of the color of his skin or the shock she felt as he walked onto the stage. She only remembered the joy of hearing about the ancient mysteries and myths. The lecture program had a bio of the speaker who was a professor at the university. Light-eyed purple were most often ignored, or outright discouraged, when attending or applying to the university. They understood that even entering Prometheus was never in their best interest. But this brochure had invited and even encouraged light-eyed participation. So much was drawing her to this experience. After reading the pamphlet several times, Daisy was convinced this was something she had to do.

Within weeks, Daisy was enrolled in the class and, not long after, received an offer to work in the cafeteria as a means of paying for it. Her Pedagogy was a young man now and often away with Ilii. The laundry was light work, and Daisy promised Pedagogy and Ilii that she would be careful. Daisy threw herself into the study and discovery of ancient Purplynd. Some of the tales she read were versions of the stories Ilii, the guardians, and Pedagogy spoke about. Some of the books she read had versions of meals she had helped prepare. They mentioned the use of mysterious roots and potions she knew exactly. It was fascinating to her. Finding out there was a field of study that spoke about these things and that there were others interested in it was a gift she had not expected. All the while, Daisy was very careful not to reveal any of her own firsthand knowledge or so she thought. She didn't want anyone to suspect she had experiences that would prove these were not just stories about the past. She did, however, question a few times why the literature was so complimentary of tinkerers and whisperers and never questioned their motives? The one class turned into three consecutive classes on the ancient life and religion of Purplynd.

Like any good instructor, the professor took interest in his star student. There were a few after-class conversations Daisy initiated and enjoyed and several classes where Daisy and the professor were on a page the rest of the class couldn't find. One such time was when Daisy questioned whether Quel was the actual son of Kha or whether there was some other meaning to the story. The professor claimed to have translated the text personally and assured her it was indeed the case. Daisy loved the classes and all she had learned. She didn't know some of the essay questions on the tests were based on her interests. She also didn't know that some of her questions revealed more about her than she intended. When the semesters were over, and she had taken all the university offered on the subject, Daisy tried to return to her life. It was difficult. She was drawn to learn more about the past and, strangely, had a growing desire to talk with others about the things she knew. As she thought about the wonderful experience, she also found herself drawn to the instructor who shared her passion for the past and had taught her so much. She was anxious for the final class papers to be graded and returned. She was sure she did her best, but she longed to see what the professor thought of her work. In his occasional notes on her work, he would often suggest readings not on the syllabus or write long letters describing his journeys into the wild to discover and uncover the past. When the package of papers came, Daisy was not surprised to see her perfect course grade. What did take her by surprise was the handwritten message from her professor. It was a beautifully written letter on his personal stationery thanking her for participating in his classes and extolling her prowess and aptitude for anthropology. The note was flattering but what made her heart skip was something else. The professor thanked Daisy for reigniting the love he had for his work and suggested she was, in part, the cause of his promotion. He ended the handwritten note inviting her to his promotion dinner. Without talking to anyone wise enough to dissuade her, she accepted.

Pedagogy and Ilii were far away when Daisy stared into the mirror, wondering why she had taken such care to dress for the banquet. She thought to herself that she would probably sit somewhere in a corner where the light-eyed purple would be ignored and ill fed. She wondered if her professor would even notice she had come. These worries were a waste of her time. At the banquet, her assigned seat was just to the right and not very far from the head table. In fact, the seat reserved for her was directly in the line of sight of the guest of honor. Being so close to the front of the room made her even more self-conscious. She was the only light-eyed purl she could see who wasn't serving food. Many, if not all, of the Prometheus elite were in attendance. And, to Daisy's surprise, she learned—far from being promoted to the head of the department—her instructor was being commissioned as the chancellor of the entire university. When the dratsab entered and sat at the table with her instructor, Daisy thought about doing her best Cinderella imitation and running home. Just as she was seriously considering her escape, the professor caught her eye. He stared into them and raised his teacup to her. She lifted hers in response, and just as she sipped her tea, a warm sense washed through her body. The gray of his temples and broadness of his shoulders stood out. He looked so handsome in his formal wear. When he rose to give his speech, Daisy thought he was taller than she remembered. His remarks about the plans for the university and the effect of those plans on the greater world were thorough and comprehensive, but Daisy didn't comprehend much of his plan. She was captured by the sound of his melodious voice. Its hidden bass tones reverberated in the core of her being and mesmerized her.

The event ended, and Daisy began to make her way out. She kept her head down to keep purple from noticing the color of her eyes. But he found her. The newly installed and powerful chancellor found her. He touched her arm and asked if she were going to leave without saying goodbye. His touch was gentle. His voice was warm yet strong. And again, the baritone pulses hidden in his expression moved through her entire being. Before she knew why or even thought it through, Daisy accepted his invitation to lunch. And that was how their relationship moved from the safe distance of student and instructor to something dangerous. The next few weeks and months were filled with phone calls, rendezvous, and sweet tea meetings at small cafés.

Daisy was swept off her feet. Never before had she fallen so fast or so hopelessly in love. They shared a deep affection for the ancient tales. The chancellor enjoyed having someone as interested in the myths and magic of the past as he was. Daisy loved learning more about the world of her son, and, as she did, she felt increasingly indebted to this man who had first inspired her those many months ago. Ilii and Pedagogy had come and gone on several trips during the courtship. Daisy attempted to keep her growing attachment to her instructor from her family. She didn't really know why it should be kept secret. And she was deliberate not to tell the purl who was capturing her heart about her son or the things she had seen and heard that were so similar to the myths and stories the chancellor studied.

Keeping secrets from the ones you love is never wise. It corrupts the light on which love is grown and secured, but Daisy couldn't help herself. She knew her growing love for the dark-eyed chancellor was dangerous. He was an important and well-connected purl who held a strategic political position. He was often in the public's view. She was a powerless, light-eyed purl with secrets. The internal tension this produced was painful. Daisy would get determined to talk things through with her family and then remember the look of his enchanting eyes. They were eyes that asked for her protection. It was a look that begged for maternal love and suggested that only she could heal his wounds. Ilii and Pedagogy could see a difference in Daisy and suspected she was keeping some secrets. The chancellor knew Daisy listened much more than she spoke and suspected Daisy had some secrets she didn't yet share with him. He was patient because he was confident. He believed, in time, she would answer any question he asked. It came suddenly.

Their rendezvous were almost always somewhere on the outskirts of Prometheus, usually in some secluded spot but always indoors and often at a table in a corner. The chancellor said it was to shield Daisy from the prying eyes of the media. Once, they met in an obscure, very high-end restaurant where everyone seemed to know him. Daisy didn't feel comfortable, and they left almost as soon as they were seated. But this day was different. The chancellor had asked Daisy to meet him for a festival sponsored by the botanical gardens called Bright-Day in the Park. He had been away on one of his trips and said he couldn't wait to share what he found. She brought the sandwiches, and he brought the wine. Being in the bright sunshine made Daisy feel wonderful. The chancellor seemed especially excited to see her and share his special news. Daisy toyed with the idea that he would propose, even though she knew that would be crazy. It surprised her that she would think about anyone in that way. She wasn't sure she did. What she was sure of was that he communicated deep feelings for her. She was sure she thought he was handsome and strong. She believed he would protect her if she needed it. She had meant to talk with Pedagogy about all these things before she left for the park. She wanted to finally tell her son everything and have the two men in her life meet, but for some reason, her conversation with Pedagogy was confusing that morning. Daisy thought it was because he was too preoccupied with his upcoming trip, and she was excited the chancellor had asked her to the park, but other things were in play.

Since living in the mountains, Daisy had grown away from cooking and eating meats. On rare occasions they would have fowl, but Pedagogy and Ilii preferred the wonderful vegetables made with love and seasoned with the roots and herbs they brought back from their adventures and journeys throughout the whole of Purplynd. But on this day, Daisy made her famous beast and bread dish. Long ago, Tepa had taught her the recipe, and whenever she made it, purple raved about it. The dish was traditionally a dark-eyed delicacy. When Pedagogy was a child, the one time that Daisy made it, he had refused to eat it. Ilii didn't care much for it either, so Daisy hadn't made the dish in what she considered forever. She thought she had done a fair job at cooking it and hoped the chancellor would like it. He loved it. The food sent him into a wonderful place. He began to share his heart and hopes for the planet. He spoke of how he had spent most of his life looking for treasures and how he thought that she was the greatest treasure of all. He said many such things and then tenderly removed Daisy's sunglasses and kissed her. The kiss made her swoon. A warm wave washed over her, and her defenses came crashing down like a child's tower of blocks.

She lay in his embrace silently as the suns slowly sailed toward the horizon. That was when he told her his news. He wanted her to be the first to know that, after years of searching, he had found another poollé tree. It would be delivered to the campus soon. When he shared the news, a strange sensation went through Daisy's body. She was sure she had kept her secrets. She was sure she had only talked about the things she read in the books. But, at that moment, she wanted to tell the one who had taken her heart everything she knew. She listened as the purl with his arms wrapped around her, talked about how difficult it was to find a poollé tree and how rare it was to find one young enough to be transplanted. He told her that he had learned many things concerning poollé trees. He knew, after years of searching, he would eventually find a poollé tree but confessed that the trees he had found in the past had all died. The three unsuccessful attempts he and his team had made over the last ten years had almost extinguished his hope of success. It had cost a fortune. This last find might be his last chance to succeed. Powerful forces were at work against him and this area of his work.

As he spoke, the chancellor was no longer talking to Daisy but was lost in his own thoughts. What he needed was someone who knew how to transplant it. As he spoke, his tenderness and brilliance entered her ears and wrapped themselves around her heart. He was vulnerable and his reputation was on the line. She wanted to help him. She wanted to never be without his arms around her. Perhaps it was the wine. Perhaps it was the kiss she could still taste on her lips. Whatever it was, Daisy did something she had never done before: She spoke without taking her thoughts through the "Pedagogy filter."

She said, "I know someone who knows how to plant it."

As those words broke the silence, a tremor moved through her body and broke her out of the trance she had fallen into with the arms wrapped around her. Daisy sat straight up. Her heart started to pound within her chest. She wasn't sure of what she had just said. The chancellor wanted to know more. Daisy began to collect her wits. She spoke of Pedagogy without revealing his relationship to her. She spoke of him as one who knew how to grow things. She told of an instance when he had found a broken amest branch and nurtured it back to life. (Amest is a very rare flowering bush that grew in the wild and was referred to in the ancient tales.) Daisy wasn't sure she should have told that story, but she was trying to help and was still a little panicked. Then, before the chancellor could ask her to give him Pedagogy's contact information, Daisy took out her phone and called her son. She left a message:

"The chancellor has brought back a rare tree, and I told him that you could grow anything. Would you come to the university and plant it for him?"

She spoke fast, and the chancellor helped her.

"The tree will be delivered in two days, and instructions will be left for you at my office." Daisy ended the message with, "Could you please try to help him with this?"

The chancellor reached to pull her back into his embrace. Daisy's mind was racing. The chancellor whispered in her ear. He kissed her on her cheek. She began to feel calm. He asked her if she would start calling him by his first name. She said yes just as the last sun set. Daisy was caught between two worlds. Her love and devotion to her son fought with the feelings that were swirling inside her. She got up and gathered her things. It was time to go.

She kissed his cheek and whispered in his ear, "Thank you for a wonderful bright-day in the park, Syng."

Syng gazed at Daisy as she walked into the distance. His eyes were fixed on her figure until she disappeared into the crowd. A strange sensation bounced between his heart and mind. He was moved by his mark. The pretty bird that had fallen into his trap had become dear to him. The ads in the papers about the lecture were designed to find and catalog all purple who had an interest in the mysteries. The ancient stories could be dangerous. They could ferment rebellion if they were left unleashed and infected with light-eyed delusions. But Syng hadn't planned on Daisy. He was drawn to her from the first time his teaching assistant showed him her work. Her papers showed a provocative depth and curiosity. He was captured by her mind. He was intrigued by her interest and intelligence. The way she approached the material was typical for a light-eyed purl, but there was something more. Syng began reading more of her work and even directed some of his lessons to address her perspectives and confusions, one being her suggestion that the plant-based diet of the ancients heightened their awareness. Syng dismissed such foolishness and incorporated nutritionists and scientific support for carnivorous diets. His desire to date her began just as it had in the past with many of his other students. The fact that his charm did not have the same effect on Daisy that it had on his impressionable, younger students attracted him to her even more. When she walked away, Syng remembered the wonderful beast and bread he had eaten. Its familiar flavor had delighted him, even if he could not remember why he found it so enjoyable. He was still convinced Daisy was his to do whatever he wished, but he was beginning to feel attached to her in strange ways. He rose to return to his vehicle, and as he did, he chuckled to himself, wondering if he was in love.

The cooled air of the limousine made Syng begin to feel himself. Undoubtedly, it had been the best few weeks of his life. At long last, he and his crew of scientists had found a stand of poollé. This was rare and had only occurred three other times in his life. Each time, he had brought the legendary prize back with fanfare and hope, only to be disappointed by the tree not accepting its transplanting. He believed this time, with the help of Daisy's gardener, he would have success. His elevation to chancellor was the result of long years of struggle and politics. He had finally climbed to the office that would allow unchecked opportunity to mete out the revenge on his enemies. The office of the chancellor was second only to the dratsab. The chancellor had his own security forces, a very positive public perception, and the minds of the young at his command and influence. The dratsab was the supreme leader of the military; he was law and punishment. He was the one purple recognized and feared, but the chancellor was loved and admired. The chancellor's office was where benevolence and hope were harbored. Purple looked to the chancellor's office for the joys and hope of life on Purplynd. What very few knew was the chancellor's office was a mix of manipulation and complicity. It worked hand in glove with the office of the dratsab. They were carrot and stick.

Syng now held the carrot, and it pleased him. He smiled to himself, took a deep breath, and sighed. As he did, Daisy came back to his mind. He wondered at the feelings that came into him as he imagined her voice and remembered her face. He had not loved anyone for so long he was not sure if that was what he was feeling. There was something special about her, and he knew she was an important piece in the puzzle of his plans. He shook his head and smiled again when he thought of the contact she had given him for the poollé tree transplant. He imagined that, at last, he would have a living poollé tree outside his office window. He told his driver to head to the Panthae, closed his eyes, and rested.

Later in the evening, Syng called to thank Daisy for the contact. Her gardener had called him, and they had spoken. Everything had been arranged. He was inspired by the young purl's knowledge and was anxious to watch the planting. He invited himself over for dinner after the tree was planted so that the two of them could celebrate.

Pedagogy and Ilii were aware of Daisy's growing fascination with an unknown purl. She didn't reveal who it was, but they knew it was someone associated with the classes she was taking. Ilii had coached Daisy carefully. They helped her guard her heart and thoughts as she interacted in her classes, and they had tutored her on which of her experiences could be shared and which could not. But their adventures abroad kept them engaged and away from home often. And recently, Ilii had been especially focused on the Poollé Kii because the time for his pairing proscribed by the guardians had come, and they wanted to get him away from the Promethean females. Had they been informed that the purl Daisy spoke of was the instructor of the class, they would have asked a lot more questions. It was during their last extended trip that Syng began the final moves to capture Daisy's heart. Pedagogy could tell from the message his mother left him that whoever this was that needed his help did not know that he was her son. She identified Syng as "her friend," but something about the inflection in her voice suggested this friend was the one Daisy had been growing attached to.

It wasn't until Pedagogy called the chancellor and spoke with him that he realized he was being asked to plant a poollé tree. That changed matters a great deal. Poollé trees held the wisdom of the past in ways that could be transferred into the present in potent manifestations. Pedagogy needed to know if the chancellor simply had an academic attachment or if his interests were more malevolent. Pedagogy was well-trained and feared no darkness. He knew he was born to fight the evil powers of the planet, and he was prepared. Still, there is a darkness that hides in happiness, and Pedagogy wondered whether the time had come for it to reveal itself. He and Ilii sensed the meeting was important, and they agreed that he should plant the tree. He wondered whether it would stand as a guardian for good or a tool for evil. He had no idea how quickly his answer would come.

The morning arrived when the tree would be delivered and planted. The chancellor was excited and rose early from his lair in the bowels of the Panthae to hurry to campus. He wouldn't make it. The ride to the campus was interrupted by an urgent call. It was a back-channel communication from an officer of the Promethean Police department. A body had been found. More accurately, the remains of a body had been found down river from a vehicle fitting the description of one for which he had been looking. The authority, one of his former enforcers, could hold off the report of what he found for a few hours, maybe for the first part of the day, but, by bright-day, the scene would be crawling with the police and the dratsab's purple.

Syng told his driver to head out of town to the location. He cursed the turn of events. He had hoped to watch the poollé tree get planted. He knew there was only a slight chance it would live, but he wanted to meet this gardener whom Daisy knew so well. Their talk on the phone had intrigued him. Although the purl did not say much, he was confident and did not get befuddled at all when Syng spoke about ancient plants and soils. Still, something that had disappeared twenty-five years ago had surfaced. And Syng was a manipulator of too many things to trust in coincidence.

Long ago, a woman and child had driven from Biscuit in a vehicle that had no registration or traceable devices. A few cameras had caught brief glimpses of it, but it had disappeared in the darkness. Such vehicles were not uncommon among the light-eyed purple. They often hobbled together vehicles out of the scraps left by the dark-eyed, and they enjoyed trying to make them undetectable to the Promethean authorities and tracking devices. It was the woman and child he had been curious about. Years ago, spies had brought him pictures of what he thought was a replica of an ancient crib design. It was the crib of a legendary warrior and master called the Poollé Kii. The Poollé Kii was said to have defeated the dark forces and vanquished evil. An ancient myth told of how Quel-Kha crafted a crib out of a poollé tree to protect his son "from death and danger" as he went to battle. He had been alerted to the existence of the crib by Tepa, another of the purple he had found through one of his lectures. She was ambitious and had approached him after he had spoken. He sensed her attraction to power and invited her to the Panthae. Not long after, she showed up wearing dark glasses. Soon after that, became one of his "projects." Her mention of the crib caught his attention. He thought it would be a nice gift for his grandson, but the more questions he asked, the more mysteries appeared. The scant records of the mother were inconclusive, and there were no records of her child. The night before his agents were to get his answers, the mother, child, and crib disappeared in the vehicle that had just been found.

The vehicle was far from Biscuit and had crashed into a ravine. Years ago, the trunk of two small trees had stopped its tumble down the steep embankment. The creeping vines and brush had, over the years, concealed its presence. It was the unusually heavy rains that had freed it from its hiding place as the swollen soil released the trees, roots, trunk, and the vehicle they held into the river below. By the time Syng arrived, the officers had positively identified the vehicle as the one that had disappeared long ago. The remains of the body were not so easy to identify. It seemed to have been partially buried for some time. Pieces of clothing were found, and their labels were being traced in hopes of confirming their original purchaser. Syng asked if the remains of a child or a crib were among the wreckage. None had been found, but he commanded the search to continue until the dratsab's purple arrived. Syng examined the vehicle and the bones for himself. He was looking for any clue that would suggest things were other than what they appeared.

The thought that the female remains had endured terrors not associated with a vehicle crash washed past his mind. But there was nothing definitive he could find to suggest something was amiss. Still, a strange caution within him attempted to reveal itself. A small, quiet feeling deep inside him suggested that he was in danger. He resolved to spend some resources in the area in an attempt to recover the crib or what may remain of it, which he surmised must be somewhere among the debris. The woman he had hoped to question was dead and the child likely eaten by bird and beasts. He left instructions to find the crib and headed back before any of the dratsab's purple could witness he was ever there. Entering the limousine reminded him of his recently elevated status and erased the small cautionary voice inside him. All was well because he was the chancellor and had the power to enforce his will and exact his revenge. The thought pleased him. He relaxed into the plush comfort of the limousine. The sight of the wreckage and the remains mingling with his newly gained power made him hungry, but not for food. His mind wandered to thoughts of Daisy, and he remembered his date. He checked the time and told his driver to ensure that he would not be tardy.

Pedagogy arrived early in the morning. He had received the message from the chancellor's assistant that the chancellor had been called away on an urgent matter. She had communicated the last of his instructions and ensured Pedagogy would receive all the help he needed. The staff, including her, was at his command and disposal. Syng also wanted Pedagogy to know that his medical staff was also nearby. Syng knew the poollé tree had life in ways that were similar to purple and wanted the pharmaceuticals the medical team had at the ready if they could be of any use. In addition, Syng wanted to keep his trip as secret as possible. Pedagogy wondered how thorough the chancellor's knowledge of poollé trees was. Such knowledge was hard to come by and was seldom simply a matter of academic interest. He found the tree being guarded on the quad in plain sight of the chancellor's office window. It was small but stood straight and strong as if it were of noble blood. It stood, a young warrior separated from the fighting family of which it was born to be a part, captured by its enemy.

Its roots were wrapped in a breathing cloth but much too tightly. The first thing Pedagogy did was to relax the cloth around the root bulb. When he did, the tree sighed, but he was the only one who was aware of it. The sigh told him that this poollé tree had strong life connections. Looking at it, Pedagogy believed it held the history of deep and strong things. There were warrior veins in the leaves, and the bark was woven in patterns of war and peace.

In a whisper only the tree could hear, he said, "I am the Poollé Kii of the line of Miis."

He then cupped his hands, and the tree dropped several leaves into it. When the leaves touched the open palms, a pulse of life flowed through his being. He closed his eyes to accept the entrance of wisdom. One of the purple guards thought the light-eyed purl was praying to the tree. The Poollé Kii allowed the power pulse to dissipate and then placed the leaves in his shirt pocket. He would take them to the guardians who would be able to reveal much more about this particular poollé tree. He dismissed the guards and began his work. The tree had been positioned "between the two suns," which was another way of the chancellor showing his knowledge. Pedagogy began to suspect the chancellor should not be trusted with the power of a poollé tree so close to him. He wondered if he should let it die. He knew he could plant it in a way that it would survive for a few months before it would begin to whither, and by that time, he could take his mother and escape to a place where no dark-eyed purl could find them. He knew the tree would suffer if it was left without other poollé trees close. He wished his guardian, or at least Ilii, were there to consult. He wondered how much the chancellor knew and whether he had the power to tap into the life forces of poollé. If he did, if he was a whisperer, it would be better to kill the poollé tree than let it fall under the use of such a one. He quieted himself and listened within. He decided that life was its own defense against death and whatever would come, this poollé tree would not die by his neglect. He trusted what was before him had come to him. He was the Poollé Kii—life and death were his to order and enforce, and in this instance, he chose life. He dug the proper hole, reached into another pouch on his belt, and, by handfuls, placed its contents into the hole in a precise pattern. A bead of sweat dropped onto his work and flashed with a light hidden to the others nearby. Then it happened.

It was faint but unmistakable. A soft breeze carried it past him. He detected the faint scent of amest. Amest was a scent used by his ancestors. The guardians had taught him to recognize the color of purple and their scent. They taught him a purl's mind and mouth could create clever disguises, but their color and their scent would always reveal who they truly were. But amest was a rare and precious scent. Later, he would learn it was the scent of Kii. It was the same scent that had woke him early one day deep in the wild. The guardian and Ilii paused in the middle of a lesson as he discovered it. They told him he must find its source and followed him as he wound his way along the invisible trail to discover the flowering plant. It was a sacred test he was unaware he was taking but one he passed with a perfect score. It was further proof that he was Kii. His mind welcomed the memory as a thirsty purl would welcome sweet, clear water. He embraced the memory yet remained aware of where he was and what he was doing. As he breathed in the scent of amest, his whole being relaxed as if he were resting on a bed of garden grass. In this bliss, his mind found and focused on the sound of approaching footsteps. The steps were timed and tuned to the beating of his hearts. Someone special was approaching, and he sensed that he knew who it was.

He was first told the stories when he was a child—the stories of Quay and Miis, of Quel-Kha and his bride, and even the cautionary tale of Phee and Tyne. They were stories of great and sometimes tragic love. The guardians used the stories to teach him that Kii were pairs. They taught him that only one purl would perfectly match and complete him. They taught him how to listen and what to recognize within himself to know when she appeared. They told him strong bonds are only made through bold acts, and he would have to face unspeakable tests to win her. They told him this was true of all Kii. They mentioned the gha would face death for his partner. He looked up to find the source of the footsteps that were walking into his hearts and the sight of two perfectly sculpted iridescent royal blue calves filled his vision. His eyes moved past the dancing hem of her skirt to meet the eyes of the most beautiful purl he had ever seen.

Pedagogy was lost in the pha of finding the one who would complete his life when the first notes of a powerful song entered his ears. He first thought the sound was part of his memory. It sounded like a woo. He smiled, knowing the contest to win the hearts of the one purl put on the planet for him was about to begin. Her first two words sunk him deeper into the confidence that she was the one. It connected her with the other female already deep in his hearts. He smiled at the symmetry. When he responded to her, the color of her skin pulsed. He knew when she spoke, the rhythms of his hearts beat strong. The sound of her voice was a warm embrace of his soul. They talked, and time stood still. The poetry that danced from her lips as she told the story of her life enchanted him. The way she held her books made Pedagogy want to embrace her as they were being held. He looked deep into her eyes and found his hearts building a home in her soul. Then, without taking his eyes from her lips, he was aware of something approaching.

It was a foul and irritating odor. Nos storming toward them entered his periphery. He was not sure whether the scent was real or if he was connecting the color of the purl's skin with the void behind his eyes and creating a smell to describe it. He could sense Nos's nefarious intent before he began to speak or reached and grasped Daisy's arm. Because Daisy knew this purl, Pedagogy stepped back into the hole to assess her reaction to, and relationship with, the darkness that had just appeared. Beauty is often attracted to beasts. There is a misplaced fantasy of romancing darkness into light by which many female purple are tricked and trapped. It was obvious the darkness Nos brought was invested in embracing the light that was Daisy. Pedagogy wanted to know what role Daisy played in the drama. He sensed the anger rise in Nos long before his hand began to swing toward Daisy's face. He could have easily stopped him. He could have dispatched the intruder from his blissful meeting without expending much effort. But the bride of the Poollé Kii would have to be a warrior, and if Daisy was the purl his hearts told him she was, to defend her against such an unworthy opponent would be an insult. He respected her. He thought she would be just fine. He would enter the fray if she asked or if she needed him. So, he thrust the shovel hard into the soil and monitored the action as a principle would a playground at recess.

Her moves were neither polished nor precise, but they were effective, and she was fearless. She had come from Noth, so the fact that she could fight was no surprise, but the way she fought revealed something deeper. Pedagogy strained his memory, searching for what was familiar about the scene in front of him. Then he remembered.

It was a dream, a vision really. Pedagogy, Ilii, and his guardian had journeyed deeper into the wild than they had ever before. It was a three-week journey along a path only the guardian knew, to a sacred place at the foot of some mountains. There he was shown the grandchildren of an ancient stand of poollé trees. After a specific ritual, Pedagogy was invited to ingest one, then another of the leaves from the poollé tree. The leaves sent him into a trance where he dreamed that he fought the mighty Kha. But it wasn't the legendary battle of Quel-Kha. It was ancient times. He was in a small area surrounded by purple, and he was wrestling with a young Kha. It was a game of sorts. They were fighting, but they were playing at the same time. Pedagogy had never heard a story of such a thing. When he woke from his trance, his guardian told him what he saw was a game of tease, tumble, and toss. It was the deepest proof that the lines of Miis converged in him.

Watching Daisy flip Nos as if he were a child took him back to that vision. Daisy moved in front of Nos much like Pedagogy had moved in his vision. She fought Nos just as he had fought the young Kha. She fought in ancient ways, and this made Pedagogy surer she was his alone. Then suddenly, danger ripped him from his memories.

Daisy dispatched her unworthy opponent with a final flip and tossed him some distance, which made the small crowd that had assembled to watch gasp in collective amazement. Daisy turned toward Pedagogy, and their eyes met. When they did, it was as if the conversation they were having had continued through the dispatching of her enemy. Daisy appreciated that her tree planter had not intervened. She needed a purl who was comfortable with her strength. She always dreamed of a purl who would fight the big battles at her side and leave the ones she preferred to her. She was in love, and she knew it. The moment and the battle filled her being with something she had never before experienced. But before the sigh of satisfaction and bliss could escape her lungs, in slow motion, Pedagogy began to fly feet first toward her. His bare feet caressed her chest and began to move her backward. She welcomed them. Then, just as the feet were moving her, something tore through her temple at the same moment an ear-piercing explosion erupted.

Syng relaxed in the plush limousine seat and released one long deep breath. The mixture of drugs, anxiety and greed allowed him only a few hours of sleep each night. The feelings of self-satisfaction and pride were the closest he got to rest. Soon, he would consummate the pursuit of his latest project. He thought that she was a uniquely rare light-eyed purl. She was bright and inquisitive and had a mysterious side that intrigued him. She didn't fawn over him or seem impressed by his power, which added to her attractiveness. She was no doubt older than his usual conquests, but her maturity gave her a power over the young sycophants he possessed. Her body curved wonderfully and was soft but firm. The thoughts of enjoying it brought a smile to his mind. He decided that this would be the evening he would have her. He opened the compartment near his left hand, took out a vial, and placed it in the inner breast pocket of his jacket. It was his insurance. The contents of that vial would bend any purl to his will. In fact, it had done so many times in the past. His thoughts began to entertain the approach he would use to lure her into his web, but as he went through the thoughts of his past and all those whom he had subdued by these devices, something strange moved through his emotions. He realized he didn't want to use any of his past practices on Daisy. He wanted Daisy to want him for who he was. And, at that moment, he thought he was willing to wait for as long as it took. For the first time in his memory, he wanted to be invited into the consummation of a female's desire rather than manipulate or drug his way there. This thought reminded him that he was in love with her. It made him chuckle. He returned the vile to its container. He wanted to talk to her again. He wanted to hear the melodious sound of her voice. He had a free moment and called her from the limousine. They talked for a long while, and he was enjoying it so much that he repeatedly ignored his driver signaling there was an important call for him from his office. After nearly an hour, he promised Daisy that he would see her soon and said goodbye.

Seconds after Syng hung up the phone, his assistant called again. He could tell by the guarded calm in her voice that something had gone wrong. The dratsab's office was demanding an immediate conversation. She asked the chancellor to hold while she connected him to the dratsab's office. It was obvious the dratsab snatched the phone from his own assistant when he began talking directly to the chancellor. The dratsab wanted to know where he was and why he was not able to be located. Nos had shot a student in bright-day on the chancellor's campus and was attacked by a gardener. Syng's brow furled and unfurled as the strange news unwrapped itself in his mind. The dratsab was filling in details between invective and curses. Syng knew Nos was not beyond shooting a purl. Syng had taught him how to do it quickly and efficiently — but Daisy? Why ever would he do such a thing? As Syng thought through the news he was receiving, the dratsab sensed that he did not have Syng's undivided attention. He raised the volume of his voice. He wanted to know how Syng had let this happen. His office was being inundated with calls from law students, and some influential law professors had gotten the prisoner released before his office had even been notified of the incident. He didn't want a light-eyed uprising or marches in the streets because the dratsab's son had killed a light-eyed law student. The roll-in nonsense was already stirring up the light-eyed purple, and he didn't need one more thing added to their energy. The dratsab reminded Syng he had been against Daisy's entrance into the law school from the beginning. He thought it best for the light-eyed to stick to things for which they were better suited, like cleaning houses, working fields, and bearing children. The dratsab warned his father that his appointment was fresh enough to be reversed. He swore in dark and convincing language that Nos could be sacrificed on the altar of expediency if there were any repercussions to his office from this incident. Syng tried to interject some calming thoughts but was rebuked by a dratsab who took the attempts as patronizing and pedantic. The dratsab wondered out loud if the tragic death of the chancellor might also be necessary one day soon. After he made it clear that the matter was to be handled before the day was over, the dratsab hung up the phone.

The conversation put Syng in an unpleasant mood. He had never been particularly fond of his son. He admired his cunning and had to respect his ruthless quest for power, but they had never been close. The dratsab had betrayed, murdered, and stole his way to power. Syng watched his son's rise to power with a mix of loathing and admiration. He knew that the dratsab's threat was a kindness. Few of his victims ever knew they were in any danger. But now Syng knew. And this was no surprise. He had taught his son what his father had taught him, namely, a ruler must be ready and willing to kill at will. Ruthlessness, his father had insisted, is the right and responsibility of those who would rule, and the dratsab was the most ruthless purl

Syng had ever known. There was one purl, however, with the potential to eclipse him, and he had just shot Daisy.

Syng sent a stream of air rushing through his nostrils and called his assistant. He told her to send him the video feeds of the event. He had ordered a number of cameras be aimed at the poollé tree, primarily for security but also to watch the tree planter. The poollé tree was key to his plans for power that most purple knew nothing about and others, like the dratsab, thought were foolish myths and a waste of time. Syng fast-forwarded through Pedagogy digging the hole and talking to Daisy. He slowed it to normal speed as Nos walked into the frame. He wished he had audio to hear what was being said. The fight began and, at first, Syng was not surprised Daisy fought back. She was, after all, light-eyed. But her moves were puzzling. He wondered if she had been trained. She avoided most of Nos's fists and had a strength and quickness that did not fit his expectations of her. She was a stray he had invited into his home and watched grow. She was his house cleaner's fatherless child. He had never imagined she was capable of such self-defensive agility. Her skill and abilities could have been deadly. But Syng didn't know if that was because she didn't know they could be or because she was playing with Nos. This made him uncomfortable. He did not like surprises, especially those that were also threats to his plans or his life. His grandson's infatuation had grown to lust, and Syng used it to teach him self-control and obedience. His grandson was his life, and to watch him be disrespected and thrown around like a rag doll made him angry. By the time the video showed Nos stand and pull his gun, Syng was convinced Daisy deserved to be shot. He began thinking of the story he would have the newspapers run about the crazed, light-eyed purl. He knew, at that range and with the skill Nos possessed, Daisy would be killed. He had seen enough. He was feeling particularly incensed. First, fury fluttered and flew within him, then disdain for the light-eyed rose like bile in his throat. These thoughts blinded him to everything until something else caught his attention. At first, it was a blur, a flash interrupting the rising anger. He slowed the video down to see exactly what was happening. And there it was. The tree planter, flying through the air. It was unnerving: the muzzle flashes from Nos's gun, Daisy falling, and the tree planter skillfully disarming his beloved grandson, knocking him out.

Confusion swirled within him. Syng studied those moments of the video over and over. The questions of a frightened purl began to race through his mind. Who was this tree planter? How did he avoid being shot? What were he and Daisy talking about? How long had they known each other? How had he done what was surely impossible to do? Were his accelerated abilities due to the poollé tree? He studied how Pedagogy interacted with the tree. The angle of the cameras could not capture what Pedagogy did when he was in the hole. But the time he spent doing it was unmistakable and created yet another unwelcome mystery.

His thoughts turned to his Daisy. He wondered how well Daisy knew the tree planter and why she recommended him. He poured himself a shot of a black intoxicant and began to brood over the course he would take next. He loved Nos as much as he hated the dratsab. The dratsab had long been his enemy, but now he wondered whether another set of enemies had just revealed themselves. After he had thought a while, he phoned his office. He spoke with Nos. By the time he had finished talking to his grandson, the limousine had reached Noth. Syng remembered his date. But things had changed. He reached into the compartment and took out two small vials. He placed them in the inner breast pocket of his sport coat.

Daisy pulled her fire-engine red hair to the back of her head with both hands. Her hair was thick and naturally curly, sometimes unruly and uncooperative. But this evening, it seemed to obey her every wish. She had chemically removed all the kinks so her hair would lie straight and smooth on her head. She intended to put in some gentle curls in just the right places so that they would bounce on her shoulders. Syng liked it that way, and she enjoyed pleasing him. She had spent the day preparing her hair just the way she knew he would like it, including coloring the increasing number of green strands. She wondered if she should be so preoccupied with the wishes of the dark-eyed professor. She knew her that infatuation and awe had become a near desperate desire but couldn't remember if it was by her will or his. A bright patch of sky pierced the darkness and threw light into the room, and she realized how dark the day had become. Just before the beam of bright-day pushed its way through the cloudiness outside, a shadow passed through Daisy's thoughts, and a cold chill ran through her veins, raising the hairs on the back of her neck. It was over as soon as it began, and Daisy didn't think long about what it might have meant or why it occurred. She did, however, pause to appreciate the beam of light streaming into the room. Bright-day was always a joy to her. As she lingered in the light, she began to question her evening plans. She thought of her child. He was no longer a child. He had grown up, and the time seemed to have gone by so fast. The light falling on her face made memories flow through her mind. She remembered the beautiful hands. She remembered the mountain home. She thought of the years and how swiftly they had passed. The thoughts brought pha, and she gave a long, deep sigh. She turned back to the mirror and released her hair. It fell just past her shoulders. The green shock of hair that had been growing more prominent was gone, and her rich, thick red hair sat awaiting her next command. Staring at the female in the mirror, she decided to abandon the curls and pulled her hair into a bun. It was, after all, less "glamour purl" and more Daisy.

The suns' light refreshed her heart, and standing in it, she was less preoccupied with preparing for her evening guest. She had been thinking that it was time the two loves of her life met. Her Pedagogy would be leaving sometime in the morning. He and Ilii were catching a ship to some faraway place they hadn't named. She had asked, but they didn't tell her. Instead, they reminded her that if she didn't know, she couldn't say. Daisy sensed their adventures were growing more dangerous. The one time she was invited on one of their trips was near his twenty-first year. There was a ceremony in the midst of the poollé trees that they had planted so many years ago. It was there that Daisy realized her child had done things she could not have imagined, and it was there that the guardians declared her Pedagogy was the Poollé Kii. Since that moment, Daisy thought that he was focused on things beyond her. She knew the day would come when he would be independent and gone. She was in no hurry for that day to come, but it seemed to have arrived, nonetheless.

The stream of light from the bright-day suns had disappeared, and the reappearing gloom outside began to seep into Daisy. She thought about her child and Ilii leaving for an extended time to a place she didn't know, and she didn't like it one bit. She didn't like them keeping information from her. She knew it was best if she didn't know. But Ilii spoke of dark forces as if they were real and present dangers. They spoke as if the myths of Tyne and Phee were of actual purple and not just stories ancient purple concocted out of their ignorance. Daisy looked at the purl in the mirror and declared her both strong and wronged. She believed she was strong enough to withstand any evil force. But she wasn't.

Her mind went back to the mountain house when the had guardians arrived. She sat and watched while the others, even her little Pedagogy, prepared for battle. She assured herself that, since then, she had become stronger and wiser. Her own studies at the university had made her aware of more than Ilii could imagine. She determined that when Pedagogy returned from planting the tree, she would press him to tell her exactly where they were going. She imagined inviting herself along and thought about asking Syng to join her. That thought jostled her back to the present. She remembered Syng was on his way and would probably be there shortly. She hurried to finish preparing herself and the beast and bread. Daisy set the table and went into the back to change her clothes. Just as her mirror inspection met her approval, the doorbell chimed.

Daisy headed to the door wondering who it might be and knowing who it was. She had not given Syng her address and expected that he would call when he got to Noth to ask her for it. The innocent part of her refused to believe it was him. If it was him, that would mean he had means she didn't realize. It would also mean other things she didn't want to think about and couldn't really imagine. Still, who else could it be? Ilii and Pedagogy would not ring the bell and would most likely use the back door anyway. Strangers were rare but did occasionally stop by. With these thoughts in her head, Daisy swung the door open and there he was, standing tall and debonair in a sport coat tailored to his frame. The shock of yellow hair at his temples highlighted his cheekbones. His dark, navy-blue eyes were pools of mystery and intrigue. Daisy fell into them sooner than she could recognize her dinner guest. A beautiful bouquet of violet sorres in Syng's right hand caught her eye, and a strong left arm wrapped around her waist. Syng pulled her close and kissed her hello. Daisy politely broke the embrace. She welcomed her guest and turned from him to put his hat on the coat hook and find a vase for the flowers. When her back was to him, Syng wiped his lips with a handkerchief.

The sweet flavor of his kiss made the questions about how he had found her home disappear. She was comforted by the assurance that Syng cared for her deeply and didn't recognize the connection between these new thoughts and the kiss. Syng sat on the love seat, and Daisy went to the kitchen to make tea. She returned and placed the tea service on the table and deliberately sat in Pedagogy's large chair across from him. Syng took a sip of tea and asked if Daisy had some honey or sugar. Blood rushed to Daisy's face as she blushed. She could not have imagined that her tea was bitter. The tea was made from roots she and Ilii had gathered and dried. They were rare and naturally sweet. She had already sipped her cup before Syng, and her tea tasted wonderful. Embarrassed, she got up and went to the kitchen to find her guest some honey. When she left, Syng emptied one of his vials into her teacup and stirred the mixture with her spoon. When she returned, she gave Syng the honey and sipped her tea. The tea was indeed bitter, and she wondered why her first sip hadn't revealed something was wrong. Syng was pleased with the honey, and they enjoyed conversing until he appeared anxious to eat. Daisy was led to believe it was because he enjoyed her beast and bread so much. But Syng had other motives entirely. He wanted to know more about Daisy. His questions sought to uncover her past. Daisy was open to telling Syng everything he wished to know about her, but for some reason, sitting in Pedagogy's chair, she didn't quite feel that it was the right moment. She assured herself and Syng that all his questions would soon be answered.

They moved to the table where Ilii, Pedagogy, and Daisy usually had their meals. It was set with Daisy's favorite tablecloth and finest china. She had set Syng's plate across from hers in one of the seats that Ilii usually sat. She, of course, always sat just to the right of Pedagogy, who always sat at the head. She went to get the first course of salad, and when she returned, Syng had moved her setting. He told her he wanted her to be closer to him. It was true but not for the reason he suggested. There was no warm intent Syng had for moving her close. Syng was suppressing the deep suspicion that had now totally replaced the feelings of love he thought he had for Daisy. He also hid very well his intention to get into the deep recesses of her mind and memory at whatever cost. He knew that which she did not. He knew his life hung in the balance and that the dratsab's warning was no empty threat. He knew his plans were more important than any imaginary love. He knew she had secrets that she had not yet shared with him. And he knew how to get to them. These thoughts and the energy required to keep them hidden took all his focus. This was why he did not notice anything special about the tablecloth or that Pedagogy's seat was made of poollé wood. When Daisy came in and saw the change, she thought it was a wonderful opportunity to tell Syng that the seat he wanted her to sit in was Pedagogy's. She welcomed the thought of sharing her heart and hopes with this one whom she loved so much. But, before she could say anything, Syng rose and took one of the dishes, and, together, they placed them on the table. He took her hand and guided her to the seat he had selected for her. His hand on hers was warm and wonderful. With his touch, her heart wanted to leap out of her chest toward him. She sat in Pedagogy's place and watched as he sat in the first of Ilii's three seats. As he sat down, his flesh flashed red before Daisy's eyes, but she didn't seem to notice.

Daisy took a bite of her salad. The power of the fresh vegetables cleared her vision for a moment. She wondered why Syng was asking so many questions and why he wasn't eating. Then she realized it. She could see it in his eyes. She had made a mistake. Why had she been so blind? What could she do to fix it? Syng was not a fan of vegetables, and he did not want the salad. Daisy accepted the shame her thoughts offered. She should have guessed that Syng would not like vegetables. She disappeared into the kitchen with his untouched plate of salad and her half-eaten one. She felt foolish and wanted to make Syng feel wonderful at any cost. A sense of shame washed over her, and she searched her mind for a way to make up for her mistake. She left the kitchen with the warm beast and bread determined to please him. She placed the meat in front of him, and an involuntary guttural sound escaped his soul. Any other purl would have heard it as a growl, but Daisy, under the influence of the tainted tea, heard only a sigh of pleasure. Syng devoured the beast and bread. The day's turn had resulted in his missing lunch, and he was hungry. It was his only pause in questioning Daisy. He was frustrated that her answers only opened more mysteries. He was growing tired of his own gentleness. He had been asking questions in a way that would still allow for the seduction of his prey but was growing weary of the little progress he was making. He could not understand why the lip tonic and the first vial had not done their work. He asked Daisy for another drink.

Daisy disappeared into the kitchen and poured them both a large glass of water from a mountain spring that Ilii had brought from their journeys. It reminded her of the water from the house by the mountains. She kept it for special bright-day celebrations when they would have guests. Every purl she had served it to had marveled at how it was beyond any other and how it seemed to wash their mind and being. She brought the glasses to the table. Syng didn't seem to enjoy it at all. His one and only sip was followed by an expression that seemed to search for a place to spit it out. Instead, he choked it down as if it were toxic fuel. He asked if there might be something else she could offer? She hurried and brought out a bottle of honey wine Ilii had made some time ago. Almost as soon as she poured the glasses, Syng's knife and fork fell from the table. Daisy heard herself apologizing and, as she returned to the kitchen to replace them, wondered why she felt obligated to take the blame. When she was out of the room, Syng poured the second vial into her wine. It turned the wine tar black and then disappeared as the fermented juices returned to their transparent golden color. Daisy returned, and together they talked and toasted until the glasses were empty and filled again.

The more they talked, the more comfortable Daisy was sharing anything with Syng. The tonic had her believing that she was in control of everything. She believed she was asking all the questions, but, in fact, she was providing answers. She had a growing intent to seduce Syng, and it surprised her. She thought herself more powerful than she had ever been. Then, as she lifted the wineglass and emptied the last of its contents into her body, she imagined that she saw a black speck at the bottom of the glass. She looked at Syng. A horror gripped her. He looked large and imposing. He began asking questions that were direct and without filter. She was frozen and barely conscious. Syng stood above her. He was yelling, but she couldn't hear anything he was saying. He slapped her. Daisy wondered why he had struck her and why she didn't feel the blow. He swung and hit her again. Daisy, or some part of Daisy, was thrown to the floor. The Daisy falling to the floor wondered at the other Daisy still sitting in Pedagogy's chair. That Daisy's mouth was moving. She was saying something, but whatever it was, it was not satisfying Syng's wishes. There was another slap, this time with the back of his hand. With that strike, the Daisy in Pedagogy's seat was thrown to meet the Daisy already on the floor.

When Daisy's body joined her spirit on the floor, a figure made up of a thick, viscous black dust began entering her body through her mouth. The black dust was holding itself together in the shape of a fully dressed purl resembling Syng. It was forcing its way into her body, and she was fighting to pull it out of her by grabbing first its chest, then its waist, and finally the legs. Daisy fought to pull out the being that was entering her. She fought as hard as she could, but her strength was waning.

She looked up and Syng was standing over her; there was dark anger in his eyes. She could smell hatred oozing from his pores. His skin glowed a demon red. She realized he was the black dust entering her. She was confused. She thought he loved her. She thought she loved him.

Realizing that she had been seduced by evil and believing that she had betrayed her true love, she released the grip she had on the calves of the figure made of dust. Instantly, it completed its journey into her. When the dust entered her, instead of feeling that something was inside her, the dust had become a cast around her. She was encased in a thick, black, putrid paste. She couldn't move. Biting pains began in various places on her body. The stinging felt as if worms were beginning to eat their way into her body. The excruciating pain made her want to scream, but her mouth would not open. She wanted to flex her muscles and break out, but she was too weak.

Ilii were in three different places in preparation for the next day's departure. They intended to meet Pedagogy on campus before he finished planting the poollé tree and take him home. But their plans were interrupted when they detected the gathering darkness heading toward Noth. They were aware that Daisy would be entertaining the chancellor and had cleared the home of any obvious items that would reveal their presence or the identity of the Poollé Kii. They were not sure how safe this particular purl was, and they planned to assess him when the Poollé Kii met him. They would observe from a hidden distance, but even from there, they would be able to see things most would miss. The chancellor was sure to have security with him, and his security had a reputation for their strength and brutality, but Ilii did not fear a confrontation with them. They also were confident the Poollé Kii could handle any threat inside the house. But they were concerned that Daisy might be injured. Her complexion was becoming pale, and a mist gathered behind her eyes. They had watched and listened with growing dismay as she prepared for their departure by investing more in her pursuits on campus. If she had not been the chosen mother of the Poollé Kii, she would have been dismissed from his presence some months ago.

As the loneliness moved toward Noth, Ilii arrived at the campus just as Pookii was being taken to the police car. They were prepared to free him but caught his eyes that told them to hold. The crowd that had gathered in his defense was arguing for his release, insisting that Nos be arrested instead. They asserted that even the dratsab's son was subject to the law. The officers who were arresting Pookii would normally disperse the crowd with their clubs and threats, but this was a crowd of dark-eyed law students and a professor or two. They were caught between the dratsab son's and a crowd of rich purple, and they were in no good mood because of it. The Poollé Kii was taken to the police station and was met there by a few lawyers and one judge, all of whom had been made aware and were sent to intercept him. The dratsab had many powerful enemies, and a few of them took this as an opportunity to put him on the defensive.

There was little that Pookii needed to do in his own defense, but the process was costing him time. He had planned to meet the chancellor before planting the tree. He thought to assess his worthiness of having both a living poollé tree and the affections of his mother, but the chancellor's unexpected engagement changed that plan. He did not like what was happening to his mother but had to be sure of the source. If the chancellor was the danger, he and Ilii would take Daisy and disappear. If the chancellor was unworthy of a poollé tree, he would plant it in a way that it would send its secrets into Purplynd and not into its leaves. Then, when all the history it held was sent through its roots into the soil, the tree would die. But little of that mattered now. There was a darkness heading toward Noth, and he would have to hurry home in order to arrive before his mother's visitor was gone.

The process with the police was complete. Ilii, who were waiting outside the station, hurried the Poollé Kii toward Noth. His calls to the house did not go through. The chancellor's purple had blocked transmissions.

Syng glared at Daisy. He was angry that she was dying. That was not his intent, at least not yet. He was confused that the potions had taken such a quick, lethal turn. She wasn't dead, but he was sure she was on her way. He decided to search the house and find his own answers. Daisy had spoken in circles, and Syng had grown weary of getting what he wanted in small pieces. What she did reveal was that the tree planter was her son, and he was on his way. She had wondered what had kept him because he was always reliably on time. Syng knew. The knowledge that the tree planter was Daisy's son was enough to extinguish any gentle thoughts about her. The connection between Daisy and the one who had attacked Nos severed any positive possibility between him and the figure on the floor. Syng sensed that his time to do whatever it was he chose to do was short. He decided to search the secret place Daisy had revealed. She had been coy and uncooperative, but when the drugs had taken their full and final effect, she mentioned her dresser. He had no idea what he would find, but he hurried there and rifled through her things until the entire dresser was empty. There was nothing. As he walked out of the room, he turned out the light for no reason other than he loved darkness. Then, out of the corner of his eye, a faint glow appeared. It was coming from the dresser. He went to it and found a drawer with a false bottom. Beneath it, he found a baby blanket. The cloth was what caused the glow. The pattern was ancient and beautiful. Syng stared at its beauty. Something in his mind was trying to connect things. His brain made him aware of the lingering flavor of beast and bread in his mouth. It connected back to the morning, to the vehicle in the woods, and to the woman's decayed bones. Then, like a boulder falling from a thousand feet growing larger in view until it crushed one's chest, he remembered Tepa.

A guttural sound reverberated through his body. He returned to the frozen, dying purl on the dining room floor. Standing over his paralyzed victim, he resolved to mutilate the body beneath him. He was angry that she was dying without his permission and without pain. He was angry that she had not answered all his questions. He was angry the tree planter had disrespected his grandson. But most of all, he was angry that she had deceived him and was the cause of the death of Tepa, his one and only true love. The anger demanded that he punish her. He thought to cut out one of her hearts before it stopped beating. He thought of simply cutting her continuously so that she would die screaming. These and darker thoughts moved through his mind. There was also a small whisper within telling him to flee before the tree planter returned. It would have been the wiser thing to do. Instead, his dark mind chose blood and screams.

He knelt down beside Daisy and took out the razor-sharp switchblade from his pocket. He flicked it open. He placed his hand beneath her breast to search for the syncopated rhythm of her two hearts. There was only one beat. He was confused. The light-eyed were double hearted. It was part of their weakness. It was impossible for Daisy to have only one heart. The thought that perhaps the drugs had stopped one of her hearts presented itself against the possibility that she was truly single-hearted. A light-eyed purl with a single heart was the subject of ancient myths and ignorant folktales of the poor. He knew he should pause and think. He knew the purl beneath him was special. He had always known it. His attraction to her was always more than physical, and now he understood why. A whisper within his soul cried for him to stop and rethink his plans, but the rage was too strong. Daisy was dying. Her paralyzed body lay stiff, but she was still alive and aware. As he looked into the eyes of his victim, the shock and fear he saw there pleased him. The flame of the table candles danced on the polished steel of the knife blade as he brought its razor-sharp edge toward her breasts.

Daisy looked into his eyes—the eyes of the one she would have given her all—in them the betrayal of all that was ever kind or good appeared as a vacuum. She gazed into the now black pupils of the one she loved, and nothing more than death and hunger remained. She saw into his soul, and it was consumed by avarice and waste. These sights filled her with sadness. She longed for his release from the living horror she imagined was his life. Her eyes welled up with water that began to roll out of their sockets. As the tears leaped off her cheek, they burst into brilliant blue light and struck the floor. Syng screamed in horror. It was a sound his voice had never made before. It was a cry constructed by a mind remembering, in a single moment, every dark deed he had ever done and connecting them with the consequences that justice would require. His scream had somehow lifted him to his feet. But before he was standing, shaking but erect, the blade held tightly in his hand had been released. The switchblade tumbled end over end out of his hand, and some part of Syng saw its tip point at the heart of his victim. Demonic glee pulsed within his panic.

Inexplicably, the path of the blade was altered, and it stuck in the floor beside Daisy. A fear he had only known through the eyes of his victims gripped Syng, and he released his bowels. He had dismissed the possibility as a myth. He had convinced himself, and many others, that it was nothing more than fantasized stories of powerless purple attempting to scare or shame those who ruled them. He had sworn with curses in conversations too numerous to count that there was no such thing as a power able to magnify and reflect back onto a purl the darkness of their soul. But there it was—just as in the ancient myths—the gha jii from a single-hearted, light-eyed purl. Syng's scream alerted the guard who took his position at the front door just after it closed Syng inside. He burst through the doorway and, in just a moment, assessed the situation. He saw Syng. He saw Daisy lying on the floor, dead. He saw a glowing cloth at his master's feet. He rushed to Syng, grabbed him, and began to pull him out of the house. The driver arrived to help. Syng pointed to the cloth on the floor. The driver obediently grabbed the blanket and Syng's coat and hat. Together, they took Syng to the limousine. The engine had never been turned off. Soiled, shaken, and scared, Syng shouted to the driver to take him to the Panthae. There, he hoped to hide in the darkness from the light of gha jii. The limousine careened out of the neighborhood with its wheels screeching and barely missed hitting a vehicle as it turned the corner and sped away.

It was only Ilii's superb driving abilities that kept them from being destroyed by the speeding limousine. The Poollé Kii was thrown into them, which kept him from seeing anything about the vehicle that sped past. Ilii was at the house seconds later, and the Poollé Kii was out of the vehicle before it stopped moving. The putrid scent of darkness had left a trail out of the front door and into the street. Pedagogy ran up the trail past the front door that hung open on one hinge. Ilii had run also but stopped as they entered the large room to read what had happened there. Pedagogy continued to where Daisy lay. Ilii stood still. Daisy was encased and still, but their attention was directed at everything else. They read all they could about where the darkness had been. Then their focus moved to the Poollé Kii. Pedagogy was kneeling beside Daisy. He saw what he knew were slap marks on her face. He saw the marks her guest had left in his home. He saw the trail he had made. He could smell that he had been frightened and was escorted out. His questions about the chancellor had all been answered. He looked at his mother and lifted her shoulders into his arms just as he had held the purl of his hopes hours before.

He called to her. She did not respond. Ilii went into the kitchen and found the chalice of the Poollé Kii. They placed something from their pouch in the cup and then filled the large glass with the cool water from the mountain spring. With the chalice in hand, they returned to stand beside the Poollé Kii. When Pedagogy lifted Daisy to cradle her in his arms, her right arm fell from her side, and the back of her hand rested against the arm of the Poollé Kii's chair. Pedagogy held her other hand and called to her lifeless body. He called her to come back to him. He called her *Mema*, which in the ancient languages meant both "my mother" and "my teacher." It was a term of the highest esteem and respect. It was an approbation Daisy had longed to hear ever since the appearance of the guardians at the mountain house. It was the signal that she, too, was ready to do battle.

With death holding her left hand and leading her into eternal darkness, Daisy heard her Poollé Kii call her *Mema*. She stopped and turned toward the sound. Ilii began to chant the lines of a poem. Daisy's mind tried to recognize the lines, but the meaning was too far from her. They chanted it again. Her Pedagogy was speaking again.

He was commanding her, "Mema, remember your promise."

She was straining to remember just what that promise was. She remembered giving a note to the guardian. There was something he said to her that was important. She couldn't remember. She remembered jumping to intercept the falling swords. The dark dust pulled hard at her hand to keep her chained in confusion and doubt. Death promised to free her from the parasites that were painfully eating into her flesh, but Daisy heard her child, and her love would accept the pain to ensure her that child was safe. Her left hand pulled against death, and her right hand rested on the arm of Pedagogy's chair.

Daisy heard the voice saying, "Mema, keep your promise."

Ilii chanted for the third time:

"Into the darkness and then return
And gather all to fight;
Deny the death that urges you
To release this hold on life.

He, your teacher and your charge,
Shall live until you see;
Promise now this oath and swear…"

Then it happened. With death leading her to the everlasting black, Daisy remembered. She snatched her hand out of death's grip and shouted the last line of the poem. Held in Pedagogy's arms, her lips moved slightly as tears welled up in his eyes. She had memorized the lines so long ago, and every time she would say them, tears would come to her eyes. But not this time. This time, something fierce awoke inside her. Her soul flexed muscles that were united with the universe, and in unison with Ilii, she shouted at death,

"I shall not die before the Poollé Kii!"

A single tear rolled off Pedagogy's cheek. It became a brilliant blue light as it splashed on Daisy's lips. Daisy gasped. In the same moment, her right hand grabbed a tight hold of the poollé wood of Pedagogy's chair.

Ilii handed the Poollé Kii the chalice, and he began to pour the water into his *mema*. Streams of black dust began to fly out of her nostrils and out the open front door. Each swallow of water brought Daisy more strength. She took the chalice in her own hand and tilted it back to consume all that was in the glass. There was a small leaf in the last bit of the mountain water. Daisy welcomed the presence of the poollé leaf. She did not chew it, and as it passed her tongue, the sweet taste of almond, mint, and mango swept past her senses. Her Pedagogy helped her to her feet, and she stood grateful, looking into the eyes of her son that glowed like a blue flame in the dim light. Then it hit her. She doubled over in pain. Spiny thors battled in her stomach. She turned to the back door, with both hands holding the rage within, and began to walk, then stumble, toward it. Ilii ran past her and opened the door. Daisy took one step. Her feet were unsteady as she placed one in front of the other. Then something urgent began in her stomach, and she ran through the door and into the middle of the yard. Her son followed. She fell to her hands and knees and began to retch. Her abdomen pulsed and heaved.

Purplynd opened to her fingers, and she grasped the planet as if it had handles. Her flesh glowed red. Then, in one long heave, Daisy expelled a thick, black tar. She gasped for air and retched again, this one interrupted by plaintive gasps. What was coming out of her was from a place far beneath her stomach. Her core was being wrung out like a sponge twisted beyond dry. When it was over, she stood up from the dark mass. It was large, as if her body had been poured out onto the ground as a thick, dense tar. It was alive, and it had a will. It sought to return to its host. Daisy would have none of it. Instead, she looked back to Ilii, who offered her the hilt of a sword. She did not wonder where it came from or how it came to be in their hand;

she just drew it from its scabbard. As it moved in her hand, she recognized that it was the sword that had hung over the fireplace in the mountain house. She knew it was hers. She lifted it with both hands and thrust it into the heart of the bubbling ooze at her feet. Instantly, what was a gelatinous, bubbling life-form became charcoal dust. The dust gathered itself quickly and, in the form of a thick rope, flew as far away from Daisy as quickly as possible. Daisy looked at Pedagogy and Ilii. They were smiling. Her eyes appeared to be back lit with bright blue lights, and her skin pulsed a royal blue. Pedagogy held out his arms. She ran into them. He welcomed her back.

As usual, Syng's guards stopped at the entrance to the Panthae and opened the car door to escort him through the restaurant to the elevators. The driver bent down to help his employer out of the vehicle. He didn't recognize the purl he saw. Syng's skin drooped, his color was gone, and there was something pale and unnatural about his flesh. He was sweating and looked frightened. His eyes were watery and strange. He stared as if something horrible had captured his gaze and would not release him. When his eyes did move, whatever they saw moved with them. He seemed genuinely afraid but unable to change what he was seeing. The guards reached for him, and his gaze found in them either the same image or one worse, for he became even more frightened. The odor had gotten worse, and the thought of walking him through the restaurant in that condition was abandoned. The guard left him in the seat and decided to drive him to the back of the Panthae.

They led him through the entrance that most purple didn't know existed. It was a small side door where they had often brought his victims and guests. Syng was not steady on his own feet, and the two guards held him up and walked him into the dark passageway to the private elevator. The further Syng got into the darkness, the weaker he became. His guards were almost carrying him when the elevator came. The doors opened, and they carried their boss, who either could not or would not walk, in and the elevator began to descend. A guttural moan they had never heard began to grow as the elevator descended. They were confused. The doors opened to the cavernous passage that led to his lair. That was when it happened.

Syng rose to his full height. His muscles began to tighten, and his full strength was felt by his assistants. They wondered if this strength would be used to harm them. They knew a fight was on the horizon or maybe had already begun. They knew the smell of darkness and death, and it rushed into the elevator as soon as the doors opened.

Syng pushed them into the walls of the small elevator and yelled, "No!" He growled and fought as if he were in the grips of an unseen power and cried again several times, "No!"

At last, the elevator doors closed. When they did, he fell to the floor as if all the bones had been removed from his body. He moaned a plaintive mix of sorrow and regret as his guards reached to lift him to his feet. He ordered them to take him home, which confused them for a moment. He had lived no other place in their immediate memory. Then they remembered the apartment.

Ilii pulled Daisy's sword out of the ground. It was in deeper than they had imagined, and it took two of them to pull it out. They smiled to themselves at the strength Daisy possessed. The Poollé Kii and his *mema* walked into the house, and Ilii cleaned the sword with fire and water from the mountains. As they walked into the house, the vision screen came on and began broadcasting. Whenever the dratsab had an announcement, he wished all purple to hear, every monitor within viewing distance of a purl came on and carried the message. Sometimes these were simple commercials that encouraged purple to eat right and exercise. Other times, short announcements told the scores of the popular teams. But when the screens came on and there was an announcer reading some statement or proclamation, purple were expected to stop whatever they were doing and listen attentively. The dratsab and his team of population control psychologists were strategic and focused on increasing their rule or quieting any discontent whenever they aired a broadcast. The broadcasts helped ensure the dark-eyed purple maintained a sense of their superiority and the light-eyed purple accepted their place in the hierarchy of beings. Many of the light-eyed purple hated the broadcasts for this very reason, and they were the ones most controlled by them. Pausing to take notice of the broadcast was just part of what everyone everywhere did, except for a few. Of course, the monitors also surveilled the activity and attention of the purple watching. Purple could receive a ticket or even be arrested for not paying sufficient attention. When arrests for not listening were made, they were always dramatic and broadly publicized.

The screens popped on, and, instead of the usual poster or rare announcer, the screen flashed the word *"Emergency"* five times before a video clip showed a purl striking the dratsab's son and then from another camera angle a gun appeared and fired. The clip showed a female purl being rushed to the hospital. Then the dratsab himself appeared on-screen. He spoke into the camera, visibly moved. He related how grateful he was that his son had survived, and the brilliant, young light-eyed law student was still fighting for her life at the University Hospital. He promised that no matter how unpopular, he would continue to advocate for light-eyed purple to climb the ladder of success. He lamented about how some light-eyed could not accept that other light-eyed purple would aspire to move into areas they believed belonged rightly to the dark-eyed race, as he called it. He then named Pedagogy a terrorist as a picture of him filled the screen and asked all Prometheus and beyond to help locate him. He related that this event was of national importance. Then the purl who had no connection with religion ended the rare broadcast with a short prayer. Pedagogy and Daisy, who were staring at the screen, quickly bowed their heads to hide their faces. Daisy didn't know what had happened, but she knew what she had just heard on the screen wasn't true. They knew, and they were sure the surveillance apparatus of the dratsab would be tuned to find them. Ilii packed the final items they would take on their journey, and the five of them disappeared into the night.

The guards took Syng back to the vehicle. As they opened the door, the odor hit them. It was as if there had been some dark death growing in the back seat while they were away. They put their employer in the back seat. He sat in the middle of the plush bench as if he were being pressed on each side by large figures. His eyes had widened in trepidation. He stared blankly as if he sat between two executioners. His shoulders were tight, his elbows were pressed close together, and his hands were pressed palm against palm between his knees.

The eyes of the two guards met. They shared the confusion. They did not know if the chancellor would live or die. They did not know if his mind would return. All they knew was something was happening they did not understand and could not control. They knew their lives were precariously tied to the health and well-being of the chancellor, and the responsibility of what would happen next could not lie solely on their shoulders. As they drove to the high-rise apartment building, they also realized they had no way of entering the apartment. The chancellor's private residence, although very rarely used, had state-of-the-art security. Access was granted through a simultaneous eye scan and voice match. They did not believe the chancellor would be able to stand with his eyes open or speak coherently enough for them to gain access; plus, they began to realize the images of them holding up the chancellor had probably already been caught by several cameras and knew they had better start making their case. One of them picked up the phone.

The night had almost exhausted its strength. The pale light of morning began to push its way onto the horizon. There was only one purl who was able to override the security system of the chancellor's apartment. Calling him at this hour and for the reasons they had to do it was as likely to cause their cruel, slow death as not calling; the thought of stopping the car and running into hiding passed through their minds more than once. They were trapped. A drop of cold sweat fell off the forehead of the purl as he pressed the speed dial to the dratsab's private phone. The short phone call took an eternity. The dratsab's voice was calm and measured, but as he spoke, the bones of the purl felt chilled. The chancellor's medical team would meet them at the apartment, and he would open the apartment when they arrived.

Syng's medical team was the best the university had. They were composed of two MD-PhDs and two former military medics who became expert emergency medical technicians. Together, they were capable of handling anything. Each had their particular interests. They often traveled with Syng on expeditions and co-authored journal articles on their journeys and research. Usually, only two of the four were on duty at any one time, but the shooting on the campus had brought the entire team together. The first EMT had responded when Nos's holster alarm went off. He was the first to run out of the building toward the gunfire. While the crowd was ducking, diving, and running away, Dow ran toward the danger. Zaup, the doctor on duty, was not too far behind. Dow instinctively ran toward the bloody body lying on the grass while Zaup was concerned with the son of the dratsab.

Burned in Dow's memory were two things. The first was seeing the green leaves turn red and begin to pulse as they stopped the bleeding wound. The second was the look in the eyes of the purl who had been pulled from the female body. The look penetrated his soul. The look carried a message that was as clear and permanent as if it had been written in granite with a diamond-tipped drill. *Do not move the leaves. They will heal her. You cannot.* Dow did not understand how his eyes met the eyes of the Poollé Kii. He didn't know who or what a Poollé Kii was. He only knew that Daisy's life depended on leaving the leaves where they had been placed. Dow and the EMTs placed Daisy on the gurney, and Dow rode to the hospital by her side. Dow felt something that he hadn't felt for a long time, not since he had left war and battlefields long ago. The purl on the gurney was his to protect, and he was committed to do that with lethal force if necessary. Any other purl would think this strange, but Dow had worn a uniform in the hot hell and putrid smell of battle, and purple of his ilk were different.

Zaup had quickly assessed that Nos was none the worse for wear. He had the scrapes and bruises of someone who had just gotten beaten up a bit and probably had a concussion from the blow that knocked him out. But this was nothing that rest and time would not put right. Zaup escorted Nos to the chancellor's outer office and completed his examination there. He gave him some meds that would reduce the swelling and speed the healing from his beating. Nos swallowed them all without water. The doctor offered him a pill that would calm his emotions, but the son of the dratsab refused to take it.

Zaup then went to the hospital to check on the female who had been shot. He had sympathy for the purl; no one should be shot, but the real attraction for him was medical. He was a scientist and wanted to know and see what was happening to the one who left the bloodstained grass at the university. When Zaup arrived at the hospital, he was ushered into the secure quarters most didn't know existed. It was where the elite of Promethean society received their care. He walked into the room and greeted Dow as he picked up the chart and started reading. Dow briefed him on all that was happening. Daisy's vital signs were fine, if a little subdued. It was as if she had been sedated, but she had not been given any medications. The dratsab had given instructions that she was to be left to die, one less mouth to contradict the story he was constructing. Zaup had no problem with the directive. Dow did. Zaup saw it as an opportunity to experiment and learn. The leaves that had, by then, begun to merge into her scalp fascinated him. It was as if they had begun reconstructing the wound. It was as if they contained the biological blueprint for her body and were replacing the missing pieces. Zaup wanted to take a sample of the leaves and begin to study the phenomenon. He gathered a sterile surgery scissor and turned toward the purl lying still.

What confronted him when he did so confused him. It was Dow. He was standing between Zaup and Daisy. Zaup thought to ask what Dow was doing, but he already knew. He thought to assert his superiority as the MD but thought it better to pause.

"You are not going to touch her," was all that he said, but the look in Dow's eyes and the quiet solemnity in his voice helped Zaup understand two lives stood in the balance at that moment, and he was not ready to give up his for a medical curiosity.

He relented and put the scissors down. He asked whether Dow was at all curious about what was going on with the leaves. They had a light conversation. Zaup and Dow were friends. They had worked together for a good while, and Zaup respected his opinion, especially when his life depended on it. He waited awhile and then left.

Dow stood guard all day and into the night. He had made friends long ago with a few of the staff and had served with one of them. More than served, actually, they were very close and had history. Together, the sympathetic staff attended to Daisy through the day. The order from the dratsab meant they would not be operating on her or giving her any of the meds a purl with her level of trauma should receive. At first, Dow thought this was a death sentence, but, as time wore on, he became convinced it was what probably saved her life. He sat beside Daisy, thinking. He was unable to shake the message planted in his hearts and could not reconcile it with the instructions from on high. As the hours passed, his connection to the one who had caught his eye at the scene of the incident increased. A bond grew between them. Dow thought he recognized him as a soldier he had served with but couldn't remember where or when. His mind told him there was some other truth for which he must look. It took some hours, and then Dow realized that the connection was one he had only made once before. It was the connection warriors make in times when death is dealt fast and furious from the hands of fate. It was the love and respect one gives and receives in the mud and blood. Dow couldn't shake it and didn't want to. Whoever the female was, she would not die while he lived. Late in the evening, everyone in the hospital paused to watch the universally broadcast announcement from the dratsab. Dow stared at the screen as the dratsab lied about what happened. He wondered who else recognized they were lies and realized things had just gotten complicated.

Early the next morning, Zaup's voice sounded through his earpiece. It happened not long after his friend had begun her shift for the day. She had gone home and gotten a good night's rest, and no one had any idea that it would be the last one she would get for a while. Dow was instructed to bring the ambulance to the rear of the chancellor's apartment. He had to check the address twice because his mind automatically began mapping out his way to the Panthae. Before he left, he made a pact with his friend to ensure that Daisy would not mysteriously expire in that hospital room.

When he arrived, the chancellor was still sitting frozen in the back seat. Zaup had been called by the dratsab and sent to care for the second most important purl on the planet. When Zaup arrived, the driver and security purl looked as if they were in danger but not from anything one could see or touch. He asked them what had happened, and they told him what they could. They didn't have to confer with each other to leave out the parts where the female was lying on the floor or the knife that was stuck in the floor. Zaup turned to the unmoving figure in the vehicle and asked some questions, to which a mumbled response came that had nothing to do with the questions the doctor had asked. Syng's body was cold and clammy, but his head was hot. His body was rigid. Not long after Zaup had finished his initial examination and just as the sedative that he had given Syng went into effect, Dow arrived with the ambulance. The four of them placed the chancellor on the gurney and took him through the private corridor to the penthouse apartment elevator. Just as they came into view of the scanner camera, the dratsab spoke. The sound of his authoritative voice startled all of them. They realized he had been watching, and the two guards broke out again in a cold sweat. The elevator doors opened, and they entered. In the bedroom of the palatial apartment, Dow and one of Syng's bodyguards cut his clothes off and washed him under the careful eye and direction of the doctor. The sheets and clothing were burned in the large fireplace in the living room.

Syng didn't move. His body remained still; his breathing measured. The sedative seemed to have had more power than expected, which Zaup thought was strange. He was one of the best and didn't make mistakes—at least that was what he kept repeating in his mind as Syng lost whatever consciousness he had and slipped beyond the reach of any available medicine. Days passed, and the doctor could not explain what was happening or why. Both teams of the chancellor's medical staff were baffled. They consulted with the dratsab's team, but they were equally confused. No traces of any poison were found. His mind had turned against his body, and no medicine helped. His team attended to him around the clock.

The dratsab wanted answers. The distraction of the incident on campus held the attention of the newspapers for the week. He had ordered all the video recordings of the incident confiscated and controlled before his doctored broadcast. Witnesses disagreed with the official account at their own peril. A few purple were brave enough to speak up, and that was one of the bones on which the media chewed. Meanwhile, the dratsab took the opportunity to push through some new measures that would enrich him and further curtail the rights and mobility of the masses. Dow had used his technical savvy and special access of the chancellor's office to obtain a copy of the actual footage before the dratsab's message had been delivered. He was in the penthouse apartment watching the video when Zaup, who had been looking over his shoulder, shouted. Something that they both had missed, even though they had viewed the video countless times glared at him. Zaup saw Pedagogy place a leaf in Daisy's mouth. They watched those moments over and over. They studied Daisy's body, frame by frame, attempting to ascertain what impact the leaf might have had. This increased Zaup's desire to experiment on the female in the hospital, but Dow would have none of it.

"That, you are not going to do," Dow said to the doctor, and it was enough.

Dow spent every free moment he had watching over Daisy. Her healing was miraculous and mysterious. He was the first to report that she was likely to die on the way to the hospital. He was the only one who had witnessed the transformation of the leaves in those first moments. He marveled at how they disappeared without leaving a scar or mark in the days that followed. But he was not about to let anything, or anyone, touch her. It was the message he got and couldn't shake from the purl who had since disappeared. Within two weeks of that fateful day, Syng was trapped in a coma, and Daisy's recovery was complete. But only a few purple knew this because the dratsab had ordered her to be kept in a drug-induced coma. He intended to "let"

her die of her wounds. At least, that was what the papers would report. But his son had persuaded him to let her live.

It took every day of those two weeks for Nos to put all the pieces together for his elaborate plan. He had convinced all but two of those attending to Daisy that he was her lover and friend. One was Dow, who knew enough about the chancellor's grandson's campus antics to doubt his story. Dow never thought much of him, and Nos was working too hard at the "concerned, grieving lover" bit. The other purl was one no one else noticed: a light-eyed janitor. Dow thought that she was a spy from the dratsab's office because she was a bit too aware to be just a janitor. No other purl thought there was anything strange about her presence, but he did. It might have been his military training. It might have been the clandestine business the chancellor was always involved in or the assignment he was on, but there was something different about her. He decided to treat her as a potential danger until two nights before Daisy went away with Nos.

Daisy was out of any danger. She was sedated, but the dratsab's son had made plans to release her from the coma. That meant she wouldn't die in the hospital. Dow was relieved at that revelation. He had completed his mission. Then, late that night when almost every other purl had gone, something happened. He was walking down the hall, and the door to the janitor's closet flew open with a bang. A tall purl appeared. It was obvious the purl's back had opened the door because he had been pushed against it. Dow recognized the purl. It was Nos. He was looking into the closet, determined. Nos took one step back toward the closet, and the business end of a mop appeared. The sound of Dow walking toward him caught the attention of the would-be rapist.

Whatever plans Nos had disappeared. He turned and walked past Dow. Nos was confident Dow would be quiet. Nos didn't know why he had stopped. He thought about dragging the purl by her hair to wherever he chose and doing to her whatever he wished. But something stopped him. He told himself it was his choice. He told himself he had just decided to change his mind. This was because he didn't want to recognize the fear. Something about the purl in the closet reminded him of the moment on campus when he realized the female, he was fighting had the power to kill him. He had pushed that memory so far away from his mind that he never thought of it. But his body would never forget, and the wisdom in his body changed his mind. He told himself he would come back and rape her another day.

Dow rushed to the closet. The female, startled by his presence, tensed her muscles and tightened her grip on the mop handle. When she realized it wasn't Nos, she relaxed and let out a sigh as if innumerable memories had been gathered together and thrown away from her body. Dow recognized her as the purl he had suspected was a spy. He took her to the break room and gave her a cup of coffee. Her name was Daisi. She told him Nos had been coming onto her for some weeks. Nos had filled the hospital room with Daisies as a way of proving his interest in her. Dow related that Nos had told him they were for Daisii, that they were her favorite flower. Daisi said Daisii's favorite flowers were sunflowers. As soon as she said it, Daisi saw something in Dow's eyes, and the look snapped her out of the Nos-induced trauma and back to the present. She realized what she had just done. She exposed that she knew Daisii, and that had never been her plan. She thanked Dow for his concern and quickly disappeared.

Dow spent the rest of the night watching over Daisii as he had the past two weeks. Then, just as the morning lights began to dawn, his comm lit up. It was Zaup. The dratsab wanted him at the apartment. Dow hopped in an ambulance and hurried over to the apartment. When he arrived, the whole team was present. The apartment was not a hospital, but every piece of medical equipment with a potential to help had been brought in over the weeks of the chancellor's decline. But Syng was dying. There was nothing they could do. They had tried everything. All their tests told them was his body was shutting down, and whatever was pulling him toward death was beyond their control. Everyone in the apartment was panicked. The dratsab had been clear. If his father died, they would die. They all were close enough to the first family to know that their deaths would not at all be pleasant. They estimated he had a day or more to live. Zaup slumped in the overstuffed chair and began to contemplate just how tortured his death would be. A few others, one of which put a strong drink in his hand, joined him. Getting inebriated seemed like a rational thing to do. Dow had arrived from his vigil over Daisy and began reviewing the tapes of the campus shooting again. Zaup was a few drinks in when he walked over to watch the video with Dow. They had viewed the recording a dozen times before. There was no reason to watch it again. Still, they were inexplicably drawn to it. The now familiar imagines presented themselves. Then they looked at each other, as the same thought burst into their minds. Zaup told the group he had an idea. Dow had grabbed the keys and was already on his way to the door.

Downstairs, in the cool morning air under the light of the first sun, Zaup slammed the passenger door, and they headed to the campus. They were going to get some of the leaves from the tree. It was as sane an idea as any other. When they arrived at the tree, Zaup put on surgical gloves. Dow held open a sterile pouch. Zaup attempted to pull a leaf off the tree with two fingers. It didn't move. He wondered if he was being too gentle or if the alcohol he had consumed was having a greater effect on him than he thought possible. After a few attempts to remove the leaf without damaging it, he grabbed one with his whole hand and tore it off its branch. He repeated this until he had four leaves. Some of the bark from the branches remained attached to the leaf stems. Crimson sap oozed into each gouge of the branches in response to the violent acts. Zaup was blind to the tree's reaction to his theft.

They rushed back to the apartment. A darkness that had been seen in the distance over Noth earlier was now directly overhead, and it began to rain. When they arrived, two guards from the dratsab's office were standing outside the door. Inside, the other medical team and those who had driven the chancellor that night he was ill were waiting. They were in the parlor. Death was sitting with them. Zaup walked past them with Dow on his heels. Syng lay still on the bed. His breath rattled. The doctor had only given him hours to live the day before. Zaup took the leaf from the pouch and opened Syng's mouth. As he moved the leaf toward him, Dow stopped him and cut off the bark with bandage scissors. Then Dow took a sponge and wet the chancellor's mouth and tongue. Zaup looked at him with gratitude. He was desperate and not thinking as clearly as he normally would. By the time this was done, and Dow held Syng's mouth open, everyone was in the room.

Zaup placed the poollé leaf in the pried-open mouth of the chancellor. When the leaf touched Syng's moistened tongue, his body snapped into a sitting position as if a hidden spring had been released in his back. His eyes opened wide as if someone had opened shutters to shatter the trapped darkness. Everyone in the room was frightened by the sudden movement of a body that had lain still for weeks. With his mouth still open, Syng released a shrill shriek that suggested his tongue was being burned by acid. Panic gripped the frightened Zaup, and, as he reached to remove the leaf, Syng's jaw snapped tight. With the terrifying sound still reverberating in their ears, they all witnessed Syng's body move to the resting position at the speed of a coffin being lowered into its grave.

Syng was awoken by an alarm that sounded like the roar of a beast. The sound was so fierce that he was on his feet instantly. He was disoriented. He began wandering, driven toward the sound. He was in the woods. He wondered why he was. He was sure he was near death. He was sure his arm was broken, and the wrist on the other arm throbbed with pain. He suspected his son had dumped him in the woods, and his hatred for him increased. His body hurt all over, which made him think that he had been thrown down some steep embankment. He suspected the dratsab wanted him to die alone. With that thought, Syng swore an oath in his dark mind to make it out of the wilderness and kill the dratsab. But even as he thought this, something was out of place. His memory began to return. A cloudy image of a female lying on the ground began to form in his mind. He remembered Daisy. There was something in his hand that his mind told him was his switchblade, but his touch told him was a spear. He was using it to walk. He remembered attempting to stab her through her hearts and the shock of realizing that she was single hearted. Two memories twisted themselves in his mind as one, and he strained to understand. He was sure she was double-hearted and was sure she was single-hearted at the same time. The two females lying on the ground dead by his hand presented themselves. He was too confused to sort things out. He was too hurt to rest. Something more urgent than a clear mind and memory called to him. He had to get somewhere. He had to keep going.

Moving away from the body that he could no longer see was a life-and-death matter. He pressed his way forward, not knowing why it was so important or where he was going. Every step convinced him that he had been in a battle for his life. He tromped through the woods, knowing he was making too much noise but not caring he did. His chest hurt. He imagined his lung had been punctured. He could not see well, but he had a clear sense of how to get to where he was going. His labored pace made the journey seem like hours, but the destination was close. He promised himself rest was not far ahead and used this hope to power his steps. There was something important to remember, and it attempted to hinder his forward movement. But someone needed him just ahead. Instead of stopping to clear his mind and weigh his thoughts, he quickened his pace. He began to feel good about getting to where he needed to be. His sense of urgency was satisfied by his actions. There was someone or something he had to save. There was a danger only he could avert. The thick woods began to thin, and the light of a clearing called to him. At last, he had made it to his destination in time. At the very moment his hope crested, a twig snapped beneath his foot. As his swollen eyes searched for the danger, the sound of something speeding through the air filled his ears. An explosion in his chest knocked him backward. His feet searched for solid ground attempting to regain his balance. But the impact of the Panthae tooth was too powerful. His foot landed on the second trap's trigger. His mind began to clear. He began to remember. The thin cloud shrouding his memory began to evaporate, and he almost knew where he was. But before it was gone, another searing explosion tore through his body. Syng sat up straight in his bed. He grabbed Zaup's arm before he could put the defibrillation paddle on his chest a third time. Syng's grip was strong. He looked at the doctor. His eyes held something strange and dark. A new danger peered into the world from within him. He was more than recovered.

ACIAM AJ

THEY LEFT NOTH THE morning after Syng's visit and by bright-day Ilii, Daisy, and the Poollé Kii were aboard a cargo ship carrying seventy thousand metric tons of corn to be processed and transformed on the giant island of Aciam Aj. The fourth-largest island in the Raci Sea was one of a family of islands formed by volcanic activity near the birth of the planet. For thousands of years, it was home to a quiet, indigenous, self-sustaining purple who referred to themselves as Aj. The oral histories told of how the Aj were created and sent to each island. They all shared similar sustainable cultures and every three-year cycle held a celebration on the big island. There, romances were begun, contests were engaged, and champions were celebrated. At least, that was what the ancient songs and stories told. But for the past five hundred years, the only lasting memory was of work, pain, and the occasional parade. Aciam Aj was paradise transformed into hell. There were parts of the island—high in the mountains and in the rough interiors where the tall trees thrust their trunks as fingers into the sky—that remained unspoiled. There were places deep in the woods where the fruits still grew wild and where the ancient songs of lament and joy were sung by the birds and carried on the breezes. But the coasts of Aciam Aj had become concrete and steel. The songs of birds had been replaced by the thud and grind of churning metal, and the wild fruits were now tamed and taught to grow quickly on plantations that produced them to be fast frozen and shipped to Prometheus.

Ilii and the Poollé Kii had planned the trip years in advance. The guardians had read the moons on the night they held the blanket to the sky in the sacred stream. They knew the year and month the Poollé Kii's hearts would open. They had instructed Ilii on the path to his final preparation, and all that needed to be completed before that time came. Through the rigorous training and the stages of change the Poollé Kii would go through, Daisy would either have proved her worth or been sent to the ancestors. When his hearts opened, he would either choose or be chosen and bond to that purl for life. If it was the right purl, the guardians were certain the Poollé Kii could become the one. It would be a long process to claim his queen and title, but the guardians believed he could be gha. Ilii were convinced that no such female existed in Noth. The interior of Aciam Aj held the oldest surviving tradition-keeping clans known. They also were known to have the most beautiful females on the planet. Ilii knew the time had come for the Poollé Kii's hearts to be opening. The choice would be made soon, and they couldn't imagine a purl with the right heritage anywhere around Prometheus.

The laundromat had become a successful community co-op. They had taught the community how to share. All their clothes were laundered without any purl profiting or pilfering. The cooperation demonstrated there began to grow into other areas. But Daisy's fascination, and then attraction, to her instructor had caused months of delay. The initial plan included her, and then it was thought best to leave her in Noth, but now she was included again. The darkness that had descended into her had been found, purged, and killed. She was now not only safe to include on the journey but had also become mema. Ilii had been instructed by the guardians that, although her eyes were light and her red flesh had turned blue, the fact she had only one heart meant she might not be able to withstand the tests that were surely to come. Daisy knew Ilii was there to protect the Poollé Kii from dangers. What she didn't know until she slayed the beast that came from within her own body was that the Poollé Kii's greatest threat was her. The thought made her eyes water, but at the same moment, a fierce sense of pride and honor tightened the muscles in her arms and chest.

It took the massive ship three weeks to traverse the distance between the Promethean mainland and Aciam Aj. The accommodations were sparse but regal. The five of them were given an entire deck just beneath the control room. It was obvious the Poollé Kii was revered, but contact with the crew was limited to Ilii. The Poollé Kii relaxed indoors and wore a hooded cloak whenever he went on the deck or a balcony so the ubiquitous eye of the dratsab would not be able to locate him.

They arrived and set up shop. There was no pretense of treating light-eyed purple with any civility on Aciam Aj; there were quotas to be made and schedules to be kept. Work was easy to find. Ilii acted as if they had just come to town from the interior and took jobs in a factory not far from the rear walls of the Promethean Embassy. Daisy accepted a position translating in the office of a factory making designer clothes for the Promethean markets. The Poollé Kii sat behind one of the sewing machines in the same factory. For months, they disappeared into the fabric of island life. Prometheus and the light-eyed communities around it would be full of purple seeking to find their way into the dratsab's graces by turning in the purl who attacked his son, but here on Aciam Aj, they were safe.

Ilii were intent on using the time away from Prometheus to introduce the Poollé Kii to potential females they thought were suitable. If the stories were half true about the females of Aciam Aj, their mission would be complete, and the guardians would be pleased. Things were looking positive. They had been invited and taken to an interior village by one of their coworkers. The small community welcomed them, and two of Ilii were quite taken by the beauty of the females they met. Almost every weekend included a trip into the interior.

On their way back from one of their trips, they stopped at a restaurant not far from a military base. It was bright-day and the place was full. The four of them went to the bar to wait for a table to clear. Ilii sat on either side of the Poollé Kii, and one stood with its back to the bar to watch the crowd. Ilii didn't like the energy. It was their job to protect the Poollé Kii, and a crowded bar was not the ideal place to do that. After about a half hour, Ilii sitting on the right side of Pedagogy went to check on the status of their table. A beautiful female took the vacant seat. She was inebriated and leaned in entirely too close to inquire if she had overheard correctly.

"Did he just call you Pookii?" she asked.

She was a striking female, obviously comfortable with males, and had a magnetic confidence. She had decided to welcome the handsome purl new to the place, and not much could stop her.

"What the buoge is a Pookii?" she chuckled.

Her beauty softened the blows of her words, and she knew it. She didn't realize Ilii were not amused. The Poollé Kii thought she was an interesting purl and signaled to Ilii not to interfere. He also thought it was funny that the mispronunciation of his title was so humorous to her. The female ordered her new friend "Pookii" a drink. They continued talking for a while, and every time she mentioned "Pookii," she chuckled. Then it happened.

The bar was usually filled with light-eyed purple, but occasionally, dark-eyed groups would invade the space. Most thought this was an attempt to take advantage of the light-eyed females. On this particular bright-day, the crowded bar was half-filled with off-duty, light-eyed soldiers and the other half with dark-eyed purple from who knows where. One very confident dark-eyed purl took it upon himself to insert himself in the conversation Pookii was enjoying with his new friend. He intended a dark-eyed seduction of the pretty purl at the bar. The female brushed him off without any pretense of politeness. It was clear she preferred her conversation with the "light-eyed miscreant" as the purl identified Pookii. Pookii smiled. He didn't think the situation was going to end up in any way the cocksure, dark-eyed purl could imagine. He was right. The dark-eyed purl swept the female's hair behind her ear and leaned into whisper or kiss her cheek or who knows what because, before his action became clear, she turned and pushed him away with both hands. The move was so abrupt and unexpected that the purl lost his balance and fell to the floor. As he fell, he knocked into a purl who spilled a green slime beer all over him. Ilii tapped the shoulder of the Poollé Kii. It was a request for him not to get involved. The dark-eyed purl was incensed and embarrassed by the rebuff, particularly because his friends burst out laughing as he wiped the slime beer off his face. The female turned back to the Poollé Kii and gave her best impression of a helpless female. He smiled. She was very attractive and seemed to be attracted to him.

As she was smiling at her new friend, the dark-eyed purl stood and slapped her from her blind side. The blow knocked her off the stool and dissipated the effect the intoxicants were having. She stood up, stone-cold sober. There was a look in her eyes the dark-eyed purl had never seen before and one he would never forget. A surreal silence blossomed outside of time itself that was soon interrupted by the sound of the female's fist smacking very hard against the dark-eyed purl's jaw. The sounds that followed began with glasses being dropped, chairs overturning, and then the full-throated, dark, destructive music of an all-out bar fight.

Pookii found himself back-to- back with his new friend. Ilii were ensuring no harm would come to the Poollé Kii by letting no more than three or four opponents attack him at a time. Less than ten minutes into the fray, two female purple ran toward them, yelling to the one they called commander. They grabbed her and started pulling her away from the direction of the front door. As she was heading out, she caught the shirt of her newest friend and pulled him along with her. They ran through a narrow, dark hallway and burst through a door into the bright-day and the parking lot behind the bar. They all jumped in a waiting vehicle with the one they called commander still holding on to the Poollé Kii. Ilii were not far behind and got into their own vehicle to follow. Pookii's new friend sat beside the driver, and Pookii was pushed into the back seat. The commander laughed and slapped her thigh as if she had just jumped off the best ride of an amusement park before it fell apart. As they drove away from the bar, military police vehicles with their lights flashing and sirens blaring sped past them. A few loud chuckles and comments were made.

The one they called commander said, "Purlenes, I want you to meet my newest friend, Pookii."

"Hey, Pookii," they said almost in unison, laughing at the name.

The Poollé Kii realized that this new name was probably going to stick and asked if his new friend would like him to call her commander.

She replied, "My name is Daisi."

Pookii smiled and wondered if his heart had room for another Daisi.

As it turned out, it did. They drove for a short while, and then the driver turned into a residential area about a mile from the military base's front gate. After a few turns, the vehicle climbed up a hill and then turned left into a cul-de-sac. As they did, the commander turned to her new friend and tapped her mouth with her index finger. The soldiers in the vehicle sat still and silent. The Poollé Kii could hear their slight breaths, but any other purl would have sworn they stopped breathing. No stranger to stealth, Pookii disappeared into the silence. Ilii, always in tune with their kii, did not need any signal to stay still in their vehicle. The commander noticed their discipline and made a mental note. The driver pulled into a driveway and got out of the vehicle as any normal purl coming home would do, and everyone else remained frozen. She disappeared into the house and, about ten minutes later, reappeared on the porch and gave the all-clear sign. When she did, the commander, her crew, and her guests got out of the vehicles and went inside. As they walked in, the Poollé Kii noticed the "4BX6" where the house number would usually be. This was the same number on the camouflaged patch on the uniform of the soldiers who had accompanied him on his ride from the bar.

As they entered, it was obvious this was no normal home. The couches, chairs, and tables were about where one would expect, but there were also pool tables, video game stations, and an oversize bar. As they entered, the purl who had opened the door and the commander walked into the back. Ilii followed the initial scent of that first soldier until they came to a corner with two large mirrors. Anyone else standing at the mirrors would have thought that they were there to give a comprehensive check on how one looked. Ilii knew the mirrors held more than their reflection. They asked what they were? The soldier looked at her commander with an expression of both wonder and danger. Without thinking, her hand went to the knife handle in the small of her back. With incredulity in her voice, she said it was a dressing mirror. Ilii clarified their question to inquire what was behind the mirror. The commander looked at her new friend. His eyes seemed to be backlit. Although her soldier was ready to fight to keep their secrets, the commander had a growing trust in her new friends. She decided to share her secrets or at least one of them. Daisi motioned to the soldier, and she pushed the side of the mirror panel; it opened to a closet filled with several odd-looking switches, boxes, and gear. The twinkling lights and almost silent hum and clicks of the hardware pulled at the hearts of Ilii. The three of them gathered at the doorway. They asked some geeky questions endearing themselves to the soldier who had opened the closet. They spent most of the rest of the night talking about frequencies, fail-safes, and satellite cycles. Ilii learned the soldiers had rigged the home so that the ubiquitous surveillance of the dratsab and military intelligence would be redirected to another location. While Ilii were engaged in learning the latest military surveillance tech, Daisi and the Poollé Kii turned their attention to other things. As the two of them talked, one of Ilii kept an eye on the Poollé Kii, and one of the soldiers kept an eye on the commander. The commander was curious about the fighting techniques her new friend used in the bar. He seemed to effortlessly transfer the power directed toward him away from him in ways that seemed poetic. They began talking about fighting and about different weapons used for hand-to-hand combat until late into the night. When they finally decided to retire, the Poollé Kii and the commander slept in separate rooms on the second floor while Ilii and one of the soldiers stood guard outside each of their doors.

The next few weekends, instead of courting trips into the interior, the Poollé Kii and Ilii met Daisi and a few of her soldiers at a gym in the middle of nowhere. The commander was interested in the fighting theory and ancient techniques Pookii had suggested were superior to the ones she was using. Daisi was also fascinated to see a maté and wanted to know if her troops or some of her troops could become as coordinated and connected as Ilii. She asked her new friend if he would train her troops. Pookii told her about the incident at the university and shared his concern of being recognized by the pervasive cameras of Prometheus. Aciam Aj only had cameras around military bases and government buildings, which made it relatively safe for him. When Pookii told her this, she smiled. Daisi had run an ID check on her new friend as they were driving from the bar fight. When her soldier gave the all-clear sign, it was not just because she had diverted the surveillance sensors to another location. She had also checked the report on Pookii from the inquiry she had initiated through the vehicle's internal surveillance systems.

The only information on Ilii had been that their antique shop in Prometheus burned down in a fire some twenty years ago. But she did see the all-points bulletin from the Promethean authority looking for "Pedagogy," but her equipment detected the bulletin had been fused together. That particular soldier had assembled the same kinds of alerts when she had worked for Promethean intelligence. The signatures of a false flag message were obvious. The commander motioned to a nearby soldier who came back with a large jar. In it was a camouflage cream. The cream contained nanotechnology that overrode any and all facial recognition software. Within two months, the commander had used her position and mission to have Pookii certified as a military training contractor. Of course, this came with the necessary privileges to get on base and other places Pookii had been cautious to avoid.

Pookii was especially delighted to learn of the existence of such a camouflage because it meant he would be able to get back to Prometheus. A darkening shadow was wrapping itself around the one he loved. The Poollé Kii had held his growing love for Daisii in his hearts alone. The night the guardians held up his blanket in the moonlight, they read the season he was to find the one purl destined to complete his journey to gha. The season of his pairing, as it was called, had begun a week before they left Noth. Ilii had planned to have him in the heart of Aciam Aj before his season began, but the Poollé Kii delayed the trip because of the shadows which descended on Daisy. The possibility for gha-love is very rare. Gha-love is a love reborn from an ancient pair. It is a love so strong it enters the poollé and remains there, waiting to enter the world again. The rituals and tests of the guardians established and proved Pedagogy was of the line of Miis. When the impure bloodlines were extinguished through his tests and purging rituals, he became the Poollé Kii. To become Gha-Poollé Kii, he would need the love of one from the line of Quay. The other challenge was that gha-love had to germinate in the soul long before it was expressed in the flesh. The connection must be made between the four hearts long before the lips touch. But time was passing, and Ilii wanted to push the Poollé Kii to find his queen and contended for more courting trips into the interior.

Daisi and the Poollé Kii were getting closer, and they feared his hearts would find their rhythm with hers. They knew the guardians would not approve and did not want to fail in their mission. Their hearts began to bend with the concern until the Poollé Kii sat them down and told them his heart had already been bound in rhythm to Daisii. Watching the anxiety drain from Ilii made the Poollé Kii smile. With their new military IDs, he was able to send Ilii to Prometheus one at a time to keep a close check on his Daisii. While Ilii would protect her person, he would visit her dreams. When the moons were aligned, the Poollé Kii would call his bride to their home in the mountains by the clear stream. Their love grew stronger and wiser in the dreams. There, beyond time, they had loved each other for eternities. It was a connection rooted in the poollé trees and stronger than the distance separating them. It was gha-love growing in their hearts.

As time passed on Aciam Aj, Pookii and Ilii introduced the female purple of the 4BX6 to a whole new approach to fighting. Ilii did most of the training during the day. Pookii met the troops after work during bright-day. There, they would eat a meal and discuss the day's lesson for hours. For their part, Daisi and her troops told Ilii the extent of the military's ability to surveil the civilian population and several techniques to avoid detection. This went on for months until it all ended abruptly.

Ilii and the Poollé Kii arrived at the training gym and was met by the purl who had driven them from the bar long ago. There had been an incident on base earlier in the week. The commander had just been taken from the hospital and was being taken to an undisclosed location. Her soldiers suspected she was near death. They were correct. Pookii insisted he could help. The purl's expression changed from anxious desperation to faint hope. She turned, began heading to a vehicle outside, and called them to follow her. She was running. Pookii followed her into the cab of the joint-light tactical vehicle, and the driver began to speed away but was told to wait. Ilii had run to their vehicle and were gathering things from the trunk. When they finished stuffing a small duffel bag, they jumped in the back of the troop-carrying vehicle, which wasted no time heading to rendezvous with their commander—or what was left of her.

Light-eyed troops were first allowed to enter the military so they could dig latrines and feed the dark-eyed forces. When the generals needed more bodies to throw at the cannons and machine guns of the enemy, they discovered light-eyed purple could be trained to fight. Decades had passed since those days, but life for the light-eyed had not greatly improved. Given the opportunity to defend themselves and obtain a higher level of respect, many young light-eyed purple signed up. Daisi joined after high school. While her friend Tu was going through college and law school, she had distinguished herself on and off the battlefield. Years had passed, and now she had a battalion at her command. But throughout the military, the predominantly dark-eyed officers still treated the light-eyed troops as "less than." As Daisi had risen through the ranks, she taught her female troops to defend themselves from the rape and abuse that had been common in the male-dominated forces. She ensured 4BX6 females were well-trained in self-defense, the youngest of the recruits were guarded, and she listened when any of them spoke out. Still, requests from a superior were to be considered orders, and there was no distinction made with the entrance of females into the service. At times, this created problems.

One of Daisi's soldiers left her friends to run back to the barracks to get something and was unexpectedly confronted by an officer when she entered. He asked her some questions, which she answered to the best of her ability, and then he made a request she was not inclined to obey. When neither his rank nor the intimidation in his voice compelled compliance, he used his muscles. After a few quick, blindsided fists, he had his way. He finished his dark mission with whispered threats in his victim's ear. He exited the barracks pulling up his zipper as he pushed himself past three 4BX6 soldiers. The soldiers seeing him coming out ran in to see what had happened. Two of them took their friend to the hospital, and the other went to tell Daisi.

Daisi was clear—rank had no privilege to rape. When she was notified of the incident, Daisi went to the hospital to see her soldier. The soldier was afraid of her rapist, but she was connected to her commander by love and respect. She told her everything. Daisi headed to the office of the perpetrator. He was high ranking, but so was she. As she entered the large anteroom of the building, he happened to be walking out. She called to him across the large hall. Her voice bounced, was amplified by the polished marble floors, and invited combat. He turned toward the sound of her voice as contempt and anger rose within him. She continued her verbal assault on his character, enumerating charges against him, and questioning his masculinity. He approached. She continued.

If words were weapons, hers were sharp, piercing, and personal. There were witnesses, and the picture Daisi painted with her words were powerful and compelling. Red rage pulsed in the one who was the target of her words. His skin shone unmistakably rouge. He was much larger than she was and moved toward her until his size advantage was obvious. He meant it as an intimidation and a threat. She welcomed both. If he had walked away, if he had ignored her, she could have been brought upon charges and jailed. If he had not responded, she would be guilty of conduct unbecoming an officer. He could have concocted any story and would have been believed, but his pride and conceit would not let him. Her words would not let him. He stood a good three sizes larger than her and stared down on her frame. His muscles were tight. She stopped her invectives and fell silent. He thought he had achieved his objective. A voice in his head told him to walk away. It suggested he had achieved his goal and there were other means of retaliation at his command. But that voice was very faint, and much louder thoughts were screaming in his mind. Those thoughts were pushing blood into his muscles. Then, breaking the eternal silence hidden in those few seconds, Daisi whispered words that broke the dam holding back his rising rage. Anger washed over him as a wave. He squeezed his fist and sent it toward Daisi.

Daisi saw the blow coming and could have avoided it altogether but chose to allow enough contact to create a loud sound and establish with the gathering crowd who had begun the physical portion of the confrontation. It cost her a tooth. He was large, strong, and powerful. He was fueled by rage seeking unrighteous revenge. She was light, fast, and calculating. Hers was a battle of countering and causing harm. His objective was clear but much simpler—he intended to kill her.

But she was too fast. What began as hand-to-hand quickly became foot-to-face. The MPs had been called and were running toward the fray, but the battle was over before they arrived, and the commander fell to his knees defeated. With the MPs in sight but out of range, he pulled a knife from his boot. It was the same knife he had held to the throat of his victim in the barracks. Rising to his feet, he swung to kill his fellow officer. Daisi was caught by surprise and did not move quick enough. The wild swing made contact and slashed Daisi across her torso. She began to bleed.

Something warm saturated her whole being with the inflicted wound. She connected it to the strange teas her new friend had been giving her. The thought took no time, and before the pain of her wound registered, Daisi caught the arm holding the knife and broke it in a jumping, twisting move that made her small frame spin around his neck. The loud crack of his bone was immediately followed by his short, involuntary scream. The knife fell to the floor. The move ended with Daisi on her feet, looking at her defeated foe, bleeding. Her blouse began to soak with blood. She put her hand on the wound and bent over.

He began to get up. The rapist, instead of giving up, was stumbling toward her. He picked up the knife with his unbroken arm to attempt a fatal lunge. Daisi, with blood dripping through her fingers, realized she might not be able to move out of the way quick enough. She tried. He quickened his pace. His knife-wielding arm raised in the air. He attempted to plant his foot for the deadly thrust but slipped on the blood he had spilled. He stretched out his arms to break the fall. One was broken. The other held the knife, which he let go. The dropped knife hit the highly polished floor the same moment as the hand on his unbroken arm. It bounced. Its blade pointed toward his chest. Justice wanted the two to meet. His hand could not hold his body away. His muscles were too weak, and the knife with which he intended to kill Daisi pierced his heart. He died at her feet. She looked down at the vanquished beneath her, and then all went black.

Daisi began to wake. The lights seemed especially bright, but that was because she had been trapped in the darkness for so long. She struggled to focus. Pain pulsed across her chest as if a line of lit cigarettes lay on her skin. She began to remember. She began to move her arm to feel her wound but, as she did, the metallic ring on her wrist stooped her movement. The sound of the handcuffs binding her to the bed helped her mind clear. She was confused. Officers don't get handcuffed to hospital beds. As she tried to sit up and see her wrists, more pain shot through her body. The move helped her realize her other hand was cuffed to the bed as well. A whispered expletive escaped her lips as she lay her head back on her pillow. Noises came in from the hallway. A large MP guarded her room. Four soldiers appeared. One was her second in command, Lieutenant Commander Aya. Daisi could see the lieutenant commander speaking to the MP at the door. She was not in a good mood. She was speaking too softly for Daisi to make out every word, but she knew the voice. It was her someone-may-have-to-die-here voice. The MP was objecting. He was asserting he had to call up the chain of command. Aya began quoting the military laws he was violating. There were some invectives involved. She was clear. No request being made of the policeman. He was being given clear orders and a choice, step aside or die.

Two additional soldiers arrived armed and as focused on violent solutions as their commanding officer. Moments later, Lieutenant Commander Aya was standing over Daisi, apologizing for taking so long to find her. The two soldiers who had followed her into the room were removing the handcuffs. Either Aya was talking too fast, or Daisi's mind was running too slow because Daisi could not grasp everything that was happening. The first pair of handcuffs and then the second hit the floor and slid until they hit the wall. Two additional soldiers entered, wheeling a brand-new military gurney. One of the team at the bed cursed out loud. The lieutenant commander looked at her. She disconnected the infusion bag from the tube going into Daisi's arm. Daisi gasped. As the long needle was carefully removed from her vein, she felt choking fingers being removed from her neck. The soldier showed Lieutenant Commander Aya what was being fed into the body of their commander. Aya cursed. The four soldiers, under the watchful eye of the lieutenant commander, lifted Daisi onto the gurney and strapped her legs. They attempted to maintain the angle Daisi was already in, but the move was painful. The wound began to seep. As they were heading out of the room, Aya looked back. The IV bag was on the floor where it had been thrown in disgust. She went and retrieved the evidence.

The soldiers, now numbering six, were all female and wore the 4BX6 patch on their shoulders. Two manned the gurney: one in the front, one in the rear. Two soldiers walked in front of them, and two took up the rear with their heads on a swivel. Lieutenant Commander Aya walked beside Daisi. A small army was positioned outside. Six joint light tactical vehicles, a troop carrier, and a gunnery loaded with enough equipment for a small war were on a hair trigger. The air was thick. If a force intent on thwarting this transfer showed up, it would get very noisy. If there were any soldiers on base who wanted to back the attempted murder of a battalion commander, they didn't want to face the 4BX6 to do it. The light-eyed, double-hearted purple under Daisi's command wanted war and preferred a hand-to-hand confrontation to a shooting one but were ready for either. They locked Daisi's gurney into the ambulance and sped off. Many miles away from the base and several miles from the nearest back road, the lead vehicle pulled out of formation and slowed until it was parallel to the passenger door where Aya was in the ambulance. Salutes were exchanged. The convoy peeled away. The ambulance and one joint light tactical vehicle continued into the darkness for another two hours.

The driver drove Pookii and Ilii through the night, avoiding detection, and arrived at the camp at the beginning of next day. Signals were exchanged with the armed sentries who had detected the vehicle heading toward them an hour before through the sensors that had been placed miles out. The hundreds of devices in all military vehicles that made them traceable had been removed, replaced, or made to malfunction to ensure no munitions would fall out of the sky to cease their existence. The small campsite about a hundred yards away from where the vehicle stopped was as safe and well defended as any modern, autonomous force could make it, but the sentries remained exposed to a danger they had not yet grasped. There was one camouflaged tent invisible to the unaided eye surrounded by a small circle of trees. Pookii's senses detected the tent and a presence the sentries had reasons to fear.

Pookii jumped down from the vehicle and walked to the door of the invisible tent. Ilii followed, carrying the bag they had packed and brought. The door opened. They entered a small field hospital. Aya stood over Daisi. She was in pain. Pookii scrubbed his hands and came to the bedside. He directed the attending purl to remove the bandage covering the wound across her chest. The flesh above and below the tear across her torso had turned her blue skin bright red. There was a clear purple ring where what was once blue was becoming red. The wound itself was a festering black line stitched with a single, thick thread. The nurse told Pookii they had attempted to remove the stitches to replace them with conventional sutures, but Daisi had reacted in such pain they chose to wait. Pookii looked at the wound. Ilii came to his side. They gave the patient a drink from a flask. Her flesh pulsed, and she calmed to a steady breathing. They placed a stick in her mouth and told her to bite down when the pain began. As soon as Pookii began removing the strange, thick vein holding the wound closed, Daisi began to bite down. Ilii watched their Poollé Kii perform an operation they had spent many days and hours in remote places teaching him. The delicate part came after the stitching vein was removed because attached to it was the true culprit and cause for concern. The Poollé Kii whispered something and then began pulling. A black thread just thicker than a spider's web was attached to the vein, and as the Poollé Kii delicately drew it out, it began to get thicker. When it was as thick as a thread, he caught it between his thumb and forefinger and began to pull harder. He continued to pull, and it continued to grow thicker and harder to remove until it was the thickness of yarn. The green-haired Ilii stood beside her Poollé Kii with a small woven basket. As the black thread was pulled from Daisi's body, she placed it in the basket. One of the 4BX6 medical team standing beside Ilii looked into the basket and began to inquire why the basket seemed to be filled with black larvae. She wanted to know whether the larvae were in the basket before the thread was placed into it. Ilii darted her eyes toward her, and she realized this was not a time for questions. The sound of her voice had provoked strange movement in the basket. Ilii blew a cooling breath into the stirring mass, and it quieted.

The Poollé Kii had reached a critical point in the operation. The living black yarn had separated into six strands and was anchored to unseen places inside Daisi. They could not remove any more without severely damaging whatever organ to which they had attached. Pookii handed the pulsing black vein to Ilii and leaned to whisper into the ear of Daisi. She nodded in affirmation to the whisper. The operation, to this point, had been painful, even with the drink that Ilii had administered, but no one but Pedagogy knew how painful this next part would be. He whispered again. Daisi bit hard into the small twig that had been placed in her mouth. She screamed through clenched teeth and rose a bit from the table. The twig bled sap from the pressure. Her blue face turned red with the strain. The Poollé Kii continued to whisper into her ear. The moment Aya stepped forward to stop what she thought was unnecessary affliction to her commander, one of the strands released whatever it was holding. Aya thought it made a sound. Its long, razor-thin tentacles withdrew itself from deep inside Daisi's body and into the strand Ilii was holding. The Poollé Kii moved to her other ear and continued whispering. Daisi opened her mouth, and Ilii took the twig from it. She began to weep. She made no sound, but her eyes revealed she was seeing something deep and dark from her past. Pookii must have asked her a question, to which she nodded in affirmation. Tears were streaming. Again, there was a pop, and another of the strands recoiled. This treatment repeated until all the black strands had released their hold on Daisi. The purple-colored ring that had outlined her wound disappeared. The wound lay open, pulsing and blood soaked, inviting the healing touch of someone gentle and loving. The Poollé Kii was there.

Pookii closed the wound with proper sutures. He then took a bandage soaked in poollé leaves and applied it to the healing wound. Daisi smiled. She knew deep pains had been healed. She knew broken and bound things within her had been cured. She touched Pookii's arm.

"Thank you," she whispered and then fell into a dream-filled sleep.

Syng released Zaup's arm and looked at his own. Strange and powerful pulses moved within him. The feelings brought him pleasure. A thought wafted into his mind, or perhaps it was a whisper in his conscious. Before he deciphered its origin, he decided to act on its behalf. His hand snapped out and caught Zaup by the throat. He began to squeeze, depriving Zaup's brain of the oxygen it needed to survive. Syng was enraptured by the power surging through his body. Zaup lost consciousness. His body went limp. The dead weight demanded more muscle, and Syng simply willed the strength required for his arm to hold him erect. His attention to his new-found strength was interrupted as he realized the panic on the faces of the purple in the room. They were yelling something to him. He perceived they were pleading for something from him. He released the body, which fell limp to the floor. Dow fell to his knees beside Zaup. He was still alive. Syng declared himself hungry. It was a command to bring him food directed at no one in particular. Everyone scrambled out of the room, some carrying Zaup's still unconscious body and the others fleeing the unwelcome spirit that had so darkly manifested in the room. Moments later, Syng appeared in the kitchen. Vegetables were being stir-fried, and a thick piece of beast had just been placed in a hot cast iron pan. Syng took the bloody, raw meat out of the pan, placed it on a plate, and began to eat as if he had not eaten for millennia.

Days passed. Syng remained suspended between his dream and reality for some time. He heard the journey of his recovery as if it was a curious tale about someone else. But the thing that drew and held his attention was the tree. He recognized and remembered his fascination with the poollé tree, but what was once a fetishized attraction to ancient myths became a passion in which all else paled. It was a full three weeks from the night he left Daisy dying on the floor in Noth before the dratsab would let him leave his apartment. There was a storyline to be followed, and the chancellor's sudden healthy appearance on campus was not a part of it. When he finally got to the poollé tree, most of the leaves had fallen off, and the few left clinging to the top branches had turned a strange lavender. The university groundskeepers had planted the tree in the hole that had been left for it but not before a storm had knocked it over, and rains had washed all its native soil from its roots. Syng feared the tree would die, and the thought angered him in a strange, unnatural way. He called for the head groundskeeper, who explained all that had been done to ensure the life of the tree. He told the chancellor these things as they walked into the building where the chancellor's office was. When they were inside and out of sight of any public, Syng took the pruning shears from the holster on the groundskeeper's belt and plunged them into the purl's chest. The terror in the groundskeeper's open eyes were the only witness to his deed.

Two additional weeks passed, and Syng began to resume some of his duties. The dratsab was informed of his father's improving condition and provided the news outlets with a narrative appropriate to his purpose. As Syng improved, he returned to the guarded and calculating chancellor vaguely aware of a new, resolute purpose he had embraced. As the months passed, he lost awareness of the presence that took residence in him on the stormy, rain-soaked night of his near death. But what continued to grow in his conscious mind was his desire for the poollé tree.

The death of the high-ranking officer required dratsab notification. Two officers flew to brief him in person. One of them was Lieutenant Commander Aya; the other was the base commander. The attempt to court-martial Daisi for the death of her fellow officer, or the fact that her troops forcibly liberated her from the hospital, failed. The illegality of her incarceration, the fact an officer of her rank had been handcuffed to a hospital bed, the unethical operation on that officer without consultation or consent, and the rape of her soldier were too much for her enemies to cover up. They never intended for her to live. The fact that her elite forces remained loyal to her and had an unmoved chip on their shoulder didn't help either. She was simply too powerful to confront.

Her enemies retreated. The dratsab demanded the truth, and no details were omitted. His office prepared press releases and described the noble battle in a fierce fight against an ambush that took the life of the high-ranking officer. The commander was outnumbered and fought valiantly. A hero's parade through the center of Prometheus and posthumous honors were conferred for his heroism. While the matter was in the limelight, Daisi took the opportunity to retire from her military service. Aya wanted to follow. Daisi had been a parent and teacher to her and had saved her life twice. Aya would do anything for her. But Daisi insisted she remain. They both knew the best way for Aya to keep her safe was to watch from the inside. There were no Promethean parades for Daisi, and that suited her. Instead, she and about a dozen of her troops boarded a troop carrier late in the night and headed to the mainland. Also, among the departing crew were a few of her contractors. Their faces were covered with the near invisible camouflage cream.

Ilii, Daisy, and the Poollé Kii were happy to be home. The soldier whom Ilii met and bonded with over the high-tech equipment was named Vii. She drove them off the base in her own vehicle. They drove to a hotel parking lot about five miles from the base, and she took a small square out of the vehicle and placed it in the bushes. They all knew why. The conversation got lighter as they left the parking lot behind them. They drove for a half an hour and stopped in the parking area of a wooded preserve. Ilii got out of the vehicle, and two of them ran into the thick with speed and without sound. They ran up into the trees, their feet making no more sound than that of a small wapiti. From high among the branches, they spotted the figure they hunted. A purl, kneeling on one knee with a cloak covering its bowed head. Together, Ilii flew down from opposite sides to attack the prayerful-looking, still figure. They intended a surprise, a quick attack. But just as the toes of their feet touched the ground and their weapons began to move toward the target, the figure leaped high in the air. There was a long pole in their hand, and it met and redirected the weapons sent toward them. The sparring match lasted only a minute or two. They had missed being together. This was the loving way Ilii said hello.

The last three months had been the green-haired purl's rotation to Prometheus. She had kept as close an eye on the DLA director as she could, but something was wrong. The maté came back to the vehicle like teenagers returning from mischief. Ilii's eyes met those of the Poollé Kii, and they confirmed what he had suspected. The rest of the ride to Noth was bathed in quiet. The Poollé Kii authored it without a request. He was not pleased with the report that had just been confirmed by the doubt in Ilii's eyes. The Poollé Kii knew that Daisii was in danger, and he had been gone too long.

They arrived at the outskirts of Noth just before the rising of the first sun. Vii dropped off her passengers, and their gear, in a wooded area on the edge of the wild and returned to the base. Pookii, Daisy, and the maté walked through the forest to a circle of six trees that had grown and matured since their ceremonious planting. Ilii set a bedroll in its center, and the Poollé Kii lay down. Daisy lay at his head, and Ilii positioned themselves outside the circle and kept watch. As the Poollé Kii closed his eyes to rest, the trees sighed. Their roots pulsed beneath the dirt. Their leaves blocked the brightening light, and the travel-weary Poollé Kii slept. It was very rare for him to rest during the day, but things were about to change, and this was its signal. As bright-day began, the Poollé Kii rose. Together, he, Daisy, and Ilii went into Noth, stopped at one of their favorite places to eat, and then headed to the laundromat. They had already been informed their home had been burned to the ground several weeks after they left. Strange, dark-eyed officials had come asking questions of the neighbors and had even sent light-eyed spies to the laundromat to find out where they had gone and any other information they could gather. It was a fool's errand. The spies came days apart, each professing themselves as new to Noth, but the clothes they brought with them barely needed washing. They put coins in the washer and dryers to do their laundry, which proved they hadn't been invited to the laundromat as they had sworn. If they had been invited by a purl from the community, they would have known no coins were necessary. Before Pedagogy left, the laundromat had become much more than a place to wash clothes. The purple of that part of Noth came to wash and fold their clothes without need of money.

Everyone shared, and no one wasted. The work of the laundry went on during the day. Purple who went into Prometheus to work dropped off their clothes in the morning, and those who stayed washed, dried, and folded them. Then, at bright-day, those who returned from work came and were joined by those who had been cooking all day. And together, the community ate and talked about their day and the challenges they faced. Often, they would sing and sometimes dance to the music that would invariably break out. The strangers who came hung around and folded clothes while everyone was eating. Then, when the new purple had returned to the laundry enough times to figure out the rhythm of the day, they still seemed more interested in asking questions than simply enjoying themselves. Their red complexion would often pulse crimson when the tables turned, and they were asked certain things.

The spies had disappeared, but Pedagogy was back. The news of his return spread through the community, and the bright-day celebration spilled out into the parking lot. Stories were told, more food was brought, and purple enjoyed themselves until the suns began to say goodbye. And just as the celebration was ending, Vii pulled up with Daisi. The commander had stayed behind on base to say some farewells to old friends and to ensure all the paperwork was right for Lieutenant Commander Aya to get the promotion she was promised. Daisy was back home, looking forward to a quiet retirement, and, for the first time in her life, considering marriage. She had never thought there would be a purl strong enough or that she loved enough to give her entire life. She learned early that strength was required to climb out of the light-eyed hell so many had insisted was her destiny. She had built up that strength and excelled. It had cost her. But in a strange twist, the military career she imagined would take her life had ended, and she was still alive.

As Vii opened the door, appreciation, love, and warmth washed over Daisi. She got out of the vehicle and, for a moment, was walking on air. She moved through the crowd, greeting old friends as she walked toward her newest. She arrived just as Ilii were discussing where they would sleep for the night. They had resolved that they would sleep in the big garage where they used to remodel cars. It was the shop where the roll-ins started and had remained a gathering place for that part of Noth. Hearing the dilemma, Daisi invited them to stay at her home. Pookii thanked her and mentioned they would find another place as soon as possible. Their eyes met. Daisi told him he was free to stay with her as long as he liked. When she said it, she realized she meant it in ways she had not intended to reveal. In fact, something resolved inside her. Her hearts found a syncopated rhythm, and she accepted something as deep and true. She loved him. The instant the thought exposed itself in her mind, a warm flush washed across her body. Her skin flashed a brilliant blue that only one purl noticed.

When the night had blossomed around them and the crowd had gone, the Poollé Kii walked to the wire fence that had been erected around the charred remains of their former home. Without a word being spoken, Ilii cut an opening through which the Poollé Kii entered. Daisy watched her son, who was now a purl of power and substance, until he disappeared into the darkness. The Poollé Kii was reading the ruins. Ilii stood guard. No one asked, but everyone knew he was neither to be disturbed nor questioned. After some time, the Poollé Kii emerged from the darkness. Satisfaction and resolve were in his eyes. Vii had pulled up her vehicle. Ilii were right behind her with a vehicle from the garage. A light conversation began on the ride across Noth, but the Poollé Kii was silent. His thoughts were buried in the events of the last day he was in that home. He was proud the circle which had formed around the laundry was well-established and thriving. During the celebration of his return, he was told the roll-ins on the other side of town were growing larger. Talk had begun of the whole city of Noth having one big roll-in. Councils from the various circles had already begun, and his wisdom was sought on a few matters. Pookii knew this would take time, perhaps more than he had.

Daisi's home was spacious and well furnished. There was a large backyard with a pool and guesthouse on the far side. Ilii unpacked their possessions as Daisi and the Poollé Kii observed. Daisi attempted gentle conversation. She looked at her friend and guest, whose eyes betrayed the fact that he was faraway. She could sense he was troubled. She had never seen him rattled or in any way, even slightly unaware of his surroundings. Something was amiss. Her hearts ached. She tenderly took his face in her hands and turned it toward her. She closed her eyes and pressed her lips against his. As their lips touched, a warm tingle flowed from the crown of her head to the soles of her feet. She floated, lost in the bliss. She fell into an eternity and wished to stay forever. With her eyes closed, a vision of something beautiful began to form, but, before she could see it, something pulled her back into the room. She opened her eyes, intending to look into the eyes and face of the one she had just embraced. Instead, the staring gaze of Ilii evaporated the momentary bliss. They were not pleased. In the second or two she had taken to kiss the Poollé Kii, she was surrounded. She wondered if they would kill her for the breech of protocol—at least, that was the first thought that filled her mind. Her hands released the Poollé Kii, and she turned to look at her friend to gather his opinion. Their eyes met, and they both laughed. His eyes said, *Thanks for bringing me back to reality.* Her eyes said, *Sure, thanks for not killing me because of it.*

Ilii didn't move. Instead, they stood in silence, surrounding their Poollé Kii. It was a request for him to retire into their care. The Poollé Kii was standing in the home of his friend, but his hearts and soul were far from Daisi's living room. So, at the silent but urgent request of Ilii, he went to the guesthouse to rest. Ilii prepared his bed, and the Poollé Kii lay down, but little rest came to the purl whose destiny called clarion. He lay still in the darkness until sleep finally came, but long before first light, he woke to the nightmare he had entered before his eyes had closed. Daisii was walking away from him. He called to her in the distance. She recognized his voice and looked over her shoulder. She stared at him as if she was searching to remember who he was. She thought to pause but instead kept walking toward a peril he knew, but she did not perceive. He began to run to her. He ran to catch her before the danger descended, but he was too late. She tumbled into an abyss. As she descended, the darkness rose to swallow her, and there was nothing he could do. That was when the Poollé Kii sat straight up in the strange new bed. His nocturnal fit had summoned his guards into the room. He opened his eyes and Ilii were there. The message was clear. Daisii was in danger, and time was running out.

When the morning arrived, the Poollé Kii dressed and went to the big house. Vii had prepared breakfast. Daisi and Pookii sat at opposite ends of the table. Ilii sat in the three seats on the left hand of their kii. Two of Daisi's team sat opposite them. His *mema* sat on his right. Vii moved in and out of the kitchen until the whole meal was set on the table. She then sat at the right hand of Daisi. Breakfast began quietly. *Mema*'s son was unusually focused elsewhere. Ilii seemed ready for war. Only Daisy noticed the pulses of royal blue illuminating the muscles of the Poollé Kii. The pulses of light moved from the kii through Ilii as a wave of the sea breaking onto the shore. Daisy did not see any change in her own flesh, but she could feel the pulses inside her body. While all was quiet, she realized they were in syncopated rhythm with her single heart.

Daisi had spent the night falling head over heels for her house guest. She went to sleep embracing her pillow as if it were him. So, she was a little shy at the table until she noticed Ilii. She mistook their focus and could not see the connection occurring between Ilii and the Poollé Kii. She was feeling light and wonderful. She looked across the table and called with her eyes to the one she had been daydreaming about. The Poollé Kii sensed her call, and his eyes turned from his inner thoughts to meet hers.

"Good morning, Pookii," she said with a sultry playfulness.

With those words, laughter burst into the room, and breakfast began.

Dreams are real. It is a deception to believe otherwise. Only those who would chain you in a world of their own manipulations will convince you that they are not. The Poollé Kii had kept Daisii and their love alive through the dream they shared, but the tie between them had become frayed and thin. The pace and pressure to produce had Daisii working without regular rest or any real joy. She was enslaved in a gilded cage and could not see the bars that bound her. She was being slowly poisoned by the myths of her own power. The idea that she alone could change the plight of her purple and shift the paradigm of their oppression was ever present. Someone was whispering these lies into her hearts.

The Poollé Kii had allowed his attention to be distracted. His work on Aciam Aj had required focus. His connection with the commander was beneficial, but her growing attraction had confused him. He knew she had the spirit of a warrior. The process of removing the darkness from her soul knit them together in ways few could understand. He had offered to fill the void created if she released the darkness that had given her strength, and she had agreed to let it go. He was now her power. She saw him as her savior. She believed that without him, she would die. And, until he taught her how to live without the darkness, he was indeed what she needed to survive. But seeing Daisii falling into the abyss awoke something deep within him. It tapped a memory far past his own life. It was a memory brought into his being by the poollé. The memory cleared his heart and focused both his mind and his muscles. Soon, Daisii would be in grave peril. This he knew before even she could perceive it. He needed to get to his gha-love before the darkness swallowed her completely. But there was danger. Power, true power, does not yield to anything except greater power, and engaging those powers always comes at great cost. Pookii, as everyone in Noth now called him, asked Daisi to take good care of his *mema*. He told her he had to go into Prometheus. Something about the tone of his voice and the look in his eyes suggested that her friend would not be returning soon.

Since his near death, Syng had been consumed by his hunt for poollé trees. The myths he had dismissed about their power had been overridden by his experience. Months began to move by as he fell deeper into the dark mysteries. His former preoccupation with purple myths had now become an obsession. The months turned into years. And those years convinced him that he was more than anyone imagined. His memory of the night at Daisy's house became tangled with his translations of the saga of Phee, and he could not unweave the storylines of Tepa, Daisy, and Phee that occupied the passionate part of his psyche. The purple part of him would have lingered to unravel the passions. Did he ever truly love? And if he did, was it Daisy or Tepa? His mind wandered in confusion when he sought to reconstruct Tepa's death. The mutilation and carnage were dissolved into a memory of power.

He did not remember it was his own hands that slayed her. Such self-reflection would have given him a slight chance for redemption. Instead, he gave his mind and attention to the supremacy which pulsed through him the night of his near death. The thoughts consumed him. He was driven by the feelings that surged through his being from the poollé leaf. He wanted to feel that power again. In fact, he wanted nothing more. Each day, the hunger for it increased. Something inside him had changed. He was not someone he had never been, but the purl he was becoming became real in powerful ways he could sense but not describe. He was not simply Syng; he was more. There was someone inside him, someone long dead but now coming alive in a welcome host. It was a commanding force within his soul. It moved restlessly within him as a muffled moan powered by mendacity. But this inner voice brought a dark clarity and focus. He had searched the planet for poollé trees and places where the ancient myths seemed to suggest were relevant. Then, after nearly three years, there was a breakthrough.

The dratsab sent him to what he believed was a godforsaken place on the edge of the empire. Some uprisings had disturbed the supply chain, and production quotas were being missed. The chancellor was sent as an ambassador of peace and gentleness. If his persuasions didn't work, the soldiers would be released, and there would be blood in the streets. Syng suspected the dratsab was setting him up for failure to diminish him in the eyes of the elite, or perhaps his son would have him killed on the journey and concoct some cover story and bring in a new, more malleable chancellor. Syng knew his powers were a threat to the dratsab but also knew he did not have all the pieces in place to protect his position as chancellor or, in fact, his own life. The plans that were in play had to be adjusted. Syng decided he would take Nos. He loved his grandson. He looked forward to spending some time with him far from the gaze of the dratsab. Somewhere, he could finish his training of the one he raised to succeed him. He had always planned to transfer all his power and secrets to Nos. From a child, Syng had guided him in the path to power and rule. He had shown Nos things no other had seen. But his suspicions of the dratsab's intentions made him wonder if, while on his journey, he might have to dispose of his grandson as well. As the thought of murdering his grandson passed through his mind, Syng smiled. He called Nos and directed him to join him; they were traveling to Aciam Aj.

Daisii woke from a pleasant dream. She lay in her bed, trying to recapture the bliss the vision brought. It had been a long time since she had dreamed about him. Years ago, when she returned from the hospital, going to sleep was like going on a date. He was always there, waiting for her. As she slept, he would take her places. They would sit by placid lakes, and he would fish while she lay in his arms. They would lay in soft grasses and listen to the birds sing to them. But the most wonderful part of her vivid dreams were the conversations. They had the most elaborate and memorable conversations. He would make her laugh in the dream, and she would wake up smiling and the joy would last the entire day. He would tell her stories of his adventures and childhood. Sometimes she would lay in his embrace as he read her ancient stories and tales of the past. Often, they would rest in their beautiful home in the mountains. It was their secret place. She wondered why sleeping and dreaming of him made her feel so whole. In those early days, her dreams were more real than life. But another reality grew to command her attention.

Work at the DLA took her away from the mountain pastures and streams of her dreams and plunked her right in the middle of Promethean politics. At first, her work was an invigorating adventure. In those initial months, she was able to accomplish so much for the light-eyed purple. As the years went by, she gained a reputation as a successful advocate for the often overlooked and oppressed. Articles were written about her, and just two weeks before Nos's marriage proposal, she made the cover story of the most read weekly magazine. Only she and a few others admitted she didn't look herself with the dark contact lenses. They were a gift from Nos, and over the years, she had come to accept them as her identity. It was the night after her picture was on the magazine when she had the dream. He had come back to her. It was the most vivid and important dream of her life, or so she thought when she woke. Their love was so strong.

The danger was so real. Daisii woke with her hearts calling her to action. Her love had made a request. She could not remember the dream, but the urgency and importance were unmistakable and stark. She took the journal out of the nightstand and grabbed the first pen she could reach. In bright purple ink, she wrote the message from her dream before it passed from her memory.

Remember, our love is stronger than life or death. I will be there when you need me, and you will always bring life to me.

Daisii stared at the words on the page. The dream began to fade, but the importance of it remained.

"I will never forget. I will always love you," she whispered as a tear wet her cheek.

The dream was gone, but the urgency and the importance of its message was grave. A chill raised the tender hairs on her arms. To remember meant life; forget, and two lives would be lost, perhaps more. She closed the book and pressed it against her chest. Her hearts seemed to welcome the embrace.

Daisii dressed for work, but her hearts lingered on the dream. Her memory went back to the last day of law school. There was something about that day she needed to remember, something connected to the dream, but what was it? She remembered her tree planter and the schoolgirl crush she had. But some important details were missing. It was urgent that she remember. She tried to press her mind past the voice of Nos and the stories he constantly told her about that day. She couldn't quite make it. Something was there, and just as she was about to reach it, the image of Nos came in its place. The impulse to fight rose as her memory was blocked. The thought of flipping Nos's body out of the way came into her mind. She smiled.

It had been a long time since she had fought. She remembered her childhood. When she was a child, she fought all the time. She couldn't remember losing. She thought of her best friend, Daisi. She remembered teaching Daisi how to defend herself. She thought of her friend's baby brother, Bud. She remembered teaching him to fight. She remembered seeing him use what she had taught him to hurt someone and her vow never to teach anyone else. She had a natural ability to fight. It was in her from birth. Her stepparents told her she fought before she could walk. They said she could flip and tumble before she learned to write her name. They loved her; there was never a doubt about that, but they never told her anything about her birth parents or the mystery of how they were chosen to be her parents. They always used the word *chosen*.

Daisii's thoughts were wandering all around the history of her life; struggle seemed to be the organizing principle. And, right at that moment, she was struggling to remember something: another fight, an important fight. It was the last fight she had. Daisii pressed her mind to find it. The concentrated search pushed the joy of the dream away. Someone or something was calling to her. A sense of urgency compelled her. Her brow furrowed and the growing frustration did more to block her memories than reveal them. She thought to sit still and calm her mind. She sat and let her back rest on the seat back of the chair. She read the bright purple words she had written in her journal. Daisii relaxed her shoulders and released a deep sigh. She let her eyelids close and went toward the bliss of her dream.

The intercom rang shattering every hope of recapturing the dream. It was the most annoying sound she had heard in a long time. Nos's voice broke into the room. He had a meeting with the dratsab, and he wanted Daisii to ride into work with him. It was the last thing Daisii wanted to do. But Nos's voice brought her back to reality. *Dreams are empty fantasies*, her mind remembered. Nos was real. Nos promised to put her in a position to help the light-eyed race. He always used that word: *race*. She never liked it. But he had managed to get her promoted to Director of Light-Eyed Affairs. It was what the feature article in the magazine was about. Daisii thought she owed Nos. She skipped her breakfast and hurried to get ready—Nos wanted to leave early. She left the journal on the dressing table. The bright purple words stared into the room with no one to read them.

"Pedagogy!" he almost shouted the name across the store but realized it was exactly the wrong thing to do.

He was just so happy to see his friend. It had been almost three years since he disappeared. Everyone who knew him understood why he was gone. No one knew where. Not even Ka Chi, Pedagogy's deepest friend. That was why all the sophisticated techniques and tests of the dratsab's men could not get any useful information from him. Every question they asked sent Ka on elaborate accounts of forests and plants and the wisdom Pedagogy had about such things. The dratsab believed in technology and relied on the accuracy of pupil dilatations and body chemistry to discover the truth. And all his devices confirmed that Ka did not know where Pedagogy had gone or even who he was. Some of the dratsab's purple used their fists and clubs for one or two of Ka's "interviews," but nothing of any use came out of those sessions either. Ka had strength and history few would understand or suspect. He seemed a gentle purl. He was known as one who tended flowers and played in gardens. He could be counted on for fixing a meal or a broken appliance, but only Pedagogy, Ilii, and he knew the depth of his strength and power. He was poollé-strong and wise. He alone could have found Pedagogy if he chose to search. He knew without being told that his friend was well and did not need him, wherever he had been. But here he was. Ka's hearts leaped at the sight of his friend, and that was why the suppressed, but excited sound of his best friend's name escaped his lips. Luckily, no one was in the store to hear him.

The store was in the middle of a long block of row houses in the poorest quarter of Prometheus. There was little to distinguish it from the other houses except the slightly modified entrance. Inside the house, racks and shelves occupied what would be the living space in the similar houses on the block, but once one entered the backyard, a vista of green and growing things filled the view. Over the years, backyards were joined together until a small, protected field of growing food and flowers created an oasis amid the concrete and gray of that part of Prometheus. Pedagogy and Ka walked to the back of the garden to a spot Ka kept for him. They sat and caught each other up on the journey of the last three years. Ka laughed out loud when Pedagogy told him what he was currently being called in Noth. Ka thought it was a good cover. The dark-eyed enjoyed all allusions to their superiority, and such a name would send Pedagogy to a category of insignificance in most dark-eyed minds. Pookii told Ka of Daisii and that he had come to join his gha. Ka knew what that meant and the seriousness of the quest.

Ka's wife and children joined them in the sacred place in the back of the garden. They ate the evening meal together and sat and sang until the long shadow of the last setting sun bid the day goodbye. The mother and children left, and Ka finished making a bed for his friend in the garden. As the Poollé Kii lay down to rest, the sweet odor of amest sent him to pleasant dreams. Ilii, never far from their kii, kept watch from the rooftops.

The Poollé Kii woke to the same disturbing dream. Ilii at his bedside, on the rooftop looking down and too far away to be seen, stood with their every muscle poised to strike. They sensed the Poollé Kii would soon be in danger, and they would not be allowed to intervene. They didn't like it. They didn't like it years ago when their kii commanded them to not interfere with his arrest. And they knew they would not like whatever was coming. The Poollé Kii was headed somewhere they would not be allowed to follow. Pedagogy rose from his garden bed and washed. He dressed, Ilii applied the camouflage cream to his face, and he went to say farewell to his friend. He kissed the children as they slept, and the touch of his lips brought smiles to their faces and filled their minds with the most wonderful dreams. As Pedagogy left, Ka gave him a bouquet of sunflowers. The beautiful arrangement had one vine-like stalk of amest.

An hour later, the hooded Poollé Kii walked through the main entrance of a tall downtown apartment building. Security was high in that part of the city because of all the wealthy residents. It was higher still in this condominium because it was where the dratsab's son lived. The building was one of the newest in Prometheus, which meant the security cameras were smaller and harder to detect. The doorman had directed Pedagogy to the front desk instead of the dock, where most deliveries were made. Pedagogy thought the slight delay would not make much of a difference. Ilii's reconnaissance report told him exactly when and where he needed to be to see and be seen by the new director of the DLA, but something was amiss.

It was time for them to meet face-to-face again. The dreams had knit their hearts together, but time, distance, and something Pedagogy could not quite understand had begun interrupting their connection. He suspected it was a whisperer. If he was correct, the danger to Daisii's life and his own were real and grave. He was disturbed by the dark eyes that stared at the world from the magazine cover. He read the article, listening between the written lines to hear her hearts. But now, he wanted to hear her voice. The dream they had shared the night before had ended frightfully, but he had managed to get a message to her. In that dream, she began to recognize him, and she welcomed his voice. She promised to remember before the black mist swallowed her. Pedagogy knew being physically closer would help heal their bond. And Pedagogy was happy to be close to whatever battle was ahead because, afterward, he would have his bride.

The chime signaling the arrival of the elevator rang sweetly. Pedagogy looked at the time. According to Ilii, he had several minutes before Daisii would arrive in the lobby. Her driver had not arrived, which was unusual. It was why Pedagogy went inside. The plan was to be walking in the building as she was walking out. He knew the sunflowers would call to her, and when they caught her attention, he would catch her eye, and that would be all he needed. But the absence of her driver suggested her routine had been altered. The Poollé Kii improvised his plan. Before the elevator doors finished opening, the sweet melody of her words rang in his ears. The sound of her heels dancing across the polished stone floors afterward was music to his hearts, and soon thereafter, the sweet fragrance of added amest met his nostrils. He closed his eyes and breathed in the scent of her presence. She was close, and the warmth of her nearness took him to the mountain home where she lay in his embrace. But the momentary pleasure disappeared, interrupted by the strain of veiled frustration in her voice. She was assuring someone on the other end of the phone. She was saying she was almost where she needed to be. He lifted his gaze, expecting to see his gha walking toward him. She was not. He did not notice. What he saw when he lifted his gaze were three guards running toward him. He looked past them to see Daisii walking away from him toward the private exit at the rear of the building.

In the brief moment between realizing that Daisii was walking away and that the guards were running toward him, Pedagogy was glad of two things—first, that he had left Ilii behind with orders not to interfere. The sight of them easily dispatching guards, in what was one of the most secure buildings in Prometheus, would have brought unwanted attention. Second, he was glad he had successfully delivered the flowers. He had connected with the purl at the desk who assured him the flowers would be delivered. The card he left with them would substitute for his presence. In it was a message he believed was powerful enough to keep her from danger. He was right to believe these things, but what he did not know was that Daisii would not see the message in time to save herself.

Pul, the newest security officer in the building, had noticed the unmarked vehicle when it drove up. It pulled to the curb in front of the building and took up half the space where the DLA's driver parked and waited for her boss to walk out the building. He was about to go outside and tell the driver to move when his partner told him that the DLA's car had been cancelled for the morning. Instead, he was told Nos's driver would pick up the DLA at the private entrance. The van stood in front of the building with its engine running as if it was waiting for something. Pul's irritation grew. Finally, a hooded figure exited the panel door of the vehicle carrying a vase with an obviously expensive arraignment of sunflowers. Pul didn't like it. There was something not right. He was fresh off the police force where he had been fired for beating a suspect senseless. Pul knew officers who had done much more and much worse without so much as a reprimand, which was information he shared with anyone who would listen. Syng had hired him the same day he had been fired. Part of Pul wanted to prove his worth to his new employer, and part of him was suspicious of all light-eyed purple. So, when the facial recognition data from three different cameras declared the purl walking into the building were four different purple, Pul's attitude moved from agitated to angry. All legitimate delivery purple had files. And the sophisticated military-grade software installed and operated by the best in the business told him that the purl at the desk talking to the receptionist didn't exist. Pul was not having it. His conversation with the other security guards in the room since the van pulled up had revved them up as well. They flipped the Code Alpha switch and ran out of the control booth toward the hooded figure at the reception desk.

Daisii fumbled around in her purse to find the fob that would open the glass doors to the private entrance. With it in her hand, she lifted her gaze from her purse to the path and saw in the opening glass doors a reflection of an image of a hooded purl. She turned her head, and her eyes locked on him. Guards were running toward him. As the scene unfolded, she wondered why he seemed unconcerned about the danger coming toward him. He removed his hood and took his face out of the shadows. She had seen him before. Something told her to stop. She felt the purl needed her. She thought it was to intervene and stop the beating of yet another light-eyed purl that was surely about to begin. Then she saw them—his eyes. They froze her. A wash of warmth radiated through her body. It called her. At the very same moment, a blast from Nos's horn commanded her attention. Her hearts pulled her toward the purl in the lobby, but her head remembered Nos was meeting the dratsab. As she passed through the portal, her pace slowed. She decided to intervene. Her hearts were pulling her toward the royal blue purl in the lobby. They knew him. Her head swirled in frustration. The glass doors had closed automatically, but she decided to return through them. She stopped to turn around, but as she did, the hand of Nos was on her arm. His touch was gentle and reassuring. His voice was calm, sweet, and urgent. He kissed her cheek and walked her to the passenger side door, which he opened. They needed to talk through his presentation to the dratsab. He needed to better understand why the growing roll-in movement among the light-eyed race was not a problem. He had informed the dratsab she would be able to handle this strange phenomenon among the poor light-eyed purple.

Pul decided he would crack the purl in his jaw. His years of working the Promethean backstreets had taught him to establish dominance and authority early in any contact with a suspect. Once, he broke a purl's jaw with one punch. That got him a reputation in the PPD. After that, word got to the streets that he was a tough purl. But his new coworkers didn't know this about him, and he wanted to impress them. Plus, he liked hitting purple. His thoughts slowed him down just a little, and one of his teammates arrived a second before he did and grabbed Pedagogy's arm. Just as he did, Pul sent his famous right cross toward Pedagogy's jaw. Pedagogy adeptly moved out of the path of the large fist. It had nowhere else to go but the face of the guard who held his arm. It hit him in his left eye and knocked his hat off. He cursed. The other guard leaped to place a choke hold on Pedagogy, but his arm caught nothing but air, and his body slid off Pedagogy's back. The swinging and missing went on for almost a minute without Pedagogy lifting his hands. The Code Alpha had alerted the PPD, who always had a car not far from the building. Two uniformed police officers were running up the steps to the lobby doors to assist. As they entered the lobby, the two guards were gathering themselves off the floor. Another guard was holding Pedagogy's arms behind his back. He was looking to the others for help. The fear on his face suggested he would rather be anywhere other than where he was. PPD ran, took his place, and handcuffed Pedagogy, who offered no resistance. Pul was helped to his feet. The officers began walking toward the doors with their prisoner held between them. Pul called out to them as if to give them some vital information. Actually, he wanted one more shot at Pedagogy. When the officers stopped, Pul fired his fist into the abdomen of the one they were holding. The Poollé Kii was unable to avoid the blow. It landed hard.

The Poollé Kii stared into Pul's soul and extinguished the small lamp that it held. The sudden and complete darkness that captured Pul's soul showed in his face as terror. The officers looking at him took note of the expression. There was something about the purl between them that was peculiar, and whatever it was, the partners decided they did not want an experience like the one Pul and the other two guards had obviously not enjoyed. They took the handcuffed purl and locked him in the squad car.

Two additional purple happened to be in the lobby to witness the entire encounter. One lived in the building and was the warden of Prometheus's largest and most notorious prison. As Pedagogy was being taken to the car, the warden made a phone call. The light-eyed delivery purl had made fools of the three guards. Their attempts to intimidate or hurt him failed completely. The warden didn't like light-eyed purple who didn't respect the order of things. This purl needed to learn how the world worked, and the warden knew just the guard to teach him. He made a call to have Pedagogy sent to his prison. Then he made a call to set up a special reception for the prisoner when he arrived.

The other purl watching the altercation was a beautiful green-haired female purl with sky blue eyes who had entered the lobby without being seen. As the disheveled and embarrassed guards gathered themselves and headed back to their hidden surveillance room, Pul approached the light-blue-eyed purl. He noticed she was very attractive, but she was a witness. In high-end buildings like this, he wanted to know who she was, what she had seen, and whether he should consider her a threat. He asked her. She smiled and wondered if they could perhaps talk about it later over drinks. Pul knew the type: females who were attracted to uniforms and power. He concluded she was no threat to him or his partners. Pul suggested they meet at bar called the Panthae. She agreed. She walked away under his gaze, and he decided he would have her later, with her permission or without.

That night, they met at the Panthae. The two of them sat at a small table in the middle of the restaurant. Ilii sat with her back towards the wall. She wore a skirt that flowed as she walked and a V-neck sweater that showed off her shape. The cut of the sweater revealed enough to keep Pul's attention. He ordered dinner and plied her with enough wine to render her malleable, or so he thought. Dinner ended, and he suggested they take a walk in the warm night air. She complied. The wine he consumed convinced him that he was strong and powerful. The conversation with the beautiful purl had restored his confidence. He thought to take her to a nearby hotel but decided instead to have her in the dark alleyway they were approaching. As these thoughts were moving in his head, the green-haired goddess suggested that he was a coward for hitting a purl being held by two others. He took her arm and turned sharply down the alley. He didn't notice she did not at all resist. He stopped at the end of the alley and, in the dim light, grabbed a fistful of sweater and sent his other fist toward the female. He decided to beat her and then rape her; perhaps he would kill her after. The fist he sent toward Ilii missed its mark, as did his many other attempts to harm her. The high-pitched screams that periodically broke out of the darkness could have been mistaken for the voice of a female. The Poollé Kii had insisted she not interfere with his arrest, but he said nothing about teaching a lesson. And Ilii could not have peace if they allowed this purl to sucker punch their kii and get away with it.

The next morning, Pul was not at work. Instead, a call from the hospital informed his boss he would not be in. Nearly every bone in the hand he used to hit the Poollé Kii was broken. It was unlikely he would be able to use it to punch anyone again. The rest of him was also in very poor shape. Pul lay in his hospital bed in casts and traction. A tear he could not wipe away rolled out of his eye; he understood he was lucky to be alive.

As the PPD officers were driving their prisoner to the downtown jail, they received instructions to take Pedagogy to the prison instead. They complied without objection. It meant a longer drive but overtime pay. After several hours, they arrived at the largest prison in Prometheus. They drove through the gates and into the underground prisoner receiving dock. Their prisoner had been quiet and peaceful. They were careful not to look in his eyes because doing so made them insecure and afraid. When they opened the back door, Pedagogy was sitting with his hands resting on his knees. They looked for the steel handcuffs that had bound his hands behind his back. They were at his feet, torn into pieces as if they had been made of papier-mâché.

The chancellor journeyed into darkness on his private aircraft. He had an official airplane nearly as large as the dratsab's but had taken a smaller aircraft. His official aircraft would draw attention, questions, and press reports anywhere it landed. And both he and the dratsab, for very different reasons, preferred the trip be clandestine. So, after announcing the need for some rest after what the press reports called a long and fruitful school year, the chancellor was off with his grandson to relax and engage his storied adventures, pursuing remnants from the ancient Purplynd past. The truth, however, was that the dratsab was sending him to Aciam Aj to quiet some unrest that had moved through several small factories and was in danger of spreading to more relevant production lines. As far as the dratsab's spies could uncover, the unrest began two and a half years prior in a small factory with handcuffs dangling from a sewing machine.

One of the tailors in the factory decided he did not need to be handcuffed to his machine and removed them. The floor boss had objected. He didn't know how the tailor managed to break the cuffs, but this was his best tailor, so he didn't say much. In addition, something about this particular purl made the floor boss both fear and admire him. Then this tailor began unlocking the handcuffs of any purl who wished to sew without them until most of the sewing machines had dangling handcuffs. Management objected, but the tailor had a conversation with the floor boss that convinced him the right choice to make was to side with the workers. The work was still getting done, and quotas were being met, so there was no real problem. Then meetings began happening, and conversations started that would have repercussions. The workers started going to the bathroom from time to time. They began taking their whole lunch break. The teaching and presence of this strange tailor had given birth to possibilities among these impoverished light-eyed workers, and the change in their self-perception was spreading. That particular purl could not be found and had not been seen for a while.

It seemed that in that part of Aciam Aj, purple began to imagine their lives could be lived without the constant presence of hatred directed toward them because of the color of their eyes or the rhythm of their two hearts. They began to believe their lives could be composed of more than incessant toil. The dratsab knew the danger of such ideas. So, he sent his solution to the problem. To Syng, Pollyannaish ideas like freedom and self-determination were easily exterminated by applying his three elements of social control: food, intoxicants, and terror. And these, he would apply according to a particular formula of his own design. It was, in fact, his social engineering prowess that authored his rise to the chancellorship. He would give food, shelter, and an understanding ear to most of the dark-eyed purple. And, while they ate, the media of their choice would fill their minds with whatever he wanted them to think about. Concurrent with this, all types of mind-salts and body-sugars would be introduced into the light-eyed communities to addict them to pleasures and keep them poor, satisfied, and working. But these first two would not work effectively enough without the third: violence. Violence was the key. Not just any violence, not just the violence of repression or of police forces. Terror was needed. Strategic, precise, heinous acts of terror that were widely publicized but never adequately explained or excused were necessary to tamp down notions that led to real uprisings.

The purple sitting on their couches consuming salts, sugars, and the information framed by Syng would create reasons to justify both the violence and their inaction while it was the fear of the terror hidden deep in their minds that truly controlled them. That was why Syng had sent his best student ahead of him a week before he arrived. This student had been developed over the years and had proved himself worthy of the large investment many times. Years earlier, Syng had recruited him into his service. They shared an affinity for enjoying the pain of others. In those early days, Syng had occasion to assign him a gruesome task that included reassembling body parts and disposing of them. It was the darkness of his eyes and the red glow of his skin that assured Syng that he was special. Syng had his records expunged and placed him as a guard in the largest Promethean prison. There, he knew Noj Burg could hone his craft and watch for possible new recruits.

Noj arrived at the island unnoticed and unseen. He began his work, and by the time the chancellor arrived, the media was awash in stories of horrible murders, rapes, and mayhem. Zaup arrived with Syng. He went to meet Noj and participated in some of his nefarious deeds. Dow and the others knew nothing about Noj or Zaup's partnership with him. Then Noj left as invisibly as he had arrived. The chancellor met with the island's governor. Soon after, the prices of salts and sugars were reduced, the island was granted a new loan to repay former debts, pensions were reduced, and everyone was talking about the deadly crime wave. In a few short days, Syng had outperformed the dratsab's expectations. The supreme leader called his father to communicate his approval. The dratsab was heralded in the paper as averting catastrophe and congratulated in the highest circles of Prometheus. While he enjoyed this prestige, the dratsab freed Syng to pursue his search for poollé trees. Syng had told him that the ancient forest in the middle of the island was a place where they might be found. This was true but not at all the real reason Syng wanted to go to the island.

His team, with a few exceptions, had been on the island for some time. Soon after the chancellor finished his work for the dratsab, they scheduled a meeting to report on their progress. Dow traveled into the port city, picked Syng up, and drove him to a bar on the edge of an ancient forest where they were to meet. When Dow and Syng arrived, the others had already begun drinking and bid their employer to catch up. Syng sat at the bar with his crew while a back room was being arranged for them to eat dinner. The conversation of his inebriated team began to center on a dispute about the alcohol content of various liquors and whose constitution could hold what amount of alcohol. While they pointed out various known and strange alcohols on the glass shelves behind the bar, Syng stared at an ornate bottle on the very top shelf. It contained a blue liquid that seemed to glow in the dark bar. He asked the bartender and found out that the very expensive liquor was called gha juice. He thought it was interesting that the local purple were still connected to the ancient stories. He ordered a shot.

It was recommended that he choose another drink. He insisted. When the very small glass of alcohol was poured, instead of taking small sips as directed, Syng took the shot glass between his thumb and forefinger, brought the glass to his lips, and while staring at the intense gaze of the bartender, began to tilt his head back, intent on drinking the whole thing. He disregarded the panicked look on the bartender's face. He thought to show the ignorant light-eyed servant his power and strength. It was another way to express the dominance of the dark-eyed race, as he called it. Syng threw his head back and drank the alcohol as if it were a shot of whiskey. Something instantly changed. His eyes were still fixed on the bartender whose lips were moving but for Syng, there was no sound. A chill shook the bones in his body. The bartender was speaking and panicked. In his periphery, Syng could see purple rushing toward him, but he could neither hear any sound nor feel the hands touching him. A constriction began beneath his skin. He was being choked from the inside. His heart felt as if it was shriveling, and the sensation sent sharp pains through his veins to every extremity. He wanted to scream like a frightened child. He tried to open his mouth, but the pain demanded it remain shut. He wanted to cry because of the terror, but before he could, a gas fire ignited and circled his mind with a blue flame. His brain began to boil with pain. His pupils flashed the color of fire, his flesh a brilliant red. His body turned out of the grasp of those attempting to attend to him, and Syng crashed to the floor dead.

It was a fitful night of tossing and turning. Syng dreamed he was falling through darkness while using every muscle in his body to prevent his descent. Zaup and Nos attended to him while he slept. They had all gotten thrown out of the bar. When Syng fell to the floor, it was only the fact that Zaup was there and that Dow had a portable crash cart to restart his heart that saved him. The purple in the bar were incensed. The bartender had given Syng the drink over the objections of many and only because Syng had offered triple the already very high price. He had cautioned Syng to sip the liquid slowly. The fact that a dark-eyed visitor to the island had come close to dying was enough to close the bar down and cause trouble for everybody. When Syng fell dead, the locals began ritualistically making signs to ward off devils, darkness, and evil. They were reacting to the myth that said one sip of the blue alcohol would judge a purl's heart. The legend of the drink was that it would kill true evil and any purl who belonged to true evil. The stories also said this same drink would bring a noble purl back from the dead. That Syng died so quickly proved to many that he was a very evil purl. Zaup inquired and learned the alcohol was made by a tribe deep in the forest of an island on which visitors were not allowed. The mixture was distilled once every hundred years. It was acquired, at a very high price, by the bar owner's father the generation before and existed as a symbol of hope and pride in the village. Zaup asked but was not told what plant or plants were used to make it. He asked for a sample but was denied as he and the whole group were rushed out of the bar. He learned later that the blood sample he took from Syng as he lay recovering had the same strange markers as the blood sample, he took years ago after Syng had ingested the poollé leaf.

Days later, Syng woke up in a cold sweat and foul mood. He had been taken to the bar owner's home, which was one of the nicer homes in a circle of houses. The bar owner's wife had nursed him back to health with a few teas and balms. The look on her face suggested she was healing him against her better judgment. Her husband had insisted that he be healed and sent on his way. Bright-day had just begun when Syng was rested and strong enough to leave. Without saying thanks or acknowledging the brush with death he had just survived, Syng and his party got in their vehicles and went on their way. The village changed from an eerie quiet to very active as purple performed communal rituals intent on chasing any residual evil from their midst as soon as they left.

Syng was alive, but it took three more days for him to stop feeling like he had been kicked in the head by a thousand-pound mule. It was a day's slow drive through brush and rock over a terrain that had neither map nor road. They drove into the trees until the forest was too thick and made camp. The next day, Syng and Nos were the last to rise from their tent. Breakfast was waiting for them, but it would be an additional two days before Syng would begin eating anything more than a small piece of bread. The troop began to hike into the forest. Syng and his grandson carried light packs on their backs while the others carried the bulk of the supplies. Dow carried the most. They were journeying to a place where they had met a tribe before Syng arrived.

The advance party had been searching for caves and stands of poollé trees when they found themselves in the company of another purl. The purl seemed old and weak and was walking seemingly with the aid of a stick, appearing to be on an invisible path intersecting their own. Dow, who was the linguist of the group, got down on one knee and gave the greeting he thought was the correct one. He knew if his research was off and his greeting was from the wrong tribal group, it might be the end of his short life. Zaup thought Dow was being much too deferential to a single unarmed native. But Dow was smart and experienced enough to know the purl they saw was the one the tribe wanted them to see. Dow knew they had been followed for the last hour, or at least the tribe wanted them to know for the last hour that they were being followed. He had made the right greeting and explained it was the respect they had for the old traditions and purple that brought them. He told them they were searching for ruins of the ancients. Dow also told him they came on behalf of their leader who wished to know if there was any purl left who could answer his questions.

Zaup was more nervous than the others of the group and managed to keep his hand away from his revolver, even though everything in him wanted to aim it at the threat he suspected. Dow was convincing enough to ease the mind of the purl who had intercepted the party. The old purl flicked his cane and sent a stone into a rock some distance away. It was a move that surprised everyone except Dow, who saw enough in his eyes to understand that the old purl was not only what he appeared. At the sound, warriors stepped out from behind trees in every direction. One warrior took the gun from Zaup's holster, but everyone else was allowed to keep their weapons. They were invited and followed the old purl deep into the forest while the warriors disappeared to the periphery. The old purl took them to a rock wall with markings on it. An entrance to a cave was not far away.

It had been weeks since Zaup and Dow had first seen the markings. They were taking Syng to them. Syng knew this and was anxious to arrive. They paused at the place where they met the old purl and described the encounter to Syng again. Zaup was doing most of the talking. They began to wander in the direction of the rock wall. They found themselves entering a clearing they neither remembered nor recognized. Dow suspected that they were not alone. Zaup took out his navigational assist. He was determined to prove he could retrace the steps to where they had been. When they were at the rock wall, Zaup had marked the spot on his device. He had used the same device to bring them to where they were, only they had never been there before. He decided to trust his technology some more and began to lead the party west. Dow objected. When they were very near the middle of the clearing, Dow sat down and encouraged the others to do the same.

Syng had a growing antipathy for Zaup. He talked too much. Plus, he hated hearing that Zaup had restarted his heart at the bar. Syng remembered the time he woke to Zaup holding defibrillator paddles. Time had persuaded him to wonder if he had needed the shocks to his heart at all. Now, the very sound of Zaup's voice tempted him to hate him even more. Syng, noticing the caution in Dow's demeanor, told Zaup to sit down and be quiet. The whole party sat near the center of the field.

Zaup continued talking quietly, but incessantly, until Syng told him to shut up. They sat for two hours. For Zaup, it was an eternity. Then, just as bright-day began to wane and Zaup was going to make his next argument for moving, a purl appeared from the shadow side of the clearing. He walked toward the group. Without words, he directed them to sit in a circle facing one another. He then helped them make a small fire in the middle of their circle. The visitor waited until the fire grew self-sustaining flames and, finally, he disappeared. The party understood they were to camp for the night. Under Dow's direction, they set up only one tent, in which Syng and Nos slept. The rest of the party bedded down in their sleeping bags in a circle surrounding the fire.

The next morning, they woke surrounded by purple. The purple who could be seen stood with long spears or poles at their sides; a few had what seemed to be small rocks between their fingers. They were clearly all warriors, but not all of them were male. Syng's men thought the females were fiercer than the males, but that was only because they looked as lethal as the males. They were. Purple were behind them and children could be heard moving in the background. The old purl who had intercepted them in the woods walked into the circle. Pitchers of water were brought, and the men were instructed to wash. One of the pitchers was sent to Syng's tent with a wooden bowl to catch the water as he and Nos washed. The old purl would speak to Dow, and Dow would communicate his instructions to the others. Zaup, in particular, was annoyed by this. He thought he was certainly smarter than his EMT. When Syng and Nos had washed, they appeared in front of their tent and waited as they were instructed. All their gear, including their holsters and guns, were gathered and placed beside the tent behind them. Syng, Nos, and his men sat cross-legged. As soon as they were settled, one of the warriors struck his pole onto the ground. The sound it made was louder than would seem logical given the laws of physics and sound. Syng took note. Zaup wondered. The action was repeated one by one around the circle, each purl striking their pole with a loud thud. As the circle of thuds was completed, the purl who began the successive actions fell to one knee. Behind him was another warrior who, as the warrior in front of him knelt, pointed his or her spear at the group. The movements were rhythmic but quick. They gave the impression that the purple surrounding Syng's party were dangerous and fearless. Two warriors who were directly in front of Syng rose and took a step toward them and then to either side. Syng's displeasure grew. He did not like being vulnerable or intimidated. The two warriors who had been behind those two moved backward and to the side, leaving an opening through which a large, cloaked purl entered. He walked toward Syng. His head was covered by an oversize hood. He walked with a cane, and Syng assumed he was an old purl. In his other hand, the barrel of the gun that had been taken from Zaup could be seen beneath the long sleeves of his cloak. Syng's sense of powerlessness increased as the large figure came close. He didn't like it. He was angry at the obvious show of power. He was angry that he was made to wait as long as he had. He was angry that he was at a place on the planet that did not know or care who he was. But he also knew this was an opportunity to get something he wanted. He suppressed his true feelings and hid them deep within.

The cloaked figure paused. The silence increased. The figure stared from the shadows of his hood. He looked at each member of Syng's team and the red hue of their flesh. He listened to the rhythms of their single-hearted selves. He learned much about who sat in front of him. The only two purple whose flesh were blue, like the hue of his entire purple, were Dow and Syng. Dow was standing, as he had been, beside the old purl he had met weeks ago. The hooded purl took his cane and wacked Dow hard against his thigh and backside. Dow grimaced. The place where the cane struck Dow glowed red and faded back to blue. He turned the cane to hold it by its shaft and stretched it out toward Syng. As he did, the figure looked into his eyes. He gently tapped Syng's knee with the handle. The touch of the cane made Syng's entire body glow crimson. None of Syng's team perceived any of this. They, like most purple, would not notice the color of a purl's skin. The figure speaking through Dow told Syng to stop hiding who he was. Dow did not understand but translated the thought, nonetheless. At those words and because he no longer cared to continue the pretense, Syng stopped masking his anger. His flesh burst into its natural red hue. The figure walked toward him. He used his cane even more than when he walked into the circle and extended Zaup's loaded gun, handle first, to Syng.

Syng reached to take the gun. He had decided to shoot the one in front of him. It would be a demonstration of *his* power. He had killed many for much less than the indignities he had borne over the last few hours. He attempted to calculate the cost. How long would it take for his purple to retrieve their weapons? How long would it take to torture the information he needed from those who remained? The gun was in his hand. The figure turned his back. Syng's finger reached the trigger. There was nothing stopping him from a clean kill. Nos looked at his grandfather. He was glad he was going to kill the indignant purl. Syng began to tighten the muscles in his forefinger and panicked. Was he sure there were bullets in the gun? If he pulled the trigger and nothing happened, they would kill him. He changed his mind, and, just as Nos thought he would hear the loud clap of gunfire, his grandfather threw the gun to the side. He told Dow to apologize for any offense that Zaup had given. The figure turned and began to sit. Syng thought he was going to sit on the ground and wondered at the awkward motion, but before his mind could grasp what the purl was doing, two of the warriors ran toward their leader. One threw himself into a roll that stopped with him on his hands and knees beneath him. The other flipped and turned until the two backs of the warriors formed a perfect seat on which the hooded purl sat. The speed at which the one turned to sit and the two created a purple chair beneath him made Dow suspect there was much more to these purple than met the eye. Syng and the hooded purl began to converse. Syng stood to his full height and revealed himself as the chancellor of all Prometheus. He expected the purple would show some surprise or deference, but they did not. Syng asked the hooded figure who he was. The old purl standing next to Dow spoke, and Dow informed Syng and his party they were in the presence of the guardian of Aciam Aj. When Dow spoke the title of the cloaked purl, the warriors surrounding them thrust their poles and spears into the ground in unison. The act made a thunderous clap. Syng sat down.

Syng shifted his tact from attempting to impress purple with his title and attempted instead to impress the guardian with his knowledge of the ancient myths and thereby win his confidence. The guardian was neither impressed nor persuaded to cooperate. Syng showed the guardian many markings which he claimed were from an ancient text but could not translate. The guardian seemed very interested in the markings and asked where Syng had found them. Syng told him they were from books he had found. It was a lie. The guardian knew he was lying but did not reveal he did. After some time, the guardian told Syng he could not help him, and he would not be allowed any further into the forest. The guardian sensed all the darkness swirling around and within Syng. He stood to leave. Syng knew his chance was slipping away.

"Wait, please!" he shouted.

The urgency and plaintive plea needed no translation. The guardian stopped. Syng ran to the backpack he alone had carried. He pulled out the blanket he had taken from Daisy's home. It had lost its light, and the colors had become dark and gray in his possession. But even Syng noticed the gray blanket seemed to revive some in the island air. He held it up in the light of the setting suns. At the instant the guardian saw the blanket of the Poollé Kii, he extended his arms, and every muscle in his body pulsed a brilliant blue. The cloak flew off high into the air behind him and was snatched by one of the warriors who leaped to catch it. The purple in the inner circle made a synchronous move so quick, it was hard for Syng or his party to perceive. It made an almost musical, thunderous clap and ended with them kneeling with their heads bowed.

A strange hush swept across the open field. The blanket seemed to breathe in the presence of the guardian like an infant returned to his mother's arms. Syng did not make the connection. The guardian looked at Syng. He peered into the darkness holding his soul. Evil slithered, and murder had made a home there. The guardian saw females abused and discarded, children abandoned and broken. He saw Daisy, but it was unclear if she was dead or alive. He stared into the eyes of Syng and asked in perfect Promethean dialect to whom the blanket belonged. Syng was startled that the guardian spoke perfect Promethean. But, before he had time to process what was happening, he asserted that he was the owner. The guardian folded his arms across his chest and, standing erect, no longer looked like an old purl but rather a fierce warrior or god of some kind. He asked how Syng had procured the blanket. Syng lied. The guardian asked why he had brought it. Syng lied again. The guardian knew he was lying. The guardian knew the blanket. He knew the infant he had wrapped in it. He did not know how it had come into the possession of the red purl in front of him. He did not know if the darkness that was choking the life out of the fabric was due to a death that had occurred or was coming. He knew what Syng suspected: There was power in the cloth and the information it held. He knew what Syng did not, the blanket was linked to the life of the Gha Poollé Kii.

Syng realized the power of the cloth as he held it. He mistook their reverence for it for deference to him. He began to assert himself as if possessing the blanket gave him authority over the purple surrounding him. The guardian stepped close to the cloth and blew a long breath over it. Some of the dark gray grime that had covered it began to flee from the cloth like dust off an old book. As the dust hit the open forest air, it became black as charcoal and fell toward the grass but hovered above it as if it and the ground shared the same magnetic polarity. It gathered in a small cloud of darkness until it began to form slender fingers that headed to the nostrils of Syng and his party. Each of them, except for Dow, inhaled the dust. None of them seemed to perceive what was happening. As Syng inhaled the black dust, he smelled a sweet odor he mistook for the smell of the guardian's breath. After the guardian had blown some of the dust away, the pattern of the blanket began to reveal itself. The guardian told Syng he held the blanket of the kii. Syng knew the word from his study of the myths. Some thought the kii was an avatar. Others thought the myths proclaimed that the kii was the creative power of the planet in purl form. Syng thought the kii was the ancient purple's explanation of a purl like himself. His understanding of the myths he had read convinced him that the blanket of the kii was like the wand of a wizard. He thought all he needed to do was to learn the correct incantations, and he would possess the power of a kii. He was wrong in both his assumption and his memory, but his lust for power and the potential of gaining more blinded him.

The guardian watched the thoughts move through Syng's mind. He understood Syng's craving and knew the danger of it. He told Syng the gray of the cloth meant its power was fading and that the life and power of all to whom it was connected would fade with it. Syng assumed that, because he was in possession of the cloth, he was the purl of whom the guardian spoke. He sensed the guardian's attachment to the cloth and his power to restore its color. He remembered how it glowed when he took it from Daisy's home and the fortune his rich friends had offered for it. He believed the restoration of the cloth would increase his power.

Still, in the delusion of his preeminence and oblivious to the company he was in, Syng commanded the guardian to restore the power to the blanket. Unseen archers stretched their loaded bows at the sound of Syng's threat. A short breath from the guardian signaled them to relax their weapons. The guardian informed Syng that the colors of the blanket would only be restored in dream water. Syng demanded dream water be brought. The guardian blew through his lip, and an almost imperceptible whistle escaped. Instantly, two purple leaped from their kneeling position and flipped over the inner circle of warriors. One landed behind Dow and, wrapping his arms under Dow's armpits, held him in a vice grip. The other stretched out his arm. Then the warrior speaking in perfect Promethean told Dow to open his hand. Dow's hearts began to race. He complied. The guardian, without removing his eyes from Syng, pulled a leather bottle from his waist. He removed the top and tilted it over the outstretched hand. A clear liquid poured from the bottle onto Dow's blue skin. It splashed and ran through his fingers as water. The warriors released Dow. One of them stooped down and, with a knife, cleared away some grass and made a bare patch of ground the size of a large hand at the guardian's feet. He loosened the dirt over the opening.

The other warrior, at the command of the guardian, brought one of Syng's party and stood him between Syng and the guardian. He was held in the same manner as Dow had been. His hand was extended and opened. The bottle was tilted to let only a few drops of liquid escape. As the drops hit the red skin of the purl, he began to scream in pain. The liquid burned as if it were an acid. His cry was plaintive. The guardian stopped and looked to see if Syng was beginning to understand. The purl's burning hand was immediately pressed into the loosened dirt. Tears from the pain dripped to the ground. The guardian then poured a little of the liquid onto the cloth. The cloth seemed to leap toward the liquid. The wetness made the fabric spark with color. The moistness spread toward Syng's fingers as a fire runs along a fuse. Syng's fingers began to get very warm. Syng, fearing being burned, threw the blanket away from his body. Before it hit the ground, a warrior caught it and presented it, folded, before the guardian. The moisture on the cloth made a small portion of the intricate pattern brighten as if the blanket had taken a deep breath of light.

Neither Syng nor his purple were aware of the difference between the flesh of Dow and themselves. What they did understand was whatever was in the pouch was dangerous. Syng suspected some sleight of hand. The guardian told Syng the cloth needed to be washed in dream waters before the colors would return or its writings could be read. The guardian told Syng the journey to the waters would take several days. He informed Syng that he would guide him to the waters if Syng wished but added that the liquid in the bottle fell from the sky in that part of the forest and, some mornings, a mist of the same liquid would linger near the ground. The guardian suggested Syng take the night to decide if he wished to face the perils to reach the waters. He looked toward the purl whose hand was burned and stated he doubted that all his party would survive. He promised to return in the morning for his answer. A loud thud of warrior spears erupted, and the guardian was gone. He left the blanket with Syng. Food was brought, and some of the purple sat in circle to eat with Syng and his team. Syng spat the few bites of food he tried into the fire and retreated into his tent. Nos never tried the food. In the tent, they talked about the possibility of extending their trip. Syng thought there was no need to suffer such perils. Nos had no interest in archeology, myths, or baby blankets. He wanted to continue the plan for his ascension to the dratsab. They agreed to send Dow. Syng noted that if they attempted to disappear with the blanket, he would have the military come in and kill as many as would be necessary to retrieve it. They ate some of the dried meat they had brought, drank some liquor, and went to sleep.

Just as the first sun began to rise, Nos left the tent to relive himself of some of the alcohol he had consumed. He almost wet himself when, as he parted the curtain to the outside world, he was confronted with the sight of the tall and imposing figure of the guardian standing several feet from the tent entrance. He was surrounded by warriors dressed for a long journey. Frightened by the sight, he retreated back into the tent and woke his grandfather. Syng disliked accommodating anyone, especially when it interrupted something he was enjoying, and he had been enjoying his sleep. Nos told of the scene outside their sleeping quarters as a purl presented them with a pitcher and bowl and left them to dress. They both washed in the water that had just been provided. Nos decided to urinate in the pitcher and bowl that had been brought for them. He thought it the proper indignity to a purple who did not sufficiently respect who he and the chancellor were. What he did not know was the villagers had already done so. Their urine was the only liquid that would not burn their red skin like acid. Plus, the scent would protect them from any kaviri they might come across in the wild. So, unknowingly scented, they presented themselves outside the tent.

Syng told the guardian he had decided not to go due to pressing matters in Prometheus. He ordered Dow to go with the guardian to restore the blanket and then bring it to him in Prometheus. He asked the guardian to send some purple with him to show his team ruins that he had come to see. The guardian agreed and left. Syng, Nos, and the rest of their party packed their gear and were led toward the ruins. Dow and the blanket were left at the campsite. Syng made sure Dow understood his life was tied to the return of the blanket and revealed his alternate military plan should the blanket not be returned. Later, Dow was taken to their village and made to sit cross-legged in its center. He suspected he was taking a test. He was correct. The guardian was nowhere to be seen. The blanket remained in his lap. He did not see any warriors but suspected he was being watched, if not guarded. He used the time to release the stress of working for Syng and to rethink some of the choices he had made.

His hands rested on the blanket in his lap. He had never held a cloth so soft. Yet, he was convinced the cloth was as strong as steel. He sat in wonder connecting his past and present. After an hour or so, he pressed his palms into the ground to release some of the pressure on his butt and legs. When he did, something pulsed through his body. The planet seemed like a gentle magnet and his hands seemed like iron fillings. He relaxed the muscles in his arms and sat back down, but he kept his hands pressed to the bare ground because it felt so good. Then the feelings began to change. What began as an attraction between his palms and the ground became an embrace. The ground began to hold his hands. Hours passed. Streams of peace moved slowly into him and with it, a clarity and calm. He thought his hearts were being recalibrated but didn't know if anything like that was possible.

He remembered the only other time he felt these sensations. It was three years ago, just a few weeks after he had begun working for the chancellor. It was a feeling that washed over him as he looked into the eyes of a stranger. Eyes that connected with something good deep within him. Dow did not know how long he sat. He didn't know if his eyes were open or closed. He didn't know his flesh pulsed red or that the red moved through him into the soil. He only knew the pains of war, with the horrors in which he had participated, passed from him. He knew tears had wet his cheeks. He knew the liquid he drank from a leather flask like the one on the guardian's belt was the freshest, wettest, and most wonderful water he had ever drunk. He woke from the dream—or trance—encircled by a group who seemed to be waiting for him. As he woke, the conversation began. He was fed the most delicious meal of leaves and roots, after which more conversation occurred. As the last sun was setting, he was led to a small hut and told to rest. The blanket was taken and placed in the largest hut in the compound. It was guarded by sentries who seemed both peaceful and deadly.

Dow woke as the first sun began its rise. He had dreamed the guardian had returned. When he looked out of his hut, he was standing just as in the dream, cloaked with his hands folded on the hilt of a powerful, long, razor-sharp sword. In Dow's dream, the guardian was searching his mind and soul to see the substance of his character. All Dow had ever done and his motivations, both good and bad, were exposed to the piercing gaze of the guardian. He left the hut where he had slept and washed in clear, clean water with others in the village. Then a party of twelve, with the guardian in the lead, headed to what Dow imagined was the rear of the small circle of huts. The blanket was retrieved, and an ornate, leather pouch with an image of a large tree in its center was brought from the large hut. The blanket was folded four times and then placed into the leather bag. It fit perfectly. Once it was ceremoniously received by the guardian, the group of warriors headed into the forest.

Their march reminded him of his military days. They moved quickly and quietly through the thickening trees. He thought the sound of his own feet was loud and clumsy. They were. He did not know the danger his noisy footsteps and Promethean scent brought to the party. He only knew that he was safe in the company of those he wished were his friends. There was a strange urgency to the pace they kept. Dow slowed them down. The group traveled all day, barely pausing to rest or eat. When they did rest, they ate a fairly large meal of nuts and dried fruits. After the meal, the group sat around the fire and conversed. Much of the attention was directed to the guardian. Dow gathered that the guardian was a special guest and not always among the tribesmen by the way they honored him and asked their questions. Dow had questions also but did not think it was his place to speak. Instead, he listened. This went on for a while until all, but Dow and the guardian busied themselves preparing places to sleep. Dow thought it strange they would be sleeping in the trees and not on the ground. He was told this was because the night would bring rain. The entire party nested in the trees like birds. Dow rested in his hammock of vines and leaves thinking he had just eaten the tastiest meal of his life again. The stories he just heard, or what he could remember of them, danced in his head. The moment he lay down, his entire body released the weariness of the day's march, and he began to drift into sleep. The sky was barely visible through the trees as he closed his eyes. The stars were bright and seemed close enough for him to grab and put in his pocket.

Dow's restful night ended when he fell out of his tree and into a fight for his life. He was unafraid to die but determined to live. He was fighting to save someone or something or someone that *was* something. It was this confusion that woke him. He was still in the tree. He was dreaming, but it wasn't just a dream. He wasn't sure what it was. The sound of rain beating against the leaves was musical, but he needed to go back to the dream and find the answers to the life-and-death questions the vision had raised. He closed his eyes and shifted his position. When he next opened his eyes, the rain was gone. The sounds he heard instead were of the warriors readying themselves for the day's march. Dow climbed out of his perch in the trees, washed, and began helping to erase the evidence the group had ever been there. They walked through a mist that hung low to the ground for much of the day. They spent bright-day descending until, near dusk, they arrived at a beach to a jigsaw-puzzle cove. Even in the fading light, the sight was breathtaking. The last setting sun shone shades of blue against the curving western wall. The turquoise water carried light from an unknown source as the far wall hid itself in the growing shadows. The twelve purple were scurrying about the guardian as if time was running out for the task they had to complete. Just as everyone had taken their place, a long, curved animal tusk was given to the guardian. He lifted it to his lips and blew three long blasts. The sound the horn made was unlike any Dow had ever heard. It was not loud or piercing to the ears but shook the body to the bones. The earth seemed to lend itself to its production, and the sky seemed to ripple like the waves in a placid lake after receiving a stone. It was a low sound which arrived at the ears after traveling from one's feet. After the guardian's third and final blast, everyone stood still. The guardian slowly moved the mouthpiece of the horn to his ear. Dow was afraid to breathe. He could hear the beating of his hearts and thought they were intrusively loud. Then, just as the last ripple from the blast dissipated, the guardian relaxed and gave the unusual horn to one of the warriors. The guardian turned and sat down. The others, after a pause in which they seemed unsure if they had permission to move, began to attend to the guardian and prepared the last meal Dow would eat for a while.

No fires were lit that night. Instead, Dow was invited to lie down on the sand. He was given the pouch to hold at his chest, and the warriors lay around him in a protective semicircle. They lay with their poles and spears at their sides, alternating the direction of their head and feet toward the trees lining the beach. Two warriors remained standing and faced the forest. Dow knew there was something to be feared from the coming darkness but was unsure if it was purl or beast he should expect to attack in the black of night. He was determined to keep vigil with the others, but the weariness of the day crept toward his consciousness and grabbed it. Then, just before sleep took total possession of his body and soul, the guardian rose. Dow widened his sleepy eyes. The guardian unsheathed the broadsword which hung by his side. It seemed to leap into the air, flashed a reflection of whatever light remained, and descended straight down into the sand in front of the guardian. The guardian placed his hands on the hilt and stared into the sea. Dow decided to let his eyes close for a moment. He was determined to do whatever he needed to help defend the party from whatever would come from the woods or the sea. He just needed a moment's rest. He tried to remember the dream of the night before, but the darkness and the weariness conspired against him. Dow lost consciousness.

A low, guttural rumble of something approaching woke him. He tried to move, but he was not yet in command of his limbs. The sound was getting louder. He opened his eyes. The light of the first sun was close but had not yet given much of its strength to the day. All was shadows and gray. The silhouette of the guardian still facing the sea filled his view. Dow commanded his body to rise, and, as it struggled to comply, he remembered the pouch on his chest. The rumble in the distance got louder. Dow thought he recognized the sound. Just as the familiarity began to ease the tension, the sea began to move.

Something beneath the waters had been awakened. The light that shone in the waters the night before had been traded for darkness. The guardian remained still. The warriors were now all erect. The two who were on the edges of the semicircle had turned toward the sea. Dow found out later that these were the quickest and most capable warriors in the group, even if they were all quite fast and lethal. Eight of the other ten purple still faced the woods. They separated into two groups and took several steps in opposite directions toward the forest. The two remaining purple helped Dow to his feet. They pressed the pouch against his chest and stood guard on either side of him. Dow's hearts pounded as if they wished to be released from his chest. He listened for the low roar in the distance, but instead, the waters exploded in white foam and darkness. A beast the size of a dragon erupted from the waters. Its neck was as long as a serpent. Its skin was as dark as a cave. It rose high into the air and began its descent. The sight made Dow want to scream in fear and cry for help at the same moment. The creature opened its mouth to reveal razor-sharp teeth. As it did, the guardian flexed every muscle of his body. This sent the cloak that had covered him into the air. This was the last thing Dow witnessed because, as this occurred, a pole to the back of his knees sent him to a kneeling position. The flying cloak fell on top of him and covered him and the two purple at his side. The guardian spun the sword in his hands. Its business end headed toward the open mouth. In the same moment, the two warriors thrust their spears into the neck of the beast from opposite sides. The guardian's blade entered between the teeth and pierced its tongue. The beast threw the warriors, whose spears dug deeper into its neck, into the waters as it reflexively bit down on the broadsword. The guardian leaped into the air, removing the blade, and descending with a blow severing the beast's head from its body. The blood of the beast splattered as its body thrashed with the involuntary muscle spasms of death. The blood burned all it hit as if it were an acid. Dow would have been likewise burned if he had not been protected by the cloak.

The carcass of the sea beast fell to the beach. Half of its dark body remained in the water. Smoke rose from the sand where the black blood was being absorbed. It carried a foul scent into the trees. Dow was helped to his feet. The cloak that had protected him was thrown to the side as the acid blood finished its work on the cloth. The guardian cleaned his blade with sea water and a piece of the cloak as others hurriedly washed the black blood from his skin. A grumbling sound went on for several seconds, and then silence. Dow looked around the guardian to what had been making the familiar sound. It was an amphibian aircraft which, by this time, had landed and was coasting with its engines off toward the beach some distance away. The aircraft had flown close to the surface of the water to avoid detection. It was a combination of yesterday's horn blast and the sound of the aircraft engines that had awakened the beast beneath the waters. The guardian and the two warriors walked toward the aircraft that had glided to a stop in the bright sand. The eight other warriors, still in a semicircle, backed up toward the plane, their eyes watching the trees. Their caution told Dow there was still danger to be faced. Dow looked toward the plane, and, in the distance, several crew members jumped from the aircraft. Two held weapons and joined the eight on the perimeter. One tall figure flanked by two purple with weapons slung over their shoulders walked to meet the guardian. As they got close, it was clear the three were female. When they were just a few feet from the guardian, two of them fell to their knees and bowed their heads in respect before the guardian of Aciam Aj. The tallest of them neither knelt nor bowed but instead ran the last few feet and almost jumped into the arms of the guardian. She kissed his cheek and hugged him as if they had been long separated. She wrapped one of her arms around his and stared into his face as they spoke. Suddenly, they both fell silent and looked toward the forest. The two kneeling guards stood, removed their weapons from their shoulders, and trained them on the trees.

The guardian shouted for Dow to run ahead of him. The pilot released the guardian's arm and began running for the aircraft. She was much faster than Dow. As she ran, her feet left no footprints and made no sound. Danger was close. War had taught Dow to sense death before it could be seen or heard, and there was no doubt: Death was coming. The only question was for whom. Dow knew his mission was to keep the blanket secure. Syng had been clear that his life was bound to the protection of the strange cloth, but Dow no longer cared about Syng's concerns. Dow understood the blanket was an important part of something bigger and more important than Syng or Prometheus. Somehow, in his dreams the past few nights, the blanket, the female purl lying in the grass bleeding, and the purl who was snatched away from her all intertwined. The blanket was the garment that kept them alive and together. It didn't make sense to Dow in any way that he could explain it out loud. He just knew the blanket in the leather pouch was worth protecting at the cost of his life and many others. And just as Dow determined not to die on the beach, fear burst through the trees. What appeared first as a dark shadow revealed itself to be streams of fierce and ravenous, serpent-like beasts running toward them. The sound of the aircraft engine and the scent of the sea beast had called them to tear flesh and dine. This, coupled with the odor of hot, black blood, had driven them into a frenzy. Dow thought they were some sort of crazed kaviri but later learned they were of a species much more dangerous. He learned they would feast on whatever flesh came between their teeth, whether it was sea-beast or purl.

The serpents streamed out of the trees toward the purple on the beach. Dow, the guardian, and those who had just met on the beach were running and almost at the aircraft. The guards who had come with the pilot began firing their weapons. The warriors met the beasts that survived the guns with their own versions of lethal force. The beasts continued to pour out of the forest. Dow realized that not all the purple with him would survive. He wanted to stay and fight. He wished he had a weapon of war. Then a stream of beasts headed toward them from the other side of the aircraft. Dow worried that he would not make it. Screams of purple being bitten and eaten began to fill the air.

The pilot was on the aircraft and started the first engine. Her guards stood in front of the door, firing at the coming horde. Dow ducked under the wing and into the aircraft. The guardian was next. The two nearest the plane called out to the others as they backed into the waters toward the moving doorway. There was no saving them. Of the two, one jumped aboard, still firing. The other caught hold of the front strut as the plane backed into the waters. As the aircraft turned to take off, that soldier climbed toward the door. She was at the door as the plane was lifting itself out of the waters. Just then, another beast—awakened by the engine's roar—leaped from the waters and caught her by the boot. The guardian leaped to grab her as she was being pulled out the door. She screamed. Dow watched the beast descend back into the waters, the boot still in its teeth. The soldier was pulled completely into the aircraft, and the door was shut. Her leg glowed red from the knee down, but her foot was still attached. Dow looked out of the window as the aircraft left the cove. There was no saving the others. The swarm of beasts were furiously eating either the sea-beast or purple carcasses.

The five purple on the plane who had survived the melee were silent for hours. There were so many things of which Dow was unsure. What he was sure of was that he no longer was in the employ of Syng. His life was bound with the blanket, and he welcomed giving his life in its service. Dow looked into the eyes of the guardian. They confirmed he was now a part of something more important than Syng, and what had cost precious lives was worth those lives, and more. And, before his piercing gaze turned to other contemplations, the guardian's eyes confirmed that they were traveling toward danger and not away from it.

DESTINY

THE POOLLÉ KII walked the length of the outer fence surrounding the prison and crossed the road to head toward the nearest town. While he was in prison, he spent his days teaching a few of the inmates means through which they could regain their power. He spent his nights dreaming of the one he loved, believing that they would be reunited soon. He could sense from the colors in his dreams that his Daisii was returning to him. The sight of her in the lobby was cemented in his mind. She looked so beautiful, even if he could see that the time she had spent in the DLA was taking a toll on her hearts. It was time for her to be delivered from her messianic crusade and welcomed into the celebration of liberation. It was time for them to be united, and the thoughts of her embrace filled him with pha. He believed that in his arms she would come to see her true destiny, and he knew that one touch from her would give him the strength to lift mountains. There were dangers ahead. He knew this better than any other. The guardians had taught him to read the time through the signs and circumstances surrounding him. He did not have the cloth of the Poollé Kii. His mother had always called it a blanket, and he never thought it necessary to correct her. She knew it was special. He knew it would guide all others to their roles in his protection. He did not know where it was, but at least it had not been burned in the suspicious house fire that consumed the home in Noth. It was finally nearing the moment of his destiny, and he welcomed the perils that would soon envelop him and those he loved most.

With these thoughts rolling in his mind, he lost track of time and distance as he walked. Then, just as he passed out of the view of the last prison camera, Ilii drove up. One of Ilii had watched the prison exit each moment the Poollé Kii was held there. They were overjoyed to see their kii. They had spent every moment thinking through how they were going to get into the prison if he fell into any danger. They had even consulted with Daisi's contacts for the possible acquisition of explosives. As they drove to Noth, Pedagogy laughed out loud as Ilii described some of the plans they had in place.

Nos got up from his table to leave the Panthae, with the warden following dutifully. As they left the restaurant, Nos insisted that one of the ladies drive the warden home. She would ensure he would rest and keep a watchful eye on him should Nos decide it was the night for him to die in his sleep. Nos seemed calm as the warden said good night. The warden took the gift of the night's companionship as an indicator that he had returned to the good graces of his friend. But Nos wanted to kill something. He walked behind the bar and reached for one of the unmarked and untraceable guns that were kept there. As he turned to walk into the night armed with a lethal heart, his actions caught the eye of the bartender who came and—putting his arm around Nos's shoulders—told him to go home and sleep it off. He had known Nos for years. He was the one who had poured the younger Nos his first drink and since cleaned up many of his messes. Nos never questioned his rare counsel. He was like the elder brother he never had. Nos dropped the revolver in the bartender's hand and headed for the door. He exhaled a deep breath as he got in the car to go home. He turned on his display and selected the trace program to see where Daisii was. The locator in her ring showed she was in her apartment, and the other surveillance monitors in her apartment recorded her moving around. Nos turned off the program, believing Daisii was exactly where she should be.

By the time he had arrived at the building, he had decided to stop by her place to speak with her. It was late, but he was impatient. He knocked on the door. There was no answer. He banged on the door, still no answer. The thought that she might have used his simulated-presence security program passed through his mind. He remembered the look in his grandfather's eyes when he described how he had made her last meal and wondered if the poisons had killed her. He dismissed that thought, knowing that if she had missed even an hour of work, he would have been notified. Then he thought she was in the apartment with Pedagogy. *They were sleeping together.* It was an insane thought that, at that moment, seemed like a rational thing for Daisii to do. The thought made his skin glow redder than it already was. He decided to use his override authority and unlocked the door. It was an unwise decision. His using the protocol would be recorded and logged into the dratsab's security notes automatically. This was true for all the important government official residences. But the inebriated impairment overrode Nos's better mind. He spoke the code and lent his iris to the eye scanner. The door opened, and he entered, angry.

Nos went through the apartment like a desperate wolf in a maze; either his prey was there, or she was not. He looked for signs of Pedagogy. Daisii was nowhere to be found. The engagement ring was sitting on the bathroom vanity. He left the apartment. He went up to his apartment and logged into his security protocols. He searched to find where, in all Prometheus, Daisii was or had been. Nothing suggested anything was out of the norm, which increased his suspicions. He knew there was something wrong. She was not where she was supposed to be. She had released the purl who had attacked him. The ring was not on her finger, which meant the poisons were not suppressing her long-term memory.

Nos called the assistant he had planted in Daisii's office. He asked her questions, to which she had insufficient answers. He ordered her to come to his apartment. He wanted to see for himself if she was lying. Nos hung up the phone and waited for Daisii's assistant to present herself. His mind began to wonder who else was a part of the conspiracy to undermine his rise to the dratsab. Nos began to suspect the dratsab had infiltrated his network and would soon know his plans. He wondered why his grandfather had insisted he go on the trip and suspected that even he was against him.

Why didn't his grandfather shoot the disrespectful old purl at the campsite? It was not like the chancellor to allow such indignities. What was Dow up to? What was so important about the rag the chancellor would not let him so much as touch it? Why was his grandfather so protective of Daisii, and where was she? Was she with him at this very moment?

There were too many questions and not enough answers. Nos sat in his apartment with these questions cycling in his mind until the assistant arrived. The peaceful power of the alcohol had gone. Nothing but the cold, calculating, and cruel son of the dratsab remained. He asked Daisii's assistant question after question. This was the second weekend Daisii had disappeared. Nothing else the assistant revealed added to his understanding of what was happening. He raped her. He thought to throw her to her death down the elevator shaft. She pleaded. He relented. She took the elevator down, shaking with fear and clinging to the shards of clothing that remained. Nos fell back into his living room and lost consciousness on the couch.

The weekend passed slowly. Nos's distemper quieted like the crust covering lava. He waited for Daisii to reappear. There was no need to attempt to call her because he had discovered her phone on the table when he had entered her apartment. The ring was of no use, and all the clothes with tracking threads were hanging in her closet or at the cleaners. If he called his grandfather for help, he would be berated for trusting too much in his tech gadgets. He contemplated engaging more of his own resources. With one phone call, he could have the apparatus of the Promethean security begin an all-resource search, but that would involve too many purple. He couldn't make that move without raising suspicion with the dratsab. He was already fearful that both the dratsab and the chancellor knew that he overrode Daisii's security to enter her apartment. He was the son of the dratsab, but Daisii was the DLA, and as such, she had some power. Besides, Nos understood, to be worthy of the dratsab meant not asking for help but being able to solve problems in ways that increased other's fear and your own power. Nos didn't trust anyone but himself. He thought his mind was clear, but it was actually awash in fear, anxiety, and anger. His mind was anything but sharp, but it did have focus. His next move was with Daisii. She was the key to unlock the mysteries that were pushing him to act. She was the center around which the danger swirled. To kill the wrong purple, or in the wrong order, would thwart the plans for his ascension. And he wasn't sure if or how the recent events were a part of those plans. After two days of these thoughts churning in his head, the signal on his desk finally alerted him that Daisii had returned.

As Daisii reached for the doorknob, time seemed to slow down. The joy and freshness she had been feeling from her trip to Noth paused. She began to sense things that pushed the bliss behind her large heart. She entered her apartment. The presence of an uninvited guest lingered in the air. The apartment seemed slightly altered. Things were not exactly where she left them. There was a slight scent she was able to follow from her front door through her whole apartment. The ring was where she left it but not exactly *how* she left it. Her phone seemed to have been shifted from where she had placed it. Her new awareness of sights and scents began after the first weekend with her old friend. Somehow, hugging the toilet bowl sick that first night had improved her vision the next day. The teas Daisi insisted she take home with her had become her favorites. Daisii had just spent the best two weeks in her memory. The second weekend in Noth was more wonderful than the first. But her second step into the apartment brought back something distasteful and dark. The slight scent was familiar. Just as her mind was about to reveal the source of the scent, there was a loud banging on the door.

It was Nos. Daisii let him in as the last bit of pha retreated into her hearts, and her lawyer mind came to the forefront. Feigning concern, Nos began with questions for Daisii's safety. But these moved to insinuations of her fidelity and then turned to accusations of conspiracy. Daisii's first impulse was to defend her actions and allay his fears. The answers came to her mind without any effort: *She had gone to visit her friend in Noth. She put the ring in a jewelry soak, and the liquid turned black. She had no friend in prison that she had released. Prisons, of all places, must abide by the law.* These answers and other thoughts came to her mind but never escaped her lips because Nos never paused. Instead, his anger rose with each revelation of his insecurity. His red skin grew crimson with his growing anxiety. Daisii wondered how she hadn't been repulsed by his red skin all this time. She was one of the rare purple who could see purple for who they were and could see their skin color.

She relaxed into letting Nos vent all his emotional energy. Everything he was saying and doing increased her confidence in the direction her hearts had been leading her for some time. But the peace and calmness Daisii was displaying enraged Nos all the more. The alcohol he had been consuming all weekend had severed the counsel of his grandfather from his conscious mind. He knew how to deal with females who didn't know their proper place. He was too important to be disrespected. If Daisii didn't know enough to be afraid of his power and position, he would show her. He grabbed her arm to command more deference and to instill the submissive fear missing in her eyes. The touch was identical to one long ago. Without knowing what he was doing, Nos grabbed Daisii exactly as he did the day he had attempted to kill her. The body remembers things the mind cannot or will not. The touch sparked something in Daisii. A curtain of impenetrable darkness shattered in her mind, and as the shards of blinding darkness dissipated, she remembered.

Daisii recalled the last time Nos grabbed her arm to threaten her. She remembered in full color. It was as if a large wave washed away the debris blocking her view of the horizon. She could finally see. The green grass of the law school lawn, the warm summer suns of the last day of law school life all opened before her. Her mind woke from a long sleep. Nos appeared as who he was and who he had always been. Something warm flowed through her. She welcomed the feeling and did not see her flesh pulse with a royal blue glow. With the feeling and warmth came an involuntary flow of blood and energy to her muscles. The tissue beneath Nos's grip flexed in response. Nos registered the resistance of Daisii's muscle. It was as if he had taken hold of warm steel. He missed the glow of her skin. His grandfather had trained him to perceive purple's skin color, but his anger was blinding him. He did notice her power. In the same moment the muscles flexed their response to his grasp, he made eye contact. Daisii's eyes held a fire he had spent three years trying to extinguish. He had boasted that the fire had been quenched. He had bragged to his grandfather that she had become pliable and soft in his hands. It had taken years to whittle away at her confidence and security. The patience he had to engage was painful for him, but she had finally submitted to his power and authority. The engagement was proof. But something had clearly changed.

The look in those eyes frightened him. A cold chill rolled over his shoulders. He had only seen eyes like that once before. The memory was not in his mind but in his body. The side of his face where the tree planter had struck him began to throb. He released Daisii's arm and loaded his fist for a strike. He began to calculate. His mind was attempting to catch up with his body.

Why had he left Daisii alive in the first place? It was his grandfather's idea. No, it was his grandfather's demand. What was so special about her? Why was he taken on the trip? Was the warden working with the dratsab? Should he kill Daisii here and now? He left his gun upstairs. Where is the tree planter?

With the last thought, an icy chill hit his bones. There were only three purple who had ever made him truly afraid—his father, his grandfather, and Pedagogy. The first two fears he understood. It was fear of raw, naked, violent power. The third was different and indescribable. He feared it far more than the others. These thoughts took time. He realized that Daisii had left when she was walking back toward him. She placed the engagement ring in his hand. With an extended arm that had the density of granite, she gently pushed him past the threshold of her door and closed it. Nos stood staring at the door. He looked at it and wondered if the dratsab was at that very moment looking at him through the ubiquitous surveillance cameras. He retreated to his lair to plan violence. There were now two purple of whom he was deathly afraid, and they were neither the dratsab nor the chancellor. He convinced himself that time was running out. He knew what he had to do and, at that moment, decided to do it.

Daisii rested her back against the closed door. Three-year-old memories danced before her as puppies released from cages. The entire fight at the law school replayed in her mind. Each blow and counter strike displayed in slow motion and full color. It was as if the fight was a game she was playing with a friend. She enjoyed the memory. She enjoyed the fact that a part of her mind had finally returned. She remembered the Nos of law school. She thought of the last two weekends and how wonderful they had been. Joy filled her cheeks, and she wondered how she had gotten so far from her roots. There were only two missing pieces. Why did the fight start in the first place, and how did it end? Daisii thought she would soon remember these also but was glad she had broken off the engagement. She felt neither alone nor afraid and did not remember any reason to be either. Bliss unfolded within her as a flower blooms in a time-lapse film. She didn't know why she had said yes to his proposal, but she knew marrying Nos was the last thing she wanted. What she did want was a cup of tea. She walked to her kitchen, smiling.

Nos left Daisii's apartment angry and confused. He returned to his luxury apartment and sat in the darkness. His grandfather had taught him to find the power he needed to solve the problems of life in darkness. He poured himself a strong black liquid and sat sipping it, expecting the questions in his mind to clear. The power of the alcohol hit like a stone. He fell into the plush leather of his couch like a tree suddenly released from its roots. His sleep was deep. His dreams were dark. Many hours later, Nos rose with clarity and purpose. He dressed and headed to the dratsab's mansion. It was where the real decisions were made for Prometheus. He knew the dratsab was there along with all those who held power. When he arrived, his position as the son of the dratsab got him through every security checkpoint except one. He found himself sitting in the office just outside the room where a meeting to decide the future of Prometheus was in full swing. He sat staring at two large ancient doors that had been hand carved into ornate patterns. His grandfather had brought them back from one of his journeys long ago. They had hung in the Panthae until his father took over his grandfather's restaurant. He had removed the doors and brought them to his mansion. They both called them the Doors of Power. It was one of the few things on which his father and grandfather agreed. The doors opened out and could not be opened from the side where Nos waited.

Behind those doors at a large oval table sat the richest and most powerful purple on the planet. Conversations occurring in that room would have consequences for billions of purple directly through them. As he stared at the carvings, Nos began to recognize symbols he had seen in his grandfather's work. The carvings pulled him into a contemplative trance as he sat staring at them. He recognized a symbol or two that were on the cloth Dow had taken into the deep with the tribe. As the recognition grew in his sight, some of the symbols began to move before his eyes. Nos wondered if the alcohol he had consumed in the past few days was returning for a visit. The symbols captured him and held him until the doors suddenly burst open. A figure dwarfed by the large doors—yet still very imposing—moved toward him.

The chancellor walked two full steps toward Nos before he recognized him. His sight had been blurred by the fury and contemplations of death swirling in his mind. Nos had risen to move toward the room as soon as the doors began to open. He watched the visage of his grandfather change from rage to wonder as he passed him. But the surprise at seeing the uninvited guest passed quickly from the chancellor's face, and another look began in his eyes and washed over his entire body. The powerful purple in the room behind him had just sent him to solve their problem. They had instructed Syng to do on the outskirts of Prometheus what he had done in the port city of Aciam Aj. He did not mind death or killing, but he did hate to clean up other purple's messes. It was the dratsab's responsibility to maintain the domestic order, and if purple were dancing instead of working, it was because of his incompetence. He did not mind the dark energy in the room; he just didn't wish to perform in any play he had not authored. His son had praised him for his work, but the manner in which he did it left a large space to interpret his intentions. Syng left the room feeling both his power and position were being threatened. He believed that there was at least one purl in the room who had been conspiring with the dratsab to have him replaced. He left but not before beginning to plot his response. These were the thoughts polluting his mind when he ran into his grandson.

Nos had his own agenda. A part of him wished to pause and confer with his grandfather, but he knew he only had a moment to make his move. He had waited hours for those doors to open. Once they closed, they locked to all beyond them. He moved past his grandfather and toward the closing doors, determined to act before he was acted on. The chancellor, recovering from the thoughts that drove him out of the room, began to catch up to the moment he and his grandson were moving through. He reversed his course and, on the heels of his grandson, slipped through the doors before they sealed themselves shut.

The uninvited, but recognized, guest commanded the attention of the room. The chancellor's return added gravity. Whatever was about to occur would come with his endorsement. A silence crept over the room as the large doors closed like a tomb on all inside. They had been finishing the discussion of tactics the coming repression would take, in addition to the deaths and violence the chancellor would author. The warden was in the room. Nos thought the level of discussion which occurred in the dratsab's mansion was far above the warden's position. Nos wanted to know what he was doing there and asked out loud. The dratsab informed Nos that it was none of his business. Nos replied. There were insinuations in his outburst. Several of the purple at the table had known Nos from when he was a child. All of them had power and influence far exceeding his own, but he was the son of the dratsab, and they chose to let the dratsab deal with the interruption. By doing so, they elevated the confrontation. Either the dratsab would handle this situation in a way that increased the fear and power he had, or the perception of his invincibility would be damaged. Nos went on weaving a slightly incoherent tale of conspiracy. It was a mix of what his grandfather had prepared him to say and some additions born of his own fears and insecurities.

The dratsab replied. When he spoke, he did so beratingly. He displayed his utter contempt for his son. He spoke of the plot to overthrow him hatched by his own son and father. He revealed some of Nos's secrets and indiscretions, particularly the ones against the families of the purple present. He called Nos weak and an embarrassment. He pressed a button, and a holographic scene appeared in the middle of the conference table. The image of Daisii throwing Nos around like a rag doll danced on the polished wooden surface. It showed his attempt to murder her. It then showed him breaking into her apartment. The dratsab spoke of a conspiracy with the light-eyed gone bad. He accused Nos of saving the life of Daisii and manipulating the bureaucracy to promote her to the DLA position. He suggested the chancellor was involved. All were silent. The case against him was unassailable.

Nos was stunned by the depth and clarity of the dratsab's case. It was as if the dratsab knew he would break into the meeting. Nos thought he had been setup. But by whom? While he was thinking, a low, guttural sound like the growl of a kaviri about to pounce on its prey came out of the dratsab, followed by a belittling whisper brilliantly clear reminding everyone in the room that Nos had been knocked out by a gardener. Nos glowed red. He only had one option. He ran and launched his body toward the dratsab, who was now standing at the end of the oval table. The force of his body knocked the dratsab backward. His legs got caught in a chair, and his body fell to the floor. His head hit the solid surface beneath the expensive carpet hard and with a thud. The dratsab was dazed, and before his head cleared, Nos's arm found its way around his neck.

No one in the room moved. Nos took complete advantage of his father's momentary incapacitation. Nos tightened his grasp, shifted his body, and heard a crack. The body of the dratsab went limp. Rage swirled in Nos's veins. He searched for another kill. Confusion stirred in the room. A few were banging on the large doors, trying to escape. Others stood at their seats, weighing the cost of intervening. As the dratsab was killed, those assembled in the room released a collective gasp. But only Syng observed that, at the sound of the breaking neck, a thin river of blackness streamed out of the open mouth of the dratsab. He continued watching as the stream flowed into the nostrils of Nos. Syng alone understood the transformation was complete with the momentary reveal of vacuous black orbs which filled the eye sockets of his grandson.

Nos stood feeling powerful and confident. The dratsab was his. When he stood, every purl in the room froze and gave him their attention. In a voice deeper than he remembered as his own, Nos declared, "The dratsab is mine."

Every purl in the room heard him say, "I am Tyne."

Daisii sat at her kitchen table, drinking her tea. It was even better brewed in the clay pot and with the mountain water Daisy had given to her. She had just enjoyed one of the most wonderful weekends of her life. She smiled as she thought of what Daisi would think of Nos—exactly what she was thinking at the moment. How had she gotten so far from her own roots? She felt wonderful about asking Nos to leave.

She looked at the teapot and wondered what few things she would take with her when she left. She knew she would have to leave. Nos was 100 percent transactional. She had managed to keep her body from him for these years but putting him out was something he would surely make her pay for in some way. When she realized that her breaking off the engagement was irreversible, he would retaliate. Sooner or later, it would be in the Promethean news, and Nos would ensure that he came out on top. How much she would have to pay she didn't know. But pay she would. That thought brought her back to the law school lawn and the fight. Daisii heard herself laugh out loud. Nos, she remembered, deserved it then and probably deserved it now. The thoughts brought her to the edge of her memory. There was something more to know, something very important. As she sat in the kitchen, she remembered Daisy, the older woman who had so much wisdom, love, and understanding. Bud had brought Daisy over from the pool house and introduced her as Pookii's mother.

Daisii's eyes watered. Bud symbolized every hope of her heart. Bud, whom life had turned into a cruel monster, had become the most loving and gentle purl she had ever encountered. Almost. There it was again: something in the way of her thoughts. Who else was loving, gentle, and kind? Who else held her heart? There was some purl her memory needed to reach. She had confided in her new mother figure and had asked Daisy to tell her more about this Pookii, but the conversation went into the formation of her own heart. Daisy was captured by this woman, and just as the conversation was to turn back to Pookii, Daisi broke into the room. She called Pookii her purl and playfully told Daisii to keep her thoughts off him. Daisii knew her friend and understood exactly what she was saying. Daisi was attracted to this purl, but he belonged to someone else. Pookii, whoever he was, must be special for her friend to even contemplate taking him from another female. It was one of their primary rules growing up, no purlfriend stealing. Daisi told her she had just missed him. He and Ilii were driving into Prometheus to pick up some final parts for their vehicles and had left minutes before she arrived. Daisi had wondered if they had met because Daisii came in just after Pookii had left. Daisii wondered about this Pookii purl who could change the hearts of Bud and be the catch Daisi couldn't charm into submission.

She looked out the window and around the apartment and realized there was nothing keeping her there. Instead, there was a call coming from her hearts. Daisy had helped her understand and see clearly some things that were happening on the planet. She had such a peaceful way of being, but Daisii believed there was so much more to learn from her. Daisii wanted to be around Daisy as much as she loved being back in the presence of Daisi. The apartment was full, but all she desired was the clothes she brought with her and the clay pot Daisy had given her. Daisii finished her tea and made another decision. She rose from the table, dressed for bed, and went to sleep.

The Poollé Kii realized Ilii had taken care of Pul; it was in their eyes. No words were said, and no questions asked. He just knew. If they had not somehow restored the balance of things, they would have no peace, and they looked very peaceful. The drive to Noth was enjoyable, even if the reports of the repression on Aciam Aj were unsettling. Pookii knew the seeds sown there had just begun to take root, but they were already too deep to die from what the chancellor had done. There was time to finish organizing the big roll-in, and then the Poollé Kii and his bride would retire to the mountain home. That was the hope.

The dreams of living with Daisii in the mountain house kept the kii at peace as the turmoil grew around him. The big roll-in was going to connect Biscuit and Noth with three stops along the way. The route would avoid all major dark-eyed roads and mainly be on the dirt back roads left for the light-eyed purple. All were welcome, and every light-eyed purl wanted to contribute something. Children were already making signs and artwork. Young purple were calculating how many cookies and pastries they would need to make, and every adult was formulating some plan to contribute what they could. They asked no one for permission. They requested no funding from any of the usual sources. They confined their journey to light-eyed territory and property. The light-eyed purple viewed it as a celebration of their independence and self-sufficiency. And light-eyed purple all over who had either heard about it or planned to attend were excited.

The big roll-in would begin as the light of the first sun began the day, at which time a caravan of show vehicles from Noth and Biscuit would head toward each other. There would be celebrations at each quarter mark and at the midpoint where the two caravans would meet. Then the vehicles would encircle a large field three times before heading back to their own city.

That was the plan as the purple of Noth and Biscuit had conceived it. But as the word began to spread, the purple who would be doing most of the preparation objected. The purple driving and riding in the vehicles would be relaxing and enjoying themselves along the way, but those preparing food and ensuring the program at the circle went smoothly thought their work was not balanced with the rest. Purple had talked and talked to no resolution. Pookii had been asked both mediate the conversation and make the decision. But only purple who didn't know the Poollé Kii believed that he would tell others what to do. That was just not his way. He didn't make the decisions for others, but he would come and show the way to pha. But even this he would not do without Ka Chi and his wife, so after a few days in Biscuit working on his vehicles, the Poollé Kii and his friends Bake, Bank, and Bud drove into Prometheus to pick up parts and Ka. They took Pookii's vehicle. One of Ilii drove. Ilii had outfitted the vehicle with all the latest tech their friends in Daisi's former unit had sent them. They stayed in pretty constant contact since they met, always talking about tech things other purple would either not understand or not care about. Ilii drove the Poollé Kii around in this vehicle, suspecting that the dratsab might still be looking for him.

It took several additional weeks of back-and-forth organizing with the leaders from Noth and Biscuit to finally agree that the big roll-in would be five days long—one day for the drive in and parades (because so many purple wanted to come), three days of celebration with games, music, and contests, and, finally, the last day to drive back to their respective homes. Without the Poollé Kii, Ka Chi, and his wife, no agreement would have been made. The respect every purl had for each of them and their ability to listen to the things that were spoken and unspoken turned what could have been contentious into meetings that were conversational and constructive. Now that all was set, the light-eyed purple had growing pha, and every one of their communities were abuzz.

Daisii was determined to tie up some loose ends before she resigned from being the DLA director. She wanted to ensure the positive things she had achieved would not easily be undone. She came in early and left late each night that last week. Her administrative assistant was not her usual self the first several days, but Daisii accepted her explanation of being under the weather. Then something changed dramatically. There was a news alert that broke. Every purl in the building paused to hear the message from the dratsab. When the image came on, seated behind the dratsab's desk was not the dratsab but Nos. Daisii's assistant became instantly ill and threw up in a trash can. She held it, shaking, not daring to move from in front of the monitor. Nos spoke. The dratsab had been assassinated by a light-eyed purl who had been recently released from prison. The purl was known as Pedagogy and had been last seen leaving the prison. A doctored picture of Pedagogy from his time in prison was shown on the screen. Just before it did, Daisii's forehead furrowed, and her eyes averted from the screen to check on her assistant. Daisii knew that Nos was lying. She didn't know why he was lying.

The broadcast ended, and purple went back to their work. Daisii's assistant went and cleaned up. When she returned, she knocked on Daisii's door, entered her office, and closed the door behind her. She was still trembling. Tears stained her cheeks. She held tissue in her hand, and sniffling, began to speak. Daisii spoke over her, calling her name loudly. The interruption caused the female to raise her head to look at her boss. Daisii was tapping her lips with her forefinger. Daisii continued to talk, instructing her assistant as if she was giving her usual tasks to perform. As she was speaking, she gathered both their coats, left her phone in the desk drawer, and led her out the back of the building. They walked under a large umbrella through the rain, and Daisii's assistant told her everything.

Hearing about the rape and the callous and calculating measures that Nos had taken on her behalf—and sometimes in her name—made Daisii wonder again why her opinion of him had changed since law school. Daisii told her assistant to take the rest of the day off and went back to the office with a renewed sense of urgency. That night, in her apartment and away from her work, her mind was troubled. The notion that a light-eyed assassin could slip past the dratsab's security, and the purl she had so often rebuffed was now the dratsab did not sit well. The peripheral glance she had of the alleged assassin was strange and unsettling. She felt uncomfortable staying in her apartment, but in the confusion, she left her cell phone at the office and wouldn't call Daisi to come pick her up without a phone that had some higher level of security. She passed the teapot and thought of her new mother figure. There was enough water and tea for one last pot. Daisii made herself sit and sip the hot brew. The tea did its work, and Daisii, feeling calm and peaceful, dressed and went to bed.

She fell asleep just as her head hit the pillow but soon after woke, fighting Nos. They were on campus. It was the last day of exams. She was walking. She saw a tree and then more trees. She wasn't on campus. The instant she realized she was in a forest, he was on her. He jumped her from behind. It wasn't Nos she was fighting, but something kept telling her it was. The fight was fierce and went on for a long time. When it was finally over, she lay nearly dead among the leaves on the forest floor. Then Nos—who was not Nos—hobbled over to her, leaning on a stick, and stabbed her with it. She closed her eyes to see darkness. She opened them, and her spirit was floating in a hut above her spiritless form. Her body was lying motionless, covered in a garment of breathing leaves. The leaves were dark and moved together as if they were waves on a rolling sea. A purl appeared and whispered in the ear of her body lying alone and still. Then suddenly, the leaves burst in an explosion of energy that lifted her body off the cooling board and suspended her in midair. Her spirit was pulled back into her flesh, and she could feel her bones. The leaves formed a cocoon around her and were no longer attached to her body. Then they gathered themselves and fell to the floor, encircling the bier.

Her body floated back to the board, and Daisii sat straight up in bed and shouted, "Pedagogy!"

It was morning. She had slept through the night, but the dream woke her with an excitement. She remembered. She remembered everything. She wanted to close her eyes to see him again and recreate the warmth of his presence, but there was something more urgent. All the pieces came together into one beautiful, big picture. She was leaving Prometheus and the DLA, and if it would take the rest of her life trying, she was going to find her tree planter. There was no need to go back to the office. Her resignation letter had been written the day she accepted the job. Nos kept it in his desk and would no doubt use it. Daisii felt whole in a way she hadn't since that conversation with her Pedagogy. She was ready to leave as first light began to create faint shadows in the darkness. She picked up her teapot and, turning to leave, decided to take one final walk through the apartment. In her bedroom, she looked at her nightstand. There was one more thing she needed to take with her. She opened the drawer and lifted out her journal. She turned to the bright purple ink and read, *Remember, our love is stronger than life or death. I will be there when you need me, and you will always bring life to me.*

A warm wash of love flowed through her, and a tear ran down her cheek and leaped onto the page. She had to find him.

All the morning papers carried headlines lamenting the assassination of the dratsab and heralding the ascension of his son: the noble, fearless, and wise Nos. Toward the end of each glowing article, it was mentioned that his only flaw was falling for the seductive devices of a light-eyed aspirant to the dark-eyed race who had pursued him through law school and almost tricked him into marriage. Investigations were underway about possible misuses of power while the famed light-eyed DLA was in office.

After Nos murdered his father, the conference room had erupted. A few purple objected. Nos told the warden to kill one of them. The warden complied and choked the man to death, believing that his chance of surviving that room depended entirely on the whims of the self-proclaimed new dratsab. Syng killed another of the room's occupants. He embraced the purl as if to reassure him of his safety and, while doing so, injected a poison into his veins through a ring he had worn to the meeting for just that purpose. He intended to kill his son and claim the dratsab for himself, but the first part of the meeting did not go as he had anticipated. Now, Nos had changed the game. Syng decided to see how it would play itself out. The warden, after killing the purl, went to his knees and bowed his head. He knew his life depended on submissive obedience. Those still alive in the room feared neither death nor Nos. They controlled facets of the media and the militia, and several were loyal to Syng.

They made it clear to the new dratsab that his life depended on his ability to remedy the employment problem and restore their profit margins. Light-eyed purple were leaving jobs in increasing numbers and living cooperatively outside the economy that had been designed for their control. They were abandoning their electronic and tech devices in favor of walks in the woods, gardening, and sitting in circles. Now, there was talk among them of a week-long general strike. The roll-in madness had to be crushed. They told Nos that his father was ineffective, and if he wished to remain the dratsab for any length of time, he needed to prove himself and crush this rebellion. Something in Nos's gut growled with pleasure. He knew that just as they let him kill his father, they would let some other purl kill him. But he delighted in the thoughts of revenge. He smiled and nodded. The purple in the room believed he was assenting to their demands, but Nos was just congratulating himself. He had killed the right purl first.

Aya taxied the seaplane to the beach. Everyone disembarked and stood on the shore. Dow had an idea where they were but wasn't sure. At least there were no creatures rising out of the sea to devour him. The soldiers were told to put their weapons back in the aircraft. They complied but returned with the look of parents who had left their children at home with a stranger. Just as the suns began to set, the guardian took the long horn and put it to his lips—again, three long blasts. The deep and low sound rose from the ground and was felt in the body without the ears registering much sound at all. Dow looked cautiously toward the sea. Aya smiled at him and made a motion that helped him realize that he was worried about the wrong thing. Dow sarcastically thanked her as if the past few days had not had enough adventure. The guardian walked to a boulder protruding onto the beach. He pressed his ear to it. He didn't have to tell the others to stand perfectly still. It was several minutes before he removed from that place. When he did move, he lay down, resting his head on smooth stone.

The soldiers anchored the plane to the beach. They brought out bedding for everyone. Aya took a bedroll and laid it like a blanket over her father. Dow thought it strange that no sentry was set, but the journey had exhausted him, and he was happy not to have to volunteer for a shift. He lay down and fell into dreamless sleep. When he awoke in the morning, the first sun had already risen. Aya and her soldiers were awake and had packed everything except the bedroll Dow used. Dow was given a wet rag and a piece of something he took to be dried fruit. He thought it was a wonderful breakfast. The guardian had not moved from the night before, and Dow asked if he was still asleep. The look Aya returned made him feel stupid. Dow knew every closed eye isn't sleep and realized the guardian was the only one who had not slept the past night.

It was an hour later that the guardian rose from listening to all that approached or was nearby. He stood about thirty yards in front of the sea plane which was bobbing gently in the rising tide. Aya stood at his side with the two soldiers behind and on their outside shoulders. Dow was in between the soldiers and behind Aya and the guardian. They waited in silence for some time. Then Dow heard it. If he had not been not with those who knew much more than him, the sound would have sent cold fear through his bones. Something was coming. There was thunder coming through the ground. Whatever was coming had hooves hitting the planet as if they intended to harm the very ground over which they moved. The sound grew louder and more intense. Flying creatures leaped from the trees on the horizon. In the distance, a cloud of dust began to grow as something approached. Dow's eyes began to focus. The shape of creatures began to reveal themselves. They headed toward the group with the power and mass of a freight train. Dow wondered if they would be able to stop or if it would be wiser to move out of their path. As they got closer, Dow began to discern the horse-like beasts from the dust that flew away from their punishing hooves. The moment he thought he would be knocked down by their power, the beasts reared up on their hind legs and danced their menacing front hooves high in the air.

There were eight of the horse-like beasts that stood before the party in ranks as precise as if they were being ridden by soldiers. One walked up to the guardian as two remained slightly behind and on either side of the one. The five others took positions as if they were sentries. The guardian and the one beast seemed to converse for some time. As they did, Dow sensed the concern of the beast increase, but Dow didn't know why he believed it. Then it happened. The guardian and the beast turned their attention to him. They walked to him, and the beast grew more massive and powerful as it came closer to Dow. The guardian motioned for Dow to open the pouch. Dow shifted the strap slung over his shoulder and moved the pouch from his back to the front of him. He could feel tensions rise. The beast's breath was hot. Dow opened the leather pouch and thought the cloth seemed less gray than when he had held it in his lap. He began to remove it from its case and to marvel at the beauty hidden beneath the gray film covering it. His fascination with the cloth was brief because when the cloth of the Poollé Kii came in view of the animal, it reared on its hind legs with its front hooves poised to strike death. Aya and her soldiers went to their knees and bowed their heads. The two beasts behind knelt. The five sentries emitted a sound that was fearsome. Dow felt as if fire was coming through the nostrils of the lead beast. The beast returned to all four hooves and demanded the pouch. At least that was what Dow understood. The guardian confirmed his understanding and directed Dow to replace the cloth in its pouch and to place the pouch around the wide neck. The pouch hung perfectly between the large muscular shoulders as if it had been made to be carried by the creature. With the pouch securely attached, the beast turned abruptly and ran toward the tree line, its hooves making thunder and leaving a cloud of dust behind. The five sentry beasts moved with their leader as if controlled by one mind.

The two kneeling beasts remained. They were inviting riders. Dow feared that they would not pause in that position too long. Aya kissed her father goodbye. There were tears in her eyes. Of the few conversations that occurred on the plane ride, the guardian had instructed his daughter in a way which suggested he believed it was his last chance to do so. He told her it was time she entered the path to become the guardian of Aciam Aj. She had many objections. None of them seemed to matter. The guardian mounted one of the beasts and told his only child to remember his last instructions. He told Dow to mount the remaining beast and hold on for dear life. It was a literal command. The beasts ran hard and fast across every plain or clearing they entered. When they entered the wood, they went as fast as the trees and terrain would let them. Dow held on tight. Night fell, and the beasts continued. Dow began to fear he would fall to his death. He didn't believe he had the strength to hold on any longer. Just as he was about to give up and accept death in the wilderness, the beasts stopped. The guardian dismounted. The lead beast lay down. The guardian and Dow lay beside it. The others formed a protective circle around them.

Dow asked about the cloth. The guardian told him its story. Dow had never heard of such things and never imagined the forms of life on the planet or how simply and intricately time and life can be woven. He learned that the life of the kii was bound to the cloth. He learned that darkness was growing on Purplynd and that the Poollé Kii was with the lead beast when it was born. The bond between them went back over lifetimes, and unless the cloth was restored to its full power and returned, the cloth and the Poollé Kii would die. If so, the beast would no longer have purpose, and many things would unravel among purple and beasts. Dow had more questions, but the guardian had not slept much for a cycle. He ended the night's lesson with Dow and closed his eyes for a deep rest.

The next day, Dow woke abruptly to the sound of thunder erupting through the ground on which he lay. As the fog of sleep dissipated and his eyesight cleared, Dow looked to see the dust of the beasts speeding away. The thought that he had been deserted began to fill his mind with a mixture of shame and abandonment. But before those emotions could register, terror snatched hold of him. Beside him, a beast reared on its hind legs about to throw its front hooves into the planet. The beast bid him to neglect every thought other than getting his body on its back. Dow knew the beast could not speak and was not speaking, but looking in the eyes of the terror, Dow's mind clearly understood that he had twelve seconds to get on its back because, after that, the beast would be gone. Dow made it in ten.

The beast Dow rode was smaller than the others and a bit faster than all but the leader. Still, most of the day was spent following the distant cloud of dust. The last four hours of the journey climbed through thick woods to a mighty stream. It was there Dow and his beast caught up to the others. The six beasts were drinking from the stream in a way Dow took to be holy. Dow dismounted and went to the bank. He had swallowed dust all day and needed the water desperately. He joined the guardian, knelt down, and thanked God for the gift of the stream. When he tasted the water, he began to weep. The taste of the stream convinced him that the clear liquids he had consumed all his life were better thought of as mud if what now entered him was water. His vision cleared when he brought the waters to his face and eyes. He believed he could see a leaf flutter on a tree branch a mile away. He wanted to fill his water-skin, but the guardian stated that the beasts had given them permission to drink the water, not take it. Dow was confused but accepted that his purl brain was not of the highest intelligence on the planet.

The lead beast breathed through its nostrils as soon as the beast that brought Dow finished drinking. It began walking up the bank. The guardian walked beside it. They seemed to be having a silent conversation. The beasts walked in single file behind their leader. The beast that had been Dow's mount was the youngest and was the last in the caravan of purl and beast. Just as the second moon added its light to the star-filled sky, the group came to a large pool not far from the base of a waterfall. Four of the beasts walked into the pool and paused. They dipped their long noses into the water three times and walked out, two on each bank, with their docks to the water and their eyes trained on the darkness behind the trees. The guardian took the leather pouch off the neck of the leader. Then the leader and the three remaining beasts walked into the water, the leader in front, one on each side, and one behind. They entered the waters, walked in a complete circle, and stopped, facing the waterfall. The third moon was rising.

The two purple entered the pool and stood in front of the beasts. When Dow entered the water, he felt a cold chill that went through his feet to his bones. It was as if his entire skeleton had been refrigerated. The cold chill pulsed through his entire body and then, warming, began to radiate heat. He was unaware that his flesh flashed red or that the redness, like ink, flowed downstream. The guardian took the cloth out of its case. He instructed Dow to dip the empty case into the waters and hold it there for a short while. The waters filled the empty pocket, and wetness moved up the strap around Dow's shoulder. He could feel something move in the leather. The darkness it had absorbed on behalf of the cloth was escaping into the waters. It descended into the waters and flowed down into the small stones at the bottom of the pool. The beasts snorted and moved their hooves so as not to allow any of the blackness to attach or touch their legs or hooves. The third moon came fully into view, and the waters shone a brilliant royal blue. Dow wanted to stare in wonder at the beauty of the waters, but the guardian's gaze called him to attention. He knew without words or explanation that there were things to be done and that there was an important role for him to play. There was no time for wondering at the sights. Dow lifted the pouch out of the waters and emptied it. The leather almost instantly felt dry, soft, and alive. The tree on its face seem to blossom; its trunk and branches shone with iridescence.

The guardian opened the cloth in the light of the three moons. He gave the blanket to Dow and told him to hold it tight.

"Whatever happens, don't let go," the guardian spoke out loud for emphasis.

Dow could see from the look in his eyes that it was critical for him to hold on. He didn't know why. There was no logical reason he could conjure to suggest he hold it any tighter, but he had long abandoned confidence in his ability to command his own actions in the presence of the guardian. He closed his fists and pressed his fingers into his palms. The guardian walked a few steps away from the group toward the center of the pool. He unsheathed his sword, which seemed to jump from his side and twirl in the air. Its blade flashed the light of the moons like a mirror, and then, with both hands, the guardian thrust its tip into the bottom of the pool.

Dow could see through the clear blue water that the blade had pierced stone and rock and entered the bed beneath. The guardian pulled back on his sword with all his strength. A black wound opened at the bottom of the pool where the sword had struck. As soon as the blade created the opening, the cloth flew toward the bottom of the pool. Dow's grip held, but the force and speed of the flying cloth pulled him off his feet and headfirst under the water. He had time to neither take a breath nor close his mouth. He felt a fine, cold sand flowing through his fingers. He tightened his grip. He thought the cloth was disintegrating, but all he could see at his fists was blackness flowing toward the opening. He didn't know how long he had held his breath or how much longer he could. He realized that he might drown. Then he was convinced that he *was* drowning and about to die. At that moment, he determined to die holding on to the cloth. His mind went blank, and the pressure to grip the cloth as he died made his forehead ache.

Just as he was about to give in to death and be sucked into the crack the guardian had made, he felt the teeth of one of the beasts lift him by the belt on his waist completely out of the waters. He gasped for air. His fists were still clenched, but he couldn't feel anything in his hands. He feared he had failed. He didn't know what he could have done differently. He shook his head and opened his eyes to see the guardian's sword flash as it twirled in the air on its way back to its sheath. Then he looked between what he thought were his empty hands, and there it was. The cloth felt as light as a feather. Its intricate patterns were woven in different colors of light. Each color seemed to have its own sound, and the blanket seemed to sing in a multidimensional harmony that could have called the heavens into being. It was thick and soft and seemed bone dry but alive with beauty and meaning. The beast lowered Dow to his feet. Dow held the cloth up to the moons instinctively. The guardian and the beasts stood together and studied the markings until the light of the moons began to wane. Suddenly, the top half of the cloth went dark. Dow's hearts paused. He wondered if he had done something. The guardian and the beasts reacted. The sentries had turned to face the cloth, and all the beasts reared on their hind legs, lifted their snouts, and made a piercingly fierce sound akin to a lion's roar and the cry of an eagle. Pain shot through Dow's bones. He looked to see the guardian's reaction, only to realize that his head was also lifted to the heavens, contributing to the clarion sound.

After those moments suspended in eternity, the beasts returned to their four hooves. The guardian folded the cloth and placed it in the leather case. The poollé tree on the face of the case glowed as it received the cloth. The beasts all began filling their bodies with water from the pool. The guardian filled two flasks and drank as well. He told Dow to do the same. The beasts' bodies glowed red and blue as if they were made of pearl. The guardian reminded Dow that the cloth, the lead beast, and the Poollé Kii were connected in intricate and dependent ways. The rapid darkening of the cloth meant death was near the kii. And if so, the guardian and the beasts were determined it would have to meet them first. Dow didn't know what the beast understood, but he was sure the beast and its guards were headed to intercept death on its way to the kii. He sensed that when they left the pool, there would be no pause until they did.

Preparations for the big roll-in were settled. The weekends before and after would be for setup and breakdown, and everyone would share equally in those activities. The first day, a parade of vehicles would head out from both Noth and Biscuit, with the show vehicles in the front and rear and service trucks and buses in between. By the beginning of bright-day, each would pause for a celebration meal and then continue to the great circle. If all went well, they would arrive at the place where the great circle would occur at the same time. The morning of the second day would begin with setting up the campsites. Children had their own area. Youth, singles, and those who wished to camp as families each had their own sections. After inspections, the parade would begin. The show cars would circle the field three times, driving slowly and with as much joy as could be shared. All the vehicles would then park, forming the outer rim of the circle, and the full-on festival would begin. It had taken one whole week just to determine the order and placement of the show vehicles. Every other thing had taken equal or more time to plan. But after the plans had been checked over and over, the day for the big roll-in was just a night's rest away.

Tu had spent the last two weeks in Noth with Daisi. She kept suggesting she look for her own place in Noth, but Daisi insisted she stay. Tu's hearts began to grow in Noth. She hadn't realized how her life had become so overwhelmed with worry and concerns about bureaucratic things that rarely made it down to the lives of the purple she cared most about. Her heart longed for Pedagogy, and she spent the weeks after leaving the DLA searching for clues of who he was and where he was. One bright-day, after working with Daisi around the house and on the big roll-in logistics, she confided in her friend that she was in love and looking for Pedagogy. Daisi thought it was funny that her friend was so head over heels in love. Daisi reminded her of their preteen days when they bet each other who would get married first. Tu told her friend she wasn't married yet and kidded that they should have a double wedding. Daisi asked who it was she was to marry in this double wedding and then had to explain that her deep love for Pookii was not the marrying kind. She told Tu how he had saved both her life and soul on Aciam Aj. And then she told her about the time she had kissed him and how Ilii almost threw her through her own window for doing it. They both laughed. And Daisi told Tu that Pookii was some sort of kii thing and that he was already in love with some purlene whom she had never met. So, Tu had better get ready to pay her debt.

Tu shared her clues that the tree planter had to have been hired to plant the tree on campus. She had never seen him before, and he had not been wearing a campus maintenance purl uniform. She deduced that he must have been hired out of the chancellor's office. But she also knew that, with her current status, she couldn't get close to the law school to ask questions. She wondered if he was anywhere on Prometheus, owing to the fact that none of the state's resources seemed to be able to find him. Tu wondered if Daisi would help her get to Aciam Aj. She knew light-eyed purple often went there to disappear from the ubiquitous surveillance of the dratsab. Daisi was unaware that Daisy had dated the chancellor at the time Tu was talking about him, and she had no idea her Pookii was Daisii's Pedagogy. What she did know was that her friend was desperately in love and that she would do anything to help her.

Conveniently, Aya had just flown onto the base and had sent Ilii a care package. Bud had told his sister he was coming to pick it up, and he was already behind the time he had set. Daisi told her friend she would call Aya and see if she could get her an unrecorded ride to Aciam Aj. She hurried to get on her secure comm unit because she thought Aya was leaving sometime that very day.

As if on cue, Bud walked in not a minute after Daisi had gone inside the house to her "comm shack," as she called it. It was a closet much like she had at the 4BX6 rec house. Bud stopped by to get the care package that had just come in from Aciam Aj. The ever-present Promethean security systems were always being improved and modified, and Ilii insisted on being apprised of the latest tech and protocols. Both Ilii and their friends believed that the security of the Poollé Kii had to be more sophisticated than camouflage cream, of which they had just run out. Their friends at the 4BX6 had fixed some gadget that Ilii had sent them months ago. It was not something one could send through the mail, and they needed it for the big roll-in. Bud walked in through the backyard and was headed to the pool house to get it when he ran into Tu. He, of course, gave her another big hug. As they exchanged hellos, Bud asked if she was really going to tear up every time. She replied that she hoped so. She asked how things were going with the big roll-in preparations. He let her know they were hectic. He was just running in to pick something up.

As he turned from their embrace to head to the pool house, their eyes met again, and Tu said, "I really want to meet the purl who helped you change."

Bud smiled as he hurried onto the house and told her that he was in the vehicle outside. He said he would ask him to come meet his other "little sister." Just then, Daisi came rushing out of the house. She told Tu that Aya agreed to take her, but she already had a flight time. If Tu really wanted to go, she would have to be at the base in an hour. Daisi told her, given the time it would take to get to the base, through security protocols, and to the aircraft, she had to leave as soon as possible. She said Aya would be back in another two months or so, and that would be her next opportunity.

It was not a question for Tu. She was desperate to find her Pedagogy. She felt that she had waited for more than a lifetime for this purl (a thought that always made her "lawyer mind" spin in circles, but it was what she really came to believe). She had lost three years, and she didn't have another minute to waste without him. She told Daisi to get the vehicle ready and ran into the house. As she ran, she thought the only thing she really needed was the teapot Daisy gave her. OK, her mind added that a few pairs of underwear would probably be good to have as well. She smiled at her own internal wit. She was excited. She began to think of the house in the mountains from her dreams. *Aciam Aj has mountains*, she thought on her way to her room. She smiled again. She was thinking insanely illogically, and she loved it.

Bud got back to the vehicle and gave Ilii the package. They took it and opened it like an eight-year-old at Christmas. Ilii were talking to Pookii about the big roll-in. Earlier in the week when Ilii, the Poollé Kii, and others were camping at the great meadow where the big roll-in would take place, they were awakened in the night by a roar in the distance. Ilii were wondering if it was a death cry. The Poollé Kii was explaining that it was akin to a death cry but something of even greater concern. Bud interrupted. He asked Pookii if he would come in to meet his "sister."

Ilii looked at him, wondering how some purple didn't really understand who the Poollé Kii was and how it was that they talked to him as if he was just another purl. Bud was oblivious. The Poollé Kii asked if she was coming to the big roll-in. Bud thought so. Pookii suggested he would meet her then. Ilii took that as their command and started up the vehicle.

Just as they began to roll, Ilii shouted, "Wait!"

They had read enough of the information that had come with the repaired part to know that they needed some special tools from the comm shack and the pool house. Ilii stopped the vehicle. They ran out.

Seconds later, Ilii in the vehicle said, "This is going to take a few minutes."

Ilii knew that Ilii had just run into an unexpected problem. Bud asked how they knew. Pookii told Bud that Ilii were a maté.

Bud asked, "What's a maté?"

Ilii looked at the Poollé Kii. Their eyes asked, *Who is this bumkin, and why is he with us?*

Pookii decided to go meet Bud's "sister." Bud and Pookii got out of the vehicle and walked past the garage to the back gate. The Poollé Kii began to explain what a maté was. As they entered the backyard, the garage door opened in the front of the house, and Daisi and Tu sped on their way to catch the plane to Aciam Aj.

The media had thoroughly laid out the case of improprieties and misuses of power in connection with the former light-eyed DLA. Their investigative reporting received assistance from some unnamed but reliable sources and had laid out a clear case of corruption and mismanagement. Most of their facts were correct, but their attribution was way off. There was no way to correct the narrative from the outside, so Daisii was made to suffer a huge amount of public shame and humiliation. This was what Nos wanted. He was still not sure of his grandfather's connection to Daisii and wanted to ensure that everything and everyone close to her was tainted. The chancellor was the closest threat to his reign as the dratsab he knew, and even though Syng had given congratulatory press and done complementary things, the power of the dratsab had to be protected from every purl on the planet. Nos sat alone at his desk and began mentally preparing for the meeting to address the roll-in rebellion. He had neither friend nor family he cared about. He was the dratsab, and the planet bowed before him. Nos loved being dratsab. He wondered why he hadn't killed his father sooner; he concluded it was his grandfather's fault.

Daisi was driving her friend to the airbase as fast as she could. Tu had packed as if she was flying on a commercial aircraft until Daisi gave her a flight bag from her military days and helped her understand the situation. The flight bag was just about the size of a small carry-on, and Tu had to adjust her thoughts on what she would take. Some things, Daisi told her, could be sent when Aya came back in a few months. Tu didn't really care about clothes or anything more than getting to the island, and Daisi had to help her think past her excitement. As they drove through the neighborhood, Tu told her friend that *he* was there or had been there. This she knew from her dreams. In some of her dreams, Daisi was there with him. In one dream she had, Daisi and her Pedagogy were fighting dark-eyed assassins in a bar.

Daisi wasn't listening to her at all. She was thinking through how to get her friend past the checkpoints and to the aircraft. Tu thought her mind was mixing up the two most important purple in her life, but the dreams convinced her that Aciam Aj was the place to continue her search for Pedagogy. Daisi thought about what the weather would be like on the island for the next few months. She reached over the seat and gave Tu the special, lightweight, all-weather jacket she said would be good in the mountains. Tu was still talking. Something inside Tu told her there was a link between the island and the love of her life. The picture she had seen of the island reminded her of the mountain house of her dreams. She visualized herself walking up to the house high in the hills and her Pedagogy leaning on the porch with a cup of hot tea, waiting for her to arrive. She closed her eyes to see it better. Then it hit her.

She screamed, "Stop!"

The urgency in her voice took Daisi back to their childhood. There was panic in the sound of her cry. She was in danger. Without processing why, Daisi slammed on the brakes. They both rocked back into their seats at the recoil. Daisi took a mental inventory of the weapons at hand—none. She gripped the wheel tightly and looked at her friend. There was no sign of trauma.

"What?" she asked.

"I forgot my teapot."

It took a minute for Daisi to clearly understand that her friend Tu was willing to miss the very rare opportunity to slip out of Prometheus over a teapot. Daisi didn't understand why it was so important to Tu. This, in part, was because Tu didn't know why it was so important; she just knew it was. Daisi turned the vehicle around and began recalculating what it would take to make the flight as she raced back to her house.

Bud thought the idea of fighting as a team was exciting. There were a couple of fights where he thought he could have used a few teammates. Pookii guessed it was every fight he lost. They both laughed. Bud remembered the first time he met Pookii. That was a fight he won by losing. His eyes watered. He was glad he was not who he had been. The Poollé Kii patted his friend's shoulder. Then Bud left to go find Tu. Pookii was content to wait. There were concerns about the security of the roll-in. The new dratsab was obsessed with ending the roll-ins. Under his father, the laws were getting increasingly restrictive and were used as an attempt to distract and capture the compliance of the light-eyed purple. Few light-eyed purple really understood the radical power of resting and sharing. Most just enjoyed the pha. It was a means of renewal. But the big roll-in was attracting thousands. The Poollé Kii knew the dark-eyed security units had infiltrated some of the families who were excited about coming and suspected that perhaps one of his own crew might be among them. He sensed violence was coming but hoped it would not occur until after the big roll-in. He had sent messages to Nos's father promising to turn himself in if the dratsab would not attack the big roll-in. Killing the better part of three thousand purple was a price the dratsab was willing to pay to keep his position, but if it could be done cheaper, he would take the bargain.

The Poollé Kii was content to face the former dratsab on his own turf and terms, but he suspected that Nos preferred spectacle. He knew Nos had less substance than his father, and the darkness that swirled within him was dangerous. The kii wished he had his cloth. With it, he could face whatever danger he had to. Without it, he might not survive. Still, he knew the light that was dawning on purple was more important than whether he lived or died. That light was needed to defeat the darkness, and if he had to die to set the light ablaze, so be it. This resolve passed through his mind, and...there it was, the faint scent of amest. He closed his eyes and followed the scent toward the house. He opened his eyes to see Bud. Ilii came hurrying toward them in both directions, apologizing for taking so long. Bud told him there was no one in the house. They all walked out of the backyard to get in the vehicle waiting to take them to Biscuit. As they walked through the gate and into the front yard, Daisi was standing at the open driver's side door of her vehicle. She walked over and greeted them and began asking about the prep for the big roll-in. As Pookii walked by, she thought to give him a love tap and balled up her fist to do so. She was immediately caught by the gaze of Ilii. She changed her mind and gave him a hug instead. Pookii smiled at her, knowing exactly what had just happened. Pookii caught the scent of amest again. It was stronger than in the backyard, and it led toward the front door. He released Daisi and turned toward the path where the amest called him. Then she appeared.

She was not looking where she was going at all. Her head was down because she was wrapping a teapot in some newspaper that had headlines about the DLA. She was fussing about the lies and saying how she probably should have gotten another page of the paper, but she knew they were in a hurry, and...she heard him call her name. She felt his voice in her hearts before she heard it in her ears.

"Daisii," was all he said, but it was the sound of angels singing to her ears. She looked up, afraid to believe it was true, but there he was.

She ran toward him, casting the pot, paper, and anything else that would slow her down up in the air. Ilii, leaping and flipping, caught the pot and its lid before they hit the ground. The newspaper flew off in the distance, and Ilii looked at Ilii, suggesting they missed something. Pookii caught his Daisii as she jumped into his arms. He twirled her. He kissed her. She kissed him. He held her as she had held her law books when they first met. Tears streamed down her cheeks. She found him. He found her. Their hearts began to beat together as Daisii's breasts pressed against his chest. She was in the arms of the love of her life. Pookii straightened his back, and Daisii's first foot touched the ground; the other, bent at the knee, told a tale of ecstasy. The Poollé Kii closed his eyes and held Daisii as their spirits danced. She buried her nose in his neck and held him. Two woos flew into a nearby tree and began to sing. The eternal power of their love had brought them together again. Their combined breath sent the scent of amest heavenward. Ilii surrounded the embracing couple as three points on a triangle. They were kneeling on one knee, heads bowed. The green-haired one had her long pole; the other two had swords. Daisi wondered how they got them and from where. Daisi knew Ilii were as dangerous on one knee with their head down as a stick of dynamite with its fuse lit. She waited until the lovers had their moment, happy that the two most important purple in her life had found their true loves but baffled that they knew each other. Her comm link rang. It was Aya asking for a status update. Daisi told her there would be no extra riders today.

Nos sat behind the dratsab's desk with his legs crossed and his feet propped up on the highly polished wood. Most of the meeting covered the plans in place to quiet the rebellion and get purple back to their toils. The plans being presented had been coordinated through the dratsab's office for months and were meticulous. His father had not left any area uncovered. The Promethean Police Department, the Department of Socialization, the Department of Prisons, and the Department of Light-Eyed Affairs were the main speakers since they had the public responsibilities for restoring order after the mass riot was put down. Each presented their plans for the coordinated attack on the light-eyed freedom movement. The top-secret plan had been in motion since the roll-ins began getting popular among the grade school children a year ago.

The presentations bored Nos. His father should have dealt with this long ago. He thought all the details were unnecessary and, in fact, didn't pay close enough attention to understand how all the pieces fit together or that they were interdependent. He daydreamed most of the meeting until Pedagogy's name was mentioned. Some purl was saying his father had accepted a deal that would have Pedagogy surrender after the big roll-in. His father had promised Pedagogy a fair trial and open hearings, but the purple in the room told Nos that, of course, those promises were empty. Now that the charges included the murder of the dratsab, no pretense to fairness was necessary. They began to describe the tortures that had been prepared for Pedagogy. Nos sat up. Of all the things that had been said, this was something in which he was invested. The tree planter had shamed him, humiliated him, and debased him in public. There were only a few purple who knew this, and the actual witnesses had been threatened or convinced they were confused. All the camera footage had been scrubbed and remastered. Nos had even destroyed the file his father had. But none of these facts made a difference. He knew. He could never forget the backhand. The place on his face where he was hit still burned when exposed in the bright-day suns. The purple who gathered at the dratsab's mansion knew. They had watched the holographic recording of it right before Nos killed his father. And some of them had seen the footage before. He felt he would never command their full respect until he dealt with Pedagogy, and he had to do it publicly. He wanted Pedagogy killed in front of the cameras and by his own hand.

He asked where Pedagogy was and did not accept that no one knew. Promethean surveillance was ubiquitous and state of the art. Its only rival was the military. Why hadn't he been found? There were many explanations offered around the table. Nos accepted none of them. He thought that some powerful purl was protecting him. He believed there was a spy among the purple in the inner circle of power, perhaps even in the room. He slowly looked around the large conference table. He asked to be reminded why the chancellor had missed the meeting. Whoever answered the question would be his second suspect. The meeting ended without Nos changing any of the plans. He did tell the assembled high-ranking officials that he would review the plans and reserved the right to change any one of them.

The Sunday before the big roll-in began, the warden went to see Nos. He had wondered why, as the new dratsab, his old friend had not yet promoted him to a cabinet position. No purl had been more loyal to him than himself. He had protected and supported Nos since law school. He knew his secrets and had covered for him when his father would have had him killed for the despoiling of one of his cabinet member's young wives. The warden had found, accused, and incarcerated an innocent purl who, of course, was tragically killed in prison. The warden knew this Pedagogy thing was important to both of their careers. He believed he fell out of Nos's good graces that night at the Panthae. He had no idea Pedagogy existed before then. And since then, he had never stopped hunting for him. He was not sure he had convinced the new dratsab he was innocent. But he had to prove it. He also knew the dratsab maintained power through fear and the perception of his invincibility. If a dratsab could not defend himself, then he has no business being the dratsab. But the warden understood every leader needed good lieutenants, and he was out to prove that he was the best lieutenant Nos could ever have. He had just gotten some key information and wanted to deliver it to the dratsab himself. Maybe after hearing it, his old friend would invite him to have a drink like old times.

He arrived at the office and asked to see the dratsab. He was made to wait forty minutes. The dratsab was careful to manage perceptions, and his gatekeepers knew not to give any purl access too quickly. Nos wasn't doing anything in his office except watching the state-produced propaganda on the vision screen. The media was singing his praises and enumerating all the good and wonderful things that had begun since he had become dratsab. He was told the warden had some important information for him, and he was in the reception area, waiting for permission to see him. Nos had a growing hatred toward the warden. He suspected he knew more than he shared. He had treated Pedagogy like a hotel guest when he was in his prison. Then he let him go free. How he colluded with the director of light-eyed affairs was still a mystery, but Nos had no doubt he had. And what was he doing in the cabinet meeting at the mansion? There were too many unanswered questions. Nos concluded the chancellor had something to do with all of it, but he hadn't yet figured out how the pieces fit together. The media moved to a series of infomercials and behavior modification shorts. Nos turned off the vision screen and signaled to his assistant he was ready to see the warden. The warden came in. Nos greeted him with a big smile and offered him a drink. The warden was grateful to be asked. It was an indication he was moving toward the good graces of the dratsab, but he declined the alcohol. *Not yet*, he thought. *Wait until it's a drink between friends.*

Nos apologized for the long wait and lied about how demanding it was to be the dratsab. After a few more comments to put his prey at ease, Nos asked why his friend had traveled so far to see him. The warden was anxious to tell the dratsab everything he knew. He told him his spies had just learned that there was going to be a wedding near the beginning of the big roll-in. He was not sure who the groom was, some poollé or Pookii. The warden suspected that it was the same purl whom Nos slapped him about, but he wasn't going to mention this suspicion.

What he did mention was that the former director of the DLA was the bride. Nos flashed red with anger and shame. The warden was saving his juiciest and most recent information for last: He had just discovered the location of his former girlfriend. She was in Noth at the home of a former military officer. He had sent purple to arrest them, but they found the house deserted. He was sure, however, they would all be at the "big roundup" where the riot would start, and his purple would be there to arrest them. The warden finished and believed he had given Nos the head of his enemy on a silver platter. He expected Nos to offer him that drink again and they would toast the death of his nemesis. Nos sensed the warden's need for affirmation. He did the best imitation of being grateful and giving praise he could. Nos insisted they drink to celebrate and went to the bar. Reaching for the decanter, he pushed a hidden button to his outer office, signaling he was ready for this meeting to be over. He poured two glasses of the dark liquor he was growing to love and brought the warden a glass. Nos sat next to him on the coach, smiling, and just as they toasted their success,

Nos's assistant interrupted them, announcing the dratsab was late for an important meeting.

Pookii and Tu, or the Poollé Kii and his gha as Ilii referred to them, were inseparable. There were embraces and gentle kisses. They sat or walked together as if they were joined at the hip. Everywhere they went, Ilii remained armed and formed that triangle around them. These first moments of their reunion were delicate. If the full presence and power of Miis were to grow in Pedagogy and the full strength and presence of Quay were to flourish in Daisii, they would need focus and quiet. Usually, the couple would retreat to sacred woods, preferably near a stream or waterfall, and allow their hearts to grow strong and syncopated. For the kii, this would occur under the watchful eye of a guardian. The cloth of the kii held in the light of the three moons would have stated how the correct guardian could be summoned. It would have also framed the time in which the gha would come. But the cloth was stolen years ago, and the Poollé Kii had chosen his mate, gha or not.

Ka Chi knew most about the ancient things and had created a space as close to a sacred wood as could be found in Prometheus, so he was called for advice. Ka told Ilii to bring the couple to his garden. Daisy, who was taking care of roll-in matters in Biscuit, was also notified and hurried to meet them. So, after the first hour in the pool house, Ilii drove the couple to Prometheus to the sacred place in Ka's garden. Daisy, who arrived from Biscuit just before the couple came, harvested from Ka's garden teas and special roots in the manner the green-haired Ilii had shown her long ago in the mountains.

This meeting of Pookii and Daisii threw off the very tight timetable for the big roll-in. Bake, Bank, and Bud got on the phones, attempting to minimize the damage of Pookii's change of plans soon after he and Daisii went into the house. One of those calls was intercepted, and that was how the warden ultimately found out where Daisii was and about the marriage that was about to take place. The mass arrest and detention of the "rioting," light-eyed participants was to happen late on the third and final day, just as the darkness began. A few family members who had been co-opted or bribed had been instructed to start trouble the first day and escalate each day until the third day, when a full-on riot would be instigated. The large, temporary holding pens had not yet arrived at the staging area, and the extra police purple, media purple, and medical purple had not yet reported for duty. These were some of the reasons the warden and others wanted Nos to wait. But the very recent photos of Daisii and a hooded figure that the warden brought Nos made the dratsab furious. He insisted the hooded figure was Pedagogy and wanted the arrest to happen immediately. His purple started scrambling. Nos waited all Monday for the departments to adjust to his orders. By Tuesday morning, he had run out of patience. He ordered the operation begin. He boarded his vehicle and headed to the circle to apprehend the most wanted purl in all Prometheus. He would confront the assassin who killed the dratsab, end the rebellion, and humiliate the purl who had shunned him in one fell swoop. He thought to leave Daisii in a life of sorrow and regret while he proved to the rest of Prometheus both his power and worth.

Everything would be recorded, and after all was edited and sanitized, it would air as a live broadcast. Nos glowed red as he sat in the armored limousine. The chancellor sat beside him; the warden sat with the driver. Both of them would be afforded the opportunity to prove their loyalty and devotion, or—Nos swore to himself—they would not survive the reckoning that had already begun. Noj rode in a vehicle directly behind with a four-legged beast trained as a reflection of his predilection to cruelty, blood, and death. Noj was now in the sole employ of the dratsab. Nos smiled. He had all the power he had ever craved, and, as the moment approached for its display, Nos felt the warmth of ecstasy flow through his body. As the power washed over him, his pupils turned black, and a deep red glow pulsed through his skin. His driver announced they were minutes away.

The bright-day celebration was just beginning as the Poollé Kii and his Daisii walked into the great circle. The first dinner meal of the big roll-in was about to commence. The Poollé Kii had taken his bride-to-be to a field of sunflowers through the woods to the north of the great circle. There, they would be wed as soon as Ka Chi returned with the guardian of that realm. Daisii didn't know what a guardian was but took it to be some sort of priest or magistrate. Whoever or whatever a guardian was, one was required for their marriage, and that was all that mattered. Ilii moved seamlessly and silently as they kept guard of their kii. Only they and the kii understood why. The celebration was pha. Hundreds of family members were returning from their small chores and labors, readying themselves for the start of the bright-day celebrations. Daisii was enraptured with her freedom from the DLA and blissful about being with her husband-to-be. But the kii and Ilii knew that there were pockets of cool air moving in and out of the circle. The sky in the distance had a gathering darkness. The air carried the scent of danger for those perceptive enough to be in tune with the planet. Small children ran and played, especially around the couple. Ilii let the children weave in and out between them. By the time the Poollé Kii reached the center of the large circle, all could see the sky was becoming an ominous gray. He signaled that the dinner be moved indoors and the children be sent to the play vehicles that had been prepared for ill weather.

Daisii released her two-handed hold on Pedagogy's arm. Something warm rose within her and moved through her veins. The pair continued to move toward the entrance to the circle. They stopped. Turning their ears toward the rear of the circle, they listened and heard a sound. It was faint. Many thought it was thunder in the distance behind them, but Ilii and the kii knew it was something else entirely. They turned their gaze toward the entrance.

Three dark and foreboding shadows of death in the form of purple were heading for the opening, intent on entering the circle with malice. The Poollé Kii recognized the scent. A few moments later, Daisii recognized the faces. It was Nos, the warden, and the chancellor. Then it happened. Just as the three were past the small entrance to the large circle of vehicles, the beast appeared. Pulling hard against its leash, it was towing a purl who—leaning back against the strain—seemed excited about the ravage of flesh and blood the beast would bring. The Poollé Kii saw the pair. Ilii's and Daisii's eyes were caught by the motion of Nos's hand reaching into his coat. His eyes were empty and dark. His face was not smiling, but the thoughts of pleasure at the evil he was bringing could not be hidden. They sensed before it appeared he had brought and was about to unleash a weapon of murder and mayhem. Ilii drew their swords. The sky darkened, and the thunder was louder. It rose from the ground and moved through their bones like small earthquakes. Children were scurrying to safety under the direction of those who were older but still too young to gather for battle. The dratsab's purple entered behind their leader. Two toddlers stood crying as the two groups moved closer to each other. They were frozen in fear at the sight and sounds around them. The two small children were looking for their parents and caught sight of the snarling beast coming their way.

The Poollé Kii recognized the purl at the end of the leash. Any purl with a soul would avoid harming small children, but he knew that Noj had sold his soul to darkness long ago. The beast lunged at the children as if they were its long-overdue meal. Pedagogy leaped to intercept the large teeth in the open mouth of the beast just before it fastened on the face of one of the children. Daisii's head turned. Her love was flying through the air. The danger was swarming into the circle. Daisii ran toward Nos behind Ilii. The beast bit hard into the forearm of the Poollé Kii. His muscles flexed in response. The children were swept up by an adult and taken to safety. The Poollé Kii twisted and hit the ground with the back of the beast's head. The move snatched the leash from Noj's grasp. Noj began to reach for his next tool. The beast bit again into the Poollé Kii as he began to rise to his feet. Noj's gun was out and pointed at the kii. He pulled the trigger again and again as the Poollé Kii approached, holding the beast as a shield.

Daisy and Ilii watched the dratsab pull his weapon. Ilii ran toward him, protecting their gha. Nos began firing. If it were just a few bullets, Ilii would have been able to withstand them. But one of Ilii fell to the ground. In the distance, what was heard and felt as thunder revealed itself, as the first large beast leaped over the vehicle at the north end of the circle and headed toward the entrance. The Poollé Kii threw the now dead beast at the feet of Noj. He saw one of Ilii fall and the second of Ilii about to go down. If the second of Ilii went down, Nos would have clear shot at Daisii.

Noj's gun was empty. He pulled a large knife from the holder on his belt and swung wildly at the approaching kii. He missed. Their eyes met. Noj looked into the eyes that had been seared into his memory. The eyes of the one purl who had neither fear of him nor the death he dealt. A black power filled his being. He lifted his arm high in the air to slaughter the one he had sworn to murder. His hand came down hard and fast. The Poollé Kii's attention was elsewhere. He was counting the bullets coming out of Nos's gun. He knew that the second of Ilii would fall and the remaining bullets would then be sent to slay his Daisii. He called to Nos with all his being and power. The sound made Nos's face burn where the Poollé Kii's backhand had struck him three years ago. Rage and fear surged in the young dratsab. The purl protecting Daisii fell. Nos desired to send two simple shots into the head of his unprotected former fiancée, but something stronger called within him. He turned the gun toward the tree planter. His mind suggested he had done this before, but there was no time to think through what his mind was attempting to recall. He only knew at that moment the most important thing to do was point his weapon at the tree planter. His aim left Daisii and looked for the one she intended to marry. Meanwhile, Noj's thrust was coming toward the kii. Pedagogy avoided his lunge and redirected the murderous momentum. Noj thrust the large blade into his own heart and began falling to the earth. Bullets from the dratsab's weapon entered his back, hastening the work of death that had already arrived to possess his soul. The dratsab kept his weapon pointing in the direction of the Poollé Kii and fired again and again.

The large horse-like beasts were nearly upon them. The beasts were plowing through the hundreds of police and mercenaries who had followed Nos into the circle.

Five beasts formed a wedge. Behind them were three beasts; two had riders. They headed to the kii with deadly fury. The Poollé Kii's attention to Nos had caused him to make an awkward move to avoid Noj's knife thrust. Although he still used most of Noj's body as a shield, the move exposed him to the danger of Nos's weapon. He knew it was a fatal decision, but without it, Daisii would have died. The bullets from Nos's automatic weapon were too many to avoid. He was hit over and over. The Poollé Kii fell. Just as his body hit the ground, Daisii—who had run behind

Ilii—was upon Nos. His hatred would not let him stop pulling the trigger on the empty weapon. Daisii kicked Nos hard in his rape tool. He dropped his weapon and bent reflexively. She jumped and, flipping, rolled over his bent back. As she did, she caught his jaw and the back of his head in her hands and held tight. The power of her body pulled Nos to a standing position. Daisii landed her move and broke his neck with a loud crack. She released Nos's head, which fell toward his back as if attached to his body by a few threads. His body stood erect, frozen by the shock of sudden death, and then fell in final reverence at the feet of Daisii. His head, twisted unnaturally at his shoulders, bounced as the body met the ground. His mouth, shut in silent death, was forced open wide from the inside as a black serpent, fleeing death's descent, came streaming out of his body. The serpent of black dust seemed afraid of the ground and, leaping away from it, spread itself into the air. The darkness increased.

Daisii ran to the side of her Pedagogy. A large horse-like beast reared above Nos's carcass. The guardian dismounted in a twisting leap from the crown of its head and, unsheathing his sword in midair, plunged it deep into the ground. He adjusted his body to gather strength and pulled hard on the hilt of his sword. Straining, he opened a crack in the planet. The darkness that had been spreading in the air, blocking out the light of the suns, began to descend unwillingly toward the hole that beckoned.

Syng had no weapon. He was not sure why Nos had kept him at his side unarmed. But now the dratsab was dead, and with his death, opportunity had arrived. The dark power he craved was descending into the planet. Syng picked up one of Ilii's swords and plunged it into the back of the guardian. The guardian could have avoided the thrust but knew burying the darkness was more important than his life. He looked down on Ilii's blade protruding through him. He summoned all the strength he had to keep the planet open. Syng twisted and then removed the blade. The guardian slumped forward over the sword, frozen. The hole closed, and the vacuum for evil ended. Syng stretched his arms wide, tilted his head, and called to the darkness. Hearing him, it gathered like an ocean in the sky, and began streaming down toward Syng's open mouth.

Daisii reached the body of her Pedagogy. She knelt beside him and cradled him in her lap, much like he had done her years ago.

"Stronger than life or death," she whispered.

But before she could call his name or listen for a beat of one of his hearts, it was upon her, another large horse-like beast. It roared as it reared high above her head. Its breath felt like dry fire. Placing its front hooves on the planet, the beast commanded through its eyes that Daisii deliver the Poollé Kii. Before Daisii could calculate the danger or respond, the rider on the beast next to this one dismounted and was at her side. Dow had unceremoniously jumped off his beast. The sights and sounds around him were familiar. He was at war. A wounded soldier was lying on the ground. He took his flask and poured the liquid onto the wounds. As the mountain water flowed in the wound, the bullets in his body rose and rolled off his body. The water increased the life left in the Poollé Kii. But Dow knew he needed something to stop the bleeding, or the Poollé Kii would be dead in minutes. Breath like fire seared his neck and called to him.

Dow looked up. The leather pouch glowed in the shoulder of the beast. Dow pulled out the blanket. It shone like a light in the swirling darkness. He moved to place it over the largest wound of the kii, but as it came more fully into the dark air and death, it opened itself like a parachute and burst into flames. The heat made Dow reflexively pull his hands away, and when he did, the blanket lowered itself and covered the bleeding chest of the Poollé Kii. Dow wondered whether the bright light and heat coming from it was actually fire. But there was no time to think or to marvel. The colors of the blanket changed where the bullet wounds were bleeding. Parts of the intricate pattern pulsed; other parts seemed to link like veins around the most serious wounds. The beast towering over Dow and Daisii demanded the Poollé Kii. Dow didn't know how he knew, but he knew that he had no choice. Daisii, sensing the gravity of the mortal wounds, realized she objected to what was about to happen. She didn't know how she knew what was about to happen, but she knew. The beast had demanded the body of the kii. Daisii felt it was exerting its right to the one who belonged to her. The confusion took the space in her hearts where fear and panic should have been. She was determined to fight purl or beast for the one she loved.

She raised her eyes to stare the hot-breathed beast in the eyes. As she did, she realized that Dow had also heard the command from the beast, and he was complying. Dow was lifting the body of the Poollé Kii onto the back of the beast, who had bent down to receive it. Daisi thought to object. The Poollé Kii's chest slumped lifelessly onto the neck of the beast. The straps to the pouch that held the cloth of the Kii were wrapped around each of his arms like they were vines. Then Dow clasped them over his back, holding him to the mount. The straps gave themselves to this in a way that made them seem alive. The blanket embraced his chest and somehow helped hold the body in place, and in the brief second it took for the beast to rise, Dow thought the beast, blanket, and body had become one flesh. The beast pivoted and launched itself across the field. Two beasts proceeded it, clearing a path. Thunder echoed from the hoof beats. Flashes of lightning danced where hooves hit stone.

The sky was dark. A strange cold grew. Many stood frozen in shock and sadness. The shock and panic began to rise in Daisii. A warm wash flowed through her veins as she stood. Her flesh pulsed a brilliant royal blue. She turned to stare at one of the beasts who turned from stomping the dratsab troops as if it had been beckoned by its master. It came straight to Daisii, who leaped to mount it without it even pausing. She grabbed its mane, and they disappeared in the cloud of dust the others had left. Dow ran to the mount that had brought him and climbed on the beast, who then immediately followed the path of the others.

Daisy arrived just as her son disappeared on the beast. The bond of love that only motherhood could make had called her to her child as soon as hatred had entered the circle. She had been bringing children into the daycare vehicles since she felt the first pocket of lonely cold enter the circle. But she heard her son call to Nos before the cry even came out of his mouth. As she began running toward the danger, she saw one and then the other of Ilii die. She saw her man-child fall from the bullets of Nos's gun and Daisii requite his murderer. After the body of her child had disappeared and his bride-to-be followed, she turned her attention to another matter. She slowed her pace and stopped at Ilii's corpse. She bent and grasped the hilt of their sword. It was heavy and felt too large for her hand. She began walking toward the chancellor. Syng stood with his arms stretched out and his head tilted back on his shoulders, drinking in the darkness. Daisy approached his side and began to circle around him until she stood facing him, dragging the heavy sword as she did. Its tip scribed a circle in the planet, and sparks jumped from its razor-sharp edge. She walked slowly until she stood in front of him. She commanded with a voice that came from the depth of a mother's resolve that he release the darkness he was imbibing. The sound of the command made him cease the flow of black dust into his being. He looked at Daisy. Black orbs filled his eye sockets. And through them, he could see Daisy was committed to removing the darkness flowing into him and wrapping his soul in the cold dark power he welcomed. At that moment, he knew all the darkness he desired she disdained. Further, he knew she was intent on releasing the darkness now inside him by any means necessary.

He bent down and picked up the sword with which he had killed the guardian. In a voice that was little more than a growl, he said, "I should have killed you at the house."

Daisy replied, "What makes you think you didn't?"

The question enraged him. She was suggesting she had somehow returned from the dead. It would mean she was gha. It would mean an ancient power lay in her that only death could reveal. He swung the sword wildly. Daisy barely had time to lift the heavy sword to deflect the swing. It knocked her back into the body of the guardian still bent over his sword. She fell to the ground. The body of the guardian fell also, hitting the planet just beside her. Daisy breathed in deeply the sweet last breath of the guardian of Aciam Aj. A bliss she could not explain washed over her. She fell into a field of amest. She thought to close her eyes and dwell forever in that dream. But death was rushing toward her in the purl of Syng.

Syng had walked up to her fallen body and was rearing back, both hands holding the hilt, the long sword blade behind him already moving with increasing speed to sever Daisy in two. Daisy saw the flash of the razor-sharp blade moving through the darkness. She thought to move, but before she could decide in which direction and how, she realized her body was already in the air. She landed in perfect fighting form just as her child had done so many years ago. The memory made her smile. The sword in Syng's hand severed a stone as it hit the ground. Daisy stood feeling powerful and calm. Syng pulled back his arm for his next swing. There was a quiet confidence that filled Daisy. She thought to deflect the coming blow with the sword she had taken from Ilii's side. She wondered if she had the strength to lift it, and as she sent the question to her muscles, panic pulsed in her heart. Her hand felt empty. She must have released the sword as she flipped in the air, or perhaps she had left it on the ground. Daisy's move had placed her just out of the path of Syng's blow, which struck the planet with such force that Daisy felt it lift her off the ground. Daisy looked for the sword. Her gaze moved to find it, and there it was. At first, she couldn't believe what she was seeing. She was confused. But at the same time, the sight made so many things become clear. At the end of her arm was a beautiful hand—the same beautiful hand that had sealed the back door shut. Within her was the powerful presence that had kept her and her child safe all these years. The muscles of her entire body flexed. They glowed a brilliant royal blue. The sword in her hand was waiting for its next command.

The dance that followed was a war between good and all the darkness that could be gathered in a purl. What was left of the dratsab's forces retreated. Fear had captured them, and they began to run through the small opening through which they had entered. They were no match for the three remaining beasts. Still, a few paused to watch the sword battle. The three beasts, having defeated the small army that followed the dratsab into the circle, began to gallop around the circle close to the vehicles. They spread themselves equal distances apart and continued to run through the cold darkness. As they did, purple moved out of their way and into the vehicles. All pressed their attention out the windows, watching the beasts and the battle. Then it appeared. It was faint at first, almost imperceptible—a sky lit by the suns above the backs of the beasts. Purple looked behind and outside the circle of vehicles; the air there was clear. The darkness began to form a column high into the sky above. The beasts began slowly closing the circle, corralling the darkness in a large invisible pen. The darkness swirled inside the boundary the beasts demanded. The few who were still in the circle, wandering beneath the concentrated gray cloud, were washed in a cold sorrow that froze them in tears and fear. Meanwhile, Daisy and the one who would be dratsab fought. Daisy sought to separate Syng from the darkness within him. Her moves were defensive and demonstrated that her counterattacks, if she chose, could have been deadly. She quickly and easily taught Syng he was no match for her. With each failed attempt to kill his opponent, Syng grew angrier. Each breath brought more of the darkness into him. Yet no matter how much focus and power the dust gave its host, Daisy countered.

A frightened child running away from the galloping beasts chose the wrong direction and ran further into the darkness. The darkness grabbed him and held him in the cold. The child began to scream. The sound annoyed Syng. He decided to kill it. If he couldn't easily kill Daisy, he could kill the child and end the irritating noise. He began to swing the fatal blow. Daisy pivoted. There was no more mercy she could extend. With a twirling, twisting move, she severed the sword-yielding arm and then the head of Syng. The darkness began to swirl with fury as it fled from his falling carcass. As his body dropped to the ground, the green-haired Ilii leaped into the darkness and grabbed the child. The black coal began to stream out of the severed head and body of Syng. The swirling blackness began to emit a foreboding sound. Ilii gave Daisi, who had been fighting by her side, the toddler and instructed her to hold him close and firmly. The beasts now fought to keep the darkness contained. Their skin glowed in the darkness. Ilii ran into the black and met Daisy at the guardian's sword. The two of them pulled against the hilt of the blade buried in the planet with all their strength. The crack began to open. The black coal-like dust began to flow against its own will into the crack.

Daisi carried the child to Bud and told him to take it to one of the vehicles. Then Daisi, understanding what was happening, ran through the darkness to join the two. The overwhelming loneliness made her scream, and tears flowed out of her eyes, but neither could stop her. She pulled with the others. The crack widened. The blackness began to rush into the middle of the planet. It did not do so willingly, and the groan it made was low, guttural, and plaintive. The two females and Ilii pulled hard. Their arms were intertwined. The loneliness and cold pulled their souls toward sorrow and despair. An eternity passed as they held open the portal to the realm of dark torment. Daisi fell first. The pain, grief, and torment that swept by her into the grave of the netherworld was finally too much for her, and as the sky began to clear of the darkness and cold, she collapsed. Ilii and Daisy kept the crack open until the last of the dust had descended beyond sight. Ilii drew strength from the radiance of Daisy and remained at her side until the task of removing the darkness was done. She released the sword hilt. She began falling toward the earth. Bud, who had returned from securing the child, caught Ilii and eased her descent to the ground. The green-haired purl was bruised from battle but not seriously injured. The maté was broken, and she felt the absence of her brothers as if it were a mortal wound. She thought to close her eyes to join them, to die as an act of her will. But, just as she began to close her eyes in consent with death, Daisy pulled her to her feet. The look in Daisy's eyes commanded there was one task that remained.

The sky was clear of all the darkness and seemed fresh as if a drenching rain had washed it bright and new. Purple began to realize the darkness was gone and the victory was complete. Daisy drank in the clean air with deep breaths of satisfaction and delight. She could smell the scent of sunflowers from the field where she had been making wedding plans. She remembered the beautiful hands that were her own and marveled as she looked at them. The bright glow was gone, but within, Daisy knew and could feel the power and wonder of her transformation. She felt as if another heart was growing within her, and she could feel its rhythm. The sky, air, and absence of evil filled her with pha. She remembered the beautiful hands that had sealed the back door so long ago and wondered if this power, this beauty, had been inside her all along. Her thoughts quickly confirmed that things were more complex. But she understood her transformation began that day, long ago. She remembered the note and the perfect poem, three stanzas each with twelve lines and six rhymes. She had memorized them. She read them to the Poollé Kii every night:

> Behold the royal seed of Miis,
> The answer to your prayers,
> And place a guarding, watchful eye
> As he enters into your care
> Still as a child into the wild
> To wander and to feast,
> To danger face or be replaced,
> Uniting purl and beast;
> Yet not alone shall you raise
> The hope of all our pha.
> And in your namesake,
> He must find the true and only gha.

The first stanza danced through her mind on the melody that had risen long ago. Her lips began to move as she began the second stanza.

> You, the child that Kha begot,
> The answer to his cries,
> Were born to send the darkness to
> The place where evil dies.

> Now guard your heart, for it is weak
> And easy to deceive;
> What you call love will you betray,
> But still, you must believe.
> Into the darkness and then return
> And gather all to fight;
> Deny the death that urges you
> To release this hold on life.

She was beginning to understand the message for the first time. She had always been confused about which part of the poem referred to her and which referred to her child. But now things began to clear. She was the descendant of Kha, not her Pedagogy. Her heart, and something else beating beneath her breasts illuminated a confidence that washed over her as her flesh gently glowed. Then she saw it.

She was drawn to the pha of victory and had begun to relax her fighting muscles, and it appeared. It began in her periphery, but she could feel the presence before she began to see it with her eyes. The urgency of the vision turned her head. And there it was, the large beast, ferocious and deadly. Daisy had seen such beasts before. The blood of the vanquished covered its hooves. It walked menacingly, checking the area for any lingering danger. Then, apparently satisfied that there were no more opponents to defeat, it walked to the body of the guardian. It seemed to Daisy it was angry. There was something in its eyes Daisy understood to be a desire to continue the trampling of the dratsab's forces. Then Daisy saw it: the circle of iridescent color in its blue mane. She began to remember. She had seen this beast before. The last verse gave her even more focus:

> He, your teacher and your charge,
> Shall live until you see;
> Promise now this oath and swear,
> "I shall not die before the Poollé Kii."
> The time will come and shall not pass
> When the battle has begun
> To rule, to rise, to bury him
> Before the setting suns
> Then find the one to him that's true
> To finally set him free

From death and danger; he must rest
Beneath the poollé trees.

Daisy's whole being pulsed with affirmation and strength. The syncopated rhythm within her made her marvel and wonder at the thin space between what was and what is, between what is not and that which will be. There was an urgency of the moment. All was not over or complete. But, at the same moment, so much had been resolved.

Her eyes passed over the carcass of Syng and rested on the fallen frames of Ilii. Evil had been vanquished at a high cost. Ilii and the guardian lay on the battlefield, having paid the ultimate price for the victory and hope that was now possible for all purple. The bodies of Syng, Nos, and Noj did not deserve to lie on the same ground as the two of Ilii. In the quiet of these contemplations, the large and menacing beast moved toward her. Daisy was snapped out of the fog of her thoughts and wondered if the last thought was hers or the beast's, which had entered her view. It caught her eye and held her gaze. The beasts were requiring the bodies. Daisy looked into the eye of the beast and recognized it. A spark in the base of her head flowed like a warm and welcome wash through her body. She remembered the mountain house and the first time she saw these very beasts. The memories of her time in the mountains began to fill her mind. Ilii, standing beside her, was not so distracted. Each of the three beasts knelt beside the bodies of the two of Ilii and the guardian. By the time the first beast had lowered its massive form, the green-haired purl was pulling the body of the guardian toward it. Bud quickly understood what she was doing and went to help. Together, they lay his body across the back of the beast and repeated this for the other two. Ilii mounted the first beast before it could rise holding the body with one hand and grasping the mane with the other. The beast began to launch itself across the field, and Ilii yelled for Daisy to follow. There was no need. Daisy had already climbed on one of the beasts, holding one of the fallen Ilii as the other departed. Daisi looked at Bud, who, in a test of wills between purl and beast, was holding the last beast for Daisi to mount. She caught his eye, which bid her to join the others. His eyes also communicated that he would not be able to hold the beast much longer. They both knew that it was more a matter of the beast's willingness to wait and not Bud's strength that held it. Daisi ran toward her brother as fast as she could. The beast flexed the muscles in its shoulder and sent Bud tumbling in the direction of Daisi. Daisi used the back of his tumbling frame as a step and mounted the only remaining beast as it began to move in the direction of the others.

The horse-like beasts thundered through the brush like a storm. The broad shoulders of the two beasts that led the way cleared a path through the uncharted and foreboding thick. The beast behind them carried the Poollé Kii. The three beasts ran as if death were chasing them. It was. An additional two beasts followed in the wake, desperate but unable to close the gap. After an hour of breathtaking speed, the two lead beasts—silently commanded by the beast that carried the Poollé Kii—slowed. A meadow opened before them. Within the meadow and off to the left of its center stood a perfect circle of six trees. The three beasts began to walk slowly toward the cathedral of trees. Minutes after they had entered the meadow, the beasts carrying Dow and Daisii broke through the tree line. The beasts that had preceded them were already at the trees. As they approached, the rhythm of Daisii's hearts made a noticeable adjustment. Anger and anxiety glued her to the beast as it had raced through the woods. She refused to accept the death of the center of her entire life and being. As they had raced, she pushed the beast to catch the one that had taken her Poollé Kii. Now that she approached it, she wondered if she had the strength to take the body from the beast. And if she did, what would she do then? She refused to believe he was dead. His strength had the power to keep her and their love alive through the years of drugs and deception, and now she was demanding that same love return life to him. She knew his resolve from the moment she fell into his eyes on campus so long ago. She didn't know what was required or what would be demanded of her in the next few moments. What she did know was that he would somehow live, or she would die.

There was something sacred about the place they had come, holy even. As she approached, Daisii recognized that the trees were the same type as the one her Pedagogy was planting the day they met. The thought carried a warmth throughout her body and with it, a renewed resolve to reclaim the body of the Poollé Kii. The ferocious beasts they had ridden knew where they were. The two that had led the way marched to the circle of trees and stood as sentries between the first, second, and third trees. The beast that carried the precious cargo waited majestically. The two beasts on which Dow and Daisii rode approached and stopped some distance away from the beast carrying the kii. Their muscles vibrated as if they were silently growling. It was their way of insisting that their riders dismount. Daisii was already anxious to dismount the beast and get to her true love. The two jumped off their mounts. Daisii rushed toward the Poollé Kii. The beasts moved to position themselves between the fourth, fifth, and sixth trees opposite the others. The beast with the body of the

Poollé Kii stood some distance from the entrance to the sanctuary, waiting as the other four took places between the six trees. The two trees directly opposite the Poollé Kii's beast was the only gap left open. There was a whisper of a memory attempting to remind Daisii where she was. But she had no time to let her mind clear or her memory return. She wanted only to get to the body on the beast in front of her. What she was going to do when she got there, she still did not know. How she was going to procure the body from the beast she had not considered. What she knew was that she and the Poollé Kii were one, in life or in death. She knew that whatever claim the beast had on the Poollé Kii, hers superseded it.

She was determined that death would not separate them. Daisii approached the beast, aware of, but indifferent to, a pageantry that was unfolding in front of her. Just as she was about two paces from the beast, it began to move toward the cathedral of trees. She quickened her pace and ran to the side of it. She stretched her hand to touch the thigh of her beloved. She wanted to feel his warmth, to gain some assurance that there was still life left in his body. Her disappointment was eclipsed by horror. There was something more important than her thoughts or intent, and it called to her. She lifted her gaze. The thoughts she refused to recognize, the memories that refused to clarify her history or declare their intent, froze her body. The beast with the Poollé Kii moved toward the entrance to the sacred circle. It walked as if a thousand purple were watching, as if the last image of the Poollé Kii that the planet would see was passing before an assembly of reverent masses. The thought that this was a death march sent a chill through Daisii that overrode the mental paralysis that had her frozen. She ran past the beast and into the circle of trees.

The horror that had pulsed through Daisii was quickly replaced by the energy that terror injects into the bloodstream. Before her eyes, in the center of the trees, lay what looked like an open grave. It was twice as wide and somewhat longer than usual for a single purl. Its base exposed roots from each of the trees that had journeyed to the center of the sacred space. The branches of the trees bent toward the center of the circle like a canopy. At the far side of the grave stood two cloaked and hooded figures, one larger than the other, their faces shrouded in shadow. As they stood somber and reverent, one rested his hands on the hilt of a large sword whose tip gently pierced Purplynd. Daisii saw but noticed none of these things. She did not see the powerful presence of the beasts staring into the sacred space. Instead, her focus was glued on the approaching beast carrying the source of her life and hope. She was not going to allow him to be buried. The beast carrying the Poollé Kii entered the circle. The beasts standing guard between the trees bristled as if they heard her thoughts and could read her intent. Their bodies shook in a simultaneous display of power. Daisii perceived that her next action would result in her death, and the thought increased her focus. The beast bearing the Poollé Kii came closer.

Daisii walked in front of the beast to block its path. The beast took no notice. Daisii reached high, placed her hands on the breasts of the beast, and pushed with all her might. She screamed as if to pull more might into her limbs. She was no match. The beast continued toward the exposed roots of the six poollé trees. Daisii fell. Fear in the form of shock and despair washed over her. There was something familiar about the grass against her skin, but she did not have time to sort through why. She watched as the beast moved to the opening in the planet. Through its legs, she saw one of the figures discard its cloak and move to the beast on the opposite side of where she lay. She began to rise and did not detect the scent of amest in the air. As she stood, she saw the second purl leap and then flip into the hole. The beast that refused to release the Poollé Kii to Daisii offered his body to the one who had come to receive it. Daisii realized that the purl and the beast were on one accord and that fighting either would mean fighting both. It was a battle she welcomed, even if she was convinced it would lead to her death. She walked in front of the beast, knowing it could sever her in two with one snap of its powerful jaws. She saw the body of the Poollé Kii cradled in arms not her own; his eyes were closed and his mouth agape. This image of his lifeless form draped in the powerful arms overwhelmed her emotions. She began to give up hope of life. Her eyes began to tear. She lifted her gaze to see the one who so lovingly held him, but he had turned toward the grave. She could only see his silhouette in the fading light of the suns. Her hearts were confused. Her mind decreed that she knew him and trusted him. Her hearts demanded she intervene. But the anger and despair were beginning to move her away from thoughts of violence. She reached out and touched the arm of the one carrying her love. He turned his head toward her. She saw his face, and the rhythm of her hearts changed.

A wave of confusion crashed over her head and washed away all but the strength to stand as she recognized Ka Chi. It had only been a few days since she first met him, but the bond between him and her Poollé Kii was unmistakable and strong. He had celebrated their engagement and had gone to find a guardian. She was sure he would not harm him but wondered why he was not attempting to revive his friend.

Involuntarily, Daisii concluded if his dearest friend and the beasts that were connected to him in ways beyond words had given up on his life, she should as well. The confusion struggling within her took the remaining strength from her limbs, and she fell to her knees. The swirl of emotions bid her to rise to her feet, but lacking the strength, her efforts left her on her hands and knees. She began to close her hands into fists. The planet opened to her fingers and made handles for her to hold. Her hands gripped Purplynd as if to pull the strength she needed from its depths. But defeat, like a receding wave of the ocean, drained all the power from her being. She felt alone, bereft of all hope, abandoned by those who would love her and those who would hate her and every purl in between. It was not a new or strange emotion. It was a memory renewing itself in the moment. It was the rebirth of a truth she knew in her bones. She was feeling the first true lesson life had taught her: Love will always leave you. Why had she ever believed she could be anything other than alone? As her soul wept with these thoughts, her flesh glowed red and the color washed from the arch of her back through her hands and feet into the planet.

Then she heard something just above a whisper but as clarion as the crack of lightning. It was a low and deep voice, as tender as it was irrefutable. There was something intimate in its sound, something sacred and familiar. It was a voice from her past speaking in the present, seeking control of her future. She welcomed the wisdom of the words, not because she understood them but because she knew they came from a source beyond question. "You are no orphan."

The words were a prompt. They were the beginning of something she was always to remember she had forgotten. It was a poem, a perfect poem, three stanzas of twelve lines that her mother read to her at bedtime every night. She had cursed the poem when her mother left and swore she would never recite it again. But here, the voice was calling to the place she had hidden from herself and all others. The pain of grief and loss brought the memory close enough for the voice to uncover. Daisii could not keep the first twelve lines from moving into her consciousness:

> You are no orphan; listen close
> And steel your heart with truth
> Between the lines of life to live
> Until you discover proof
> The ancient seed of warriors past
> Flows within your veins,
> And you were born to take your place
> Beside your kii to reign.
> It is not for you to fear the death
> Of all that must not live
> Nor doubt the power love possess
> Which you were born to give.

With the memory came clarity and breath. A waft of something pleasant passed through her being. Daisii imagined it was a scent but knew it was something more.

The planet in her hands began growing and opened her fists until her fingers were spread and her palms flat. The grass was soft and warm in a way that welcomed pha. Memories swept into the present to replace reality. She, though still on the ground by the grave, was transported to the home near the mountains. She heard the steady song of the stream flowing in the backyard. The taste of its cold, clear mountain water was so real she could feel it move through her being. It refreshed her. And then there it was, the scent of amest. A warmth of love burst from the syncopation of her hearts and moved through her body. She knew he was there. She knew all was right and well or soon would be. Then a gentle confidence emerged in a voice which rose from the fabric of her thoughts. This voice had the same gravity and power of the first but added a visceral pulse of love that was essential and supreme. The words that erupted into her were warm, welcome, and creative.

Her entire being shone a brilliant royal blue as she heard, "Dreams are real."

Daisii rose to her feet. The lines of the poem continued flowing through her hearts.

> Dreams are real, forever know;
> When all around has died
> The breath of life awaits the light
> Of truth's redeeming sigh.
> Once past the door all living take,
> Your history is the key
> Within the place no purl can find
> Among the poollé trees;
> Now hold your hearts and give them once
> This, strange as it may seem,
> All that's true and comes to be
> Embedded in the dream.
> You, child, are born to find the way
> For purple to be home
> To right the laws that all may live;
> Although you feel alone,
> Your life to save is his to own,
> And his to yours will be
> When you have finally learned the truth
> That only closed eyes can see.
> Child of Quay, united now,
> Within your hearts find peace;

Betrothed, betrayed, belong, bereft,
You are the bride of Miis.

During that time and in those moments, Daisii began to realize the reason for her being. The truth of what her life meant, the reason for every moment of heart break and triumph came into her being with the veracity of the first cry of a newborn. All the pain of life's labor was eclipsed by the dawn that burst through the dark night that comprised so much of her life's journey. Wisdom welcomed her with a warm embrace, and Daisii sighed as if she was finally in its arms. She walked to the foot of the opening in Purplynd. Several roots from each of the six poollé trees that formed the sacred circle came together in the exposed grave; from there, they reached up to support the body of their kii. He was held above the bottom of the womb cut into Purplynd, covered in leaves from the poollé trees. The leaves were six distinct, iridescent hues and pulsed in shades of red. They moved as if they were a sextet singing a song of ages. Daisii could see the glow of the intricate pattern of the blanket peek through from beneath the leaves. These signs of life were undeniable and filled Daisii with hope. She knew the poollé trees were at work healing the love of her life. She knew when their work was done, he would rise and return to her side. As she waited, the song of the leaves began to move in her hearts. The rhythms were so sweet and familiar that she felt she could sing the words. It was the song of Quay and Miis and the thousand generations between them, her, and the purl for whom she waited. Hope guided her through the starless night and danger without fear or fret. The first whispers of morning unmasked the silhouettes of two figures on the other side of Purplynd's womb, keeping vigil with the same sense of assurance.

There, beasts and purple kept watch throughout the day. Then, the moment the second sun revealed its strength and bright-day began, Daisii's hearts jumped. Simultaneously, the beasts rose to their hind legs and released a sound greater than a lion's roar and as clarion as a trumpet's blast. The sound reverberated through the planet. It was loud enough to be heard for miles without being harsh or painful. The arms of Ka and the guardian lifted high in the air, and at that same moment, the poollé leaves burst from the body of the Poollé Kii. Daisii watched with joy as the leaves sent themselves to the inner edge of the trees, forming a ring just inside the sacred circle. The cloth of the kii had also taken to the air in the burst of life. It shone brighter than the day its beauty was first seen. Its descent momentarily obscured the face of the groom for whom Daisii had waited. When it appeared, the love in his eyes was unmistakable. It called to her more powerfully than it had ever before. It was love that existed before any time she knew and would last longer than life. Daisii leaped at the behest of his sky-blue eyes. His arms held open as he called to her, the Poollé

Kii caught his bride as she floated into his arms. They twirled in the embrace. Daisii fell into the sweet taste of love as they kissed.

"You bring life to me," he whispered.

"Our love is stronger than life or death," she replied.

Moments later, they presented themselves before the guardian. Pedagogy was adorned in a robe woven with threads that shone with diamonds and topaz. Daisii was in the wedding gown of her childhood dreams. There, before the beasts in that sacred place, they were married. Ka stood by the Poollé Kii as his best purl and brother. Two woos perched on trees to either side as the sole observers to the marriage. And Daisii could feel a thousand witnesses affirming the blessing of the union that came from the guardian. After the vows came the kiss and embrace, and Daisii lost herself in the contours of her husband's muscles as he held her. As she was held, she loved the wisdom confirming any future battles would find them inseparable. Then Daisii's new husband put his hands on her shoulders and separated himself far enough to look into her eyes. His words only reiterated what his eyes were saying.

"Let's go home."

Daisii knew he was speaking of the only home she had ever known, the home at the foot of the mountains, the place they shared in dreams. As if on command, at those words, the beast of the kii came with another beast beside it. Daisii's new husband jumped on his mount with the strength of new life. Daisii knew he was anxious to get to his honeymoon, and the thoughts made her flesh flash violet. But as she prepared to mount her beast, she heard an alarming sound. It took her a moment to realize it was a voice. She began to clear her thoughts and connect the voice to a purl or experience. The voice was welcome and familiar but strange and disturbing at the same time. Then it dawned on her; it was the voice from her dream.

Daisii awoke. She was still on her hands and knees. She turned her head toward the sound and saw two figures facing the setting suns on the far side of the opening in Purplynd. Daisii rose to her feet slowly. Her mind was accepting the pha that was present. The body of the Poollé Kii lay still in the hole, but Daisy knew it was no grave. She walked as a queen ascending her throne and stood in the place she had in the dream.

"I am the bride of Miis," she declared.

Immediately, the cloaks of Ka and the guardian flew off their frames. They flipped in the air and landed together on one knee with their heads bowed. The sword that the guardian had thrown into the air pierced the planet between them. The moment the sword entered Purplynd, the roots beneath the Poollé Kii lifted his body. Then leaves from each of the trees trickled then flew to the body of the kii. Daisii watched as the leaves contributed their distinct, iridescent hue to the body of the kii. They attached themselves to the body and began to pulse red. Daisii, watching the beauty of the flying leaves, did not see Ka or the guardian rise to leave but noticed their return. In their arms was a robe woven with threads that shone with diamonds and topaz and the wedding gown of her dreams.

To be continued . . .

APPRECIATION

Someone practiced at deploying words in the service of his thoughts should be able to express appreciation and thanks, but I am sure that if given another lifetime to learn, I would still fail to communicate the deep sense of gratitude, debt, and love I have for these who helped bring this story to life.

Thank you to the first readers who read comma-less drafts laden with far too many typos: Kathryn Carter, Gary Gray, Terri McWilliams, Dawn Raymond, Shirley Shelby-Watson, Kristine Smith, Susan Smith, Nichola Torbett, Joyce Whitfield, and Cheryl Wicks. Angie Noel provided invaluable help coordinating readers and mailing multiple manuscripts all over the country—you are incredible. Berena Hughes coordinated the final steps to publishing the first edition, managing the cover design, and proofreading the manuscript multiple times. It would have taken another year without her. Thank you to Lance Pettiford for your collaboration on the cover artwork. Thanks to Meg Calvin and MLC Consulting whose expertise took *Purplynd* out of the shadows and put it on a platform otherwise impossible. Thank you to Anna Rhea of Joppa Editing and her team of copyeditors for ensuring that the second edition is even more exciting than the first. Thank you to Rafael Polendo, Matthew Distefano, and Keith Giles of Quoir Publishing—finding a partner in the radical adventure of freeing Christ from stale imaginations that entomb the Gospel is nothing less than a miracle.

Thank you to Frankie Carrie, the pastor who taught me the wisdom that "if it's gentle, it's Jesus." Your prayers for me are precious. Thank you to Donna Hayes, who has always been the angel from heaven who believed, encouraged, and inspired me. I live everyday trying to become who she sees me to be. Cassandry Keys cheered every scene as they were written. Her encouragement kept me writing when I might have given up. Her faith that *Purplynd* was a story that had to be finished and published was much stronger than mine. Anyone who enjoys this story has her to thank. Valerie Annette McCann Woodson, the constant beat of my heart, you hold it all together as my imagination wanders in and out of what is and what could be. Finally, my undying love to the brown baby boy born on the back side of Bethlehem, who all of the powers of the world ignored until right before they crucified him. Because he is alive, we all have hope.

For more information about Brian K. Woodson, Sr.,
or to contact him for speaking engagements,
please visit www.purplyndtrilogy.com.

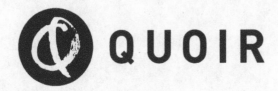

Many Voices. One Message.

Quoir is a boutique publisher
with a singular message: *Christ is all*.
Venture beyond your boundaries to discover Christ
in ways you never thought possible.

For more information, please visit *www.quoir.com*

CPSIA information can be obtained
at www.ICGtesting.com
Printed in the USA
BVHW081947171222
654235BV00005B/251